REBELLION GROUND

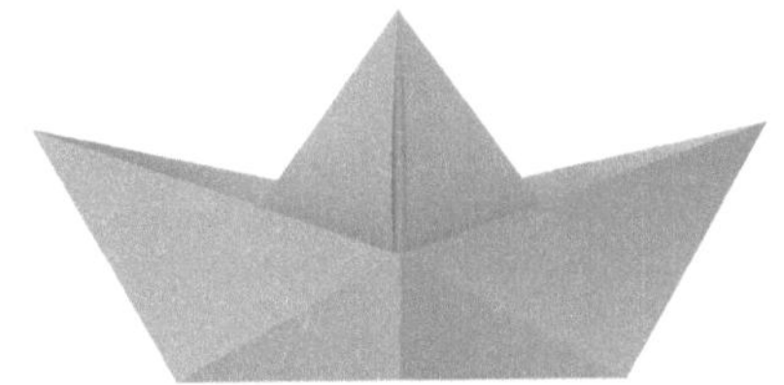

Book 2

The Newland Trilogy

E.M. CARTER

ISBN: 978-1-915981-34-9

Published by Resolute Books
www.resolutebooks.co.uk

"There may be times when we are
powerless to prevent injustice,
but there must never be a time
when we fail to protest."

Elie Wiesel

PREVIOUSLY, FROM REPRESSION GROUND

CARYS, AMY, AND Jacob have found a way out of the heavily barricaded Midlands Compound, hotly pursued by NForce and their trainers from Ashton Training House, after discovering an explosive secret that could blow up the whole of Newland: the truth about the Home, where Unproductive people are supposedly sent to live out their days in comfort.

The sickening truth is hidden away behind a veil of secrecy and an oppressive regime: no one questions the New Day Party, who claim to have saved the nation and set them on a better path. The three teenagers and Jacob's sick grandfather, Aiden, who was almost murdered in the Compound jail due to his perceived unproductivity, are now fugitives on the run, wanted for treason and heading for the ruins of an old city on the Outside named Birmingham, hoping they might find shelter, safety – and more answers.

CARYS

I STAND IN the road, the dusk of the evening beginning to fall around me. I watch as the coach disappears over the horizon and listen to the silence, punctuated by Aiden's laboured breathing. I glance at him, take in his sunken cheeks and yellowed eyes, and wonder how we are going to get through.

Jacob stands with me, his head thrown back, breathing in the air outside the Compound. His eyes are closed, a slight smile playing around his full, cracked lips. I cautiously take his hand and feel a squeeze in response. I shiver, the heat of the day dissipating by the second.

Amy stands next to Aiden, her arm linked with his. Her wide eyes sweep over the area, filled with the shock of what has gone before but newly radiant with hope.

Someone else is with us, too. Sim is here, his happy face soaring through my mind, his blue eyes sparkling and mischievous. He's large in my heart, and it swells with pain. Jacob turns to me as if he reads my mind and lifts his hand to my face. Slowly, he tracks the path of my tears.

We turn towards the ruined city cast in shadows in the distance. It looks like it's going to be another long walk. I clutch the stone in my pocket and sigh as I resume the forward trudge, shouldering our backpack.

We stagger with the fading light, with our pain and our baggage, with our brokenness and our freedom.

Fifteen Years Ago

MIDLANDS COMPOUND

SHOUTS INVADED THE heavy thickness of the woods, echoing through the distance and shattering the frigid night air, spurring Benedict on as he ran. Belting through the forest, squeezing between unyielding trees, he frantically scanned the ground ahead. The barrier was in sight now, looming tall and grey through the gloom. Benedict clutched the warm bundle to his chest, his heart pounding harder with each stride.

Don't look back.

He thought fleetingly of Sarah, taken last week. 'She's safe now,' they'd said. 'She'll be well cared for.' They called her by that other name, but he never would. She was his Sarah. Always and forever.

That was before he'd found the files.

Keep running.

His breath escaped in ragged gasps. *I will get through. I will get you out of here.*

The shouts drew closer. A sharp bark rang through the stillness, and Benedict froze for seconds.

They came quickly, crashing through trees, their dazzling torches dancing crazily through the murk. Then came the shot, splintering the remaining silence and slamming into Benedict's broad back.

The ground thundered towards him, the air punched from him. Just in time, he shifted the bundle, his last ounce of strength concentrated on keeping it safe.

Benedict lay gasping on the cold earth, his hand outstretched, cupping the baby's face. For a moment, he held her shining, slate-grey gaze.

Be strong, Carys.

They caught him there, surrounding him, their malevolent presence colder than the icy air. A young officer stepped over to him. Stooped to pick up the baby.

Benedict reached out. Grabbed the young man's ankle. *Please.* 'My daughter. Carys—'

One of the other officers snorted then spat on the ground.

'Please.'

The young officer paused for a moment, his face in shadow. He caught Benedict's eye and looked away. 'We won't hurt her.' His tone was almost kindly, a stark contrast to the frost oozing from the others. 'She'll be cared for.'

'Use my money.'

The officer had her in his arms. Her eyes widened and she began to flail, a thin cry escaping from her tiny mouth.

'Please tell her… tell her I went to the Home.'

A pause.

Then, 'I will make sure of it.'

Benedict groaned as he reached to his pocket and drew something out then tucked it into his daughter's blanket. 'Please keep it for her,' he said, and then his words were drowned in a rising hot tide that swamped him and snatched away his breath.

The young officer said no more. His superior gripped his elbow, heaved him away from Benedict. 'Update his details.'

Benedict strained to watch them, to grab one more glimpse of his daughter. *She is so loved.*

The shadows of the night blurred with rushes of pain, twisting the scene around him. He peered through fading vision at the young officer handing his baby girl to the grizzled one, the one with the narrowed eyes and mouth set in thin lines.

Be strong, Carys.

The young officer took his NSlate and pulled up the relevant page. *Benedict Clerk, age 24.*

He took a glance at the fallen man, still as stone on the frozen, callous earth, and his wailing child, straining away from the aggravated chief. He thumbed in the final details.

Status: Unproductive.

PART I

RUINS

1

BIRMINGHAM RUINS

CARYS

EVERYTHING HURTS. We're covered in grazes and open wounds, stumbling under the weight of what's just happened.

Darkness closes in as we reach the outer edge of the old, ruined city. We stare in numbed exhaustion at the gloomy shapes around us, poor shadows of what they were. Remains of buildings of every shape and size, long ago destroyed. Twisted structures of steel, reaching to the sky as they died then forever frozen. Weeds curl through the ruins, clawing their way through windows without glass and doorways without doors. The place is oppressive; I shudder as I almost sense the ghosts of the people from the Before, screaming as they lost their homes and their lives.

The silent night presses on us like a weighty blanket. The light is fading, and Jacob's NSlate is almost out of battery. No charge pads out here on the Outside.

Aiden stumbles at Jacob's side, his face drawn and sallow, and fatigue chases the rest of us hard. Grief twists my insides into a churning mass, and something in me wants to lie down and curl up, here among the weeds and the ghosts, and never get up again.

'How about there?' Amy is pointing at a half-crumbled edifice. It looks like it was once some kind of public building. An office block, perhaps. Maybe a training house of some kind. I remember Jacob saying that they were once called "schools". The blank windows gape at me, lifeless and unwelcoming, but there's nowhere else to go.

Amy leads us to the building, skirting around ancient rubble and tangled weeds, and we discover a complete doorway at the top of what were once some kind of stone steps. They're little but a pile of debris now, and we scramble up over them and stoop through the doorway. 'Careful,' Amy says, gripping the partially collapsed lintel. 'It's a bit wobbly.'

We pick our way through more rubble inside the building and settle into a dusky corner surrounded by walls that look sort of intact. There's no ceiling left, but the night is warm. Darkness cloaks the place, and shadows throw odd shapes. The balmy sky is clouded over, promising rain to scatter the sticky humidity of the day.

We all busy ourselves, taking the remaining food from the backpack and helping a reluctant Aiden to eat and drink. I pluck the one blanket remaining from the pack and wrap it round his chilled body, trying not to think about where the other blanket rests now. We sit in silence, soon cold despite the muggy air, taking small sips of water and finally, intermittently dozing.

I wake to a sound somewhere to the north, the sky above illuminated in too-bright light. I bolt up, disorientated, and shake Jacob awake. 'What's that?'

Jacob rubs his eyes, searching the lit-up sky, and then he gasps, jumping up. 'Get up. Not Baba. I can carry him.'

Now I hear the noise again. The throbbing, tell-tale thumping of Copter blades.

They're out here. On the Outside. And they're looking for us.

Amy is scrambling to her feet, her eyes wide as she gazes upwards. We glance at one another and begin to move away from the corner, leaving the bag and provisions scattered over the rock-strewn ground. *No time.* This ramshackle building is open to the sky, and the searching light is moving closer, brighter than any light I have ever seen. Nothing will be hidden.

'Need some… shelter,' pants Jacob as he hefts a groaning Aiden to his feet and takes the weight of him, still wrapped in the moss-green blanket. We struggle back through the doorway and stop outside, taking stock of our surroundings. Lit by brilliant light, the forsaken landscape stretches out around us in all directions. It will only be seconds until they see us. We duck for cover by the broken-down walls, desperately dodging the probing light.

'Try there.' Amy points at a confusing grey stone structure away to our right. Most of it is collapsed in on itself but there's part of it standing, a huge arched window and some kind of massive cone-shaped structure lying smashed beside it, great chunks of stone abandoned forever on the ruptured ground. We follow Amy towards it, scrambling over obstacles in our path, keeping beneath the shadow of other buildings.

I throw a wild glance upwards, my pulse pounding my throat. The Copter is over to our east, throwing its unearthly light over every niche, every remnant of every ruin. 'Hurry.'

We can't see any kind of doorway, so we clamber through the window space, Jacob helping Aiden through to Amy and me and then climbing in himself. The searchlight continues to sweep the area we ran from. Perhaps they've spotted some of our belongings. I swallow hard. *It won't be long.*

Inside the building it's dimmer. There isn't much remaining of the roof, but further away in one corner the shadows speak of a more sheltered area, so we make our way towards it, tripping on chunks of splintered stone and detritus under our feet. Amy cries out as she falls hard on her knees, but is up in seconds, brushing herself down and picking up her pace. Through the dusk, her brown eyes shine wide with fear.

When we come to the corner, we discover a confused mountain of rubble, but there seems to be a crawl space underneath one side. Jacob leans on the stone, and nothing moves. 'It's good,' he says, and crouches down. 'I'll get in first, then you help Baba… just drag him to me.'

I hop from one leg to the other, willing him to hurry. With a great deal of difficulty, we manage to help Aiden under the gap through to the space where Jacob waits, his arms outstretched and ready to draw his grandfather towards him. We follow, and just as Amy struggles through behind me the whumping blades and the dazzling light make themselves known directly above the structure.

A chilling sound now adds itself to the mix. A voice, heavily amplified. 'We know you're here somewhere. We've located your items. Make yourself known, or it will go badly for you.'

Swallowing, I glance around, taking in the cramped space. It's entirely covered over by a ceiling of fallen stone, so at least we are invisible to the Copter. If they search on the ground, however, things will get significantly worse. I clench my teeth hard. *Just keep breathing.*

Jacob pokes around the space. It's slightly lit, the rays from the searchlight penetrating small gaps in the stone. 'It kind of reminds me of the Think at Oak Tree Pre-training.' He smiles, and I frown at him.

This is no time for nostalgia.

'I think there's something here.' Jacob grabs my arm. I glance at Aiden, who is slumped on the ground, breathing raggedly, his eyes hooded and slightly wild in the half light.

I crawl after Jacob to the far side of the small space and see that he's unearthed the shattered remains of an old wooden door. The doorway must extend up beyond the pile of fallen stone, but we can access the lower half. We poke our heads through, and see what looks like ancient steps, descending into further darkness. We look at each other and nod, but my heart is hammering. I don't like underground spaces.

'It's some kind of old cellar,' I say.

'What's to stop them finding us if they land and start scouting? We'll be sitting ducks down there, surely,' Amy calls.

Jacob begins to speak, but just as he opens his mouth an ear-splitting crash shakes the unsteady crawl space. The ground shifts under our feet, and the stone above us begins to move, small pebbles detaching themselves and raining on our heads. I throw my hands over my ears and squeeze my eyes tight shut. Jacob's face is grim as he shuffles over to Aiden and drags him over to the doorway. 'Quick.'

Will the cellar stay intact? If we try and get out, they'll see us. They're not wanting to take us alive, that's for certain. Nausea rises, burning through my body, and I gulp it down.

Abject fear infuses the tiny space. Frantically, we haul Aiden through the juddering entrance. I grab his feet, helping Jacob pull him down the stairs, half slipping and sliding as we go. The steps are worn, as if centuries of feet have trod a path down here. We land in an unsteady heap at the bottom, panting hard and glancing back up the stairway. Tiny pieces of shingle continue to shower over us, covering us in dust and muck.

Sound is muted down here, the whump of the blades quieter, but the crashes increase, coming thick and fast now, the ground shaking with each great bang. My chest tightens, an iron band snaking around me, crushing my bones. *Breathe.*

Jacob swipes his dusty forehead. 'Must've seen us… trying to wipe us out.'

A terrifying boom, even closer now, right above our heads. Then heavy thuds of crashing rock, stones collapsing, cracking into thousands of pieces. It sounds like the entire structure above us is caving in on itself, imploding in a great pile of ancient masonry, trapping us.

I suck in a gasping breath.

More crashes. Thunderous explosions all around us. The acrid smell of smoke. The remnant of the building above us is alight, like a tragic replay of its first death.

I begin to hyperventilate, winded and wheezing. Jacob's hand is on my shoulder. 'Breathe, Carys,' he whispers in my ear. 'Breathe.'

I choke, the stench of smoke drawing nearer and nearer still, and then cascading over me, blinding me and catching in my throat. I'm back in the chimney at the Compound Think, fire beneath me, lungs searing and useless. Only there, there was a way out ahead, stars beckoning to me, sparkling with freedom. Here, there's nothing. *Breathe.*

'Come on.' Jacob has Aiden hefted over his shoulder. Amy takes my arm, and we stumble further into the underground room. I follow blindly, staggering through the pungent darkness, my breath coming thick and fast. Further on into a space we cannot see.

Amy is quiet, and I remember her tale of the dark passages and the black well back at Ashton. She's holding her fear inside herself. I squeeze her hand. We slip on unknown items on the ground, and then bump into some kind of form in the centre of the room. The flames above cast dim, flickering light through the ruptured ceiling, and I see it looks like some kind of large rectangular box, constructed of stone, with an intact statue stretched out on the top, hands crossed over its chest as if in death. I brace myself against it, my swirling head bowed down, getting some breath back.

The flames lick at cracking timber somewhere over our heads in the outside world.

I stand, wobbling, taking a closer look at the statue and the box.

'It's an old tomb,' Aiden says, breathing heavily. 'We're in a crypt.'

'What's a crypt?' Jacob asks.

'It's a place where they laid their dead in the Before. The ancient dead, really. I remember my mother telling me something about old buildings where they practised the old religion, and under those buildings they sometimes had these places. Crypts. Her grandmother told her that kind of stuff.'

'Great. So we're trapped in our own tomb with some centuries old dead dudes.' Jacob is deadpan, but something in his tone releases a tension in us.

'Put it this way,' Amy says, 'at least we've not been blown up by NForce explosives.'

'Yet,' I say, pursing my lips.

I hear an audible wheeze. It's not just me; Aiden is in trouble, his face drawn and yellowed as he struggles for oxygen. 'Move him away from the smoke,' I say, grabbing his hand. We skirt around the tomb further into the old crypt, and come to another doorway, this one with a thick oak door intact, leading into a similar space.

It's quieter in here. The air is clearer, but it's darker. It's a safer place for now, away from the worst of the flames above. We explore the boundary of the room and find nothing aside from unyielding cool stone walls. There's no way out of here.

'I say we stay here until the fire burns itself out.' Amy's voice is trembling.

'Not like we have any choice,' Jacob says. He lowers Aiden to the ground in the far corner, props him up against the wall. Aiden coughs, and coughs again, until he is lost in a cacophony of racking coughs. Amy picks her way over to him, sinks to the floor next to him. 'Get it out. Spit it up.' She rubs his back as he bends over, hacking and gasping. Spent, he leans back against the wall. Even through the murk I can see his drained face and sallow features. Jacob must know he can't be with us much longer.

But there may be no way out for any of us, in any case. Fear batters me again in a violent wave.

'Leave me here,' Aiden says. 'I can't do any more. This seems—' he coughs, '—a good place, to go. A place of peace. My mother could never talk about the old religions, you know… it was forbidden. But I know she had some sort of faith, passed down from her mother and hers. I feel close to her here—' he breaks off, rasping.

'I'm never leaving you,' Jacob says, his voice cracking. 'You're coming with us. We're all getting out.'

'No.' Aiden slumps against the wall, closing heavily veined eyelids. Jacob says nothing but crouches with him, stroking his wasted arms, his sunken face, his sparse hair.

We remain there, cowering on the cold stone floor in the darkness, for so long I cannot tell what time of day or night it is. The

Copter has gone. I doze fitfully, jolting awake at cracks and bangs above us, my sleep uneasy and dream filled. I listen as the flames consume, then crackle, and eventually as they fade to silence.

Hours later, I wake again, my stomach sinking like a stone as I recall our situation. A raging thirst is on me, and my eyes are sore and gritty. I lick my cracked lips. Jacob is awake, holding Aiden to him gently. The darkness seems less all-encompassing, somehow, and I wonder if it is daylight somewhere above us in the unreachable world.

'We should try and get out.' Amy stands over me, stretching and yawning. She pulls on my arm.

Jacob says, 'I can't leave him.'

'Let's bring him, then.'

'No.' Aiden rasps the word, his eyes tightly shut. 'Leave… me.'

'I can't.'

Amy and I stand in silence for a few moments. Jacob sits, rocks Aiden. Cradles him. 'I'm here, Baba,' he says.

'Why don't we look, Amy and me?' I suggest. 'We'll find a way out. Come back for you.'

Jacob nods. I glance at Aiden and my heart twists at the sight of him.

We pick our way cautiously back through the doorway to the first crypt. It's lighter in here, cracks in the ceiling revealing beams of light penetrating fallen rock and burnt timber. Most of the ceiling itself is still intact, by some great miracle.

We skirt around the large tomb, which gives me the shivers now it is more visible, the figure forever conserved a female, cold stone lips slightly curved upwards, eyes closed, her face in repose a picture of peace. We tiptoe over to the steps, mindful not to disturb our precarious surroundings. They're still there, to some extent. The bottom few are undamaged, and we begin to climb but soon come to a confused space where steps used to be, now covered with fallen masonry. The stones are blocking the exit.

Amy bites on her lip. I gaze at her, her white, drawn face framed in a beam of light from above, and a resolution overtakes me. 'There's light coming through. There must be gaps. If there are gaps, we can find them.' I remove pieces of stone, pitching them down the steps. As I take some from the pile more shift.

'Careful,' warns Amy. 'It might all fall…' Nonetheless, she's with me, plucking at the stones, dropping them into the room below.

We make good progress, tugging away the broken rubble. Shafts of bright sunlight break through as we progress further into the rock fall, and dust motes dance in the disturbed air. 'Keep going.' My heart swells with hope, though my voice sounds gravelly and raw.

I pull at a particularly large piece of shattered stone. This one looks different to the others. Part of a grotesque face is carved into it. 'Look at this,' I say to Amy, smirking. 'Looks a bit like Principal.'

As I heave it out, I sense a shift in the stones above, and suddenly there's a loosening. Piles of stone begin to rain down, the entire mass of rubble sliding. I find myself wrenched off my feet, and simultaneously feel a sharp pain in my shoulder as something heavy and sharp hits me. Then I'm sliding down, falling, and Amy screams.

I'm at the bottom of the stairway, covered in an avalanche of rock, and Amy is sprawled in a heap on top of me. She's pale in the now dazzling sunlight beating down on us, and she winces as she attempts to move. 'My arm,' she croaks.

'Oh, heck, Amy,' I say, struggling to get up and hitting my palm to my forehead, 'Your arm… and you've been helping me with these rocks. I'm so sorry.'

'It's okay.'

We brush the detritus off us. I examine my smarting shoulder and find blood, my Think jumpsuit torn to tatters around the top. I wipe some of the blood away with one of its shredded rags then look up at the doorway, framed in sunshine, open and welcoming. A moment of panic snatches at me, and I check my pocket for my name stone; it's still there, still close with me, still giving me strength I never knew I had. I exhale slowly.

'What are we waiting for?' Amy pushes herself up, cradling her arm close. We make our way up over the pile of fallen rock and through the doorway.

My gut sinks at the desolate sight.

Heaps of debris everywhere, rubble and ashes. The old walls have fully collapsed inwards, the window we climbed through the night before is gone. The structure is utterly ruined, bleak in its final destruction. Small fires still burn, dotted around the sad remains of ruins.

'Wow.' Amy steps out of the doorway and into the ruins. Walking is difficult; fallen rock lies everywhere. We pick our way through until we reach the boundary of the old building and scramble outside. Looking around, we see that most of the buildings around us have met the same fate, including the one we initially took shelter in. Our belongings – all gone. We have no food, no water, no shelter. The NSlate is gone, not that it has a lot of use out here on the Outside. Everything is gone, lost in a huge conflagration meant to consume us.

Amy and I stand there, warmed in the blazing sunshine, gazing round in utter despair. I swallow, and slivers of pain scream through my ragged throat.

We survived, but now we have nothing. What hope do we have?

2

BIRMINGHAM RUINS

JACOB

JACOB TRADER'S GRANDFATHER is fading. His eyes are sunken and bloodshot, his body all scrawny and wasted. Jacob can't stand to see him like this.

They did this. Productives. Tried to kill him. Made him even sicker.

Baba squirms beside him, tries to sit up. 'I'll help you,' Jacob says, gulping over the great lump lodged in his throat, and places his arm carefully around his grandfather's torso. Baba leans gasping against him, spent and broken, but he's still trying to speak.

'Shh.'

'No. You need to listen… Jacob. Please.' He breaks off, catching his breath, then coughs. Tries to hide it, but Jacob can see blood on his hands.

No. His insides churn into a great storm.

'I am listening.'

'I want you to leave me here.'

'I can't.'

'I'm no use to you—'

'I don't care about use.' Jacob clenches his jaw so tight it aches. Like the ache deeper still.

'I'm holding you back. Please, Jacob.'

Jacob says nothing for a moment, staring ahead at the doorway, watching rays of the sun slitting through cracks. Hammers thump his head. His thinking is too foggy.

He takes a breath. 'Then I'll just stay. Here, with you. The girls can carry on. I'll stay.'

'No.'

'I'm not leaving you.' He gazes into his grandfather's yellowed eyes. They're red-veined and watery, fatigue clear in their depths.

'I want you to go,' Baba says. And then he closes his eyes, as if he is done, as if it's all too much. He's said all he wants to say.

But Jacob will not go.

⤸

LATER HE HEARS footsteps, and shadows fill the doorway as Carys and Amy return. He heard them earlier, fighting with rock in their battle to find a way out. He couldn't help them. Couldn't leave Baba. Felt strangely detached from it all.

He looks at Carys. Her face is ashen, her lips all cracked. His heart plummets at the sight of her. 'Hey,' he says. 'Brought me a burger?'

No one raises a smile.

'There's nothing out there,' Carys says. 'Everything's gone. All our stuff.'

He reaches to his pocket, pulls out the two guns, one from his father, one he took from Gardener. 'Not quite.'

'They're not going to feed us,' Carys says, her voice hoarse.

Amy speaks up. 'We have to go. Find food and water. For Aiden, too.'

'I'm not coming.' Baba again, his voice barely audible.

'What?' Amy walks over to him and crouches down. 'Aiden?'

He says nothing but stares into her eyes, willing her to understand.

'I'm staying with him,' Jacob says. 'He wants us to leave him here to… anyway. I'm not going.'

That lump in his throat is growing. Clawing. Choking.

'You'll both die.' Amy furrows her brow at him. 'Of thirst, before anything else.'

'If he won't come, I'm not coming.'

Carys stands over him, face all flushed. Crosses her arms. 'You're being stupid. Stubborn. You've got to come. We'll just all carry him, like before.'

'No.' Baba again.

'You go,' Jacob says. 'You're good for this. Go and scout around. Get some water, and if you can, bring it back for us. If you can't… well, you can't.'

Carys sighs. Pinches her nose. 'What if we can't find any at all? Let alone enough?'

'Then we die,' he says, shrugging. 'We got this far. We can be proud.'

He doesn't want to die.

'But we achieved nothing,' she says, voice rising. 'We haven't even told anyone. The truth, I mean, about the Home. We can't give up now.'

'No.'

Amy stands up. 'Let's go, Carys. While the sun is high. The longer we leave it, the longer we don't have anything to drink.'

Carys narrows her eyes at Jacob, and he scowls at her. Why can't she see that he can't leave Baba? She's being the difficult one. He turns to the wall, irritation creeping through his body.

'Come on, then, Amy.' Her voice is huffy.

He shrugs.

'Goodbye, Aiden,' Amy says softly. She crouches down again, hugs him gently. He smiles at her. 'I'll see you in a while,' she says, stroking his cheek.

Something twists a knife under Jacob's heart.

Carys flounces out with Amy following more slowly, and Jacob sits in silence, Baba leaning on his shoulder. His breaths seem smaller, somehow, but faster. His eyelids flicker slightly, his emaciated limbs trembling, and Jacob holds him, sorrow pinching his gut.

He was going to get him to a safe place, a comfortable place. He was going to get him strong, well again.

He suddenly realises the girls didn't even take one of the guns. The NDart is gone along with their other belongings, not that it would be any good to them here; they've had no chance to charge it since Carys used it on Gardener back in the Compound. Jacob swears softly. His anger-filled confusion stopped him thinking clearly and now they may be in danger.

He feels so stupid.

HE WAITS THROUGH the day for their return. He gets up, walks around, stretches his legs. He never leaves the underground space, never leaves Baba alone. He knows daylight is up there, in his reach, but there are more important things down here.

By nightfall they haven't returned, and he's stressing. Blaming himself for sending them out on their own. Carys wasn't breathing so well; the smoke was getting to her, and she looked so knackered, so pale. They may be out there, dead, for all he knows. He pictures Carys in a heap somewhere out there in the abandoned city, and his stomach clenches.

Baba shifts again, his breath now coming in tiny, shallow gasps, his eyes firmly closed. Jacob can't swallow over the rock in his throat. 'Baba,' he croaks, cradling him. He's slipped down the wall, lying flat in the blanket. It's soaked through; he's wet himself, Jacob couldn't even help with that. He sighs, disgusted at himself.

Sometime in the middle of the night, Baba wakes again. Jacob can't see much of him through the thick darkness but can see his eyes. His heart swells up; they're shining now, as if he is better, as if he has hope. His cracked lips curve into a smile and he looks up at Jacob then past him, above him.

Then back at him. Pinning his gaze. Faded brown depths, so loved. 'I'm okay, dearest boy.'

His words are a raw whisper Jacob can barely hear.

'S… search the old ways… the crossroads… find the ancient… p… paths—'

'Shh.' Jacob takes Baba's hand and brings it close to his chest.

'Promise me…'

Jacob leans into him. 'I promise. I love you…'

He drowns in his words.

Baba exhales

and then there's nothing.

Baba slips away from him, breaths ceasing, eyes clouding.

Gone.

'No.' Jacob's choking, all alone in the murk. 'No.'

He weeps, but no one is here to comfort him.

Baba lies in his arms, gone away elsewhere.

3

BIRMINGHAM RUINS

CARYS

JACOB'S NOT THINKING straight. He can't stay here. We need to move on, move further into the city, find water. Take Aiden with us. I'm trembling with anger, and I leave without saying goodbye.

Later, I hate myself and my stupid temper. I can understand how Jacob felt confined. And now he thinks I'm angry with him, that I left him alone without bothering to comfort him in what must be the most hideous thing anyone could face.

Though I wouldn't know. I never had anyone to lose.

Then why do I feel so cold inside?

Amy keeps me going, gamely pressing on through the heat of the day. We leave the remains of the ruins and make our way towards the centre of the old city, hoping we'll find something, maybe some kind of stream. Anything. The ground has been too parched so far. Even the weather is set against us, the sun burning down on us, blistering our arms and drying our throats. I wish for rain.

I'm starting to feel disorientated by the time the sun is low in the sky. Shapes swim ahead of me, making no sense, my head lost in mist. The ground spins and swirls, and I feel Amy's arm through mine, pulling me back up. 'Carys.' Her brow is creased in concern. Her lips are dry and cracked, her brown eyes dulled. 'Carys, fight it, please. We'll find water soon. I promise.'

That's when we hear the shouts up ahead.

I grip Amy's arm. Voices are incongruent with the desolate surroundings of the abandoned city. Someone is out there, and they have seen us. Indistinct words float towards us, and then figures appear in view, hazy in the sun. 'Who are you?' I hear someone shout. A deep voice. My swimming head refuses to decode anything more, and I begin to sway.

The world is blissful and hushed, the ground soft and welcoming, Amy's concerned cries heard only somewhere in a dream.

LATER I WAKE up drenched in sweat. I lie there in sudden panic, throwing wild glances round at my unfamiliar surroundings. I seem to be in some kind of wooden shed-like structure, but I'm on a bed. It's squishy and comfortable, and my tired, aching limbs sink into the softness. White sheets cover me, and something more. I try to move my arms, and fear batters me. They're strapped down, long sheaths of duct tape pinning me to the iron-framed bed. I strain at them frantically, but they're too strong. Panting, I lie back and take in the rest of my environment.

My wrist prickles at me. I look down and see the cannula inserted there, some kind of drug flowing through an attached tube. I notice an old-fashioned drip stand next to me, a bag of clear fluid hanging from it. I beat at my bonds, gritting my teeth at the pain in my head. *What are they giving me?*

'Carys?' Amy's voice. I turn to see her in the next bed, also bound, also cannulated. 'You've woken up.' She breathes out on a long sigh.

'Where are we?' I can't get my thoughts together, but despite my fetters I feel stronger. More focused.

'Some guys saw you faint, came to help us, I thought. They asked who we were but didn't really seem to want to know. I tried to explain. Tried to tell them about Jacob, but they didn't listen. They were okay at first, got us here, set up these fluids—'

'Fluids?'

She nods. I stare at the drip bag, puzzled. They've imprisoned us, but they are rehydrating us?

Amy continues. 'I kept on trying to explain, but they said they'd be back later with food for us. And then they started taping us both down, and I tried to get away, but they said it was for safety. And that's it.'

'Damn.'

'Yeah. But Carys, in one way, this is the best thing that could've happened, surely? You were literally passing out. Dying of thirst. They saved you.'

I struggle against the tape in a vain attempt to sit up. 'I can't really see how it's the best thing to be shackled to some bed in a place we know nothing of. What about Jacob? And Aiden? They won't survive, not if we don't get back to them. Soon.'

'I know.' She too is straining at her bonds, but it's no good.

'Do you think it's Productives? From the Compound?' I say, dread creeping through my chest.

'I don't think so. They'd have killed us, not hydrated us, surely? They tried to kill us last night… probably think they have. And these guys – they were dressed differently, in old clothes, not like Compound clothes. I think they live here. On the Outside.'

I gaze around the room, contemplating our situation. The shed is constructed from warm umber pine panels, a mid-sized space with four beds, looks like some kind of hospital ward. Rough shelves at the back contain medical supplies, and each bed has an overbed table for patients. It reminds me a little of Miss Warden's sick bay.

Don't want to be back in that memory.

'We can't do anything but wait and then try to explain,' Amy says.

'But we need to get to Jacob. We can't leave him all alone. I didn't say goodbye.' I hurl myself up, as if I might tear the duct tape with force of will, but it hardly shifts.

'Just try and get some rest. We'll be better for Jacob and Aiden if we're rested.'

I purse my lips.

I struggle against the heavy sleep that calls to me, drawing me down and down as I sink into its heedless embrace. The balmy evening sun warms the shed, the bed swallows me up in its comfort, and I give in. I dream of Jacob, lying on the cold stone floor in the crypt, his bones sticking out at all angles and his slack mouth forming shapes of words. *You left me.*

Later I wake abruptly, my pulse racing as the door opens. Sweat is dripping from my brow, and I can't even wipe it away. This time I feel fully awake; my limbs feel like they are ready to function again, and my mind is at full capacity. I glance over at Amy, lying there with a worried frown on her face, eyes on the creaking door.

'Ah.' A grey-bearded man wearing old-fashioned brown corduroy trousers comes into the room balancing a tray, closely followed by a small woman with long grey hair and faded blue eyes, holding a large flask. 'Our visitors are awake,' the man says, smiling. 'I'm guessing you're probably hungry.'

There are two plates on the tray, and my stomach gurgles despite my reticence. Succulent ham, steaming potatoes and peas. I scowl up at the man, straining rigidly at the tape.

'In a moment,' he says, his face inscrutable. 'They were just for security, you understand? We don't know anything about you. You might have come to rob us. Kill us. A convict and a Think nurse, right?'

Amy looks at me, and we both look down at our outfits, the battered Compound Think jumpsuit and the torn stolen nurse's uniform, and we laugh, something released inside us. 'Not quite,' I say. The man's lined face creases.

'Be careful with them,' the woman hisses, narrowing her eyes. 'They're Productives. Can't trust them. You know that.'

'Help me get these tapes off, Sarah,' the man says, and something in me stirs at the sound of her name. Like I've heard it before, somewhere in the dim and distant past; it resonates with me. *Sarah.*

I wince as he peels the tape from my arms. 'Sorry,' he says. 'By the way, I am Stephen.'

'You don't have Newland names,' Amy says, staring at them.

'That's because we are not Productives,' says the woman.

'What do you mean?' I say.

'Time for that later. Maybe.' She glares at us, puckering up her mouth. 'Stephen,' she says, as she helps him rip Amy's tape away, 'can you get Matt and Will and ask them to stand guard? Just to be sure.'

'Will do.' The man disappears, and I hear shouting.

'Our sons.' Sarah glances back at the door, eyes suddenly shining.

'Sons?' Amy says, bringing a hand slowly to her mouth. 'You have more than one child?'

Sarah contemplates Amy and nods. Her tone softens a little. 'We don't follow the draconian rules of Productives here, child. Yes, we have two sons. Brothers.'

Brothers. The word is new but rings bells of resonance, just as Sarah's name did. Brothers. I suppose that is the word for what Amy called 'soul-children'. My mind whirls over the word; the concept. The rightness.

There's a great clamour, and two tall young men squeeze through the low doorway. 'Yes, sir,' one of them says, a mop of light brown curls tumbling over sparkling brown eyes. He salutes his father.

'Hey, Mum,' the other says. He's taller than his brother but has the same brown eyes. His father's eyes. 'They've woken up, then.'

'Yep. When they've eaten, we can see what they have to say for themselves.'

The two lads loiter by the door, slouching and grinning. The one with the brown curls stares intensely at Amy, who doesn't seem to notice.

'Jacob,' I say, an image of him rushing into my head and thumping my stomach. 'We have to go and get Jacob.'

'Who's Jacob? That's not a permitted name, is it?' Sarah brings me one of the plates. She hands me some cutlery and places the plate on the table, then pours steaming liquid into a mug. 'Tea,' she says. 'Tuck in.'

'None of us have permitted names,' Amy says through a mouthful of ham. 'We've all got Before names.' She nods at me. 'She's Carys, and I'm Amy.'

The four stare at us. 'Really?' Sarah says. 'I didn't think trainees had any names?'

'It's a long story,' I say.

The food is simple but appetising, the tea sweet and good, and for moments I am lost in its warm comfort. But then I remember, and guilt prods my gut. 'Jacob. And his sick grandfather, Aiden. They're way back. We couldn't find water. Hours away…' My words fall over one another in their haste.

'You're saying there are more of you?' Stephen's hands rest on his hips, his eyes narrowing. 'More Productives?'

Sarah takes him aside and whispers, but I can just about make out what she's saying. 'I don't want more of them. Could be dangerous. These two look all right, but two men?'

My temper rises. 'It's a boy and a really old man. And you need to hear our story before you judge us. We're just trainees, and—'

'Are they armed?' Stephen interrupts.

I hesitate.

'Crossbow?'

I shake my head. 'Well… we have… guns, but for defence.'

Sarah and Stephen gaze at each other then at me. Stephen strokes his beard. 'Hmm. Well, it's getting late. If you need to get this… Jacob, you must wait until the morning.' He gives Sarah another inscrutable look, and she nods just slightly.

Heat rises in my belly. 'We have to go now.'

The curly haired lad in the corner speaks up. 'We can help. We have a horse and cart—' He cuts off abruptly at his mother's sharp glance.

'The morning will probably be too late, though,' Amy says, frowning. 'They haven't had food or water since yesterday, and hardly any then. We've had a bit of a time of it, see.'

'I'm sure. Banished, were you?'

Amy's eyes widen. 'I wasn't, no. We were… chased. But they send banished people out here? It's true?' Hope lights her face.

'Some, yes. Now and then,' Stephen says. 'Generally criminals, though. They tend to join the gangs. We don't want them here. We're a peaceful community.'

'Community?' I glance around.

'A few families live peacefully here,' Sarah says. 'We don't want any trouble. We've always been here, see. We made our own way. Didn't want anything to do with those New Day types.'

'I want to hear more.' I fling my legs out of the bed and clamber to my feet, but my head hasn't caught up with the rest of me and spins hard, forcing me to sink back into the plump pillows.

'Time enough. You must sleep again now,' Sarah says.

'But Jacob—'

'It's too dangerous at night. The gangs… and last night, we saw Productives, right out at the western borders. Saw them blowing up the place in their helicopters—'

'Copters, you mean?' I say. 'NCopters, really, but we all call them Copters.'

Stephen wrinkles his nose. 'They changed everything, didn't they. Bunch of loons, the lot.'

Sarah smiles and begins to gather the empty plates and cups. 'We'll help you in the morning,' she says kindly.

'It was for us,' I shout, trying to get their attention. 'The Copter… helicopter, whatever. They were trying to kill us. We found out stuff about them.'

'In that case, it's more important than ever you don't go out at night. They'll be out there again, no doubt. You stay here, and then you can find your friends, and then you can leave us in peace, yes?'

I stare at Sarah, unbelieving. 'You want us to leave?'

'I don't want Productives. And definitely not Productives who are being pursued by other Productives.'

'We're not even Productives. Only kids in training,' Amy says. 'Please. Let us go and find our friend.'

'No.' Sarah folds her arms and regards us. 'Sleep, now.' She takes her husband's hand and leads him out of the room. The lads follow, the curly haired one throwing a lopsided grin and a shrug at Amy. She blushes and looks down. The door closes with a resolute click and then another.

'No!' I scramble out of the bed, holding my spinning head, and wobble over to the door. It is firmly locked. I shuffle over to the only other door in the room, and see it leads into a small bathroom.

'We're just going to have to wait until morning,' Amy says. 'At least it's comfortable here. The beds… the pillows. Ashton wasn't like this. It reminds me of… home.'

I clench my fists and gaze again around the place.

Nothing.

No way out.

I sit back on the bed, beaten. Amy is right. There's nothing more we can do tonight.

Amy

AMY PLUMBER WAKES to a scratching sound. The place is in darkness, and she can just see Carys, her mouth agape, snoring slightly on her bed. Amy can't help feeling a huge sense of relief at their rescue, however odd. At least they are safe. Jacob and Aiden, however…

The scratching intensifies, and she realises someone is unlocking the door. She sits up, expecting the place to flood with morning light, but when the door opens a figure is framed in gloom. It's still night.

The figure creeps in, shutting the door behind him. He switches one of the dim bedside lamps on. He spots her sitting up and smiles. 'Shh. It's okay. I'm Will. You know, one of the sons.' It's the boy with the brown curly hair, the one who grinned at her. She notices his eyes. Soft, kind brown eyes.

'What are you doing?' she whispers, glancing over at Carys.

'I'm going to help you find your friend,' he says.

'Why?'

He hesitates. Looks to the ground. 'I… I want to help you. I was lying in bed, just, and got to thinking about your friend, and how he might be dying out there. I can't just leave him.'

She stares open mouthed at him. 'Thank you.'

His eyes shift to the side and he looks away, twisting his hands. 'We'll take horses. Not the cart, it's too noisy. We'll take Shadow and Rainbow, they're both gentle. You can ride with me on Shadow and your friend can have Rainbow. Have you ever ridden?'

'Once or twice. At Ashton. I'm not very good, though.'

Carys sits up, rubbing her eyes. 'What's happening?'

Amy fills her in quickly, and she scrambles out of bed like a fire's lit beneath her. 'Come on then.'

Will leads them to a block of stables around the back of the shed. They can see signs of habitation here; low cottages, slumbering in darkness. 'How come they survived the riots?' Amy whispers.

'They didn't,' Will says. 'My ancestors built them. We've lived here ever since.'

'Wow.'

'Come on.' They follow him into the stables. Two horses are already saddled and bridled, their eyes shining through the murk. 'This is Shadow.' He points to the first, a beautiful alert grey with a black mane and tail, who tosses his head at the sight of Will and whinnies. 'And Rainbow.' She's white with brown socks, a stunning mare, her brown eyes flashing in her eagerness for this unexpected nocturnal walk. She strains at the rope, and Will laughs. 'Come now, girl.' Amy watches him as he coaxes both the horses out and helps Carys onto Rainbow. 'Can you manage her?'

'I think so.' Carys has had a lot more experience than Amy, having attended an elite Infant House and pre-training house. They'll have given her riding lessons. She slides her feet into the stirrups as if a natural to it and takes up the reins. 'I'm ready,' she says, smiling widely.

Amy's not so confident, hidden away in a tiny house until just three years ago and with little experience with horses since. Will helps her onto Shadow, but she feels stiff and uncomfortable, Shadow's great glossy back shifting beneath her as he skitters and grunts. She sits ramrod straight, relieved when Will leaps on in front of her with the limber ease of an experienced horseman. 'Hold onto me.' She places her arms tentatively around his waist. His body is warm and solid and smells of straw and sleep. Her cheeks infuse with sudden heat.

Will gently nudges Shadow, and he trots off in a westerly direction away from the stables. Carys guides Rainbow after him, the two fluid together, made for each other already. They make quick time over the parched ground, Amy watching the ghostly ruins flash by as Shadow canters on, holding tight to Will, afraid she will fall as she braces herself against the unfamiliar jolting. They soon settle into a rhythm, and the forgotten city streaks by as they race through the night. Carys draws up next to Amy and Will and urges Rainbow on, a determined set to her face. Her hair is wild, streaming behind her in a mass of tangles, the tatters on her jumpsuit fluttering in the wind. She looks happy. Free.

Will is quiet. His profile seems grim, his body set stiff. Amy attempts to engage him in conversation, asking him breathlessly about his family, his childhood, how he spends his time, about the history of their community, but he grunts. Says nothing. His character seems changed from earlier when he came to their rescue.

The ruins thin out as they come to the western edge of the city. She's finding it difficult to get her bearings. The building Jacob and Aiden are in will be difficult to find as it has been so much decimated from the night before, when it was distinctive with its arched window and smashed cone. This morning these were gone, as were most of the buildings around. The place was unrecognisable, just more rubble among the wreckage.

Frustrated, she gazes around, desperately trying to find some familiar landmark, but there's nothing. She's getting tired, her bones aching, her entire body stiffening up. Her arm aches and pounds with each step, but she sets her face and holds on. She glances at Carys. Her face seems drawn, like the hope is all draining out. 'Where are we?' she asks, finally.

Will draws Shadow to a halt and signals to Carys to stop then dismounts, helping Amy down. 'Maybe we should look around on foot for a while,' he says. 'You might see something more down here. This is where the helicopters were… you can see some smouldering heaps around, so it must be around here somewhere.'

Carys slides off Rainbow and strokes the length of her muzzle, her frown deepening. She says nothing. Will tethers the horses to a steel post nearby. It was part of a building once, but stands alone now, firmly anchored in the ground but reaching to nothing, supporting nothing. Will plucks a bag from the saddle and slings it over his shoulder.

Carys picks her way towards a smouldering pile of rubble in front of them. Will and Amy follow, and then they stand still, attempting to get some kind of bearings. But the night is too dark, the landscape too desolate in its destruction. 'How are we going to find him?' Carys paces, her hands in her hair. 'We need to find him, Amy.'

'I know. We just need to keep looking.'

The silence is absolute, any wildlife subdued by the legacy of the explosions from the night before. It's eerie out here, the darkness like a heavy cloak. They make their way through ruins of ruins, searching for something. Circling aimlessly.

Will stops and bends over. He picks something up, examines it, holds it closely to his face by the light of his torch. 'Do you know what this is?' He passes the item to Carys. She almost squeals.

'It's part of an NSlate. Looks like the internal card. See, there's part of the screen still attached here…' She shows it to Amy.

'What is it?' Will's brow is creased in the torchlight.

'An NSlate. You know, a tablet?'

'Oh… well, we don't really have that sort of thing in our community,' he says, his eyes turned to the horizon. He sounds almost wistful. 'Haven't got electricity, for one thing… well, we have this old generator, works when it feels like it. We rely on solar power for energy. What does it do?'

'All sorts,' Carys says. 'We use it for work, at our training house, and it has all the info we need on it—' she stops, falters, '—well, I used to think that, anyway. It's basically a communication device, but kind of programmed by Productives, so it's got all the stuff they want us to think on it.'

'Right.' Will scratches his chin.

'The thing is,' Amy says, 'this must be where we were last night, before we went into that cellar. This must've been smashed to bits with the explosive devices. So, if it's somehow landed in the same sort of place, then I reckon the cellar should be over there.' She points to the right, where just a day back a towering ruin with an arched window stood proudly against the lit-up night sky. Now just more black nothingness.

Carys grabs her hand and starts off towards their right, tripping over detritus on the floor and almost falling flat on her face but righting herself in time and shaking her head. 'Come on.'

They come to the place Amy thinks must lead to their cellar. A whole pile of stones in the corner look a little familiar, but it's hard to tell in the gloom. They inch their way over the rubble, and then she sees it. The empty doorway, which is not really a doorway anymore. There are two planks of wood remaining in the door frame, no sign of the lintel, and one rusty hinge barely hanging from the right side. The remainder of the space is taken up by piles of ancient stone. Peeking through the door, she spots the staircase and the landslide that nearly buried Carys and her alive yesterday. She breathes a sigh of relief.

Carys smiles, but her grin turns to a confused frown as Will steps around her and stands in front of them both. He's holding a crossbow, and he's pointing it at them. 'Down the steps, then,' he mumbles, his chin set and his eyes blank.

4

BIRMINGHAM RUINS

CARYS

TERROR COURSES THROUGH my body as I gape at Will. My fear of what I might find down in the crypt is magnified a hundred-fold as I take in the strange weapon aimed at us. I've only seen a crossbow in story books. It's so much bigger than our little NDart and looks capable of far more significant damage. Will trembles as he levels it at Amy and then swings it round to me. We stand frozen by the decimated doorway, unsure how to react.

Amy breaks the uneasy silence. 'What are you doing?' Her temple is wrinkled tight, her voice soaked in shock and indignance.

Will says nothing, refusing to meet our eyes. He pushes me through the doorway, gesturing to the ruined steps. I move, throwing glances back at him, holding tight to Amy's hand. We scramble down through the piles of rubble, picking our way slowly to the bottom. We stand there, waiting for Will as he follows us, wielding the crossbow.

'Where's your friend?' His voice sounds different. Harsh. I point towards the door in the far end of the crypt, lit only by the small torch Will is carrying. A slight shadow crosses the gloomy entrance. He shoves at me again, and I make my way through the crypt, skirting the tomb, through into the other underground room.

My hands are sweating.

The shadows in here refuse to form decipherable shapes, and I gaze around, straining my eyes into the darkness, listening for the slightest sound.

'Jacob?'

No response.

There's a sudden ache in the back of my throat.

'Shine the torch into the corner.' Amy steps forward, pulling Will with her. I freeze as he resists, brandishing the crossbow, but then she lays her hand on his arm and he stops, closes his eyes; he relents and sweeps the beam around the far-right corner, the corner where we left Aiden.

'There.' Amy hurries towards a mass, a shape I still cannot make out. I follow her, and by the light of the torch I spot the corner of a filthy green blanket.

Aiden.

And then I see him. Lying stretched out next to his grandfather, inert, eyes tightly closed. In the torchlight he looks sunken, his cheekbones prominent, his chest too still.

I don't think he's breathing.

Cold fingers run down my spine.

'Jacob.' Amy crouches next to him. She checks Aiden's pulse and shakes her head at me, her eyes filmy in the dancing beam.

The cold lump in my throat that started with Sim and never left me hardens further, and I struggle to swallow. 'He's gone?'

She nods slowly. 'But Jacob... he's breathing. He's unconscious.' She checks Jacob's pulse and gently draws his eyelids up. 'Pupils reactive. Needs water. Will...'

Will frowns and steps forward, reaching into the bag slung over his shoulder. What is his game? Is he helping us or hounding us to our deaths? He tugs out a battered aluminium bottle of water and unscrews the cap then hands it to Amy, who puts it to Jacob's lips. He barely responds, the liquid spilling from his cracked mouth, running down his chin and down his body, but his eyelids flicker, and then he's coughing, choking, spitting out water.

I breathe.

I crouch down next to Amy. 'Jacob,' I say. 'It's me. I'm so sorry...'

Jacob opens his eyes and raises himself. Gasping, he reaches for the water bottle and drinks deeply, choking and spewing liquid everywhere. 'Another?' His voice is cracked. Will passes another bottle to me, and I give it to Jacob.

'Slowly, now.' Amy wrenches it from his resistant hand. 'You need to take sips. You'll make yourself sick.'

Jacob sits himself up more fully. 'You came back.'

'Aiden...' Amy strokes his arm.

'Gone.' Jacob's eyes shimmer in the dim light, rivers of tears waiting to burst their banks. But he does not cry.

'I'm so sorry,' I say. I have no words for him. My insides are sawn apart.

'He was... the most wonderful man I ever knew,' Amy says. Jacob swallows, grimacing, but says nothing.

It's then he notices Will, holding the torch. He frowns. 'Who are you?'

Will hesitates for a moment, but then he flattens his lips out, places the torch under one arm and directs the crossbow at the three of us in our huddle in the corner.

'This is Will,' Amy says dully. 'He helped us. Was helping us. I don't know why...' She shrugs, raising her eyebrows.

Will drags in a long breath. 'They made me. I have to...' His eyes are on the stone-strewn ground, avoiding our incredulous gazes.

An icy band of fear curls around my body. 'What do you mean?'

Will does not look at me. His arm trembles.

A lump of hot rage wedges in my throat, and I look at Jacob, casting my eyes to his pocket. He's making for one of the guns.

Something isn't right.

Why is Will doing this?

Amy gets to her feet, brushing down her clothes and taking in a shuddering breath. She steps slowly over to Will, her eyes on the quivering crossbow, lays her hand on his arm, bravery shining through fear. 'Will, look. Y… you seem a nice boy.' She stares straight into his eyes. 'You helped us. You saved Jacob's life. What are you doing?'

He falters, his hands quaking. He tears his gaze away from Amy's and shifts his eyes to the left. 'I have to do this. They sent me.'

'Who sent you?'

'My parents… my family. They don't want Productives… we get rid of any of them we find. They let one in once. Seemed to want to be one of us – worked with us, took on our values. But he turned on us. Escaped, running back to the Compound to tell the Party about us. We found him in time… stopped him. Our lives are fragile, Amy. We can't let anything break us. We have children to think about. I'm sorry.' He lifts the crossbow, swallowing hard.

Jacob lifts the gun.

'No!' Amy cries at Jacob. 'He's not bad.'

Will hesitates.

Amy keeps her hand on his arm, coaxing. 'Wait. We're not like that. We escaped from Productives… we're wanted by them. We just need some help; we won't disturb you anymore. I promise, Will.'

Confusion crosses his features.

'Besides,' Amy continues, 'why didn't you just finish me and Carys off straight away, then, if you just kill off anyone you find?' He flinches, avoiding her gaze. 'Why keep us alive? Why feed us? I don't get it.'

He shrugs. 'We aren't evil, you know. We saw you there, and… and saw you needed help. That's what we do, first and foremost—'

'Then why…?'

He looks down at his feet. 'They're just scared. My parents. My community. I wanted to help more, but when you said about the boy…' he glances at Jacob, who shivers on the ground, his lips cracked and his eyes dulled, '… they said we couldn't afford to leave loose ends.'

Amy glances at the crossbow. 'You don't need to do this.'

'I'm sorry,' he says. His finger hovers over the trigger.

'We'll go,' I say. 'We'll never bother you again.'

Will stares at us like a frightened deer. 'I don't know—'

Amy reaches out and lays her hand on the crossbow. 'You do.'

He looks at her. Then looks away. Then falls to his knees, slamming the weapon on the ground and his face in his hands. The torch spins across the floor, and I pick it up.

Amy tugs my arm. 'We need to go.'

Jacob's face crumples.

'We can say goodbye to him,' I say, following his gaze to the inert mound in the dank corner. 'Like we did for Sim.'

We all crouch down, surrounding Aiden's body. Will hunches in the far corner, curled up on himself, a trembling shadow. Jacob wraps the blanket more tightly around him and strokes his sparse hair, his grey face, now smoothed in almost tranquil lines. 'Be at peace now, my Baba,' he croaks.

We remain there in silence, holding hands. I switch the torch off, and we linger in the darkness, waiting there with Aiden.

Finally, Jacob speaks. 'I couldn't save him.'

'But you did,' Amy says softly. 'You saved him from a death of indignity. You gave him value. Showed that he mattered. The Think death was just a disposal system, and you gave him back his humanity, Jacob. You saved him.'

'And he died in the arms of the one he loved most,' I add. 'In this place, where he seemed at peace, an ancient place of lying loved ones to rest. You gave him so much.' As I say the words the longing in me stretches, the yearning for such love.

I hear the choke at the back of Jacob's throat, and then he's crying, weeping, stretching himself out over Aiden, his tears soaking the blanket. The world spins as I stroke Jacob's heaving back and join my tears with his.

Amy goes to Will, touches his back. 'Will you come with us?' But he stays on his knees, his forehead to the ground, hands over his ears.

I slip his bag from his shoulder and sling it over my own. 'We'll be going, then.' Amy looks at me, her eyes wide with pleading. 'We need to go,' I say. 'He'll be okay. He was going to kill us, Amy.'

She stares at him and then removes her hand from his back, setting her face hard.

With one last goodbye to Aiden, we make our way into the next room and over to the wrecked steps. 'Wait.' Jacob stops still. 'That thing you did, Amy, for Sim – that thing with the twine. Can we do something for Baba?'

'There's some fragments of doorpost around here,' I say, shining the torch over the rock fall. I scrabble through the rubble and find a couple of shards of scorched wood. 'Here.'

We retrace our steps, and Amy places the wood in a cross shape on top of Aiden's blanket, his burial shroud.

The shape mesmerises me. Soothes and fires me inside all at once.

We cling together, saying a final goodbye.

Two hours later we've travelled far away from the outskirts of the city. Shadow and Rainbow were reluctant to come with us, tossing their heads and searching for Will, but I fed them sugar lumps from Will's bag and they grudgingly allowed us to mount. Jacob is riding in front of Amy on a skittish Shadow, and I am on Rainbow, who is more compliant.

'Should we return them?' I call, suddenly worried Will's family will pursue us.

'No,' Amy shouts back at me. 'We'll be in enough trouble from them. He'll be fine, but the best thing we can do is to get away from their part of the city. See if we can find others who will be more… open to us.'

I know she's right, practical Amy, but I feel guilty for leaving Will, who was clearly experiencing some kind of emotional collapse, and guilty for stealing their beautiful horses. But I know they could be our salvation. She is right.

We ride on through the remainder of the night, and as the light dawns with the morning we dismount by a cluster of hollowed out buildings and sink to the ground, watching the colours of a summer daybreak painting the sky. We fish the remainder of the food from Will's bag and drink the rest of the water, though Jacob didn't leave much back in the crypt. We are not sated, but we are surviving.

Exhausted, we sleep through the morning on the dusty ground and wake as the sun is high in the sky, beating down on us, torturing us with its unrelenting heat. We finish the water and move onwards through the ruins.

The city is thickening. Burned out buildings with vacant doorways loom at us from all directions, the silence eerie, even in dazzling sunlight. Twisted steel and shattered concrete form sculptures of anguish and torment, forever cemented in their tragic demise. Some buildings retain more of their original structure than others. It's obvious that this is the centre of the old city, the buildings representing business premises more than dwellings. In front of us is the remainder of an entirely cylindrical building, cut off after three or four storeys, wrecked and crumbling stonework lying all around as if waiting patiently to be picked up and rebuilt. Weeds snake through cracks in the smashed-up concrete, growing tall but sickly and yellow in the summer heat. I wonder what this place looked like, once upon a time. We trudge through the destruction, depressed. Jacob is silent, his usual upbeat nature in hiding, Amy seems lost in thought, and the two horses are slowing. They need water, and we have none.

As the afternoon draws on the sky begins to cloud over, a relief from the blistering heat. My neck and my scalp are burned, and I welcome the cool breeze. I rub my sore neck and gaze at the sky. The clouds darken quickly, and a drop of rain falls on my nose. Eagerly,

I bring Rainbow to a halt and dismount. The rain begins to fall, first in a slow, warm drizzle, and then in a steady downpour as the heavens turn to grey and the thunder roars. Seconds later, lightning splits the grey, dramatically lighting the leaden sky. Amy and Jacob join me, mouths open to the falling rain, water cascading off our chins. The horses stand patiently, their drenched skin glistening in the half light. I open Will's bag, which is constructed from some kind of hide. It might retain some water for the horses. Most of it drips through, but it collects a puddle, and Shadow and Rainbow poke their grateful noses in.

Refreshed, we walk for a while beside the horses. The deluge increases, our clothes soaked through, hair dripping. It feels good, and then it feels heavy and cold. Wearily, we carry on.

'What's that?' Amy stops still, pulling Shadow to a halt by her side. I can see and hear nothing but gushing rain.

'What?' I say.

'I heard voices. Shouts.'

'Where?'

'Over there, I think.' She points towards some buildings over to our right. I can't see anything unusual, and Jacob stands slumped, face turned to the ground.

'Come on, then, we should go and see,' I say, massaging my aching temples. I've had enough of this hike, and I'm ready to find some kind of shelter. They can't all be like Will's family out here, surely?

Amy takes my arm. 'Be careful. Keep hidden. If we skirt round that building there—' She points to a low-lying ruin dead ahead of us, '—then we should stay fairly well covered, I think.'

I tentatively take Jacob's arm, but he shrugs me off. Stung, I trudge towards the building, keeping Rainbow by my side. Amy follows, and I glance back to see Jacob dragging in our wake, eyes down, shoulders stooped.

We come to the old ruin and slow to a halt. The horses look exhausted, the terrain too much for them. 'We should leave them here while we check it out,' Amy says. We tether them to the sad remains of a steel frame and continue to creep around the building. The rain is finally beginning to die down, and with the lessening of the torrent comes the sound of voices.

Children's voices.

'Can you hear them?' Amy's eyes are widened.

'Yes,' I say, and move a little faster towards the shouts.

I hear delight, joy in high voices, and when we round the final corner of the building, we see them. A group of them, clad in rain gear, bounding from puddle to puddle, scooping up water in cups and flinging it over one another. They are screeching, running, skipping, splashing. They leap over rock piles and in and out of doorways. I watch in fascination, a craving gripping me. If we ever showed such behaviour when we were in pre-training we would be smacked, sent to the Think, told that we were displaying immature and inappropriate conduct, unseemly for children being brought up to be Productives.

I glance at Jacob, who is watching the children, his eyes set and chin jutting out, rain running down his face. He won't return my stare. Amy hauls me back. 'They might see us.'

'They're only children.'

'So there must be Productives… I mean adults… around, somewhere. They can't be out here on their own, surely? They're only little. Pre-training age, really. Some smaller than that, even. They seem so…'

'Happy,' I say, something twisting deep inside me.

'Look at that one,' Amy says, and I follow her gaze. A small girl dances in the midst of the others, twirling and spinning, her rain cover displaced, her face open to the sky. Her arms are flung wide in abandon. Her long brown hair tumbles in soaking ringlets, but it's not that I notice. Her face seems different. I've never seen a face like it. Her dark eyes are rounder than usual, her cheeks dimpled, her forehead high. She shines with a kind of joy I've never seen.

'She has an Unproductive disease,' Amy whispers slowly, her brown eyes wide. 'I've seen it, in a medical textbook. It never gave it a name, though. It was just in a list, with others like it. Conditions that trigger immediate removal to the Home.'

I stare at her in horror. 'But why?'

'They cannot lead Productive lives. So says the book, anyway. But look at her. She's so alive.'

'We've been so deceived,' I mutter, as I watch the little girl puddle jumping, pushing a child next to her, squealing in ecstasy as the child nudges her back, throwing water over her upturned face.

She splutters, giggling. 'Do it again!'

We remain there, watching the children play. Watching them do what they are supposed to do. My shrunken heart responds with desperate longing and even more desperate rage at those who took this from me.

We hear a shout. A man's voice, loud and booming. 'Get in, kids. Teatime.' I watch as a tall figure emerges from the dark doorway of the ruined building opposite us. He laughs as children rush over to him, giggling, some of them hurling their cups of water at him. They disappear, one by one, through the doorway, and then they're gone, the sudden silence jolting me back to the reality of our lives.

'Perhaps we should go there, too,' I say, then throw my hand over my mouth. I spoke too soon. Too loudly. The man's face jerks around.

'Hey!' He rushes over the ground between us, the joy-filled space turning malevolent as he shouts back towards the doorway. 'Wade! Drew! Jake!' In no time, three other men appear, taller and broader than the first one.

We are paralysed, but Amy breaks the spell. 'Run,' she says, and we turn, hurtling back around the building towards Shadow and Rainbow. But in our weakened state we are no match for these men. They are on us as we turn the next corner, the horses in sight ahead. 'Stop!' The first one grabs Jacob, pinning his arms around his back. My pulse quickens.

Two of the others restrain Amy and me, and the last one goes to the horses. 'Nice colt,' he says, stroking Shadow's nose. 'And this mare! Beautiful creature.' He pats Rainbow's flank. Rainbow nuzzles him, blatantly begging for food. 'You're hungry, girl?' The man takes hold of both horses' reins and walks them over to us. Shadow and Rainbow come docilely, their eyes dulled with fatigue.

The man behind me firmly pins both hands around my back. I wriggle, my heart pounding. To my left, Amy winces as one of the men does the same. 'My wrist,' she gasps. 'It's injured.' To my surprise, the man visibly softens his grip.

'Frisk them,' one of the men says.

It doesn't take them long to find the two weapons. The man holding Amy says, 'Who the hell are you kids? Where did you come from?'

Jacob says nothing.

I swallow over a lump of fear. 'It's a long story. But could… would you be able to give us any water, please? And food?'

The first man, a tall guy with sparkling blue eyes, stares at me, not unkindly. 'Come with us, then,' he says, as if we have a choice. They lead us back towards the doorway. I can't imagine where everyone is. It seems to lead into a shallow ruin. No walls remain, and sporadic rain patters the moss-covered walls.

'Careful on this bit. There are steps down. Go slowly.'

I pick my way gingerly down the narrow, pitted stone stairway. We're going underground. Maybe it's another crypt? I shiver, my rain-soaked jumpsuit clinging to me in chafing dampness.

Down at the bottom the ground is smooth, unblemished by debris. Jacob and Amy's feet slap behind me. I'm not sure what the man has done with the horses, but guess he is looking after them. His reaction to them seemed so positive. Loving, almost.

We are guided along a dimly lit passageway, through to a larger space. Blinking, I stare around the room. It's nothing like the crypt we were in with Aiden. The large space is filled with bright light and soft furnishings. Two battered brown squishy sofas sit in the centre of the room, facing each other. They've seen better days but look welcoming. A large red rug lies on the floor. It's not like the immaculate fringed rug back in Miss Principal's cloying study, but ancient and soft looking, as inviting as the sofas.

A huge, scrubbed oak table dominates one side of the room, shabby and beaten-up benches lining both sides. On the walls there are paintings. Children's paintings. Rainbows, trees, flowers, people. I've never seen a space like it. At pre-training, any pictures we did were kept in regimented folders, ordered to show progress to the inspectors, critical comments scrawled over each one. To hang one on a wall would be unthinkable. Walls were for gilt-framed pictures of Commanders and other famous Productives to aspire to. At my pre-training house there were large posters of all *The S Word* judges. But never children's work.

Amy is staring around just as I am, her eyes wide, mesmerised. I remember that she once said her mother used to fasten her pictures to the wall. But Jacob's eyes are still pinned to the floor. I try to catch his gaze but cannot reach him.

Our detainers pause, scrutinising us closely, arms folded. Finally, the first man speaks. 'I am Cory.'

I immediately think of the child murdered by the Party, Principal's baby, the one who wasn't "proper".

Amy asks, 'Are you in charge?'

He laughs. 'Not quite.' Tall and fair, his clothing is casual and old-fashioned. His chin is covered in days old stubble, which he rubs as he watches us.

'Well, who is?'

'We'll take you to her. She needs to hear what you have to say, as we do. I have to warn you. If you've come here to disrupt us, to spy on us for Productives, or to harm us in any way, the consequences will be severe.'

'We haven't.' I raise my chin.

Cory's blue gaze sweeps over me. 'Hmm. Follow me, then.'

The other men push us gently after Cory. We follow him through to a long, gloomy corridor, lit with the occasional halogen light. The walls and the floor are constructed of smooth stone. The effect is polished and cold, a contrast to the room we just left.

We enter a small room at the end. Mirrors line the walls, a thousand reflections gawping back at us. 'The antechamber,' Cory announces, and strides across the room. He knocks on a huge walnut door in the far wall.

'Come.' A female voice. Cory pushes open the door with a loud creak, beckoning us in. He turns to an imposing figure stationed on a large wooden chair with intricate carvings and inclines his head.

'Good afternoon, Cory. And who do we have here?' The woman's voice is cold, her gaze colder. She has ebony skin and dark brown, almost black eyes. Her head is shaven, and she is covered in tattoos. Her nose and bottom lip are pierced, her ears heavy with multiple gold rings in varying sizes, from lobe to tip. She's wearing a black leather jumpsuit and black buckled boots. Her scarlet-tipped fingers heave with yet more gold.

Cory smiles. 'Good afternoon, Your Majesty.'

5

THE BUNKER

'THIS IS OUR Queen.' The man called Cory examines them, gauging their reaction. Carys is excitable and fidgety, picking at the loose skin around her nails. Amy feels a momentary irritation towards her, the one who landed them down here with her lack of self-control. Jacob's quiet, saying nothing to anyone, refusing to catch anyone's eye.

Amy stares back at Cory. 'Oh. You mean like the Commander?'

'No. Not at all like that. She is our Queen.'

Amy's gaze shifts to the woman on the chair. She looks scary. All in black. She doesn't look too happy to see them.

'Well?' The Queen's voice is sharp.

Carys speaks up, and Amy cringes. 'What does "Queen" mean? I mean, I know about queen bees, of course, but...'

Amy knows what it is. Her mother had told her about when England had kings and queens. In the Before. They were the rulers, sort of. Much longer ago, kings and queens were more like Commanders now. When the New Day Party took power, the King disappeared. He was the son of a queen, from what she remembers. Or the grandson, possibly. She's a little muddled. Mum didn't know many details, and she could never ask Trainers. If she did, she'd be sent to the Think.

Now, the Queen's face remains stern. 'I am the one who looks after my people,' she says. Her words belie her tone. 'They are my subjects, but they are also my family.'

Amy is fascinated. This Queen talks about family, and it wrenches at her. She remembers the reason she is out here, on the Outside. She wants to ask these people if they know of her parents, but she can see that she needs to tread carefully. See what happens. So she holds back.

Carys stares at the Queen, eyes widened. 'What, all those children belong to you?'

The Queen says nothing, gazing down at Carys, whose energy seems to drain as she is scrutinised. She opens her mouth to speak, then closes it. Amy breathes a sigh of relief and tries to catch Jacob's eye, but he is studiously avoiding her. She stands and she waits.

After a few moments of uncomfortable silence, the Queen summons Cory, who walks to her side. She beckons him closer, and Cory bends down slightly so she can whisper in his ear. Amy can't hear what she is saying.

'She wants to know where you came from, why you are here, and what your intentions are,' he says. 'And your names. Well, your surnames, as you're obviously trainees, right?'

Carys jumps in again. 'Why can't she ask herself?'

Cory gives her a look that could freeze fire, and she stops short again. Amy thinks for a moment then decides to comply with his request. She doesn't know why, but she trusts these people. 'Your Majesty,' she begins. 'I am Amy Plumber, this is Jacob Trader, and this is Carys Clerk.' She stops as she hears a sharp indrawn breath but can't see who it is. She clasps her hands together. 'We all have illegal names, I know… it's a bit of a long story. We were all trainees at a house called Ashton, in the Midlands Compound. Well, I wasn't actually brought up in state training…' she pauses, gathering her thoughts. 'To cut this long story short, we all felt that what our Trainers were telling us about how we should live our lives didn't seem right.' Amy stops, watching the Queen, whose face is inscrutable. She takes a deep breath. 'Carys was arrested and Jacob and I rescued her, and… and in the process we discovered some information, about the Before – they didn't let us learn about the Before, see, at Ashton. So we found out that there was once something called a Human Rights Act, that the death penalty had been abolished, that there was freedom to vote in elections and other things like that. Realised this country was once very different.' She stops again for breath and watches the others. The Queen makes no movement, but Cory nods slightly.

'We were looking for the Home, where Carys's parents, Jacob's mother and our friend had all been taken at various points. But we found out that there is no Home anywhere in Newland.' Her stomach rolls even as she says the words. 'Everyone sent to the Home is actually sent to the Compound Think, drugged and murdered. In a furnace. It's hideous.'

Carys presses her fist against her mouth.

'So then, we managed to escape the Compound. Ended up here. There's another community in this city, and someone from there tried to get rid of us. Said they couldn't have Productives anywhere near them.'

'That'll be Stephen's place,' Cory says. 'They don't let any incomers in. They're pretty aggressive. We avoid them, and they avoid us, and it works fine that way. You had a lucky escape.'

Amy glances at Jacob. 'On the way, Jacob's grandfather, Aiden, died. They'd tried to murder him in the Think. He was very weak, very old, but at least he didn't die in the Think.'

The Queen speaks at last, her voice low and steady. 'He had a good death, then.'

Jacob looks up sharply at her, and their eyes lock for a moment, but he quickly turns away, shrugging.

The Queen whispers to Cory. Amy shifts, trying to support her arm, her wrist sending waves of pain towards her shoulder.

Carys says, 'We're not here to do anything bad. We just came to escape. Productives were after us, trying to kill us. Seriously, we were wanted for treason, and they were firing on us with Copters, trying to blow us up. We're not safe in the Compound.' She curls her lip. 'They don't want their little secret out.'

'It's not really a secret,' the Queen says. 'Most Productives are aware of the true situation. A very wise man once said that all that is necessary for the triumph of evil is that good men do nothing, and that is what has become the case.'

Carys stares to her left. 'I believed it. They took me there... told me it was the Home.'

Cory spits on the ground. 'They brainwash little kids.'

'But why try to kill us?' Amy asks. 'If loads know it anyway?'

'Because you are doing something. Everyone else does nothing. You are a threat.'

'So what about you all here? What are you doing?'

The Queen says nothing but looks at Cory and nods once.

'You do not need to know about us,' he says. 'If you are willing to work with us a while, you may prove your innocence. For now, you can eat. Sleep, then. You seem tired... especially the young man.'

Carys opens her mouth to speak, but Amy catches her eye and shakes her head slightly. Carys narrows her eyes but remains hushed.

Cory nods to the Queen again, then leads them back out of the room, through the antechamber and into the hallway, where he takes them through another door. 'I'll see if I can find room for you in the girls' sleeping quarters,' he says to Carys and Amy. He looks at Jacob. 'And then you can come with me. There's a bed for you in the boys' room.'

'Do all the girls sleep in together, then?' Carys asks. 'Like in a big room?'

'Not really. Most of us have family rooms, but there are orphans here, and older people who aren't in families, though we are their family. Those people have dormitories, but you'll find they are comfortable.'

Amy's eyes fill with tears, taking her by surprise. People living in families. Like she once did, before the Productives smashed her life into tiny pieces. She's still trying to gather up those shards off the floor, and occasionally one slices into her, leaving her gasping.

They leave Jacob waiting in the hallway. Carys tries one more time to grab his attention, to reach out to him, but he's gone to another place, and he's not letting her in. Her face shadowed in gloom, she turns from him and trails after Cory. Amy strokes her arm. 'He's deep in grief.' She looks like a wounded animal, and Amy wonders if she cannot yet comprehend grief, not in the way Amy and Jacob can. Not if she never knew love.

Cory guides them through a door that leads into another dimly lit hallway of polished stone. Several doors lead off this one. 'Family rooms,' Cory says, waving his hand at some of the doors. They follow him right to the end and through the last door on the right. 'The girls' dorm.'

The room is fairly small. It has a cosy feel, lit with warm lamps and fairy lights strung around the ceiling. The stone walls are broken up with more pictures, this time large paintings of animals. Horses, mainly. There are four sets of bunk beds in the room, and deep beanbags lie in scattered mounds around the carpeted floor. There are other things on the floor, as well.

They look like books.

They never had books at Ashton, other than the Sacred Book, of course. Everything was on their NSlates. But Amy knows about them. Her parents had some in their house. Very few, and very well read by her soul-child Lewis and her. They were children's books, mainly, telling tales of heroic children accomplishing great things for Newland. They were highly unsatisfying, but she devoured them nonetheless. Her heart skips a beat now, in excitement at the thought of the books in this room. Perhaps she will be allowed to read them.

'Hello, Hannah.' She hadn't noticed the child sitting on one of the bottom bunks, her nose in a brightly coloured book. She looks about ten. She's wearing glasses and her curly dark hair tumbles down her back.

She grins and sits up, placing her book by her side. 'Hey. Who's this?'

'There's room for two in here, isn't there, Hannah?' Cory says.

She nods. 'Yep. Only five of us in here. The others are still at dinner, greedy pigs. I wanted to finish this…' She holds up her book. Amy can just about make out part of the title. It looks like it begins "Harry Potter". Nothing she's ever seen or heard of, but she can't wait to find out.

Cory ushers them into the room. 'This is Amy and Carys. They've escaped from the Midlands Compound.'

Hannah's eyes widen. 'They're Productives?'

'No,' Carys says quickly. 'We were in training. Not anymore. We don't want anything to do with it. We're not Productives, never will be.' Her face darkens.

'Oh. Well, okay, then. Come in. Got any luggage?'

'Nothing. Oh, but our horses. Shadow and Rainbow – where are they?' Carys looks at Cory.

Hannah jumps off the bed. 'You brought horses?' Her voice is eager, and a warm smile spreads across her face.

Cory grins. 'Don't worry about them. Drew took them to the stables. They'll be well indulged there. I promise.' He exchanges a grin with Hannah. 'I'll leave these two in your capable hands, then, Hannah. Can you settle them here then bring them to the dining hall? They'll be hungry.'

Hannah nods as Cory leaves the room. The door closes softly behind him, and they stand in the centre of the room, taking in their new surroundings and watching their new roommate. She smiles at them and takes Carys's hand. 'Here,' she says, leading her over to one of the sets of bunk beds. 'You two can have this bed. No one's in this one.'

Carys glances at Amy, and they simultaneously dive for the bottom bunk, their laughter breaking the tension. Amy makes it first, and Carys punches her. She always punches harder than she realises, but Amy takes it in good spirit. Perhaps everything will be alright. Amy stretches out, feeling the weight of exhaustion creeping through her body.

'You can have some clothes from the store,' Hannah says. 'There are nightclothes in there, too, and it looks like you need new outfits. That what you've got on needs binning.' She giggles at us, her green eyes lost in lines of merriment. 'What have you been doing?'

Amy looks down at her tattered nurse's uniform. 'It's a long story. But we'll tell you about it soon.'

'Who else sleeps in here?' Carys asks her.

'Well, it's me, then it's Anna who is like fifty, but she's nice and everything. Then Emma and Ella. They're twins—'

'What does that mean?' Carys says.

Hannah stares at her. 'You don't know about twins? No… I suppose you wouldn't, really. We only know the word 'cos it's in a couple of Daniel's books…'

Daniel's books? A strange kind of lightness courses through Amy.

Carys frowns. 'What are twins, then?'

Hannah laughs. 'They are two babies that grew together. In the womb.'

Carys's eyes widen. 'That's impossible.'

'No,' Hannah says, sitting on her bunk and swinging her feet. 'It's just that Newland doesn't ever let it happen. I mean, they don't let one of the babies be born. I think.'

Amy's stomach churns. 'Like my mother,' she says, staring at the wall. 'She was never given a choice to keep me, but she had me anyway. In secret.'

'Where are their parents, though? And yours?' Carys asks.

Hannah's grin fades. 'They died.'

Carys gazes at her. 'Mine, too.'

'And the last one is Raza,' Hannah says. 'You want to watch out for her; she's really grumpy. She's not far from your age, though. She's seventeen. How old are you?'

'I'm sixteen,' Carys says. 'Only just. But Amy here, and Jacob, they'll be seventeen soon.'

'Oh. Well, Raza's almost eighteen. She ran away from the Centre. She's got a story to tell, but she won't tell it you unless she trusts you. That's like the Queen… oops.' Hannah flings her hands over her mouth and flushes. 'Pretend I didn't say that.'

Hannah leads them to a storeroom and shows them where to find some clothes. There are piles and piles in here. Mostly casual, old-fashioned clothes, but comfortable and clean. Hannah shows them the bathroom and finds them both a new toothbrush. Amy cleans her teeth for the first time in days and feels refreshed. Carys's pale cheeks show spots of colour.

They follow Hannah to the dining hall. Amy wonders if it will be the room with the large table they were taken to first, but it's a different place. This one is flooded with light; a smeared glass ceiling soars high above the sunken space, the evening sky saturating the room with vibrant oranges and corals. It's like sitting outside. There are groups of tables in here, each one heaving with bright-faced folk. She curls her shoulders around her chest as dozens of eyes fall on them and the excitable buzz of conversation draws to an abrupt halt. Footsteps sound in the sudden silence; Cory and Jacob walking through the doorway to join them. Everyone stares.

The children are here. The small girl who so charmed Amy, her euphoric face thrown to the cascading rain, is sitting at a table with a mixture of adults and children. Most of them gaze at the newcomers, but she clambers off her seat and runs to them, stumbling through the space, hips thrown forward awkwardly. She lumbers up to Amy and tugs on her injured hand. 'Sit with me! I'm called Esther. What's your name?'

People begin to talk again, though much more quietly, all eager for information about these strangers. Thankfully, they have little opportunity to account for themselves, as the little girl and her friends chatter nonstop, the adults looking on indulgently. They sneak stares at them, and occasionally soft smiles, but no one asks them their business, and that's fine with Amy. All that matters to her right now is food and then sleep. The egg and chips doesn't disappoint, and as she eats every last morsel she finds herself wondering where they get it. How are they surviving down here under this deserted, ruined city? Where are they getting power from, and how are they sourcing their food?

Jacob stares at his plate, his brows knitted closely, pushing the food around with a fork.

Cory tells them that in the morning, he will present them with their list of duties and introduce them to everyone. 'You look so tired,' he says. 'You need sleep.' Gratefully, they slink off in their different directions, Carys and Amy to the girls' dorm and Jacob away to wherever he has been placed, his face heavy with pain. He won't even acknowledge them to say goodnight.

In the dormitory, all is quiet, with only Carys and Amy there. Amy sinks into her new bed and sighs; it's like no other bed she's ever slept in, even the one back at home. She gazes around the room, taking it all in, but her eyelids are heavy and sleep steals upon her quickly, pinning her down in a nest of relief. She sleeps peacefully, with no shrill alarm to startle her and keep her brain trained for productivity.

₢JACOB

HE'S IN A place far away. It's like he's peering through a dusty glass and seeing a blurry version of his surroundings in this strange place, people all around him, things he's never seen or imagined. The Queen, her dark eyes pinning his down, her skin so like his. Somewhere inside him, he knows Carys is reaching to him, but she can't get to him and he can't get to her. He can't feel anything. He's numb, and when he tries to feel, to respond, nothing happens. Just one great big stinking stupor.

Baba died. He couldn't stop him dying.

He couldn't save Sim.

His mother is not in the Home. She is dead.

And his Baba died, and he did not save him.

6

THE BUNKER

CARYS

WHEN I WAKE up the room is alive with movement, and I stay there for a moment, blurry and confused, getting my bearings. My heart leaps as I realise that I am free and I am safe, I am warm, clothed and fed. And then sinks as I remember Jacob's morose face last night and my inability to help him. I felt feeble, powerless; I desperately wanted to break through to him, but it was like he wasn't there. Perhaps today things will be different. I yawn and stretch and then hang over the bunk, looking at Amy. She's still fast asleep.

Hannah is getting dressed while reading her book. She seems permanently attached to that thing. I've never actually read a whole book; I'm not good at reading, that's what the Carers and Trainers told me. They said I was too slow, that I missed words when I read out loud, that I was stupid. I've read stuff on NSlates, of course, but books are boring. The ones they forced us to read in training, at least, and they're the only ones I've known. Amy used to read medical textbooks in bed at Ashton, and I didn't get that either.

Two little girls are bouncing around the place. Everything about them radiates energy, from their wiry dark curls to their bright brown eyes to their jumping feet. They look about seven. Emma and Ella, I presume. An older lady is sitting on a chair by the dressing table, applying make-up. I catch her gaze in the mirror. A map of crow's feet extends from the corners of her eyes, and she looks peaceful. Happy.

A small cough sounds from the shadows behind me, and I turn to the girl on the top bunk opposite mine. She's lying on her front, her gaze melancholy, her forehead furrowed as she contemplates me and Amy. I'm directly in her line of sight, and I smile tentatively at her. She remains still, her face stone like. She has jet black hair hanging in straggly threads, and a sharp, thin face. She's tall, lanky, and remains of black eye make-up dot her eyes and cheeks. A silver ring pierces her nose, something I've never seen on Compound kids. That would be strictly forbidden. We are only allowed pierced ears when we reach Productivity. This girl has multiple piercings in both ears.

'Hello,' I say to her.

She lifts her chin at me.

'I'm Carys.'

'Raza.'

I don't know what else to say. She scares me a little, so I turn away and hoik myself down from my bunk, waking Amy in the process. She stretches and sits up, rubbing her eyes. We've caught the attention of the two balls of energy, who bound over to us as one. 'What's your name?' they ask together.

'I'm Carys, and this is Amy,' I say.

'Well, I'm Emma, and this is Ella.'

The other one says, 'No, I'm Emma, and this is Ella.' They break into giggles, and I can't help laughing along with them. 'Pleased to meet you, Emma and Ella, or is it Ella and Emma?' I think about how I like the names, names from the Before, and wonder again why the Party decided to ban most names. It seems so odd, now I am looking at it from the outside. I never really questioned it before, but now I think on it, and it all mixes into the bubbling pot of my anger, each ingredient intensifying the taste of it.

I'm not sure about Raza, though. I don't know if it's a Before name, and it's definitely not a permitted Productivity name. I don't like to ask, though.

The twins splutter with laughter and bounce off around the room again. The woman at the dressing table turns to them, frowning. 'Girls. Get dressed. You'll be late for lessons.' They groan and begin to pick up items of clothing scattered around the floor.

Jacob isn't at breakfast. Others welcome us with smiles and more curious glances. I see Cory across the room, but no sign of the Queen. Maybe she eats her meals in private, brought to her by servants. She certainly doesn't seem the type to enjoy socialising very much.

I sit between Amy and Raza. Raza's face is slathered in make-up; her face pale as a ghost, her eyes thickly lined with jet-black kohl, her lips black and lined with scarlet. She wears wristbands, both covered with barbs, reminding me uncomfortably of the flail. Studying her further I notice a large knife, sheathed at her waist. She catches me staring and throws me a glare full of rancour. I feel my temper flaring and, as she throws me another look, I turn to her. 'Do you have a problem?'

She shrugs.

'It's just, you keep looking at me.' Amy nudges me, but I ignore her.

'Really.' She spears her bacon with conviction.

'Yes. Really.' What is her deal? I haven't done anything to her.

Amy nudges me again, harder this time. I shrug her off.

'Have I done something?' I say to Raza. Her sharp face is hard. Cold.

'No.'

'Then please stop staring at me like that.'

'Whatever.'

Amy digs me in the ribs. 'Just leave it. We don't know anything about her. Please, don't make an enemy on our first day here.'

After breakfast, Cory takes us into the room with the sofas and the table and invites us to sit. Children gather around the table, taking out books and pens. 'This is where they have their lessons,' Cory says. 'They learn about the Before, as well as maths, science and everything else.'

'I'd like to learn about the Before,' I say.

Cory studies me, his gaze narrowed. 'Time enough. For now, we'll wait for your friend, and I'll tell you how things work around here.'

'Can you tell me about the Queen?'

'Not really. That's up to her.'

'Oh, right.' I am disappointed. There is so much to know here, much to learn, but no one is in a hurry to help. I drum my fingers on my knees.

When Jacob finally arrives, face as long as ever, Cory takes out a folder with written sheets of information. He clears his throat. 'Our community here has been established for many years, with people coming and going. At present, there are sixty-one members, or sixty-four if you three are going to be included.' He pauses, looks at each of us, his gaze lingering on me for longer. I shift on my seat in discomfort.

'Are you called anything? I mean, your community?' Amy says.

He sniffs and then lets out a slow breath, shaking his head. 'You only need to think of us as the community at present.'

Amy asks all these practical questions, like how they survive and where they get their food from. They have a farm, apparently, on the surface. They have cows and horses, chickens and pigs, sheep and dogs. They grow a variety of foods up there. Amy asks how they can grow food in the middle of a ruined city, and Cory explains that their fields are further out on the edges, where they have more rural land without ruins. The land is far from any Compound routes, so unlikely to be spotted by NForce, unless they are deliberately scouting in Copters. They've avoided being seen as yet and plan to keep it that way.

'Why don't you all live up there, then?' Amy asks. 'With the animals?'

Cory smiles softly. 'We're safer in the bunker if there does happen to be a raid on the farm. We have children to think about. Everyone is up on the surface in the daytime, going about various farm business, but nights are spent in the bunker, safe from harm.'

This sounds good to me right now.

'Where is everyone here from?' I say.

Cory is silent for a few moments. He temples his hands under his chin and glances around the room at the children, busy at work with a couple of the adults helping them. He lowers his voice. 'Most of us are fugitives from various Compounds, some from the Centre. Some escaped, some were banished from Compounds.'

Amy lifts her head and stares at him.

'What about the twins?' I say.

'You don't need any further information,' he says firmly. I sigh in frustration.

Cory tells us about the reservoir on the outskirts of the city, bordering the farm. They get their water from there, having designed a system of pipes and filters which lead to the bunker. He tells us that the water is safe for drinking but is always boiled first then stored in big refrigerators in the back of the kitchen. 'How do you get the power?' Amy asks.

'We generate our own electricity on the farm with wind turbines, and we have generators here too.'

Amy raises her eyebrows. 'It looks like you're really self-sufficient. And you just share everything? No one has more than anyone else?'

'Not even the Queen,' Cory says, his chin high. 'We are not like Productives. They pretend to have this amazing fair system, where everyone is in work, but in reality they just have the rich and poor, just like it's always been, and the rich just get richer on the back of the productivity of the poor. Here, everyone gets the same, everyone contributes. And those who are weak, or ill, or elderly – like Daniel, who you'll probably meet soon – they get what they need, too. We look after them. I know that sounds like what you were told all your lives about the Home. But here… this is different. We really do.'

I look down, thinking about the room with the computers and the sickening truth Jacob and I found just a few days ago. I swallow rising bile and glance at Jacob, who is also staring at the ground, his mouth flattened.

'It's not perfect. We have our ups and downs. People come and go, argue, cause schisms then leave. But in the main we make it work. The Queen does, really. She's wise, and she's been through a hell of a lot… I shouldn't say more.'

Cory talks about what our duties will be. Turns out there's a weekly rota, and everyone checks it at the beginning of the week. Some folks have the same job all the time, like the child carers and the shepherds, but others share the jobs out. 'You'll be in the laundry today. Sorting out washing, hanging it out, ironing, collecting and replacing sheets and towels.'

Amy nods, and Jacob lifts his shoulders. I think it sounds okay. Better than Newday Instruction, which we'd usually be in this time on a Tuesday morning.

The laundry smells of clean, warm damp. I like the feel of it, the slightly floral aroma. 'This is Kate,' Cory says, nodding at a grey-haired woman folding a large blanket, 'and you know Raza.'

Great. A day full of dark looks for me, then.

It isn't so bad in the end. Raza works hard, saying little. Kate, a warm older woman, chatters away merrily, telling us that she was brought up here on the Outside and never knew life in a Compound. Her ancestors kept their names from the Before and passed the names down through the generations. Her great-great-grandparents were some of the founders of this community, along with Daniel's great-great-grandparents. Outcasts from the Re-Ordering, survivors of the great Scourge. Kate and Daniel have been married for over fifty years. 'You should talk to Daniel,' she says, smiling at me, 'he knows everything about everything, because he has books. You should ask him to show you them sometime. He has a library. Locked up, because the books are so precious, antiques from the Before.'

Amy's eyes widen. 'Books from the Before?'

Kate nods. 'After the riots, the New Day Party ordered mass burnings of all books. Books were unhelpful to Productive life, they said, they promoted rebellion and gave people ideas above their station.' Her mouth twists. 'Better to make a clean slate, start anew, write their own Party-endorsed books to give us pride in our new country.'

'How do you know all this?' I ask.

'My grandparents told me what happened when the New Days took power. Their grandparents fled to live among the ruins, along with Daniel's great-great-grandparents, who saved a number of books and hid them away. They took a few others with them, people who couldn't stand to live under Party rule.'

Amy's gaze is pinned on Kate. I wonder if she's thinking about the books and what it will feel like to see them, to hold them. They're just books, though. They can't be that special.

Jacob gets on with his work in silence. Him and Raza make a great pair, with faces like storms, body language prickly and stooped. I know he's really hurting and wish I could help. Wish he'd let me in, wish he'd help me understand. I want to know what it's like to love someone so much that losing them is so very unbearable.

When I think about Jacob, I think I might understand it a little more than I did before.

But he's closed to me.

7

THE COMMUNITY

AMY

A MY CAN'T STOP thinking about books and can't stop dreaming about books.

'Would you mind if I read that?' she says to Hannah the second night in the dorm, and Hannah smiles and hands her battered blue book over. *Harry Potter and the Goblet of Fire.* Amy opens it carefully, reverently, sensing something different to all she's ever known. 'There are more of them?' she says, reading down the list of titles in the front.

Hannah pouts. 'Yeah. This is book four. We don't have any of the others, and that sucks. But it's still awesome. I just make up the other stories in my head.'

Amy spends most of that night and her free time the next day reading it. She's quickly immersed in the world of Hogwarts, Quidditch, dragons and the Ministry of Magic and, when she has read it, she begins it again, gorging on every word. 'You should give this a go,' she says to Carys.

Carys purses her lips. 'I can't really read properly, you know that.'

Amy huffs. 'You know that's bull the Trainers made you believe, right? Just 'cos you read differently doesn't mean you can't. And also, you've never seen a good book before. This'll blow your mind.'

'Maybe,' Carys says, but she doesn't pick up the book when Amy leaves it lying on her bed later that night.

The three refugees soon settle into the rhythm of life in the Community. After a week, they've rotated around several different jobs. They've been in the laundry, they've been on the cleaning and cooking teams, they've stood and washed up pots for hours at a time. On the surface, they have been fruit picking, standing and stooping at gooseberry bushes until their fingers bleed and their backs stiffen; they've mucked out pigs and chickens and collected milk from the cow barn, hefting huge buckets over to the horses and carts and back to the bunker. Shadow and Rainbow are well employed around the fields and to and from the bunker and seem frisky and healthy. Every morning one of Amy's jobs is to collect eggs from the henhouse, and she loves the walk through the early morning, picking her way through the ruins to the stables. Drew always has Shadow ready for her, and she's learned to handle him fairly well, trotting through the rubble out to the fields, dismounting and making her way through the squawking chickens to recover their gifts. Carys went with her on the first morning and dropped a bag full of eggs, smashing them all, so she's avoided that one since. She loves mucking out the horses and is to be found in the stables at every opportunity, chatting with Drew and Hannah.

Amy is desperate to talk to Daniel. She hasn't been able to sit with him at a meal yet; he's not too well and takes most meals in his room with Kate. He's riddled with arthritis and Amy thinks it's likely he has heart disease, but there's no suitable medication here. Kate seems to have energy enough for the pair of them, working in the laundry and the kitchen day in, day out, chatting away to anyone who will listen. Amy enjoys hearing Kate's opinions on everything from the football tournament to the Queen, although she doesn't say a lot about her.

In their second week at the bunker, she gets her opportunity. She's early for dinner and spots Daniel in his wheelchair in the far corner of the dining room. Kate is fetching his food from the hatch and nattering away to one of the other women. Amy scampers over to her. 'Shall I take it for you?'

Kate glances at her and nods, shoving the tray at her and barely taking a pause in her stream of consciousness. Amy quickly grabs a plateful for herself and takes the two meals to the table. She's just in time. The hall is filling up quickly with hot, thirsty, exhausted people, fresh from the fields and the bunker.

'Here you go,' she says to the old man. 'Kate gave me this for you.'

'Thank you, young lady,' Daniel says, his voice raspy. His faded blue eyes shine with merriment, his white hair sparse, more of it on his grizzled sideburns than on his head. His teeth are mostly gone, but it doesn't stop him smiling. 'Amy, isn't it?' He returns her analysis, looking her straight in the eye.

She nods. 'It's nice to finally meet you. Kate has told me all about you.'

He wheezes a phlegmy laugh. 'Ha! I'll bet she has. Never stops talking, that woman.' His eyes shine brighter.

They eat for a while, listening to the hum around the place. Amy sees Carys and Jacob come in together, but they sit elsewhere. Jacob's still brooding, but he seems to like Carys near him, although she keeps getting frustrated with him and asking him to talk to her. She needs to give him time, just be with him. Amy keeps telling her that, but Carys won't listen.

'Kate told me about your books,' she says, turning back to Daniel. 'Your library… and I've read the book you lent Hannah. The *Harry Potter* book.'

'Ah, yes,' Daniel says. 'It's a great shame my ancestors saved only one. It's in very poor condition now, too, mainly due to young Hannah and her love for it.' He pauses, staring at the window above. 'I would very much like to have read the others.'

'May I look at your books sometime?' Amy tries to be polite. He may be very protective of his books.

Instead, he beams. 'Of course, dear. My books are my joy. You must come and see them. Bring your friends – there are a lot to see. You'll get lost in them, though… they'll eat your time up. They do mine, still, and I've read every one of them a hundred times.' His eyes crinkle as he grins, and Amy can't help smiling just as widely.

'I'd love to,' she says. 'I'll ask Carys and Jacob. I think they'll be interested to see them, but they don't want to read as much as I do.'

'Ah. They haven't had the chance to experience the joy it brings, perhaps?'

'I think you're right.'

'Come now. Tonight. After dinner.'

'Wow. Really?'

'Yes.'

'Thank you.' She can hardly contain her excitement and crams the remainder of her food down as quickly as she can.

Daniel watches her, chuckling. 'It's good to see such enthusiasm at the thought of books,' he says. 'Most Productives who come here have no idea about books. Something is different with you.'

Amy tells him some of her story as he slowly picks at the tiny amount of food on his plate; she tells him about her parents bringing her up illegally, about her soul-child – brother, the word she has learned since – who was murdered for being complicit in the deception. 'They might be somewhere on the Outside, my parents,' she says. 'I don't suppose… Lois Retail and Alwin Plumber?'

Daniel shakes his head. 'Not here, at least,' he says. 'But don't give up hope. They may be in another Outside community. You may find them.'

'I will try.' She doesn't know how, but she will.

Daniel signals to Kate. 'I'm taking these kids to the library. Can you fetch my keys?'

Kate rustles away and Amy beckons to Jacob and Carys. 'Daniel's going to show us the books,' she calls.

Jacob shrugs, but Carys drags him over, regarding Daniel with interest. 'Will they tell us some history?'

Daniel nods. 'There are all manner of books in my library. History books, fiction books, religious books. Everything you can think of.'

'How many books do you have?' Carys asks.

'I have sixty-seven books. My ancestors saved them all from the Burnings, you see. Put themselves at great risk. Anyone found with a book was immediately put to death for insurrection against the new government. Most of them are in poor shape, but they are still there. Come and see.'

They follow Daniel as he wheels himself out of the dining hall and down the corridor towards the dormitories. He pushes through a door to the left marked "supplies". Amy has never been in there, thinking it was simply a cupboard. It turns out it leads to another double door, and that leads to a very ancient looking wooden mechanical elevator, surrounded by a rusted iron lattice cage. Amy glances at Jacob; he'd usually be all over something like this, but he stays silent, his face turned to the ground. Not even a flicker.

'You have a lift here?' Amy says, staring at Kate, who is standing by the doors, waiting for them with a bunch of keys.

'We have some great engineers in our midst, you know,' Kate says, smiling. 'You may think we're just some backwater bumpkins out here, but we can do stuff. Besides, this thing comes from way back in the Before, we just keep the old beast going. Come on.' They crowd reluctantly into the musty, narrow box and Kate presses the lower button, which simply says "B".

The lift descends into the bowels of the earth, clanking and screeching and shaking their bones. 'Is it safe?' Carys says, and Daniel laughs.

Amy wonders about the origins of this place. Did the original community here dig it out, or was there some kind of bunker here already, in the Before? How did they fit an archaic lift, of all things, down here? The bunker certainly stretches wider and deeper than she'd realised.

The lift judders to a halt and Kate pushes the door open with a loud creak. This time they are facing another door, a huge oak one, ornately carved with meticulous depictions of roses and grapes. It seems incongruous with its surroundings. Where did it come from?

Kate selects a brass key and inserts it into the large, ancient lock. The door swings open silently, as if well oiled. It's a small room, cosy and dimly lit, warm, but not like Principal's study is warm. A different, almost friendly quality to the warmth. Four large squishy red chairs form a circle around a low table, and the floor is carpeted in dark, feet-sinking, red plush. The polished stone walls don't seem so stark in this room. Gentle light spills from several uplighters placed around the walls.

Then Amy sees the books.

She knows about libraries. Her mother once told her that in the Before, every town had a library where anyone could borrow any book. Each library contained thousands of books. She could hardly comprehend it. This room is nothing like that, but she still catches her breath at the shelves of books. Someone has lovingly carved a bookcase from cedar, and it has pride of place in the room, sitting flush to the back wall behind the chairs. Books fill every shelf, and there are books on the table as well, as if waiting to be picked up and read.

'Welcome to my library,' Daniel says, smiling and sweeping his arms wide. 'You are all welcome to borrow my books, but you must sign them out and back again. It would be a tragedy if one were to go missing. And you must treat them very carefully. They are irreplaceable.'

'Does everyone here borrow books?' Amy asks, awestruck by the surroundings.

'Quite a few. Some more than others. Young Hannah, for example. Now there's a girl who loves books. Warms my heart to see. She's read that *Harry Potter* book at least fifty times, I would say.'

'I've already read it twice,' Amy says.

'Have a seat,' says Daniel. 'Have a look at some of these books on the table. I'll show you some more, too. What would you be interested in?'

Carys frowns. 'I don't know a lot about books. The books on my NSlate at Ashton… they were all about Newland heroes – men – who made sure everyone was Productive. It got so boring. I never bothered finishing them, and then got in trouble with Trainer One when I couldn't review them properly.'

'Well, young lady, I think you'll find if you try these you may feel differently about reading.'

Jacob slumps down in one of the red chairs and selects a book from the table. It looks shabby, well read. It has a black cover that has been taped back on multiple times by the look of it.

'Ah yes,' says Daniel, wheeling himself over to Jacob. 'This is one of my favourites. *To Kill a Mockingbird*. An outstanding book. I can't imagine why the New Day fools wanted to outlaw things like this. Well, actually, I know exactly why, thinking about it. I think you'll like it.'

Jacob says nothing. He flicks the book open, his eyes moving back and forth over the first page. Carys sits next to him, and Amy wanders over to the bookshelf, running her hand down the carvings of birds and trees. She wants to savour each moment in here. It's a place that feels as close to home as she has experienced since that awful day when everything was shattered. She wants to stay here and absorb the atmosphere. She's almost too afraid to pick up a book, worrying she will lose the moment.

But they lure her. They invite her into them, enticing her in as if from a cold night into a warm house with a blazing fire. She sighs contentedly and begins to scan the titles. Daniel has the books separated into sections. Fiction, history, religion, poetry, plays. She has a look at the "Fiction" section.

The Secret Garden. Treasure Island. 1984. The Fellowship of the Ring. Dracula. A Passage to India. Pride and Prejudice. Wuthering Heights. A Christmas Carol. The Lion, The Witch and The Wardrobe.

Alice's Adventures in Wonderland. Watership Down. Anne of Green Gables. Gone With the Wind. The Hunger Games. The Book Thief. Brave New World. The Hobbit. Black Beauty. The Kite Runner. The Stand.

She pauses a second, wondering about some of the words in the titles. What does 'wuthering' mean? Where is India? What is a Hobbit? What is Christmas?

The titles go on, tantalising her further. In the "plays" section she sees titles like *Romeo and Juliet, An Inspector Calls* and *Much Ado About Nothing*. The "history" section contains some larger books; *Guinness World Records 2028, Nothing to Envy, The Kings and Queens of England, History of Britain and Ireland, The Slave Trade, Rotten Romans, The History of Medicine*. The "religion" section has only two books, one a thick battered book with no cover and scorched, thin pages, which Daniel informs her is a holy book of one of the old religions that narrowly missed the Burnings, and *A History of the World's Religions*.

There is so much here. A new world to learn about. She is on the precipice of something; poised ready to leap into the unknown.

Carys wanders over and gazes at the titles with her. Her eyes are wide, and Amy knows the books are already working their magic, even unread. Carys pulls out *Black Beauty* and examines it, opening it in the middle then flicking back to the start. The words reel her in, and she walks with it, head buried in it, back to the chair.

Amy takes *The History of Medicine* and sinks into the chair next to Carys, curling her feet under her, embracing this new, exquisite feeling of excitement and discovery. She knows that, for all of them, life will never be quite the same again.

8

THE COMMUNITY

CARYS

N THE END, it's the books that bring Jacob back.

They reach into that dark place, the place he guards so carefully. I witness the glorious shattering of his defences first hand, sitting in Daniel's library one humid August evening.

Jacob's in the library every night, devouring *To Kill a Mockingbird*, saying little. Amy's been happily accompanying him, and so, to my surprise, have I. From the moment I picked up *Black Beauty* I have been captivated. I read that in three evenings – and Trainer Three said I was useless at reading – and now I'm halfway through the first book Amy kept trying to make me read, *Harry Potter and the Goblet of Fire*. It's like something inside of myself is waking, something I never knew was there. There is a new world here, and I'm ready for it. Just in these two books, I've learned more about friendship than I learned right through Infant House, pre-training and training. I've learned that in the Before, people were more important than economics and productivity. I want that, and I want to know more.

I've noticed the tattered remains of an old religious book sitting on the bookshelf. There's no cover left, it's been partially burned;

Daniel's ancestors must have grabbed it from the Burnings. It makes me think of Newday Instruction and the Sacred Book, the words of Commander Lucan, inspired by the Illumen, so we were told. I always wanted to know about the old religions, and so I read through the *World Religions* book. It fascinates me to see such a great swathe of cultures and beliefs, so much colour and life and celebration, joy and sorrow. Something more the Party took away from us.

We're sitting in companionable silence, curled up in Daniel's chairs. Daniel himself is in his room, too tired to join us tonight, but has trusted us with the keys. I'm caught up in Harry's battle with the Hungarian Horntail when I hear a slight sniff. I ignore it, absorbed in the tale, and then hear another, louder. Then a choking sob, deep and pained. I glance up this time and stare at Jacob. His eyes are bloodshot and brimming and, as I watch, tears begin to creep down his cheeks. The stony face I have come to expect over the past few weeks softens as I watch, his expression morphing into to something more raw and vulnerable. Stirred, I place my book down on the table and crouch next to him.

'Jacob?' I search his face. He looks at me, pins his watery eyes on mine. For the first time since Aiden died, he looks at me.

'They were treated so badly,' he says. 'In this place, where this book was set. But it—' he stops, swallows.

'What?' I prompt, daring to lay my hand on his. Amy watches us, nodding slightly at me.

'It… the characters in here… they're like learning that you can't judge by appearances. And Atticus, he's just, well, he shows what justice is, you know? He got this guy free. Tom Robinson. He was innocent and he got him free. Everyone was just awful to him because of his colour. But then he was freed… but he died. Tom. But now everyone's different, Scout's different… more thoughtful. More understanding.'

I have no idea what he is talking about, but something is changing in him. The impatience and frustration that have been building in me are calmed, as if they are chased away.

'You'll just have to read it,' he says, smiling through the tears. I smile back at him, feeling tears prick my own eyes. I squeeze his hand, wincing slightly, waiting for the inevitable rebuff. But this time it doesn't come. This time he squeezes back.

Amy murmurs something about needing the loo. She leaves the room, closing the door quietly, and Jacob and I are alone in this strange new sea of emotion. I crouch there, his hand in mine, eyes locked on one another. He raises his other hand to his face to rub away tears, but more fall, and more, and then his shoulders are shaking. Deep, primal sobs rumble his body, rocking him, healing him. I know he's not crying for the book, but for Aiden, and for all we have seen and lost. Before I know it he moves closer to me, and then he's kneeling on the floor with me and we are in one another's arms, saying nothing as the sobbing runs its course.

As his body shudders into stillness I hold his face gently between my hands. 'Are you okay?' It seems a stupid question, but I don't seem to have words.

He wipes tears and snot away. 'Kind of,' he says, and he smiles, and it's like the sun has broken through ragged storm clouds.

We stay there on the floor, arms around one another, for a long time, and I don't want this moment to end. I whisper to him, 'Your love for Aiden. His for you. It's more powerful than anything I've ever seen.' I hear the catch of longing in my voice.

Jacob strokes my face. 'You can know that too,' he says softly, and my heart swells. Perhaps it is something I already do have. Here and now, in this safe and astonishing place.

For the next few weeks, we settle more into community life. We work and we read, and we play. We run free through the old ruins and the fields of the farm. Jacob and Amy play football with some of the others, and I play board games with the children. They inspire me, with their delight in all that is around them, their innocent animation in all they do and learn. So different from the children of the pre-training houses, working like automatons, lost in their assurance that all is well and Newland is good. I do not want to lose my resolve to bring this freedom to others, to tell the nation about the atrocities the Party are performing, but at the moment I just want to stay here in this place.

We still talk about our next steps, but I know we are becoming more half-hearted, more lethargic about it. Putting it off for longer. We'll go when we have helped with the harvest, oh but then it will be the winter and it will be too cold. We should build up a team around us, take them with us. Maybe next spring… we'll be so much stronger, then, from the hard work in the community.

I see that we are losing our intention, but I can't seem to find the strength to do anything about it, and I know Amy and Jacob feel the same. It's like we're slipping down a comfortable slope; to clamber back up would be too much for us after all we have been through. We'll stay here and mend for as long as it takes.

Jacob

Jacob can see beyond himself and his darkness again. He misses Baba, and it's always going to hurt like hell, but the books and the work are doing something deep inside him and he feels like he is waking up.

He's getting busy here. Not just with the reading, but they've discovered his love for all things tech and asked him to take a look at their stuff. They've got this room here with a load of super ancient NComs. They say they reclaimed them from junk tips just outside Compounds and got them working again to some degree. Their power here is a bit flaky. They've got turbines and generators and solar panels and such but they're not always reliable, so the power's liable to cut out at a moment's notice. Because of this, they've not done a whole lot with their NComs. They've tried to set up some kind of internal communication system, but it's not up to much. It looks like something pre-training kids might design in their IT lessons. He doesn't say this, though. He makes impressed noises and asks them if they'd like him to update their systems. Cory, the dude who seems to be most in charge apart from the Queen, says that they would appreciate that. He says that what they would really like is if they could somehow establish communications with other Outsiders from other cities. Jacob tells him that will be pretty hard. There's no Newday net out here, no wireless coms, so getting anything like that up and running would be dependent on radio systems, old telecommunications type of stuff they had way back in the Before. Cory says they don't mind, anything will be better than nothing.

Jacob unearths a pile of ancient, dust-covered equipment that's evidently way back from the Before in a musty storeroom deep in the bowels of their bunker. It's some kind of radio transmission equipment, a couple of hefty machines with dials, headsets and attached transceiver mouthpieces of some sort. It's even pre digital display – tattered remains of labels are stuck on the dials, but he can't read them. Seems they're old HAM sets, so can be used here on the outside with no cell or wireless coverage. He has a lot to learn about how to operate these beauties, what MHz frequencies to tune to, how to set them up. Knows a little about short-wave radio communications just from tinkering with some of his grandfather's old stuff (Baba let him keep it at Ashton). Not a lot, though, but he's confident he can work it out. He learned some basic stuff about the history of communications and electro-magnetic fields and such in science lessons, but the Trainers never went very far.

Looks like these bad boys can be powered with 12v, so he hooks them up to a generator. They need some kind of antenna outside to work. There are some seriously archaic UHF TV antennas stowed down there among other piles of junk – obviously made for the old analogue TV frequencies, so not transmitters, but he's convinced he can make some modifications – as well as some vertical copper coiled aerials, some old satellite dishes, and a bunch of other useful looking kit, including a load of random cables, so he's playing with all of that. It's kind of fun, but he wishes he had a manual. He can only hope that there might be someone else, somewhere on the Outside, who has another of these set-ups and has it working. He might be able to find a channel somehow where they can communicate. It'll be patchy and probably come to nothing, but it's worth a try. He starts to think about how he can get something going that might attract communications from other people on the Outside, without interference from Productives. The worst thing that could happen is for him to give away their existence and whereabouts.

So, while the girls are working on the farm and around the bunker, he gets to mess round in a tech room, all he's ever wanted to do. He feels more chilled by the day, feels like this could be somewhere he could settle. The Productives and Ashton seem like a lifetime ago, even though it's only been weeks. Maybe it wouldn't be so bad if they hang out here for a while.

He updates their internal systems. This is easy, as he can link all their NComs manually. They don't have any NSlates or any other kit, so it's a case of making sure every unit is up and running. He suggests that they place units in other places, so people can communicate. So one goes in the main sitting room, one in the office, one in the dining room, and so on. Soon enough he's got a system going, and they seem to think he's some kind of genius. He's really not.

He's chatting to Cory one day in the office – he hangs out there most of the time. Jacob's helping him get all his paperwork onto the NDrives and set up NSheets and files to get all their information more streamlined and accessible. They're just talking about the personal files. Cory has one for every member of the community.

'So you can get these files on the NCom like this one? For every Subversive?' Cory seems distracted, staring at the file Jacob's demonstrating.

'What d'you mean, every Subversive?'

Cory looks at him, slaps his head lightly with his palm. 'Oh, hell, I didn't mean to say that. The Queen didn't want you to know. I don't really see any harm, though. It's what we call ourselves here. They're called the Productives, so we're called the Subversives. We started calling ourselves that fairly early on, when we were all fired up to do something. To actually *be* subversive. But we kind of got distracted with survival, and then we got this place going, and it turned out to be a pretty good place to live, so...' he shrugs.

'Right, yeah, so you were going to be like a resistance movement, you mean?' Jacob says.

'Kind of. Yes, actually. When the Queen got here she kind of got us all together again, and we were really up for it. We were all hurting in some way from the actions of the Productives. So we were going to be the ones who went in, led the rebellion, overthrew the Party. Balanced things out again, made it fair. I guess we've done that for our own community here. Most of us still call it the Subversives, or often the Subs for short, but we don't really mean it in a wider sense anymore. Maybe one day...' Cory gazes off into the distance.

'That's sort of our plan,' Jacob says. 'To sort of restore things, almost, to what they once were, or could be.'

'You're one of us now,' says Cory, and slaps Jacob on the back. 'You can be a lukewarm Sub, like the rest of us.' He grins.

Jacob smiles back, but inside he's grimacing. *Lukewarm.* That's it. Complacent. He's lost an edge. But there's something inside stirring again at the thought of being a Subversive. Of leading a rebellion.

AMY

'HAPPY BIRTHDAY, AMY!'

Esther, the little girl she noticed dancing in the rain on their first day here, bounces up to her with a handmade card and a small piece of fabric. She holds it out to her, a shy smile curving her mouth. 'I made it for you.'

Amy turns the fabric over in her hands and smiles. 'Oh, Esther. It's beautiful. You made this all by yourself?'

Esther giggles. 'Kate helped only a little bit. I'm a big girl an' I can do things like that.'

Amy looks at it again. A cross-stitch picture of a cat, roughly sewn in vibrant and clashing orange and purple wool. 'I love it. I will treasure it always. You worked so hard on it!'

Esther beams. 'An' we have 'nother surprise for you too.' She turns her head, makes a dramatic beckoning motion towards the door, where Emma and Ella are hovering with a tray. They walk slowly towards her, carrying a cake with colourful candles lit on top. 'I counted them,' Esther says, sticking out her chest. 'Seventeen. You're big now.'

Amy stares into the tiny flames, mesmerised by the dancing colours. Seventeen. The day she should become Productive. She's missing her Productivity ceremony, with the new dress Miss Warden would give her, the handwritten vows she must make to the Party and the champagne toast to how far she has come and how far she will go. She'd still have to complete her final year at Ashton, of course, but with Productivity comes status. She'd be given a Newland approved name. She'd be someone at last.

She twists her mouth into a wry grin and wonders if she'll ever attain Productivity now and if she'll ever care.

Esther hops up and down beside her. 'You have to blow them out,' she says, pushing her tangled hair away from her face. 'Or they'll burn the cake down.' She giggles again and prods Amy's arm. Amy looks at the cake, the candles, the gifts in wonder, thinking about how once upon a time birthdays were something special, how her mother always made her something new to wear, how they made a big fuss of her, and then how when she went to Ashton she quickly learned that birthdays were only to be marked because they meant one year closer to Productivity. There was to be no cake, no gifts. Such self-indulgence was not conducive to being in training or learning the value of hard work and sacrifice for their great nation.

She takes a deep breath in and blows on the candles, Esther dancing delightedly next to her. 'You left one! You left one!' she says, giving Amy a huge, gap-toothed grin.

'Ah well, I'm a bit out of breath. I think I need someone to do that one for me.'

'Me! Me! I can do it!'

'Of course you can.'

Esther gathers all her breath and then splutters all over the candle and the cake, her face alight with joy. Amy is hit with a feeling of safety; like she's come home and can't imagine leaving again. How can they go further with this half-formed quest? They're just three kids in a world of Productives. They'd be stupid to try anything without more backing.

Daniel wheels over to her and presents her with a gift wrapped in a silk scarf and a ribbon. 'I've saved this especially for this day.' She gazes at it, turning it over and over in her hands. 'Open it, then!'

She raises her eyebrows at Daniel as she carefully removes the wrapping. It's a small, tattered book with just one word printed in faded letters on the cover: *Scourge*.

'It's a very rare book,' he says, then laughs. 'Well, of course, all my books are extremely rare. What I mean is, very few of these were printed. It was a book that was squashed very quickly.'

'What do you mean?' She examines the book. The cover is plain and grey, the title small, as if to hide itself. There is nothing written on the back cover, and no author is listed.

'A scientist named May Samson wrote this in the old year 2030,' Daniel says. 'She wrote it to cover the Scourge that was sweeping the nation. By then the internet was down and the remaining newspapers in thrall to the New Day Party, so people had to get their news from other sources. She had a theory... well, you'll have to read it. Suffice to say, all copies of this were hunted down and destroyed… apart from this one, of course, which my great-great-grandparents saved with the others. I thought you'd like it, being medical and all.' His lips curve in a shy smile.

'Thank you,' she says, holding the book close to her chest. 'I'd like to know about the Scourge… the Trainers taught us so little. Only that it came on the back of the riots, that it spread quickly, and the population was severely decimated. That it was the fault of all the Unproductive people, of course.'

'You must read it, then,' says Daniel, patting her hand.

She feels as if she is teetering on the edge of something. It's not a long book, and the print is faded as if it was once submerged in water. She reads the first paragraph and freezes:

> "This book describes the events leading up to the Great Scourge of 2030 and the author's contention that the plague is man-made, spread deliberately by members of the New Day Party who are at present rallying for complete control in Parliament. It is vital that this book should not fall into unsafe hands."

> May Samson, November 2030

Amy reads on, hooked. She can't put it down, although the writing is clunky and rushed, and the science full of technicalities she's never learned though would dearly love to. So much was kept from them.

The book details some of the events of the riots but mostly concentrates on the so-called Scourge, which they have always been taught was spread through bad hygiene caused by the post-riot chaos. Only ten years before, the book says, another pandemic swept the world but was kept in check, the mortality rate far lower. There were questions with that one: whether it was man-made or introduced by poor hygiene in the wet markets of China. (Amy wishes she knew where China is, and what wet markets are.) This time, this author alleges that a contaminant was introduced to England's water supply and that most of the population then succumbed to the bovine influenza virus. The New Day Party cultivated cultures of the virus and added extra pathogens that meant death occurred in 99% of cases. When added to the water supply, most of the population perished within a week.

Amy sits in shock as she reads that the riots alone were not the cause of England falling into ruin. Samson wrote that the New Days destroyed cities, towns, and villages by planting bombs, dropping explosive devices, and setting large scale fires. Only nuclear power stations and their surrounding areas were spared, with New Day Party members staging coups and taking over. There must have been so many of them, organised to a high degree. It's little wonder the country was so completely flattened. Samson shared how it was her belief that they wanted to start afresh; to have a blank canvas to start Newland as it was going to go on. They were mad, she wrote. Brainwashed. Many of them had roots in nationalism and many were tied to neo-Nazi parties, whatever that means. It seemed they believed that in order to make the country a new, pure place, most of the infrastructure needed to be eradicated.

And they succeeded in their endeavour. Millions of people joined their efforts when they believed their rhetoric, and the country was razed to the ground.

May Samson, one of the lucky few who survived, was a research scientist in the old city of Oxford. She was highly suspicious of the New Day Party and particularly a man named James Hamlin, who later changed his name to Lucan. Her suspicions were further raised when she found out that all members of the New Day Party survived the "Scourge" – having stayed away from the main water supply. Samson collated her findings and produced this book, managing to get several hundred copies printed before the New Days got hold of a copy, and May was summarily arrested and publicly executed in the year N3.

Amy has no way of knowing if May's sinister assertions were true, but something tells her she was right. That the New Day Party's murderous schemes were not saved only for the new nation of Newland, but that they wiped out sixty million people. So that they could then take power over a tiny, battered remnant of people who had all lost loved ones, whose economy had tanked and whose health care systems were shattered. So that they could reign supreme in a country they created; a country of people who would bend to their will rather than face execution.

Amy gazes at the words, swimming before her in horrific shapes, taking on a reality almost too horrific to consider.

The New Day Party committed mass genocide even before they came to power.

9

THE COMMUNITY

I AM SHOCKED back to reality when Amy shows me the contents of the book Daniel gave her for her birthday the previous day. 'I feel sick,' I say to her after reading every word, though there's much I don't understand.

Her face is set in grim lines. 'We can't just forget all that has happened.'

'No,' I say.

Later on, after working in the fields all day and trying not to think about the book, I make my way to the library as usual. I'm reading *Soul Music*, which is part of a series of books about the imaginary Discworld. Again, I long to be able to access the other books in the series. I shrug off my frustration and a creeping sense of foreboding as I push the great oak door open.

Jacob's nowhere to be found, but Amy is down there, and as I enter I notice her face seems even paler than usual. She's perching on the edge of one of the chairs, her back stiff and straight, a thick book open in her lap. I recognise it as the tattered remains of the old holy book, which I've flicked through but not taken too much notice of, putting off reading until I've read the shorter books.

'What is it?' She looks up at me, her eyes wide and haunted. 'What's happened?'

'Nothing, really,' she says, shrugging and looking down at the holy book again. 'I just found something. It's made me feel even more angry.'

'Oh?' I glance down at the book. The words are too small to see from here.

'Here, look.' She points, and I crouch down to see. 'Read this section.'

I slowly read the words she is pointing at aloud: "He chose the weak things of the world to shame the strong." That sounds kind of familiar…' I say, biting on my lip. Something isn't quite right.

'And this one,' she says. She has marked another page with a card. I just came across this… it actually opened at this page. This says, "My grace is enough for you, for my power is made perfect in weakness". She pauses. 'Have you remembered yet?'

I sit back on my haunches, considering the words. They spin in my head, churning around as if trying to piece themselves together in a different order with a different meaning. It doesn't take too long for it to come to me: the Newland Sacred Book. Commander Lucan's words, inspired by the Divine Light, the Illumen.

'"His Power is made Stronger in our Strength"', I say. 'And "He chose the strong things of the world to shame the weak"'. I stare at Amy, a red rush of anger pounding my chest. 'They didn't make their divisive crap up from nothing. They took these old words from this holy book, and they twisted them to form something else. These words… these words are about upholding the weak, right? They took these words and turned them to something oppressive.'

'Yes,' says Amy. 'And then they burned the evidence.'

We contemplate one another, deep in thought.

Amy says, 'There's more in here. About defending the weak, about kindness and such. And a whole load of stuff I don't understand but want to know more about, just like everything else they hid away.' She gazes up at me, spittle forming on her lips and hands flying around as she pushes her words out. 'They were completely power crazed lunatics. Made everyone think they were good, but actually all they've done is create a society that condones murder and the vilification of the weak. Carys, we can't let them get away with this. We must take these words… to defend the weak… and do them.'

I gaze at her, awestruck by her passion. She's the pragmatic one, and here she is, breathing the fire I usually breathe. I stare at the words and I feel it rising again, and with it, a stirring of excitement. 'We need to show Jacob. We've been here too long, Amy. We've stopped bothering.'

Amy nods slowly, and we clasp hands, and it's as if the world is sliding back into focus.

AT SUPPER, CORY enters the room and marches to the centre of the hall, raising his hands. The room fades to silence almost immediately. 'The Queen has requested that we practise our yearly act of remembrance tonight,' he says shortly. People around us nod, and with serious demeanours and quietened voices, finish their food and drink.

I whisper to Hannah, 'What does he mean?'

Hannah shrugs. 'I've been here less than a year,' she says. 'I don't know.'

Raza is sitting opposite, her eyes darker and scowl heavier than ever. She's wearing a black leather jacket and heavy black buckled boots covered in mud from the days' work. 'It's when we remember people, duh,' she says, but won't say any more.

People begin to traipse out of the room, not in dribs and drabs as usual, but as a whole group. Glancing at each other, Jacob, Amy and I get up to follow the others. I'm surprised when they turn right down the corridor and then even more so when they take the hallway towards the main stairs. 'They're heading for the surface,' I say. That's unusual for an evening. Occasionally the little ones play out while it is still light, but most of the time we stay below ground after the day's work is done.

We follow the crowd as they slowly walk across the battered landscape, heading out towards the farm and the lake. I glance around, looking for the Queen, but see no sign of her. Maybe she gets to come on one of the horses.

The September evening light is beginning to draw in as we make our way through the old ruins. Orange and grey scurry together across the sky, twisting and darkening as we walk. There is a beauty in the sky tonight, an ethereal quality which reaches to me, stirs me. After about an hour we come close to the reservoir, and as we turn the final curve before we get to the western shore I see a strange light ahead, a flickering against the grey. Crackling pierces the silence; a small fire in a pit, old logs strewn all around in a rough circle. People are streaming to the logs and sitting down, warming their hands. Opposite us, directly behind the fire as I face it, I see the shadowed face of the Queen, her dark eyes glinting in the uncertain light, her long nose and sharp cheekbones noble in profile.

Everyone is seated. The entire Subversives Community is here, from Daniel in his wheelchair down to the smallest child, a toddler, sitting quietly with her mother. The crowd falls silent, and all I can hear is the sound of the fire, wood snapping as sparks fly. I lean forward in nervous anticipation.

Finally, the Queen speaks. 'Welcome, my family,' she says in sombre tones. 'Welcome to our night of remembrance. The time is right, and so we are gathered here to remember, to tell our stories and to give honour to those who went before.'

Jacob takes my hand in the fire-lit darkness, and I snuggle against him, wheezing a little from the walk and the smoke curling through the air.

'We will begin in our usual manner,' the Queen continues. 'No one is to be left out. All will be remembered. At the end, at dawn, we will be making our usual act of remembrance. You have supplies, Cory?'

Cory and his crew move around the fire, handing out blankets then pouring hot chocolate from large flasks. No one says a word.

'We will start with Ella and Emma's story tonight,' says the Queen. 'Girls. Come.' She beckons, and the twins go straight to her side. One stands on her left, and one on her right. 'As is our custom, when the parents are not with us, I tell the child's story. So please be still and hear Ella and Emma's tale.'

The tension in the air is palpable. People are sitting forward, straining to hear the words. I sit up straighter. I can feel the Queen's low voice drumming inside of me.

'The twins' parents lived in the Eastern Compound. They were good Productives, working hard at their jobs. Their mother was a baker, their father a solicitor. They met at Drew's place of work when Flora took sandwiches in every lunchtime. Within a year, Flora Baker was pregnant, and all was well in their world, looking forward to their one allotted child, destined to enter the most elite training and pre-training facilities.'

The Queen pauses, squeezing the twins' shoulders and allowing silence to fall like a blanket for moments.

'At the twelve-week scan, everything went wrong for Flora and Drew. The sonographer told them they were pregnant with twins, which was one more baby than the Party allowed. She would book them in as soon as possible, and then they could go on as normal, grateful for their chance at parenthood.'

One of the twins – Ella, I think – sniffs, and the Queen draws her closer. 'Flora found herself appalled at the reality of her situation and begged Drew to help her avoid the removal, but Drew was unwilling to go against the Party directive. His job meant power, and he didn't wish to lose it. Desperate and alone, Flora ran away, determined to keep both babies. She fled to the Outside, where she met up with Cory and the Subs. They gave her a home, and when dear Emma and Ella were born she gave them names from the

Before in honour of her new found way of life.' She hugs both girls close to her. 'She was happy here, in the bunker, and lived for her girls, but she missed her husband. She decided to find him, to bring him back.'

The Queen looks down. 'Sadly, Flora's plan did not work out. She did go back to the Centre and search for Drew, but when she found him, he was not amenable to her story or her plan. He had been promoted in recognition of outstanding service to the New Day Party and had no wish to jeopardise his position. Instead, he reported Flora immediately to the NForce, who threw her in the Think. We only found this out when another escapee from the Eastern Compound joined us and knew of Flora and her fate. We all know what happens to those in the Think.'

Jacob and I look at each other.

Ella and Emma are crying softly, and she strokes their cheeks in turn. 'So tonight we remember Flora Baker,' she says. 'We remember her courage and her loyalty, and we remember her love for her girls. We honour her.'

'We honour her.' The entire crowd say this aloud, and more than one face displays tell-tale streaks.

'Go and sit, dear girls,' the Queen says. 'We will honour her fully in our act later on. Be at peace now. Her story is told.'

The next story told is that of Esther, the girl of joy, as I think of her, and her mother, Lora, who tells her story in a cracked and faltering voice. 'When Esther was born with obvious Unproductivity markers, our joy turned to terror as the nurse's face turned grim. I'll never forget her words: "She will be taken immediately to the Home."' She pauses as a ripple runs through the crowd. 'We ran with our baby and escaped through the barrier, hiding her in the trunk of the car. Praying she wouldn't cry. But then we were pursued; news of the escape had reached the NForce, and their squad gained on us in no time.' Lora wipes her brow. 'The noise… the dread… they shot at us.' She chokes on her words. 'Rowe—' she gulps, '—he didn't make it.' The Queen lays her hand on her arm. 'The car spun out of control and down this hill at the side of the road, and I braced myself, waiting for certain death. By some miracle, Esther and I were unscathed, so we ran from the car and eventually found our way here.' She gazes down at her little girl, who is jingling up and down by her side. She smiles. 'I found the name *Esther* in the old holy book in Daniel's library. I knew this was who my baby was supposed to be. A woman of courage.'

The Queen speaks, holding Esther and her trembling mother close. 'Be at peace now,' she says. 'Rowe's story is told. We honour him.'

This time, we join in, our voices swelling with the rest. 'We honour him.'

Esther and her mother pick their way through the crowd and take their seats on one of the logs, and the Queen nods slightly.

Cory stands and makes his way to the Queen's side, his grizzled face in shadow. He stands for a moment, studying the ground in front of him. He clears his throat nervously. I look up, startled. Cory is the confident one. The self-assured one.

His voice is shaky as he begins his tale. 'I was an NForce officer,' he mumbles, 'in the Midlands Compound.'

The three of us lean forward.

Cory continues, his voice a little stronger. 'I was brought up to be an officer. It was all I was ever going to do. My father was a chief, and he was so incredibly proud of me when I qualified. I had all I'd ever wanted.' He pauses, his face inscrutable. Jacob catches my eye.

'I was a rising star. I was ripe for promotion. I was only twenty-one, but I was ambitious. Everyone around me cheered me on. I was an exemplary Productive, going far because of my work ethic. Life was good. B… but one day, everything changed for me. We were pursuing this guy, not much older than me. I wasn't really aware of what he'd done – was told he'd hacked some important files. We needed to apprehend him, throw him in the Think, and there he'd face justice. I was so up for it. I was on a team with my father, he was the chief investigating officer in the case.' He swallows, wrings his hands. This is not the Cory we've come to know, Cory the leader. I gaze at him, and I can see the young officer in him, eager to please his father and his superiors.

He takes a deep breath. 'We got a tip off that he was trying to escape the barrier. He was in the eastern forest, fleeing. We went after him quick and hard.' Again, he pauses, his nervous gaze taking in the attentive community. He glances at me for a second but looks away swiftly as he meets my eyes. 'He was slow. He was hindered by something, but I couldn't see what. We were gaining on him. We had dogs, and they were almost on him. And then my father… he took out a gun. I shouted at him. We nearly had him, I said, we didn't need to shoot. He'd only hacked files, after all. But my father… it was like he was looking through me. He just… just kept going. And then he raised the gun, and that's when I saw it. The baby. He had a baby. I remember screaming at Father to stop. But he didn't listen to me. He shot him anyway…'

I gasp, shocked at his story, but not completely surprised. I've had my own brush with the NForce.

Cory continues, his face ashen in the firelight. 'He fell, I remember, so quickly, so hard. But I saw him twist himself as he fell, holding out this tiny bundle, laying it on the ground. And then he collapsed. I ran to him. I was going to pick up the baby, but this man, he grabbed me. Stared straight at me. Asked me to tell her… to tell her he was in the Home. And to make sure she was okay.' He pauses. Swallows. 'And he asked me to keep this little box safe for her. He tucked it into her blanket. That's when everything sort of stopped for me. I looked round at my father, and I could see he just couldn't care less about this child, didn't care he'd just killed her father. I saw him for who he was. I saw all Productives for who they were. For who they'd been forced to be. And I knew right then that I didn't want a part of it.'

We sit in silence, mesmerised by his story.

'I set up the child in Infant House. Made sure she had enough money to see her through all her training. I gave more, so she could go to good training houses. Eventually, so she could go to Ashton. Kept my promise, too, I made sure that little box went with her.'

I sense Jacob stiffening. I can't seem to look at him. Can't look away from Cory. I trace the etched lines on the stone in my pocket and breathe.

'I kind of wish I'd taken the baby. Not left her to be brought up by unfeeling Productives. I got it wrong. But I was so young. After I sorted her out, I made plans to leave. My father was disappointed with the way I'd behaved and was blocking my imminent promotion, but I didn't care, so on a cold January night I fled the Compound and ended up here, eventually, where I found Daniel and Kate. I'm not proud of what I did but can only say I knew no better. Now, of course, I feel sick to my stomach about all I was a part of in the NForce.' He brings his hands to his face, resting his head in them for a time. We are silent.

After a minute, the Queen touches him gently on the shoulder. 'Cory,' she says gently, 'as usual we will honour him. The fallen man. Please state his name.'

Cory takes his hands from his face and looks up. His faded blue gaze is pinned directly on me.

'His name was Benedict,' he says, almost in a whisper. 'Benedict Clerk.'

I SEEM TO be in another place. I am a slab of stone, cold and unfeeling. I hear the Queen's next words echoing through to me as if from far away. 'Be at peace now,' she says to Cory, 'Benedict's story is told. We honour him.'

We honour him, the crowd around me chant, and it rings in my ears. *We honour him. We honour him.* And then something happens in me; I'm standing, I'm running to Cory. It's involuntary; I cannot control it.

'When was this?' I'm aware I'm shouting at him. Pushing at him.

He regards me sadly, his eyes shining with tears. 'It was about fifteen and a half years ago,' he mumbles. And then he places his hands on my shoulders. 'Carys Clerk. I knew who you were as soon as I found out your name. Your father – he was the bravest man I ever knew. He saved you. He… he called you by your name… Carys. He loved you so very, very much.'

'You killed him,' I hear myself crying, my voice stringent, cutting harshly into the uneasy silence. 'You… you murdered him.'

'I'm so sorry, Carys.' Cory drops his hands. 'I was responsible. As much as my father. I chose to ignore things I felt uneasy about. Chose to go with what everyone else was saying and doing. So yes, I did. I killed him. And he saved me.'

I find myself sinking to the ground and hear the great, desperate sobs rather than feel them. Then Jacob is by my side, stroking my hair, my back, then his hands are cupping my face. 'Carys,' he whispers, his eyes locked on mine in deep pools of darkness, 'let Cory honour your father. You can honour him too. Then you must let everyone here finish what is started. You must let them remember.'

I hold his gaze for a moment, then look away, my emotions in a turmoil. In that moment, the love of my father, Benedict Clerk, cascades over me in a great gush, like a pounding waterfall, the untold depths of it consuming me. I'm drowning in it, the knowledge that I was loved. *I was loved.*

I let Jacob walk me back to our log, tears pouring down my cheeks. Glancing back, I see Cory, standing alone, his posture bent.

I honour him.

'I honour him,' I say aloud, and I look away from Cory, the man who murdered the one who loved me. Turning back to Jacob's waiting arms, I sink down onto the log, my heart beating rapidly. And I feel closer to something called home than I have ever done in my life.

WE SIT IN silence for minutes as we wait for the Queen to call up the next Subversive. I take the time to gather myself, but there is a new feeling swimming within: a lightness of spirit.

I listen in attentive horror to story after story. Stories of rejection for weakness, stories of dawning realisation of the vile scheme we live under in Newland. As I listen, my resolve increases. Glancing at Jacob and Amy, I sense their own unease and itchy feet. The three of us are called up towards the end as dawn paints the sky with streaks of gold. We tell our story, and the community are entranced then horrified.

We're coming to the last of the stories when the Queen calls Raza. I watch as she picks her way to the Queen's side, her stance bent, shoulders bowed down. Her face is paler than usual, her dark, kohl-lined eyes huge and lost. She fingers the knife at her belt. The Queen places her hand on her shoulder. 'In your time, Raza.'

Raza keeps her eyes to the ground, stumbling over her words. 'I was in a training house in the Centre Compound, on my way to becoming a good Productive.' She sneers. 'My chemistry Trainer told me I was the most intelligent trainee he had come across. Said he wanted to have private study periods with me 'cos I'd go far, said usually girls couldn't be scientists, but he could see such potential in me he knew the Party would make an exception.' Her voice cracks and she pauses, gathering herself. 'I believed his bullshit, dumb that I am. I worked harder than ever, longing to please him.'

I search her face. Under the make-up I see a scared young girl, eyes wide, mouth trembling. The Queen clasps her hand. 'Go on.'

Raza shrugs. 'Well, you can imagine. Dr Chemist began to cross lines. A pat on the shoulder here, a squeeze there. Then more. I went to my principal, and she was outraged, but not at Chemist.' She sticks out her chin. 'Here I was, she said, with a chance no one else ever had, and I was telling petty tales on the good man who was bothering to give me so much time. She said I'd lose my tutoring sessions and be just like the other trainees again with little hope of excelling if I kept on with this… tattle-telling, she called it.'

Raza stops, rakes her hand through her hair, spits on the ground. 'I was pathetic. Thought I should keep quiet about it so I could get my opportunity. But yeah, he kept doing what he was doing, said I was special, said he just wanted to help me. But he hurt me.'

'And when you reported him?' the Queen prompts softly.

Raza sighs. 'I was thrown into the Think at my training house for spreading vicious lies about an esteemed Productive. And then I found out I was pregnant, but I was in denial. I just hid it as best I could; my so-called friends teased me for getting fat. Anyway, I went into premature labour and was rushed into hospital and gave birth to a perfect daughter.' She scuffs the ground with her feet, setting her jaw tight. 'She was breathing. She was crying. But the midwife took her away. She was too small, too weak; she would be taken to the Home.'

We are silent as Raza swallows back the tears.

'I… I tried to keep her. But they took her. They murdered her.' She looks up at the Queen, her eyes reddened. 'Then I was expelled,' she says bitterly. 'I'd sullied their good name. They banished me to the Outside and, well, here I am. I will never forget her.' Raza's face is set like flint, her blackened mouth a hard line. 'And I will avenge her.' She quietens, hugging her wasted arms to her sides.

The Queen touches her lightly. 'What was your darling girl's name?'

'I called her Carys,' says Raza, staring at me, and my heart thumps. 'It was a name I heard from my grandmother. It was the name of one of my ancestors, and I knew it meant "beloved".'

I finally know what my crime is. I return her gaze.

'Be at peace now,' the Queen says softly. 'Carys's story is told. We honour her.'

We honour her.

This time I join in, full voiced and full intentioned. I will honour her. I will not forget. I glance at Raza again, take in her hardened features. *I am with you.*

ALL THE STORIES have been told. All except one.

After Raza has returned to her log and silence once again draws in, the Queen stands. Her tall, slim figure is majestically framed against the slowly awakening sky, her dark eyes shining in the remains of the firelight. She stands straight and silent, and I watch her, waiting.

'It is nearly time for our ceremony,' she says, her voice low and husky. 'But before that, if I may, I will share my story. As with all the stories shared tonight, I ask that you do not refer to it or tell others who may join our community before our next Remembrance Night. May I trust you?'

You may. The community chant the words, sure and firm.

'And you?' She points to the three of us.

You may.

She nods slowly then takes up her tale, weaving her words carefully, evocatively. I am captivated by her.

'I was working in the council offices in the Centre Compound. I was a lowly clerk—' she glances at me, her eyes soft, '—because I was just a woman, and a woman who looked like I do at that. My given Newland name was Barbra, because it means stranger, foreigner.' She pauses, screwing up her face. 'I thought I could raise myself through the ranks, but I was never promoted. My job was to support the men around me who had more important work to do. I was Productive, but I wanted more.'

She lets the silence fall and takes in a deep breath. 'They told me I should get married and have a baby, that then I would reach peak Productivity. But I had no interest in men or babies. I wanted a family, but not like they forced it there. I knew I was made for more than this, so I began to look beyond things I was told. I was quiet and unseen so I could dig into things without suspicion. I thought I could bring stuff out into the light, that I'd be praised because of it, that the Party would reward me for uncovering discrepancies in the office's financial records and injustices that were going on under their noses.' She laughs sourly. 'How wrong I was. I was reprimanded for bringing this petty stuff to my superiors' attention, told that I had no idea of how to run things, that I was just there to file their records and make their coffee like a good little woman.'

Raza snorts.

'My pay was docked, and my Productivity score lowered. But I didn't care anymore, because I had a feeling I'd just touched the tip of the iceberg; I ended up finding out more than I'd bargained for. Much like your story—' she nods towards us, '—I found out the truth. I didn't know what to do but knew I couldn't stay there and keep contributing to this insidious murder system.' She spits out her words, her face hardening. 'Anyway, I was there late one night, ordered to stay behind by my boss to sort out some NSheets he'd messed up, when I happened to look out of the window and saw this kid being dragged in through the Think doors below my office. I knew exactly what was going to happen to him, and something snapped in me right that moment; I knew I couldn't let this kid die. It was like a fire lit up my body, like I suddenly knew what I was supposed to do. I went down there like I couldn't give a damn with a whole load of files under my arm, blagged my way through to the Think offices. He'd not been processed yet; he was just right there in a holding cell with the key in the door. I walked right in and then walked right out with him next to me.'

I edge forward on my log, watching her closely. The lines around her eyes crease as she exhales on a long breath. 'We didn't get caught that time. I got him out. Never saw him again, though. He must have been all of fourteen.'

For a moment I think of Sim and stiffen.

'That's how it started. We got a thing going, or more accurately I joined in with the thing some others had going, right there in the Centre Compound. We got kids out and I'd hide them out at my place; no one came out there anyway because they didn't like me. It was like… like I had a family. All these different kids. Some of them stayed longer, some went straight away. Some too sick to make it. Some got caught on the way out when the network was compromised.' She stops, shudders, presses her hands together in front of her. 'It all came crashing down one day when my boss caught me communicating with a known underground Unproductive. We'd only been able to communicate via dropped notes, handwritten, because as you know the NPhone system is closely monitored, but he found some notes in my desk. I was stupid; I hadn't hidden them well enough.' She lowers her head to her hands for a moment. 'But that was it for me and for a number of other resistance workers, and a couple of kids we had in the system too. I got them all killed.'

We are silent.

She shakes her head. 'I got out by the skin of my teeth, escaped then and there before they could arrest me and found my way to the Outside. I know of some others who made it too—' she gazes around the community, nodding at one or two of them, '—and those who didn't. I hope there's still a resistance there, but the truth is I don't know.'

I think about Wade, the jittery man in the cell with me back at the Think, and wonder.

'I wandered around the ruins, devastated, and that's when Cory found me; he was on an errand near the Centre. Their community needed a leader, he said, and I was it. And I had that feeling again, like it was what I was meant to do. But I never forgot my children. The ones who made it and the ones who didn't. So many of them taken, so many murdered. I will never forget them. And now I will protect these ones until I die for it.'

Emma, Ella, Esther, and Hannah walk silently to her side and place their hands on her arms. Then comes the weeping, starting slowly then spreading through the gathering like a tsunami, smashing into one after another in its power. The three of us are pounded by it, and I am rocked by its force. The Queen stands at the front of us, silent, a solitary tear crawling down her cheek.

Cory stands now and goes to her, lays his hand on her head. 'Be at peace now,' he whispers, the sobs of the people fading to broken silence. 'The children of Newland's story is told. We honour them.'

This time, the community stands as one. 'We honour them,' we chant with conviction.

The Queen sinks to her seat, exhaustion evident on her lined face, her shaven head glinting in the flickering light as she holds it in her hands.

Cory remains standing. 'It is time,' he says, gazing at the colour-streaked sky. We follow the community as they make their way to the shore of the lake, leaving the dying fire behind. They stand in a long line, spread out along the shore. The water before us laps peacefully, the dancing colours of the dawn casting ripples over the calm surface. We take our place in the row and wait.

The Queen is walking along the line, handing something out. She approaches me and catches my eye as she presses something light into my hand. I keep her gaze a moment, attempting to communicate something to her. She nods slightly and moves on to Jacob. I unfurl my fist and examine the item. It's a small boat, made from heavy card, an unlit candle set in the centre. I gaze around, watching the others. None of them move, all waiting for the Queen to finish handing out the boats and come back to take her place next to Cory at the head of the line.

At last, all is ready and all is quiet. The lake, gently lapping, curls over my feet.

'Now,' says the Queen, and the community move forward as one, wading into the lake, further and further in. The surface ripples more violently, disturbed by the sudden onslaught. Finally we stand there, waist deep in the bitter water, holding out our boats. In the corner of my eye I notice a flickering light, gaining in momentum as it moves down the line towards me. People are lighting their candles, one from another, all along until all are lit, a long line of light reflected in the wavering surface.

We stand quiet for another minute, holding our candle-boat, the tiny flame hypnotising me.

'Whisper your names.' The Queen's command bounces lightly down the line, and all around me are whispers and echoes of whispers, name upon name, names breathed lovingly, names sobbed brokenly. Quickly, the three of us catch on, and begin to whisper our names. Our names of Remembrance.

I close my eyes and clasp my boat. *Benedict,* I breathe first, his name so fresh in my mind, a name that fills me up with a joy I never knew. *Ora.* My mother's name. *Girl S.* The girl who never lived to get her own name.

For a second I pause, listening to the decreasing whispers around me. Amy is crying softly to my right. *Lewis,* I hear her say. Jacob is silent, standing to my right, seemingly mesmerised by his boat.

I take a deep breath in.

Sim, I exhale, his image flying through my head, his wild red hair blowing in the wind of my soul.

The whispers die, and the people launch their boats. Jacob follows, and then Amy, and then I push mine out over the silent, billowing lake. I watch as sixty-four boats sail out over the water, propelled by an unknown force, the candles shining through the early morning murk and, as I watch, a sound echoes over the waters, an ethereal, eerily beautiful sound.

I look up, searching the source, and I see her, standing alone, away from the Queen at the top of the line. Raza. Her black hair waving in the gentle breeze, she stands tall, the usual slump in her shoulders gone, and she sings of her loss, of all our losses, her voice low and husky but straining with a haunting power borne in pain, containing all that we are and have been.

I see you all around
In dreams of morning you'll be found
Eternal echoes ever true
I call your name, I run to you

I hear now as you sing
Your voice streaming through the wind
In deepest beauty always new
I call your name, I run to you

They threw you away
Like you could never shine your light
Flung you far out into the night
Now you're flying out of time
They stole you from life
But now I see you in the stars
See you shining through the dark
Always with me from the start

As the last plaintive note sounds over the still waters, the colours of day reach across the sky and the lights on the paper boats fade away.

And nothing will ever be the same, for any of us.

PART II

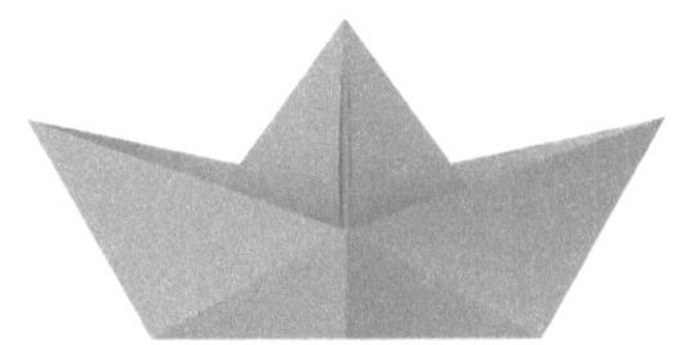

THE CENTRE

10

THE BUNKER

AMY

JACOB COMES TEARING into the kitchen where Amy is chopping vegetables for dinner, a huge grin spread over his face. She can't help smiling back, thrilled at the transformation in him these past few days. 'What is it?' She lays her knife down, wipes her forearm across her brow.

'It's a group near the Centre Compound,' he says, waving his arms around emphatically. 'Someone responded to this channel I set up a while back, on the old radio equipment we unearthed in the basement. I'd been sending various beacons, but nothing had come of it, then this morning—'

'You mean there are others out there? How d'you know they're not Productives?'

'I doubt any Productives would be faffing round with obsolete machinery from the Before,' he says. 'I've received this message – just this morning. Someone trying to get through. Someone on the Outside… near the Centre. The frustrating thing was, I could hear them, but they couldn't hear me. I kept trying. They knew I was there, though.'

'Wow – so some more Outsiders?'

'Yeah, anyway, they said to be at the radio at 7pm, and we'd try again to communicate, so I thought you might want in on that. If we can get a two-way thing going. I'm going to tinker with it a bit more before then.'

Amy's heart skips a beat. 'You think—?'

'It's always possible, Amy. So meet me there, yeah? Get Carys, too. She's chopping wood, I think.'

'I'll try.'

He dances off, triumphant in his discovery. Amy stands there a moment, the impact of what might be hitting her. What if they're out there? In some Outsider community near the Centre? What if she can find them?

Her stomach churns at the thought, her hand clammy as she grips the knife and prepares to chop more carrots.

JUST BEFORE SEVEN o'clock, Amy downs tools and skips through the kitchen, throwing Kate a smile. 'I'll be back soon,' she says, but doesn't wait for Kate's reaction. She runs through the corridors down to the room Jacob's taken over for his mass of equipment. She stops, inhales slowly.

Carys is already there, sitting in one of the ancient office chairs, spinning around. Each rotation affords a high-pitched squeak. It's annoying. Amy starts biting down on her thumbnail.

'It's nearly time. All set up,' Jacob says, his brow wrinkled in concentration. 'Carys, will you quit that?'

She stops, pulls herself up. 'Well, I'm so sorry.' She laughs, pulls Jacob's arm.

He wrenches away, irritated. 'Come on. They might be trying to get through.'

'Okay,' she says, exaggerating the "K". She sits again but keeps the seat still.

The radio crackles.

Jacob picks up this mouthpiece thing, like a microphone but much thicker, with some sort of grille covering it. 'Hello?'

It crackles again. There are definitely voices, but they make no sense.

'Can you hear me? My name is Jacob Trader, and I am close to the ruins of Birmingham...' he trails off when there is no response. 'Hello?'

Nothing. No more crackles.

Jacob flings the speaker instrument down on the desk in front of him 'Damn.'

The instrument crackles again.

'Hello?' The voice is muted, faraway sounding. 'Is anyone there?'

Jacob seizes the mouthpiece, rams it against his lips. 'Yes. Yes. This is Jacob Trader. Hello? Hello?'

More crackles. Jacob curses. 'Hello?'

'This is Bruce Medic. I'm in...' the transmission is breaking up.

'Where are you?' Jacob is shouting. 'Bruce?'

More interference, then his voice again. '... the Centre. Most of... fugitives. Some from *The S Word*... about you?'

'Mostly runaways. Some banned,' Jacob says, gripping the transmitter. 'I have run from the Midlands Compound. We found out things about Productives and the Home.'

'... know about the Home.'

This is frustrating to listen to. Bruce's voice floats over the airwaves to them in bits and starts, broken and jagged. They can't make out all he is saying.

But it is something.

There are others out there.

'Please ask,' Amy hisses at Jacob.

'Do you have anyone there name of Alwin Plumber, and Lois...' Jacob breaks off, looks at Amy.

'Retail,' she says and hangs her head as if in shame, although she has no reason for it. Not here. Not ever.

'… Retail. Lois Retail,' Jacob repeats, enunciating each word slowly and clearly.

There's a pause.

Then, '… and Lois? … course. They… us. Three years…'

Amy grips the back of Carys's chair, swallowing hard over the lump that has formed in her throat. She gapes at Jacob, finding no words.

'Please repeat. Alwin Plumber and Lois Retail are with you, in your community near the Centre?' Jacob winks at Amy.

'… confirm that. They are here.'

Amy sinks down onto a chair, pressing her hand over her mouth as tears form, spilling over as she takes it in.

Her parents. Her beloved parents.

They are alive.

'Could we talk to them?' Jacob's eyes are bright as he leans forward, bellows into the mouthpiece.

There is no response.

No crackles.

'Hello?'

Nothing.

Jacob slowly places the transmitter into its cradle on the desk in front of him. 'They've gone. But Amy… they're alive.' He reaches forward. Places his hands on her shoulders. 'They're alive, Amy.'

'I… I can't believe it.' She brushes tears away. Her heart thumps at her chest, and she stands again, on shaky legs. 'We have to go there, Jacob!'

Carys grabs her hand, squeezes it. Too hard, in the way she always does. Amy winces but grins at her through tears.

'We will,' Carys says. 'It's time.'

'We'll go tomorrow. After work,' Jacob says, and it's sealed between them.

After all these years, Amy will be home again. In the only place she's ever wanted to be. With those who love her most.

CARYS

THE NEXT DAY we're all sent off on woodcutting duty. Winter is approaching, and the Subs Community need to stockpile a good amount of fuel to get through to spring. The three of us start towards the forest, leading a horse with a cart for loading the wood, axes slung on our belts, chatting and laughing, making our plans in anticipation. I slept badly, too excited, too stirred up. We don't even know where this other community is based, but we will find it – we know it's somewhere near the Centre. We're planning to ask Cory if we can borrow Shadow and Rainbow and one of the carts used by the Subs Community; they have more than they need. Cory will comply with us when we tell him why.

A sharp crack behind us. I whirl round.

Raza.

She slinks towards us, arms crossed, blackened eyes narrowed. She looks strangely beautiful, wafting through the autumn breeze, her buckled boots loose on her skinny, leather clad legs, her black hair in multiple braids down her back.

What does she want?

I thought things would change after the night of Remembrance when she shared her deepest secrets with us, when we shared a moment of understanding as she told us her lost baby's name and looked directly at me. Even more so after hearing her song, the haunting melody that has stayed with me since, weaving its way through my dreams. But the next day, after the community slept the day away, Raza was unchanged. She closed down, her face taking on the sullen look I knew so well.

She approaches us now, dragging her feet and sighing. 'I'm to come with you. Cory sent me.'

I shrug. 'Come on, then. We have to get on with it, if we're to get a good load before dusk.'

We continue our forward trudge, but the joy is sucked out of the day with the brooding presence behind us. I wish I could break through to her. I feel desperately sorry for her, of course, but can't help feeling slightly annoyed with her. Why does she have to be so moody?

We make our way to the woods on the eastern edge of the city, beyond the farm. The ruins thin out here; occasional clusters of bombed-out shells slump lonely and foreboding along the dusty road. It's a forsaken place, and I shiver.

The forest folds us into its murky depths, the thin light of the autumn morning barely breaking through the canopy above. The colours are vibrant inside; burnt umbers and golds and vital oranges all around us, leaves clinging by a thread then breaking loose and floating to the spongy forest floor, mixing to a mulch under our feet. Damp and woody scents curl through the air as we tramp through to the clearing where the Subs have been chopping pine trees down. We slump to the ground for a rest, the horse tossing his head and straining at his bonds.

'Come on,' Amy says, after a few minutes of heavy silence. 'Let's get this done.'

These hatchets are not like the streamlined tools I remember seeing Gardener using back at Ashton; they're rough-hewn and blunt, but they do the job well enough. We put our backs into the work, hacking into the wood, and soon a respectable pile of logs lies next to us, ready to be piled into our cart. It'll be a long slog back to the bunker.

After an hour or so, we break for snacks and once again sink to the mossy ground. Jacob grabs the pack from the cart and flings biscuits and water bottles at us. We drink deeply, leaning back, listening to the sounds of the forest, the creaking of the trees. Birds chirrup around us, unperturbed by the sound of our hacking, filling the space with their joyous song. Leaves wave gently in the autumnal breeze. I sigh, a feeling of contentment stealing over me for just a second.

That's when I hear something else.

Screams.

I sit up, immediately on guard.

The others clamber to their feet. 'What was that?' Jacob spins around, searching the area. We can't see anything.

The screams sound again. Someone is utterly panicked. The screaming forms into a word, echoing again and again through the mulchy silence of the forest.

'HELP!'

'Someone's in trouble.' Jacob moves towards the cacophony, which seems to come from further back towards the perimeter of the woods.

The screams thin out. A desperate rasping sound floats through the trees to us. 'Hurry,' I say, and we begin to run, crashing back through the forest. The sounds fade away.

As we approach the boundary of the woods, another sound reaches us. Deep, this time. A male voice. No, more than one. Laughter. Harsh, mocking laughter.

'Now we have her,' one of them says, and as he does, we see him. The back of a thin man, clad in a checked shirt and faded jeans. I peer around him and see another one. And another. Three men, their faces rough with stubble, their eyes widened with excitement. They're bending over something on the ground. Something inert.

'Oh no,' I say, and without thinking I break out of the trees and sprint towards them.

Jacob shouts and grabs hold of my shirt. 'Don't be stupid.'

I pull away. 'They've got a girl.'

'I know. Look. I'll go,' he says, and tugs me back, but I resist.

All the commotion has alerted the attackers, and they look our way. They snigger. One of them, the one who had his back to me, begins to stomp towards us. 'Dear oh dear,' he chants. 'Little kids, out in a place they shouldn't be. Whatever shall we do with them?' His grizzled face is half lost in shadow. His thick, wavy hair falls over his collar, his thin mouth turned down in a grim line.

The others snicker.

'Perhaps we can have some fun with them, as well,' their leader says, baring his teeth. He pins his brown eyes on mine and slowly breaks into a grin that reminds me of Gardener's ferret smile. Two of his front teeth are missing, the others stained brown. His sour breath courses over my face, and I take a step back, almost tripping over a root.

Jacob squares up to him. Jacob's tall but is nothing on this guy. He stands inches over Jacob and makes the most of it, towering over him, crossing his arms. 'You got a problem?' He turns his face to the side, spits on the ground. 'Come now, friends,' he says, beckoning to the two others, 'let's get these ones tethered, shall we?'

Jacob throws a punch square in his gut.

He barely reacts.

Jacob punches him again, and this time he throws his elbow up, catching Jacob's nose, and then kicks Jacob's knee. Jacob crumples to the ground.

The leader smiles.

The others are inching towards us, something like delight etched on their thin, weathered faces. I throw a glance at the still figure on the ground. I can see it's a girl, but I don't know if she's alive or dead. Her blonde hair is matted with autumn leaves and mud, and something else.

Blood.

Amy and I shrink back but then look at each other and, making a split-second decision, we sprint forwards. Run into the men full pelt. One of them staggers backwards, winded. I glance round wildly, searching for Raza, but can't see her. She's gone. She's run off.

Coward.

She was the only one with a weapon. Her ever-present knife.

We've walked straight into their trap. The big one, the leader, grabs me and shoves me towards the bundle on the ground. Jacob moans and starts to pull himself up, but one of the others, a thin, small man with watery blue eyes, kicks him hard in the gut and he bends double. Amy is fighting the other one, a wild-looking man with streaked blond hair and hairy hands. He wrestles with her and quickly overcomes her, wrenching her arms around her back. She winces; her old injury coming back to haunt her.

All three of us restrained, I gaze round in dawning horror. These thugs have us surrounded and we can't do anything. We're trapped.

The men laugh harshly, calling out to one another, bragging about what they are going to do with us.

But they don't reckon on Raza.

She comes like a cat, creeping stealthily through the trees then pouncing hard. A flash of something metallic catches my eye as she sweeps it through the air, its arc leaving an impression for a split second before it plants itself solidly into the arm of the man gripping Amy's wrists.

Raza has an axe.

She didn't run away from us.

In her other hand, she wields her knife, cutting through the air, bringing it hard down on the man's shoulder. He screams and falls to the ground.

I do a double take as I notice she has another axe, attached roughly to her belt. As she wrenches hers out of the stunned man's arm and his blood spurts, she chucks one at me and I whirl into action, grabbing the handle and swiping the air around me, with little skill and no precision but plenty of passion.

I wince as my hatchet meets a soft target; my captor, the leader of them. I've caught his leg and he's doubled up, choking, his eyes dark with fury. He lets go of me and I stagger backwards, tugging the axe with me, and glance around at the carnage. Jacob is still stretched out on the ground, severely winded but trying to get himself up, and Raza stabs the last bandit, the blade of her knife embedding itself in the muscles of his calf, as he lunges for Amy. He roars and throws himself at Raza, enraged, but she has it. She raises the axe high, and he flinches away, covering his face with his arm and stumbling against the watery-eyed man. All three of them sink to the ground, moaning, grimacing in pain. Raza brandishes the axe high again, the knife gripped tight in her other hand.

'Wait,' I shriek, grabbing her arm. 'It's enough.'

'I'll kill them,' she roars, shaking my hand away, shoving at me. 'They've killed someone.'

'We don't know that. And look… don't be like them, Raza.'

Jacob gets on his feet. He takes Raza's hand, lowers her knife, looks into her eyes. 'Stop, now,' he whispers. 'We can go. We are safe.'

'Thanks to you,' puts in Amy, whose face has turned a deathly shade.

The three men squirm on the dampened ground, their blood mingled with the dank soil. None of them can form words.

I turn my attention to the supine figure behind us. I crouch next to her, lift her matted hair. Her face is covered in dirt and caked blood, and one eye is swollen and purple. Remains of make-up streak her cheeks, clumps of mascara blending with tracks of tears.

I lift her wrist. 'Amy,' I say. 'Come over. I think she's alive.'

Amy hunkers down with us. She takes the girl's hand, places her thumb on her inner wrist. She keeps still, biting her lip.

'There's a pulse. A bit thready, but there.'

'The cart,' says Jacob. 'I'll go get it. We can put her in there. Take her back—'

'But we don't know who she is,' Amy says, her brow furrowed.

'She's been attacked, Amy,' I shout. 'We can't really do anything else, can we? Hurry, please, Jacob.'

Gradually, Amy and I turn the girl over and sit her up slightly. She slumps against me. I cradle her, stroking the tangled hair from her brow. Her face is a ghastly mess. Underneath the bruises and the muck, she is white as a sheet.

Amy is peering closely at her. 'She seems familiar.'

'In what way?'

'I don't know.'

I try to study the girl's face, but it is so broken that I cannot see anything in it that would make me think I knew her. 'I wonder how old she is.'

'I think she's older than I thought, actually,' muses Amy. 'In her twenties, I would say, wouldn't you?'

'I really can't tell.'

'She's fairly tall. Thin, but there are some lines around her eyes. Look closely, Carys.'

I scrutinise the woman's face. To me, the lines are lost in dirt and blood and make-up.

Amy is still studying her. 'You know, she really looks like—'

Raza interrupts her, 'It's Lora,' she says, standing over us, hands on hips. 'Her from *The S Word.*'

I stare. 'It can't be.'

Amy inhales sharply. 'It is.'

I look again at the matted, long blonde hair, the clumps of mascara hanging from the long lashes, the heart-shaped face so battered, and I see what they see.

It is.

It's Lora Dancer.

JACOB RETURNS, CRASHING through the trees, leaves flying wildly in all directions. He's dragging the reluctant-looking horse with its cart unburdened of logs. He takes us in, crouching there, awestruck. He glances at the three fallen, groaning men.

'What?' Jacob says, looking at me. 'Why are you gawping like a goldfish?'

'Have you seen who it is?'

'No,' murmurs Jacob, drawing closer. 'But now you say it, she looks kind of—'

He breaks off.

'Familiar?' Raza says, almost grinning.

'I suppose,' he says, cocking his head and searching Lora's features.

'Got it?' I ask.

'Um…'

Amy stands up, brushes herself down. 'We've no time for this.' She sighs. 'It's Lora Dancer, Jacob.'

Jacob stumbles, catches himself. *'Shit!'*

'Yep.'

'We can't take her to the Subs,' Amy says. 'It's too risky.'

'But we can't leave her here,' I cry. 'She'll die!'

'No loss,' Raza mutters. I stare at her, but she shrugs.

'Come on,' says Amy, ever the practical one. 'Get her in the cart, at least. Then we can think about what to do. Carys is right. We can't leave her here.'

We set to, lifting Lora and lowering her gently into the cart. She's so light. She groans slightly as we move her, and one eye opens briefly then closes again.

'Lora?' I say, stroking her forehead. 'Lora… you're safe now.'

She's unresponsive.

We lead the horse onwards, two of us on each side, gripping the reins and traipsing back over the desolate land, the watery noonday sun high above us. As we round a curve in the old road, an unexpected sight greets us.

It's a silver NCV, abandoned in the road at an odd angle, the doors flung wide open. I study it and, looking closer, I spot several dents in the aluminium body panels. It looks like it's been attacked by sticks, or something with some weight.

This must be Lora's car.

'There's someone in there,' Raza says, making her way gingerly over to the car. She bends into the front and reels back immediately, slapping her hand to her mouth. 'He's dead. His head is all…' She breaks off, gagging.

Jacob says, 'I see what happened here. That gang… they stopped the car somehow. Murdered the chauffeur. Took Lora. We should use it to get her back quickly.'

We leave the cart where it is and make our way to the car. Flies buzz around the front and I won't look. Jacob and Raza tug the dead man out of the seat and leave him by the roadside.

'That doesn't seem right, somehow,' I say. 'We should put him in the trunk, at least… give him a burial.'

Raza huffs at me. 'You're so goody-goody.' But she lifts his feet and helps Jacob settle him in the boot, then turns away to the roadside and vomits. She wipes her mouth, catches me watching her and stares back, her face set. 'What now?'

A groaning noise from the cart. 'Who…'

I turn back towards Lora, run over to her. Her good eye is open, and she's shading it against the sun. Her other eye is swollen shut, the bruise blackening by the second. She scrambles, panicking. 'Where…?'

'Don't worry,' I say. 'You're safe. Those men are… incapacitated, for now.'

'They were trying… trying to…'

'I know.'

She grabs hold of my arm. 'Where am I?'

'You're on the Birmingham road. Looks like you got hijacked.'

Her eyes widen. 'My driver. Tolan—'

'I'm so sorry. They… they killed him.'

'Oh, dear Lucan, no.' She grasps hold of my other arm, tugs herself up. 'Help me, please.'

I support her as she stands on shaky legs, her knotted hair falling over her face and down her back in tangled strands. She leans heavily on me as she steps out of the cart.

'Who are you?' She gazes at me, seeing me as if for the first time.

'I'm… Girl C. Was,' I say, and leave it at that.

'You… you are an Outsider?'

'Sort of.'

'Listen.' Her tone turns urgent, her mouth twisting. 'You have to help me. To get me home… and Tolan. Look. Please. Anything you've done… don't worry. Just get me back to the Centre. I'll pay you… give you anything. I can't drive myself… I can barely see.'

Jacob and Amy wander over and stand with me, watching her. Raza remains by the car, still as a statue, arms crossed and countenance sour.

'We don't want paying.' Amy steps forward, places her hand on Lora's. 'You've had a terrible shock, Lora.'

Lora's eyes widen. 'You know who I am.'

'Of course.'

'Look… you won't be in any trouble.'

I gaze at her. Her brow is wrinkled. She's the kindly judge, the one who seems to care – I wonder if she really does, or if it's all an act. I suppose we'll be finding out.

I sigh. 'We should take her to her home.'

Jacob rubs his face. 'They'll arrest us.'

Lora glances up at him. 'I promise you. Whatever you've done… I am loved, you see. I can help you. Did you steal? Murder, even? I can get you off. Send you home. Are you trainees? You look young enough…' she breaks off, sweating. The pain is etched on her broken face.

'We come from Ashton,' I say, and Amy narrows her eyes at me. But I've done it, now. I might as well continue. 'We're under arrest – runaways – they said for treason. But we didn't do anything bad. Not really. We escaped from the Compound Think.'

Lora breathes out. 'I've heard about you. You're all over the news. From the Midlands Compound, right? There are wanted NCasts all over the place for you. You're in deep—' she pauses, '—but however deep, I can save you. If you just help me now, you won't regret it. I can't do this on my own. I can't…' She is sweating relentlessly now, the fluid pouring from her. She coughs, and blood splatters on her hand as she begins to shake and then to shudder violently.

'Sheesh,' Jacob says, wiping his brow.

'She's convulsing,' Amy says. 'Lie her down. Hold her.'

Jacob lowers her to the cart, and we hold her down as she judders, her eyes wild. Foam forms at her mouth, merging with the blood, and I wonder if she is going to die.

'Wait,' Amy says, and we do.

Lora calms, and the convulsions come to a stop, and she is slumped there like a rag doll, floppy but breathing.

'Get her in the car.'

We lift her to the NCV and place her carefully in the front seat. She slouches into the soft grey leather, unconscious.

'What now?' Jacob glances at his watch. 'They'll be expecting us back in an hour or two. With logs.'

'I don't think we have any choice,' Amy says.

Raza pipes up, and this time she takes me by surprise. A look of purpose crosses her face. 'We take her to the Centre.'

'But we might get arrested,' I say.

'Look. Lora will sort it for us,' Raza says. 'And if she doesn't, we'll work something out. Look… I've long been wanting to go there. There's someone I need to see.'

'Who?' Jacob says.

She remains tight lipped, but I think I know. Dr Chemist. Perhaps the nurse who delivered – and murdered – her child.

Amy looks at Jacob. 'Perhaps one of us should go back to the Subs with the horse. Tell them what happened.'

No one says anything for a few moments, then Raza breaks the silence. 'I'm going to the Centre. This is my opportunity.'

I scuff my foot on the dusty ground, thinking. 'I don't want to go back there alone with some of us separating off, and to the Centre, of all places.'

'Nor me,' Jacob says. 'Look, we were going to go that way today anyway, right?'

Amy sighs. 'Yeah.'

'We can slip a note under the saddle,' I say, but no one has paper or pens or anything of the sort.

Amy shakes her head. 'They'll figure we've gone to join the resistance. They knew we'd be off eventually. Daniel knew, anyway, as soon as I read that book, and Cory knew when I got hold of that community where my parents are. They'll know.'

She slaps the horse on his rump. 'Go home, boy,' she says, and he trots off quickly, the cart wending and squealing and kicking up dust in his wake.

11

THE CENTRE

AMY

AMY IS SQUEEZED between Carys and Raza, brooding. She knows this is the right thing – the only thing – to do. They can't take Lora back to the Subs Community. She would give away their position, and all the work there would be lost. They can't leave her to die. They have to take her to the Centre.

But it scuppers their plans, the plans they made only hours ago, the plans that infused Amy with hope and a tinge of something like joy. Now she might never see her parents, she might never leave the Centre alive.

In the front, Lora dozes, her thin body slumped, head back against the rest. She was brutally attacked, possibly assaulted. No one deserves something like that, even an *S Word* judge who sends people off to the Think to be murdered every week. But does she even know about what happens at Thinks? She must do, surely.

But Amy didn't know, for many years.

Raza mopes next to her, her pale face drawn in, heavy eyebrows knitted together. She exudes bitterness, a grudge against the world. Amy can only guess at her plans in the Centre and knows she wants no part of them. She thinks of the Subs Community, so abruptly abandoned, and wonders if she will see them again. If Lora isn't true to her word, they will be dead by tomorrow. The Subs have been good to them, nourished them when they were utterly broken; the Queen and Cory and their followers gave them hope for something more, for a life of contentment and giving to others. Amy will miss the children there.

As Jacob drives them away from the ruins of the old city, the sun begins to lower in the sky and grey clouds chase it away. Rain spatters on the windscreen, then drizzle turns to deluge and Jacob flicks the wipers to the fastest setting. The rainswept landscape is barren, empty of life.

Lora stirs, her hand snaking to the edge of the seat, gripping hold of it. 'Where are we?'

'Don't worry.' Carys leans forward and grasps Lora's hand. 'We're taking you back to the Centre.'

Lora slumps back down. 'Thank you. Thank you so much. I… I don't know what to say.' She starts to weep, the tears falling fast, soaking her filthy collar, imprinting tracks on her mud-streaked face. 'I…'

'Don't,' Carys says. 'We'll take you, and then you said… you'd help.'

'I will,' Lora says, wiping her hand across her face. 'So tell me,' she says, 'what exactly did you do? I saw it was treason, but why were you in the Think?'

Amy's initial reaction is to say nothing, but Carys plunges in with her usual impetuosity. 'It started back at Ashton, with a girl called Mercia Manager.'

Amy grits her teeth. Still, it can't harm them any more now, so she tries to relax, leans back and closes her eyes as Carys tells their story once again.

ᴊACOB

Cᴀʀʏs ɪs sᴘɪʟʟɪɴɢ everything to Lora. Jacob bites his cheek, half annoyed and half proud of the way she tells it, drawing Lora right in, brimming over with emotion and passion. He watches her through his rear-view mirror. Her face is so animated, shining like she's got some joy or something. He saw her on Remembrance Night when Cory told the story of her father. It was like she was infused with something then, with something new. Different. He's into it.

Lora's agog, but she's not buying it. She keeps blowing out her cheeks, like she's totally outraged. 'No,' she says, over and over. 'No. You're wrong. You've got it wrong.' When Carys gets to the part about the underground office and their repulsive discovery there, Lora screws her face right up. 'Look. That's just not true,' she says, almost spitting the words.

Carys comes to the part where Sim was killed, and she falters. In the mirror, Jacob watches as her grey eyes fill and she chokes on the words. Lora stays silent, pursing her lips, says nothing more until Carys finishes the story with their escape. Leaves out everything about the Subversives Community, thankfully.

Lora remains quiet for minutes, the atmosphere in the car heavy with her shock. Jacob figures she actually didn't know about this stuff, that she's an innocent in all this. Here they are, telling her she's been sending people to be murdered; of course she'll be in denial about it.

'I don't believe you,' she says eventually, breathing the words out on a long sigh. 'I don't know why you'd say such things, and I don't want to know why. The fact remains, though, that you saved me, and I will honour my words. I mean what I say, I always have, so I will assure you now that you will not be arrested. I have… ties… with Anson. The Commander, I mean… I can talk with him. You don't need to fear.'

She goes silent again.

Then, 'I must ask you, though, to not mention all of this… this… *story*, again. I must make this a condition of my helping you, when we arrive at my home. You will keep silent about these lies. I'm afraid to say that if you are not able to uphold your end of this… agreement, that I will not be able to prevent events taking their natural course.' She exhales, clearly exhausted, closing her good eye and touching her hand to her swollen eye. She winces, bends her head low, bringing both hands to her forehead. 'Is this clear?'

Jacob can almost feel Carys's indignation, pouring from her in palpable waves. He has to get in before she speaks. 'Yes,' he says. 'It's clear. We'll say nothing.'

Carys bristles, sits herself up straight, opens her mouth, but Amy nudges her and she gets the hint and closes it again, her face a picture of outrage.

The rest of the journey passes uneventfully. Lora is fading before them, her pallor increasing, and Jacob starts to stress about her. What if she buys it before they can get her home? They'll be in serious trouble if that happens.

But they can't just dump her. It's not who they are.

The NCV is a premium model, even more high-end than the one they stole back in the Compound, and it's awesome to drive, so it's not too bad from Jacob's point of view. He kind of feels for Amy, though. They'd made all these plans to go and find her parents, and now they might have sacrificed all of that – for Lora Dancer, who represents all they despise most about Newland.

They come close to the Centre Compound as the rainy night draws in around them. The barriers are even more imposing here, more substantial, soaring above them. Giant NScreens lashed to the barriers display projected Centre bulletins and sport, and he's dismayed to see images of himself, Amy, and Carys, underpinned by scrolling updates of their status ("Wanted for Treason"). Coiled barbed wire stretches along the top in both directions as far as he can see, and the border gates are manned with several mean-looking NForce officers, strutting around with their automatic weapons slung over their shoulders, scouting the horizon for incomers. No other vehicles are in sight, and the guards all gather at the gates, waiting.

Lora is sprawled on the seat next to Jacob, her eyes closed, her breathing shallow. She looks really sick. 'I think this could go badly,' he says.

'We just tell the truth,' Amy says. 'Lora will keep her word.'

Carys bites her thumbnail. 'I'm glad someone's optimistic.'

One of the officers steps out from the crowd towards them, holding his palm flat out. Jacob brakes to a halt, takes a deep breath, touches the window control.

The man strolls round to his window, whistling. He glances in at them, then seems to gather himself and scrutinises them more closely. Takes in Lora, who seems unconscious. Carys tries to rouse her, stroking her shoulder, but she's oblivious.

The officer stares at Jacob, then calls a colleague over. This officer is obviously a superior of the first, with triple-banded epaulettes and several medals pinned to the chest of his khaki uniform. He struts over, swinging his weapon, his gait confident as if he's proud of his intimidating presence. 'Is there a problem?'

'I'm not sure.' The first officer is gazing at Jacob, narrowing his eyes. He takes a slow and deliberate step away, turns his face to the side, and hacks a glob of spittle onto the ground. 'I don't recognise this driver.'

His commander bends, examines them closely, brow furrowing as he clocks Lora. 'Is that—?'

The first officer takes his NSlate. 'I'll enter the vehicle specs.'

Everything is silent as they wait, the commanding officer standing with legs planted far apart, arms crossed, surveying Jacob with suspicion.

'It's Lora Dancer's private NCV,' the first officer says, raising his eyebrows at his superior. 'The driver is named as Tolan Driver, her personal chauffeur, and he looks nothing like this… this *person*.'

It's time to speak up. Jacob swallows, gathering his grit together, but breaks off as a commotion in the back interrupts him. Carys. She's unclicking her belt, flinging her door open. She clambers out of the NCV. *What the hell?*

'Hello, Mr Officer,' she says, plastering a wide smile on her face. 'We have something to tell you, but we really need to get Lora to hospital. As you can see, she is in a severe condition, so the best thing to do would be to get there as quickly as possible. We will tell you everything that has happened, but can we make Lora first priority, please?'

Jacob relaxes, admiring her audacity. The officer strokes his stubble and watches her, then bends again to look at Lora. 'Cad!' he yells, beckoning to another officer from the crowd forming at the gates. 'Get your car and blue light Ms Dancer to Commander Lucan Hospital. She is in a critical condition and unresponsive.'

The officer breaks away from the others. 'Right away, sir,' he says, sprinting off towards a black NCV parked over to the side of the border gates. He climbs in, screeches it over to them in seconds. Meanwhile, the two officers are over to the passenger door, yanking it open, and the first one bends over Lora, releasing her belt. They lift her out gently, transferring her to the NCV, and all the time the battered group say nothing. What can they say, or do?

Moments later, the black NCV reverses, shrieks through a turn and speeds away, tyres slewing, surface spray flying up in its wake. They watch as it disappears over the horizon.

At least Lora will be in good hands soon.

But they remain in deep trouble. They have a dead body in the boot of Lora Dancer's NCV, and they're well known wanted fugitives. Jacob's usually laid back, but sweat prickles on his forehead as he faces the reality of what's happening here.

'Get out of the car.' The commanding officer wrenches Jacob's door open, drags him out roughly. He stands by Carys's side, places his hand in the small of her back. She glances at him, eyes wide with panic.

The other guard hauls Amy and Raza out. Raza grouses at him, then struggles with him. Goes for her knife, still on her belt, but he gets there first, yanking it from its sheath and holding it to the sun, peering at it. 'Pretty.' Raza grits her teeth, lunges for him. He grabs her wrists, and she brings her knee up sharply into his groin. He doubles up, groaning, but he's angrier now, shoves her against the car and cuffs her. He holds more cuffs aloft at them and sneers. 'Did you want to make a fuss too?'

'No,' Amy says.

A sound Jacob had hoped he wouldn't hear crashes into his consciousness.

The trunk. One of the officers has opened the trunk.

Shouts. A scramble of feet, and then they're all being wrestled to the ground. Cuffed. Nowhere to go.

Carys is desperately trying to get the attention of the first officer. 'Please. Listen to us. We found him. Dead. We rescued Lora – she was being attacked by bandits, east of the Birmingham ruins…' she trails off, clocking the fruitlessness of her words. No one's listening.

They're done for.

Dead.

12

THE CENTRE

CARYS

W E'RE TAKEN STRAIGHT to the Centre Think.

They don't waste any time, and they don't stop to hear our side of the story. All they see is a battered Lora Dancer and her dead driver. All the way through the rain-washed streets of the Centre, I try to make them listen, but my attempts prove futile. The others don't even bother, just stare out of the windows of the NForce reinforced vehicle. Raza's eyes are darkened and her hands balled into fists; I catch her eye, but she looks away. Amy responds to my smile with her own tiny one, but it's clear she is terrified. Jacob broods next to me, his presence a warm comfort.

The Centre Think is incomparable to the Midlands Compound Think. It's colossal, a building on a scale I have never seen. It climbs to tens of storeys high and forms an L shape around a courtyard at the front, the fascia all mirrored glass, giving an imposing impression. The car pulls into the courtyard, and we're hauled out one by one and marched into the building.

'Here they are,' says the commanding officer to a burly man with a florid face and a slack jaw clad in the uniform of a Chief NForce Inspector. His eyes are blank, but he smiles widely.

'So. It seems the Midlands fugitives have turned up here – with one extra. And have continued their crime spree, of course – attacking Ms Dancer and killing her driver. Matters will be swiftly resolved from here on in.'

We glance at one another. *They know who we are.* Of course.

The chief grabs hold of Jacob's arm and nods at the two officers who drove us here to follow, bringing the rest of us. Amy goes docilely, her eyes cast downwards, and I follow, desperately seeking a solution that isn't there. Raza, though, is more resistant. She struggles and bites the officer who is gripping her shoulder. He roars, snaps round and slaps her face. She recoils but brings her head forward hard, butting his forehead. 'Little wildcat,' he yells and brings his fist up rapidly, catching her nose. She staggers back, unable to bring her hands to her nose, which is pouring with blood. She shakes her head back and forth, choking. The guard laughs.

We're taken through double doors and down a long, red-bricked corridor. Multiple doors lead from the hallway, but they march us to the very end, through a further set of doors. Stairs lead to a basement level, much like the Compound Think, and we're dragged down. I trip and fall against the officer in front of me, who shoves back at me, catching me in the stomach. I double up, winded.

The stairway turns a corner down to a further level, where the lights are dimmed and the walls are dark grey and the oppressive air is damp and choking. They shove us into a small room on the left of the hallway. 'This won't take long,' the chief says. 'I am calling the nurse now.'

My blood runs cold. I know exactly what that means.

Amy's eyes widen. 'You mean…?'

'Wait!' I cry, clinging to the officer on my left. 'Look. You gave us no chance to actually explain. We saved Lora—'

The officer shrugs me off, his teeth bared at me. 'Get off me, vermin,' he growls. 'You do not deserve a chance to account for yourselves. The directive from Midlands is clear. You are to be executed at the first opportunity. Goodbye.' He gives me one last disdainful glare and exits the room, slamming the heavy steel door tight.

Sealing our fate.

We stand in the soulless room, gazing around at one another. Fear is palpable, squeezing hard at all of us. I look at my hands, glistening with sweat, and wipe them on my jeans. The room is uncannily like the holding cell I was taken to in the Compound Think, down to the battered table, the rickety chairs and the overflowing box labelled "for incineration" in the corner. I didn't know then that it wasn't only our clothes that were bound for the furnace. I shiver.

Raza starts pummelling her fists on the steel door, her jaw set tight and her eyes blazing with fury. 'No,' she shrieks. 'This is not how it will end. I will get my revenge. This is not how it is meant to be.' With each word she slams on the door, her knuckles bruised then bleeding. After a time, she breaks off and throws her head into her battered hands, sobbing.

'What shall we do?' I say, panicked, staring round the tiny cell.

'There's nothing we can do,' Jacob says, his brown eyes large with dread.

Terror floods the room, overwhelming us and stunning us into silence. One by one, we sink to the frigid concrete floor, beaten.

'Carys.' Jacob sidles up to me, places his hand over mine. With the other, he cups my chin, turning me to face him, the horror in his eyes matching mine. I search his face. So loved. It's only now I see how much, and my heart swells in my chest, I cannot contain the hugeness of it.

'I love you,' I whisper, and his eyes penetrate to my very soul.

'I love you,' he says, so softly, and leans into me, his face buried in my neck.

Raza snorts from the corner and ruins the moment, but she can't take it from us. We remain for moments, lost in one another at the end of it all. I notice Amy, alone in another corner, her head in her hands. I stretch out my hand. 'Come here,' I say, and she shuffles over to us, and then we're all leaning into one another. I beckon to Raza, but she shakes her head, turns her back on me, crossing her arms. Prickly to the last.

We sit for a while, waiting for the sound that will herald one of the Think nurses coming to deliver our ultimate sentence. It comes soon, a sound of a key card dragged through a scanner; no archaic locks here in the Centre Think. We stiffen as one and pull ourselves to our feet, forming a futile defensive posture.

A male nurse enters the room flanked by two officers gripping solid N98 automatics, trained on us. The nurse is a small, heavily bearded man with glassy light blue eyes. He opens his pack and plucks out four syringes.

I think I'm going to be sick. I glance wildly at Jacob. He grips my hand tight. 'Be strong,' he whispers, his mouth tickling my ear, the intimacy of it at odds with the sheer wretchedness of our situation. For seconds, I allow myself to sink into it, to be subsumed by his love.

I'm snapped back to reality as Amy begins to sob. Her tenacity has brought us so very far, and she is at the end of it. Her weeping is as contained as she is, but it breaks me.

Raza remains silent, her hooded eyes black with hot rage.

The nurse takes the first syringe and tugs a small vial from his pack. He tears the syringe packet with his teeth, fastens a needle on the syringe and plunges it into the vial, drawing the drug up and then pushing the liquid to the top of the syringe. He doesn't stop to check for air bubbles.

He comes close to us and grabs Amy.

Oh, no. Oh, God, help us. I call to the God of the old holy book from the Subs bunker. I don't want to call on the Illumen anymore. Not now. Not ever.

'No!' A howl of raw emotion. Jacob crashes forward, head bent, straight at the nurse.

One of the guards is quicker. The butt of the N98 arcs round, smashing into Jacob's head, stunning him and knocking him to the floor.

The nurse continues his preparation, grabbing Amy's arm and pulsing her wrist for a vein. She shrinks back, tugging her arm away, her screams high and frantic. This time, I pile in, rushing at him, but I have no more luck. The guard simply sniggers and grabs hold of both my wrists, wrenching them painfully behind my back. He glares at me, then throws a glance at Raza. 'Don't even think about it,' he snarls.

The nurse ties a tourniquet then pulses the vein a little more. He plunges the needle into Amy's arm and depresses the syringe. In seconds, she slumps to the floor, unconscious.

Oh, God, where are you?

He goes to Raza next. Grabs her arms, and she seems to wake from her slumber. She kicks him, pinches him, sinks her teeth into his hand, but it's no good. The other guard grabs her; restrains her, and the nurse repeats his well-practised procedure, knocking her out in seconds.

It's only Jacob and me now. When we're both drugged, it is the end.

The nurse fills the third syringe and stoops, grabbing Jacob's arm. Jacob's still fairly knocked out but groaning slightly. He's soon fast unconscious.

I stare at the nurse in abject, wild fear.

'Please,' I cry, but he simply stares at me, no emotion written on his face. Hauntingly vacant eyes. He picks up the final syringe.

That's when I hear a commotion. Down the hall, past the two guards. Yelling. 'Wait!'

The nurse halts, holding the syringe in the vial, drawing up the liquid. The guards whirl round. 'Sir,' one of them says, his hand held to his forehead in obeisance. The other follows hastily.

'Stop.' The voice I now recognise as belonging to the chief draws closer, in time with heavy, hobnailed footsteps, tearing through the corridor. 'Wait.'

He arrives at the open doorway and shoves through, the guards stepping aside. He takes in the scene and strides over to the nurse. He grabs his hand, yanks the vial and the syringe from him, throws them on the table. 'You can't.' He's breathless and he's angry. His eyes are two narrow slits. He stares at me and at the three others, sprawled on the ground, drugged. 'They're to be freed,' he growls through gritted teeth. 'Released into the care of Lora Dancer.'

A rush of warmth cascades over me. *She woke up. She told them. She was true to her word.* I sag to the floor, place my hands on Jacob's inert back. *We're free.*

I can't quite believe it. Not until the officers and the nurse stir into action and lift the others into their arms, one each. The chief motions to me to follow, his glance heavy with disdain. I get to my feet and follow them out of the room, back along the corridor and up the stairs, back through the long red brick hallway to the main entrance where a large crowd of people lurk, waiting.

All is confusion. As we approach, a bunch of people break free from the crowd and start tearing towards us. Some of them have cameras, thrust into our faces, panning round my three drugged friends, shouting at us. 'Do you have any comment?' 'Can you tell us what happened with Lora Dancer?' 'Why were you taken to the Think?' 'How do you feel now?' They come thick and fast, pounding at me. It's relentless, and I say nothing.

The chief steps into action, shoving the reporters away. 'There will be no comment at this time,' he states, his air of authority commanding immediate respect and obedience. They step back, disappointed.

A figure emerges from the mass of excited faces, stepping forwards. He's a tall man of middle age, his dark hair gelled back, a precise pencil moustache balanced over thin lips. He is dressed in a purple pinstriped suit, the elongated collar tapering to a theatrical point. He tilts his head to one side, places a well-manicured hand on his hip, smiles widely at me and holds his other hand out. 'Coran Butler,' he says, shaking my hand rather limply. 'Lora Dancer's butler and personal assistant. Pleased to meet you. Dear Lora has told me about your daring rescue, and I'm thrilled to be able to take you to her.' He turns to the chief and wipes the smile from his face. 'I'm less pleased with you. Lora will be furious when she learns of the treatment these children have received from you. They have done nothing but good. They saved my dear Lora from a terribly brutal attack. I can promise you that you will be severely reprimanded. After all, you know of Lora's… associations.'

The blood drains from the chief's face, and he steps back. 'I was merely following the Midlands Compound directive,' he stutters, but Coran Butler shakes his head at him and he halts, his hands in the air. 'Look, I was just doing my job—'

Coran Butler grabs hold of my hand. 'So. You must be Girl Clerk. The one who caused all the trouble in the first place, hey?' He chuckles. I cannot bring myself to even smile back, the shock and panic still fresh on me.

'Come, now,' he says and pivots, keeping hold of me and strutting through the crowds, swivelling his thin hips as he sashays along. He turns his head, beckons to the officers. 'Bring them. We will care for them now.'

Amy, Jacob and Raza are brought to a gold NCV idling outside the Think entrance. It's an extra-large model, stretching out to include three rows of luxurious seats. The others are placed gently in the back seats, and I take the front passenger seat, next to Coran Butler, who slides in and squeezes my hand. 'So nice that I was able to find you, before…'

He starts the car, and we're away from the repugnant place that so nearly claimed our lives. For the first time, I exhale, a long sigh of absolute relief, and relax into the velvet upholstery.

We are free.

13

THE CENTRE

CORAN BUTLER LIKES a bit of drama. The journey to Lora's home is something of a trial when all I want is some quiet thinking space. He delights in filling me in on every detail of Lora's revival from her "coma", as he calls it, and her absolute horror to hear that we, her saviours, had been dragged to the Centre Think and almost executed. She was most insistent that he, Coran, should be the one to make rapid tracks over to the Think and rescue us from our fate, because he is the one she trusts most in the world. And he is so delighted to see us.

He rattles on for the twenty-minute journey, and I nod and smile but decline to join the conversation. When we reach the arched golden gates to Lora Dancer's famous mansion, I am relieved. The gates glide open soundlessly, leading to a sweeping driveway stretching far ahead of us. Rounding a curve, I see the white stone house so familiar from *The S Word*, majestic even through the darkness of the autumn night. Full height windows in the front centre of the house reflect the black night sky, lending the place a slightly eerie look.

'Now,' Coran says, 'here we are, then. Dear Lora is in hospital still, of course, the poor darling. She really was very badly hurt. If it wasn't for you, I dread to think…' he stops. Shivers dramatically. 'But as for now,' he continues, gathering himself and bringing the car to a sudden stop, 'I am in charge. I have had the maids prepare rooms for you. Your friends here can sleep off the effects of the drug, and you can join me for an impromptu late-night dinner. What a treat!' He turns to me, smiling, his mouth full of very large, very white teeth. 'You can tell me all about your little adventure with my poor dear girl.'

I nod, although all I want now is to sleep.

Coran flounces up to the carved double doors of Lora's mansion, touches the scanner and waits, hand on hip, tapping his pointed boot. Despite my fatigue, I smile. I like him. He's a welcome reprieve from other Productives I've met lately.

The door swings open, and he leans in, pinching his thumb and fingers to pursed lips and producing a piercing whistle. Two women come dashing out of the house, straightening white aprons and smoothing hair. They skid to a halt when they see the NCV and its occupants. Coran beckons them, curling his finger. 'We'll need to make several journeys. We need to get these poor dear children into their beds. I do trust they are ready, as I instructed?'

'Yes, Mr Butler,' one of them says, bowing slightly.

After three expeditions back and forth, Jacob, Amy and Raza are installed in sumptuous bedrooms, soundly sleeping, unaware of their extravagant surroundings. Coran takes my hand and drags me along the upstairs hallway to another room. He flings the door open with a flourish and spreads his hands. 'Your room, my lady.'

I step over the threshold into the most opulent space I've ever seen. A huge, lavish four poster bed takes centre stage, plush cushions sitting atop a velvet throw matching the midnight blue velvet curtains. A white deep-pile carpet covers the floor. One wall is taken up with fully fitted mirrored wardrobes, and another door leads to a large bathroom, a claw foot bath in the centre, soft, fluffy towels folded over a warm rail. A large gilt-framed portrait of Commander Anson hangs on the wall between two deep sash windows.

I inhale. 'Wow.'

Coran squeezes my arm. 'I do hope you like it, dear. It's one of dear Lora's favourite guest rooms. Please, make yourself at home. I will arrange for a little supper in half an hour or so and will send one of the maids for you.' He stands back, a satisfied expression on his face.

Supper is served in a large dining room, Coran and I sitting at a buffed mahogany table meant for twenty-four, diamond chandeliers throwing spectacular patterns on the highly polished surface. I'm served with delicious soup followed by a meal I've never come across or even imagined, some kind of meat wrapped in light, flaky pastry accompanied by vegetables tender but not overdone like they always are at Ashton. Despite my anxiety, I tuck into the meal. Coran enjoys my appreciation of it all, and afterwards, he wants to talk, and offers me oak-aged whisky, but I decline. 'I'm just sixteen,' I say, and he nods vigorously. I have a headache and ask to go to bed. He concurs, slightly sulkily, and insists on accompanying me back to my room.

'Till the morning, then,' he says, and swaggers away down the corridor, smoothing his gelled hair back.

I sleep as soon as I lie down.

AMY

AMY PLUMBER DOESN'T know where she is.

She wakes slowly, painfully, her head spinning and her stomach lurching. Gradually, she becomes aware of her surroundings and construes that she must be in a dream. Sunlight streams through white voile panels at wide windows in front of her bed, which is softer than she's ever known. She's lying on silken pillows and covered by a vast, warm duvet. It's like being deep in a nest. She sinks into it, luxuriating, and then sits ramrod straight.

The Centre Think. The nurse. The syringe.

Am I dead?

A soft knocking sounds at the door, and she swings her legs out of bed and walks over, her bare feet sinking into the plush cream carpet. Cautiously, she creaks the door open and breathes a sigh of relief.

Carys.

Amy falls into her embrace, briefly wondering if her addled mind has dreamed her up as well as these lavish surroundings. But Carys quickly fills her in on the events of the night before and takes her by the hand, dragging her along the hallway and waking Jacob, whose forehead is knotted with confusion. Last of all, Carys knocks on the door of the next-door room to Jacob's.

No reply.

Carys cracks the door open. 'Raza?'

No answer.

'She must be in the bathroom,' Carys says, wandering into the room and through to the bathroom. But she isn't there, either.

She must be exploring the house. Searching for breakfast, perhaps? Carys leads them down the sweeping stairway, burnished oak banisters curving down to a spacious entrance hall. A maid clatters through a doorway to the rear of the hall, holding a tray, and startles at the sight of them. 'Oh!'

At the commotion, the door to another room cracks open and a thin man with a thin moustache peeks out then slinks through. He's dressed in a velvet forest-green dressing gown and goatskin slippers. 'Well, good morning, my dears,' he says and twirls, grabbing Amy's hand, dragging her through the doorway. 'Come, then!'

She follows him into another sumptuous room, this one laid out with breakfast dishes. All talk is suspended as they eat, and then, finally, they catch up, unbelieving as to their timely rescue. Carys introduces the thin man as Coran Butler, who seems overjoyed at their presence, though a little perturbed by Raza's absence. 'Is she still asleep? Having a lie in?' he says, smiling.

'We can't find her,' Carys says. 'We thought she might be down here.'

Coran clatters his bone china teacup into its saucer. 'She's gone?'

Carys shrugs.

Coran stands abruptly, scraping his chair on the polished floorboards. 'We must search everywhere for her. Now. Every room. All the grounds.'

But she is nowhere to be found.

'Where is she?' Coran says, flapping dramatically as he dashes in and out of rooms. 'We must find her. She can't just go, Lora will—' he stops, twisting his hands.

'Lora will what?' Amy says.

'She must be found,' he says. 'I will have to make a report, and they will blame me for letting her go.' The colour has drained from his face.

CORAN BUTLER FINDS fresh clothes for them; clothes of a quality Amy has never known (they look brand new). After showering and donning their new outfits, they join him in what he calls the morning room, a sun-filled space with deep sofas and shaggy rugs, and perch together on one of the couches, not yet at ease. She wonders what they will do now. Perhaps they can leave here. Perhaps they can go and search for her mother and father after all.

'Dear Lora is so grateful to you all. She wants you to know that,' Coran says, and Amy is relieved that he seems to have regained his composure. 'She has plans to reward you, and she would like you to stay as guests in her home for as long as you please. You should help yourselves to anything you like and have free rein of the house and grounds.' He pauses, beaming round at them, his face flushed and eager. 'Lora is talking to Commander Anson himself about a pardon for you, such is her strong feeling of indebtedness. You are not to worry at all. The officers at the border gates and the Centre Think have been severely reprimanded for their rash actions. Of course, the other girl will also receive a pardon if she returns quickly. If not—'

A sudden knock on the door. One of the maids enters, her face reddened and her hair wild. 'There are reporters out there. Hundreds of them.'

Coran leaps up, smooths his velvet trousers. 'The drama queens,' he says, pushing out his cheeks. 'They can't leave poor dear Lora alone.' Carys catches Amy's eye, and they suppress a giggle. But then they follow a tutting Coran over to the window and see a huge crowd of Productives milling around, camera equipment in tow. Some of them are peering through the window, but Coran scoffs at them. 'One way glass,' he says. 'They can't see in, thank dear Lucan.'

Amy realises they are big news in the Centre Compound. 'Can we have NBC on?' she asks Coran, and he rolls his eyes at her then nods and clicks his fingers. A screen over the fireplace lights up, and it's their faces they see first. Different shots of them; some in their Ashton uniforms, one of Carys in an MCT jumpsuit, a photo of Jacob as a boy with his grandfather. His face hardens at the sight of the image.

'Turn it up,' Carys says, digging her nails into her palm. 'What are they saying about us?'

Coran complies, and a voice booms into the room: '… the daring rescue of the nation's sweetheart, Lora Dancer, who is at present in her suite in the Commander Lucan Hospital, said to be doing well. Ms Dancer issued a statement this morning, stating that the three fugitives and the unknown girl would be released without charge, by order of Commander Anson. The story is front page news in all the papers and on every netpage today. Again, I can confirm that Boy Trader, Girl Plumber, and Girl Clerk, previously wanted for treason in the Midlands Compound, are released without charge today after mounting an intrepid rescue of Lora Dancer. Lora had fallen into the clutches of lawless Outsiders, and the three fugitives, who had been hiding out in the area, along with a fourth, unknown girl, stumbled across Lora mid attack. Lora has told of how the three fearlessly tackled the thugs and bore Lora away from the scene. Sadly, they were too late to save Lora's valued chauffeur, Tolan Driver, but were thoughtful enough to bring his body home to the Centre for his family. His wife, Mercia Carer, is here with me now.'

The images of them are replaced by a studio set, the newsreader sitting with a pale woman on a low red sofa. 'Mercia,' says the newsreader, 'can you tell us what it means to you that the ex-fugitives brought home your husband?'

The woman brings her hands to her eyes and rubs at them. 'It means… everything. I can't tell you… Tolan was a good Productive, you know? He worshipped Lora.' Her eyes shift to the side, her hands trembling in her lap. 'He was so… so lucky to work for her. I just want to thank her, and to thank the four children who cared enough to bring him home to me.' She stops there, tears spilling over.

Coran mutes the sound. 'So you see,' he says, grinning widely, 'you are indeed free! My poor dear Lora – she has saved you, in return for your act of valour.'

They stare at one another, not quite believing this turn of events. If they are, in fact, free, then they can go. They can finish training. Be Productives. Live their lives.

But there's a problem with that.

They don't want to. Too much is already lost, and there is still much to do.

It is a temporary reprieve.

14

THE CENTRE

$\mathcal{C}$ARYS

THREE DAYS LATER, Lora Dancer returns home. Coran flaps about the house, ordering the maids around, bellowing at deliverymen. He builds up her homecoming like she is the most important Productive who ever lived. I suppose she is, to him, and to many others in Newland. After all, as we keep being reminded, she is the nation's sweetheart. The one with the heart.

She is brought into the house in a wheelchair. Bandages envelop her left arm and left ankle, and the bruise on her eye is rainbow coloured. Her cheeks are rosier than when we last saw her, and her good eye twinkles at Coran as he flings wide the double doors for her, ushering in the nurse pushing the chair and calling maids to bring drinks and food. She laughs at him. 'Relax, Coran. Let me be a while. Let me get into my own home.' He stands back, clasping his hands, practically hopping from one foot to another in his agitation.

The three of us stand in the hallway, awkward and uncertain. Lora catches sight of us and breaks into a wide smile. 'I'm so glad you are here! I was very much hoping you would be—' she stops, her smile fading, '—the other girl is still not here?' She narrows her eyes at Coran.

He fiddles with a large gold signet ring and clears his throat. 'She hasn't returned, no. The NForce have an alert out. She will be found, I assure you. They are in touch with her old training house here in the Centre and tracking various leads from there.'

Lora sighs. 'Ans… the Commander won't be happy. They'd better find her quickly.' She looks back at the three of us and twists her lips into a pained smile. 'It's good to see you three have accepted my hospitality, though. I have some things to ask of you, you see. But time enough. Please, go and relax. You've no need to be standing there all stiffly.'

I'm reminded of her in full flow on *The S Word*, making the contestants feel at ease, even the Skivers. She has a gift with words, and no one ever feels threatened by her, as they do by the others, particularly Raulf and Portia.

That afternoon, she joins us out on the deck as we enjoy some autumnal sunshine. She's walking by herself now, hobbling slightly, grimacing as she places weight on her left foot. She limps out of the patio doors and sinks gracefully onto a rattan sofa. She props her foot up and surveys us. 'I have some ideas,' she says, folding her hands on her lap. 'Ideas to help you, and to help me, and… the Commander.'

I watch her closely. She is smiling, but there is a slight twitch to her left eye. I wonder if she is nervous. She never seems nervous on the show.

'The first thing that I must say… and I'm sorry that I have to, but I just need to make sure, you understand—' she breaks off, enquiring of us with her eyes, '—the promise you made to me, back in… in the car. You will hold to it?'

I feel like challenging her. Asking her what promise she means, but Jacob jumps in before I can, and I feel a prickle of irritation. 'We promised,' he says. 'We will hold to it.' I try to catch Amy's eye, but she won't look at me.

'And the missing girl? She won't be spreading those… lies?'

Jacob shakes his head. 'I think she's just looking for someone from her past. She'll be too busy with that. Don't worry.' He says it with confidence, but I see the shift in his eyes. Where *is* Raza? What is she doing? Could she get us all into trouble once again? I'm not sure I trust her, even after hearing her story. But she's one of us, now, even so, and I hate to think of her out there in the Centre on her own. Why couldn't she stay with us? Trust us?

'Well, you must tell us if you hear anything from her. The Commander doesn't like… loose ends, you see.'

Jacob nods. 'Understood.'

Lora sighs and relaxes, dropping her hands to her sides. 'Having got that over with, I have a couple of… propositions.'

We say nothing.

'The first one is that you are seen out with me. The media is very keen to see you. Get your side of the story, as it were. We are eager to satisfy this need. It would be very advantageous from all sides. The country would be able to gain a picture of you, and of mine – and the Commander's – benevolence, in this matter. It would be valuable to us. There have been some… rumblings, lately, around Party HQ, and, shall we say, things are not all rosy in the garden. But a situation like this would prove to our people how compassionate we are. Which is all absolutely true, as you know.'

For a second, she seems flustered. 'Look, I realise I might seem to be… *spinning* things here, but I can assure you, I am just making the most of things. You are free from your charges, and life is so much better for it – that's true, yes?'

We nod, wordless.

'So now, you can help me. The Commander is… close to me. Very close. I want to please him, and I know this will. I am therefore asking you to assist me.'

We stare at her, then I ask, 'What do you mean by us being "seen out with you"?'

She smiles softly. 'Merely that Coran will take me for my afternoon walk, in my wheelchair. My constitutional, if you like. To rebuild my health. You will be with me… keeping me company. The press will be alerted, prior to the event, so that we have the best possible opportunity for coverage.'

She makes it sound so cold, somehow. Calculated. I am not at all sure I want to help Commander Anson look good and squash any political unrest. A few days ago, we were ready to stir up more unrest ourselves, and now we're colluding in a plan to big him up. Heat infuses me. *I can't do this.*

Amy takes my hand, squeezes it. 'Shh,' she whispers, well aware of my discomfort. Out loud, to Lora, she says, 'Of course. We owe you our lives.'

Lora nods firmly. 'I knew you would. I'll tell Coran. He'll help you dress suitably for the occasion—' she breaks off, giggling slightly. 'It'll be fun!'

'And the other idea?' Jacob says. 'You said you had a couple of thoughts.'

'Oh, yes, of course,' says Lora, sitting forward. 'This is the best one, but I'm afraid you might not be so… comfortable, with this.'

I stiffen. I'm already uncomfortable with the photo opportunity; if she thinks I won't like this one I know I'll hate it. Amy keeps hold of my hand. 'Just keep calm,' she hisses in my ear. Jacob shoots me a warning look. I stand cautioned and button my mouth.

'I need you to publicly denounce what you have been saying,' she begins, and my blood begins to boil. 'We cannot have… rumours… flying around. There is some unrest because of your actions, and it is vitally important that you tell the nation you were wrong. That you made things up – you were bored, perhaps? And to do this, you must appear on *The S Word.*'

I boil over. 'What?'

Amy shakes her head at me.

'It will be a wonderful thing for you,' Lora says, smiling at me. 'Most children your age would give anything for such an opportunity. You will be national treasures. You will say sorry, and we, the *S Word* judges, will pronounce forgiveness and speak of the Commander's absolute insistence that Newland has compassion on you. You will publicly proclaim your regret and apologise to all those you hurt.'

I dig my nails into my palm, drawing blood, as my stomach clenches.

'And all will be well. Any unrest will be quashed and rumours quelled. You will be safe to go about your lives, and things will be as they were.'

Jacob speaks up. 'But how do people know… about us, I mean? About what we found out?'

'Of course, you've been hiding out,' Lora says. 'It was all over the news that you had broken into confidential files and twisted the words in them to make up a heinous story about Newland.'

'But how did they know what we found in the files? We didn't exactly have a chance to shout it from the rooftops, you know.'

She shifts on her seat. 'Hmm. It seems there may have been leaks… at your Compound Think, perhaps. Someone with an axe to grind, maybe; someone who knew how to get the press to listen. We feel it was perhaps… *misguided,* of the media, to spread your lies so wide, but they did, and so the damage was done. Most people didn't believe what you said you'd found for a minute, but there were those who did, unfortunately, and some have been causing trouble. But you are in the position to stop what you started. I am so glad. Aren't you?'

She smiles again, and her smile is innocent. She firmly believes what she is saying.

I know my face is flushed. I am hot to the core with rage, but I somehow manage to keep it in. Jacob and Amy murmur their assent, and we drag indoors, in no mood for sunbathing.

JACOB

CARYS IS INCENSED. Her face looks like she's been in a boiling hot bath for an hour. She's stewing over, and Jacob doesn't blame her; what Lora has asked of them is crazy. But he can totally see why she's doing it. They're pawns to her, just pieces on a game board to be pushed around, used to help her and her precious Anson. Jacob has no desire to help her.

But he doesn't know what else they are supposed to do.

The next afternoon, Lora organises her little press party. Coran Butler comes flouncing up to them after lunch holding a load of clothes over his arms. 'I've got such treats in store,' he says, and Jacob rolls his eyes.

Coran hands some stuff over to Jacob. 'You get yourself sorted, darling,' he says. 'You're going to look amazing.' Jacob checks out the clothes. They're so OTT. Blue shiny skinnies and a white top. He shrugs and goes to get them on.

He's waiting around for the girls in the huge white entrance hall, not sure what to do with himself. Feels a bit stupid. But then he sees them. Amy first, coming down the stairway. She looks nice, dressed in black jeans and a red cold-shoulder top, and her hair has been done so it sticks out in tufts, it looks kind of cool. Jacob whistles at her, and she blushes then kicks him when she gets to the bottom.

When Carys appears at the top, he can't help drawing his breath in. She looks beautiful. She's wearing a turquoise dress, nipped in at the waist then flared to above her knee, then she has these silver sandals on. Carys and heels don't tend to mix, but she looks damn gorgeous. She's got some stuff on her face too; it brings out her grey eyes, which look even larger and more luminous than ever. He whisks her into his arms and kisses her. Can't hold back. She gasps and pushes at him, spots of red appearing on her cheeks. 'Oy,' she says, but then he can see she's checking him out, too.

'Get a room,' Amy says, and they all snicker, pushing each other round.

Coran turns up then, pushing Lora in her wheelchair. She looks stunning too, clad in white wide leg linens and a white top, her hair arranged artfully over her bruised eye but not completely covering it. Coran gasps at them and staggers back, one hand to his mouth in this super exaggerated gesture. 'Woah,' he says. 'You look… astounding.' He grabs Lora's chair and twirls her, dancing her around the foyer. 'Ready for your afternoon stroll, dear one?'

She smiles widely. 'All ready.'

Jacob takes Carys's hand, and they amble out of the house and down the driveway. At the gates, there are a bunch of Productives, some with NSlates, some with cameras. Lora smiles at them all, spreading her hands wide. 'Welcome.'

They almost bow to her. Then they spot the group and start on the photos and the shouted questions. 'Tell us about your time with Lora!' 'What happened when you rescued her?' 'Describe her attackers.' 'What will you do now?' And so on and so forth. Amy and Jacob do their best to field them and answer them as Lora wants, but Carys stays silent, bristling beside Jacob. He keeps his hand clamped round hers. *Just keep quiet.*

They exit the gates and follow Coran and Lora down a footpath across the road, through a woodland area and out next to a broad river. This is the River Thames, Jacob realises, one of the rivers left from the Before. Most of the nation's rivers were flooded out and never recovered. There are still traces of ruins of the old city here, but most of them are cleared, with new buildings sitting on the riverbanks in state.

There's an NBC cameraman who keeps shoving his camera in their faces, but apart from that, it's not so bad. Lora says all this stuff about how amazing they are and how grateful she is and slips in garbage about Anson's heart of forgiveness and mercy. Towards the end, she tells them the three trainees will be featuring on *The S Word* next week and that all worries will be laid to rest. They pose for group photos, the three of them crouching behind Lora in her chair, then Lora holding Amy and Carys's hands, then Jacob and Lora in deep conversation.

The next day, the papers are full of them and they're on NBC. Carys is stormily silent throughout, and Jacob can tell Lora is a bit annoyed with her for not getting into the spirit of it all. 'Thing is,' Carys says later when they're alone in the morning room, 'it comes across like we love Newland and Anson and that we're looking forward to being good Productives. Makes me sick.'

Jacob hugs her. 'I know. But what choice do we have?'

Carys sulks. 'Since when did we get so gutless?'

Amy just hangs her head.

But all this is nothing compared to the thought of what they'll go through next week, when they appear on *The S Word*.

Before that, though, it turns out that Lora has another little surprise for them.

THE NEXT EVENING they're slumped out round the den, watching mindless drivel on the NScreen, some old film with a typical Newland butch hero rescuing the poor feeble girl. Lora hobbles into the room, dressed in a red silk dressing gown. 'I've got another treat for you.' She clasps her hands together. 'You'll never guess.' She's like a little kid waiting for a present. Not that Newland kids tend to get many presents.

'What is it?' Amy asks politely. Carys rolls her eyes at Jacob.

'Guess who's coming to dinner tomorrow?'

'I can't guess,' Carys says, her eyes hard and her jaw tight. Lora's brow creases, momentarily nonplussed by her hostility.

'Tell us,' Amy says, knitting her eyebrows at Carys.

Lora smiles, drawn back in. 'It's such an honour for you. It was his idea. The Commander's.'

The three of them stiffen as one.

Commander Anson is having dinner with them?

Carys bursts. 'No way.' She stomps from the room. Lora watches her, eyes widened.

Amy steps forward. Takes Lora's hand. 'Don't worry. Ca… Girl C just gets a little… hot-headed, sometimes. She doesn't mean anything by it. She'll cool down—'

'I can't have her near the Commander with that attitude.' Lora twists her hands. 'That would be… disastrous.'

'She will be fine,' Amy says. Lora casts her gaze to the floor, unconvinced.

'Tomorrow evening, then,' she says, and walks stiffly out of the room.

Amy and Jacob glance at one another. 'We need to make her behave,' Amy says. 'I don't like it any more than she does. All I think of when I see Anson is that he killed Lewis. My brother. But we mustn't show our real feelings – if we do, we're screwed, you know that. It feels like we're just a step away from making a huge mistake and then Lora going back on her word.'

'I know.'

They have to get Carys to put up the pretence. It's the only way.

CARYS

I CAN'T BELIEVE Jacob and Amy didn't walk out with me.

Dinner with that monster? I'd rather go back to the Centre Think. He's the one who's behind all the injustice, all the suffering. The deaths of so many. He knows exactly what is happening, even if he's managed to delude Lora.

How can I sit and eat with this man?

Jacob catches up with me later, moping in my room. 'Listen,' he says, sinking onto the bed next to me and sliding his arm round my waist. I stiffen.

'What?'

'Look. We hate this as much as you—'

'Could have fooled me.'

'Come on, Carys. You know us better than that. It's just… we value our lives. Your life. This is all so precarious. Surely you can see that? Lora's a puppet on a string. She'll dance to Anson's tune, whatever it is. At the moment, it's in our favour, but that could tip at any minute. Soon as we make trouble we'll be for the chop again. You can see that, right?'

I contemplate my bitten down nails. 'I suppose.'

'We're not sucking up to her just for the fun of it.'

'I know.'

'Listen. If we get all this over with – this dinner, then *The S Word* – then we can leave. Carry on our plan, find Amy's parents, then do something about all of this. I haven't forgotten, Carys. I haven't abandoned all this, you know?'

I gaze at him, the sulks forgotten. 'I do know. I'm sorry. It's just… just that I get so *angry*. You know? I can't help it. It's like this red-hot thing gets hold of me and I can't stop it. It takes over me. I hate all this so much. I just want to shout the truth from the rooftops, Jacob! Make Lora see it, tell her to stop being so *stupid*. But I can't. And it's so frustrating.'

'I know. But you're strong. You can do it. Just one more week, and it will all be worth it. If we lose it now, we'll lose the long battle. We'll lose the fight. Everything will go on the way it was because we won't be there to rally up troops and get some resistance off the ground.'

'We are so few.'

'But there will be more. Remember the Queen's story? We just need to convince them it's time to fight.'

'How?'

'I don't know.'

I stare at him, and it all seems hopeless. I know he is right. I must stay with the pretence for my own good and for Amy's and Jacob's good. I curl my hands into fists, bring them to my face. 'I will be good,' I say, and Jacob leans into me. Hugs me tight. My pent-up rage drains from me in the warmth of his love, and I'm ready to go on.

15

THE CENTRE

AMY

THE NEXT EVENING, Coran fusses around, getting them all dressed up again. He's in a strange mood, and Amy soon surmises what his problem is. He's not keen on Anson. He doesn't admit it, but it's there in his actions and his expressions, his nuances. He tuts and he sulks, and he preens himself when he speaks of Lora. 'She's going to look astonishing,' he states. 'I have a new dress for her. It only arrived today – custom made for her. It's silver – wait till you see it.'

Amy gathers together the new clothes from the walk with the press, but he grabs them from her and flings them to the other side of the room. 'Don't be *silly*,' he breathes. 'They are *day* clothes. You will go to the ball, my dear!'

She smiles at this reference to one of the few stories from the Before her parents read to her as a child. Coran takes another garment out of a bag, and she gasps. It's a green velvet dress, floor length. 'We need to get you properly dressed for such an important occasion,' he says, holding the dress out.

She meets Carys and Jacob in the hallway outside their rooms. They've also had the comprehensive Coran treatment. They only have eyes for each other, though. Carys wears another floor length gown, this one in midnight blue silk, and Jacob's all done up in a dinner suit with white tie. 'It's only dinner,' Carys huffs, wriggling to straighten her dress. 'This is pathetic.'

'You don't look pathetic to me,' Jacob says, and Amy screws her nose up.

When Amy arrives in the entrance hall, she's shocked to see that there are more Productives than she expected. They'd been given the impression that the dinner would be only for them with Lora and Anson, but there are six or seven other people milling around, air kissing one another, posing for photographs for someone who looks suspiciously like one of the media Productives from the "constitutional" the other day. They all turn as the three descend, staring at them.

With a hard heart thump, Amy recognises three of them immediately.

Raulf Singer. Edwin Runner. Portia Equine.

Lora didn't say anything about the *S Word* judges coming to the dinner party.

Amy glances at Carys. Pink blotches colour her cheeks and the tips of her ears, but she's keeping it in. For now. Jacob stays calm, plasters a smile on his face and saunters over to them, hand outstretched. 'Boy Trader,' he says, and his confidence pays off. They smile back at him and take his hand politely, although Amy notices that Portia's face is sharp with thinly veiled contempt.

They turn to Amy and Carys, and Raulf draws near to kiss their cheeks, followed closely by Edwin. Portia hangs back, regarding them coldly, but says, 'Pleased to meet you.'

Edwin is friendly and giddy and introduces the other Productives. Raulf's girlfriend looks like a model, and Amy recognises Edwin's wife as another Newland sports star. Portia's boyfriend looks about as friendly as Portia herself and stands in the corner, watching everyone with a sardonic expression twisting his sharp features.

Lora drifts in, as stunning as Coran predicted in a silver dress, her long blonde hair set in curls cascading down her slender back. It looks like only Anson hasn't arrived yet. 'Ah, you're all here,' Lora says, dancing between them, twirling and laughing. 'Did you like my surprise, then?'

Amy nods. 'Yes, thank you.'

Lora laughs widely, displaying small pearl-white teeth. 'I knew you would.'

Carys stands next to Amy, rigid and silent. 'Try to relax,' Amy whispers.

The double doors to the front are flung open, and Coran struts in, holding the door for a Productive behind him. Coran's face is like thunder, but he sweeps his arm towards the gathering, almost bowing. 'May I present the Commander,' he says stiffly.

Commander Anson marches into the hall like he owns it. He is not an especially tall man, but he has a powerful presence, his blue eyes mesmerising, like diamond ice, and he has the gift of making you feel like you are the only person in the world. His eyes sweep the room, searching for Lora, who skitters to his side. 'Commander,' she says, 'you look incredible.'

Anson doesn't return the compliment. He merely nods and lays his hand on Lora's tiny waist. 'Introduce me, then.'

Lora giggles. Amy watches her closely. She's behaving differently round Anson, like a child eager to please a Trainer. 'Of course,' she says, taking his hand and bringing him over. 'Commander, this is Girl Plumber, this is Boy Trader, and this is Girl Clerk. The children who saved me. And children – this is Commander Anson.'

Amy knows that the correct thing to do at this moment is to bow, even to cross her hands across her belly, but she cannot bring herself to, so she manages a nod of her head and accepts his hand held out to shake hers. He has a bone-crushing handshake, and as he takes her hand, he stares into her soul, his eyes glittering as he scrutinises her. She can't hold his gaze and looks away, confused.

'A pleasure to meet you,' he says. 'I'm very much looking forward to hearing something of your… story. I know what you have done for Lora, and I am thankful.'

Amy nods, tongue tied.

Coran is standing at the doors to the dining room. 'Dinner is served,' he announces. Amy follows the others into the room, which is transformed for the party. The chandeliers sparkle in the candlelight; silver dinnerware and solid silver cutlery are placed precisely at eleven table settings. Linen napkins in rings are arranged at the centre of each place, and names are inscribed in intricate script on cards. Amy had hoped the three would be together, but they are scattered. Carys is next to Raulf, Jacob is with Portia and Amy is between Edwin and Anson. She shivers.

Just get through this.

They stand awkwardly behind their designated chairs, waiting for a command. Lora seems as awkward as them, but Anson sweeps in, plucks his napkin from its ring and installs himself on the plush chair, and they follow. Lora is on Anson's other side, with Portia's petulant boyfriend next to her. She gazes up at Anson adoringly, but he ignores her and turns to Amy. 'So. Girl Plumber,' he says, with a twist of his lip at her lowly name, 'I believe you are illegal, by birth?'

Shocked, she gapes at him for seconds, then remembers her vow. *Just keep going. Pretend.* She raises a smile. 'Yes.'

'But you have redeemed yourself, with your studies at Ashton. Until, of course, this ridiculous escapade of yours.' He chuckles as if he has said something highly amusing, and Amy tries to laugh.

'However, you have managed to atone for that bit of silliness with your actions regarding my girl here,' he says, clutching Lora's shoulder. Lora winces, then giggles.

'We were just in the right place at the right time,' Amy says.

'No just about it. You made a courageous decision. I won't have you downplaying it. After all, you will be seen nationwide, receiving my forgiveness because of your... tenacity.'

'Yes.'

His intense blue gaze stays on her. 'You are interested in politics, Ms Plumber?'

'Um... well, yes, I suppose so.'

'Of course you are. You are from Ashton. Only the keenest minds there, of course.'

Or the richest parents.

'I am interested in most things.'

'You have studied our history?'

'Well... yes, most of it, from the Re-Ordering.'

'Of course. Nothing before that matters, after all. Only to establish the fact that things had been going dreadfully wrong and no one had the gumption to do anything about it. Until Lucan, that was.'

At the mention of his name, everyone crosses their hands and bows their head. Amy joins in, watching Carys from the corner of her eye. She participates, but her hands are clenched so tight her knuckles show white.

'You do understand, don't you, about the way things are in Newland? The way that is well established?'

Amy nods, not trusting herself to speak.

'You can be assured that all we want, all I want as your Commander, is to ensure that everyone has a good quality of life. But in order to achieve that we must all do our bit. Isn't that right?'

Everyone is listening to Anson now. They all acquiesce.

'We have a society now where people really do have compassion on those less... fortunate than themselves. Our structures are well set up, are they not, to care for those who need it. I think it would be a shame if that were to be challenged at all. We don't want people suffering needlessly, do we?'

Amy is well aware that Commander Anson is forming his words for an audience of three.

'Some may say that we have been somewhat austere in reaching our goals for Newland, but austerity can be a positive when it is part of achieving something of greatness. Many world states are envious of the system we have here.'

'How do you know that?' Jacob breaks in. Indrawn breaths sound round the table.

Anson chuckles again. 'Well, young man. I have my spies, you know. You may think we are cut off. But I can assure you, I am well aware of goings on in the world, and I can tell you that you are in the best place, here in Newland. The safest place. On that matter, you may well think that I wished you gone from here, on account of your skin colour. But I must assure you that it makes no odds to me. That view is an old fashioned one. I have no tolerance with it. You will find me more open minded than you perhaps thought. I believe in a Newland of peace. Of acceptance and broad-mindedness. You and your kind are welcome here.'

Jacob remains silent, but Carys is bursting with something. Amy shoots her a glance. *Don't.*

The dinner is served: salmon, which Amy's not keen on but she picks at, answering questions politely. Anson talks for the majority of the time and Lora hardly at all.

Raulf Singer gives Anson a run for his money, and they're soon embroiled in a good-natured but robust disagreement on inter-Compound trading laws. Raulf thinks each Compound should be self-sufficient, and Anson takes a more lenient view to trade. 'Each person should do all they can to better themselves,' he says. 'Trade laws or not. Newland is increasingly prosperous, and more so because of the entrepreneurial spirit of the nation and of so many Productives who make it their life's work to make money – and to make everything better for the next generation.'

After a while, Anson seems to grow bored, his intense eyes searching the three of them for entertainment. 'But do tell me,' he says, looking straight at Amy, 'whatever possessed you to make up such a… pernicious story about us?' He grins as he speaks, and his manner turns playful. He wants to spar.

Be careful.

Jacob jumps in before Carys. 'We needed something to… make everything worth it. The escape and everything,' he says, eyes downcast. Is that all he can come up with?

Amy can't do any better.

Carys speaks up. *Oh no…*

'It was my fault,' she says, gazing straight at Anson, who holds her gaze steadily, unblinkingly. She falters, glances away. 'I… I attacked a fellow trainee. I am not claiming innocence, but she provoked me—'

Amy kicks her under the table, and she stares daggers at her.

'—Anyway, I was sent to the Compound Think. My friends were brave enough to break me out, and we wanted to get away, so we told ourselves a story that would help us leave.'

Amy gasps. She's doing it. She's in the game.

'It was kind of like… that we needed a narrative. To tell ourselves things were bad, so that we could get out, because we didn't like being at Ashton. I guess we took things too far.' She stops there, stares at Anson.

He stands up and applauds her. Slow handclaps. Lora looks distinctly uncomfortable.

'I'm impressed,' bellows Anson. Amy glances at his glass; drained once again. He's drunk a good bottle and a half of vintage wine by now. 'You have been prepared to share your… pretence with us. That takes some guts. Come on, everyone, join me!' He lifts his glass, motions to Carys. 'To Girl C, Girl P and Boy T, the saviours of the nation's sweetheart and the spreaders of treasonous lies.' He guffaws at himself, but everyone takes up their glass, raises it.

'To Girl C, Girl P and Boy T.'

Amy sits rigidly, making no eye contact with the others.

CARYS

I RELAX BACK into my chair, exhausted by my attempt to placate Anson. He repulses me with his deadly gaze and thick lips, his silver hair, slicked back and slightly receding at the temples, and his rather portly belly. He keeps catching my eye through the evening, and even more so when I have joined in the charade. Surely everyone here knows?

The other judges are incredibly shallow. No substance whatsoever. It's all 'Yes, Commander, no, Commander, whatever you say, Commander.' Lora is completely overshadowed by him and has no personality of her own since he arrived. He takes little notice of her. It's painful to watch; she keeps touching him, brushing his ear with her lips. It's like she's desperate for his attention, but he casts it elsewhere. A couple of times I see him reprimanding her; a sharp squeeze of her hand here, a small pinch on her elbow there.

He's a bully.

I can't be doing with the whole thing. I'm feeling mutinous, and I know I'm playing with fire, but I don't care. 'Can you tell me why our country is cut off from the rest of the world?' I ask, smiling up at him. He gazes at me, his full lips slightly uplifted. I can sense Jacob and Amy's irritated discomfort.

'I like that,' he says, gesticulating at me with his fork. 'I like people who aren't afraid to ask questions.' He pauses, takes a great glug of his wine. A waitress hovering in the shadows steps forward to top his glass up. He raises it to me, his eyes pinned hard on me. 'You need to understand what a precarious position we were in,' he says. 'At the time of the riots, the three countries of Wales, Northern Ireland and Scotland had formed a united coalition. They didn't want England in on it. England had lost Northern Ireland, Wales and Scotland years before this and there was a massive amount of unrest. England had left the European Union – the continent nearest us – years before, and that was supposed to help things along with immigration and trade laws but really didn't. The government had no clue what they were doing. We were in some mess; foreigners pouring through our poorly manned borders. The coalition countries took a harder stance on immigration and left us behind.'

He takes a forkful of fish and smacks his lips together. My stomach churns.

'When the riots happened, then the Scourge, as you know we were severely decimated. It's a wonder there were survivors, to be honest. We were left in a severely compromised position with no help from the coalition countries, our government gone – they were all killed in the riots or escaped the country – and immigrants still remaining and, in some cases, still coming in. It was chaos, as you can imagine.'

I think about Amy's book and swallow my bile. 'But surely that would be the time to seek support from Europe – and the rest of the world? I don't understand why we shut ourselves away, right to the extent of erecting coastal barriers, and grounding those things people used to fly in?'

'Aeroplanes,' prompts Anson, grinning.

'Yes. Those. Why?'

He sighs. 'It's complex, especially for someone of your youth. When the New Day Party came to power, they made some brave decisions. They saw that the only way for Newland to grow again and to eventually thrive would be to choose self-sufficiency. There could be no more immigrants and no more co-operation with other nations. There would be less chance of war with others, less chance of any kind of interference if we simply looked after our own. In many ways, it's actually very simple. We started from the ground up, as it were. We grew our own food, began to manufacture our own goods. Of course, for the first years of Newland things were harsh. Many goods and utilities were simply no longer available. People had to cope with a very different way of life. But the New Days made this possible—'

By murdering everyone who challenged them, I think, but don't say.

'—And after a while, things began to improve. I think we can see that the correct decision was made, and we now have a growing nation to be proud of. Productivity is high and we have all the goods we need, our technology is cutting edge, there is enough food to go round. Of course, there were… sacrifices… to achieve this.'

'You mean like sending all the "foreigners" away?' I curl my fingers in quotation marks.

He sniffs. 'I wouldn't have put it like that, my dear girl. More that we… *rationalised*. We merely gave people a chance to return to their natural homes, and so made enough room for all survivors to start anew.'

I glance at Jacob. He is examining the table, his hands clenched hard in his lap.

'And the one child rule?' I'm on a roll now. Amy glares at me, but I studiously ignore her.

Anson studies me, stroking his silver beard. 'Hmm. It should be obvious to you that repopulating had to be undertaken in a measured manner. To leave anyone and everyone to reproduce as many times as they desired would have been catastrophic. It was simply a matter of resources. We needed to ensure that everyone had enough. One child per family meant that we could… keep things under control. It was all about compassion. Compassion for the most vulnerable. It was a question of austerity in a time that needed austerity.'

'And now?'

'We are not out of the woods yet, dear girl. We have built much, but much remains to be done. If our population explodes, there is no telling what would happen, but I can assure you of this: many, many will go without.'

He makes it all sound so reasonable. So caring. But I remember Amy, and the Queen and her dead children, and the millions upon millions murdered by the Scourge, and it doesn't seem compassionate at all.

After dessert he focuses once again on me, interrupting a light conversation with Raulf's girlfriend, and I sigh inwardly as he raises his glass at me. 'So. Girl Clerk. Tell me about your parents.' His words are an arrow, and I think he knows it. He knows about my father. About the files he found, whatever they were.

I shrug. 'I don't know them. They're in the Home.'

'Ah. Well, at least you have no cause to worry for them, then.'

I grit my teeth. 'No.'

'What did they do before they became Unproductive?'

'My father was a clerk in the local Party headquarters. My mother, I actually don't know, I was never told.'

'What a shame for you. Still, I presume she had a good job, seeing as you were sent to Ashton. You can be grateful to them for that.'

'I am.'

He smiles at me, his hypnotising gaze holding mine. He is a charmer, but underneath is a chilling indifference.

In the drawing room for after dinner drinks, I slip into an easier conversation with Edwin. I ask him about his running, telling him that I too enjoy running, and we're off to a good start. It's evident he loves to talk about himself, and he's soon telling me in great detail about his last marathon win. I breathe out in relief. Edwin is not interested in me, but he has no agenda beyond boasting to me of his prowess. I can take that. But out of the corner of my eye I spot Anson making a beeline for me, strutting over slightly unsteadily, champagne flute in hand. He stretches it out to me. 'Bubbly?'

I shake my head.

'Too young? Such a shame.' He downs his champagne in two gulps and clicks his fingers at a passing waitress who replenishes his glass speedily.

'Will you take some air with me?' He draws close to me, searching my eyes. Without waiting on an answer, he places a proprietary hand on my shoulder and spins me around, propelling me towards the door. I have no choice but to go with him. I leave Edwin in mid flow and search round frantically for Jacob or Amy, but they are taken up in conversation with Raulf and Portia. Portia's boyfriend lurks in the corner, catches my eye and smirks at me.

I stumble as I exit the room, cursing these high-heeled sandals. Anson laughs at me and takes my arm; too firmly. 'Come.' He leads me to the decking area at the back of the house. It's a pleasant autumn evening, the sky clear, stars winking. He pulls me onwards to a section of lawn in darkness, far from the French doors and surrounded by mature pear trees. It's too quiet. No one else is around.

He lifts his hand slowly. Touches my face.

I recoil, and his brows knit. 'Is there a problem?'

'No, I just… I—'

'I couldn't help noticing how beautiful you are.'

I shudder. *I can't do this.*

'And how intelligent. How tenacious,' he continues, his eyes hard on mine. 'Not many are brave enough to challenge me. To ask interesting questions. I like it, Ms Clerk. I like you.'

'I'm grateful to you,' I mumble. 'For the pardon.'

'I should hope so.' His smile turns to a leer.

I try to contain the situation. 'How long have you and Lora been together?'

He waves his hand dismissively. 'Oh, Lora. I'm fond of her, and she's useful to me.'

He is so calculating. He's even admitting it to me: Lora is his puppet, politically valuable. The nation's sweetheart and all that.

'She's been very kind to us,' I say, backing away, but there is a tree behind me, and he creeps towards me until I am pinned against it. I draw my breath in, feeling the prickle of sweat under my arms.

He brings his hand to my face again, traces my cheekbone then the fading scar left from the flailing Miss Principal gave me the day I was evicted from Ashton. 'You poor dear girl,' he whispers in tones too intimate. I quake, my heart thumping hard against my chest. *Someone please come.*

'You know,' he says, leaning into me so our faces are inches apart, his sour, alcohol laden breath cascading over my face, 'it would be… expedient for you to please me.'

I freeze.

'I can give you things. I can make sure various charges never come back to haunt you.'

I knew it. Our pardons are only temporary; only while politically convenient.

I turn my face to the side as he leans in further, his full, wet lips parting. My skin crawls. He grabs my jaw, irate now. 'You could, of course, decide to displease me instead. And you may find that is to your great detriment.'

I gape at him in terror, searching his eyes, so captivating, so empty. 'Please—'

He squeezes my jaw and crushes his mouth onto mine. I squirm, revolted, but he pins my arms behind my back.

A voice. Calling through the night, a blessed sound; my salvation. 'Anson?'

It's Lora.

'Anson, darling, we're missing you! Raulf wanted to ask you about the new New Day Tax Bill. Everyone wants to see you.'

He leaves go of me, shoving me back against the tree, his face purple with rage. 'Ludicrous woman,' he snarls, stomping away from me towards Lora, who has spotted us. A look of confusion crosses her face at the sight of me, dishevelled and reddened, propped against the tree.

'Girl C?'

'I… I—'

'Pay no heed, woman,' Anson says, gripping Lora's bare arm. 'She's just a child, playing a silly game. I'm not upset.'

I remain motionless. Outraged.

'Get inside,' barks Lora, narrowing her eyes at me.

I slink away from them and into the house, where I find Jacob talking with Edwin. I long to fall into his arms and spill it all out, but

I can't. I know what he would do if I did, so I stay silent. I play the game.

16

THE CENTRE

<JACOB

SOMETHING'S OFF WITH Carys. She says she doesn't feel well, and she is coughing a lot. Coran called a doctor for her because she wouldn't get out of bed this morning. He's given her some kind of medicine, but Lora says she can't have much as it's expensive. Lora seems hacked off as well, and Jacob gets the feeling those two have fallen out in some way.

Carys won't talk to him. He goes into her room to take her some lunch, but she turns her face away. She is proper pale, so he figures she's pretty sick, but there's something else. He asks her what's wrong, but she just buttons her lips; infuriating in the way only Carys can be.

In the end Jacob shrugs and gives up and goes to find Amy, who is reading a book in the den, as they call the morning room now. 'You okay?'

She sighs. 'I suppose. I feel so sick after last night. It was so...'

'Fake?'

'Yep. And it was obvious that we were being warned again.'

'Yeah. I think we have the message now.'

'What did you think to the lauded judges?'

Jacob grimaces. 'Thought they were fairly fake, actually, too. Raulf – he's all swagger, and a bit scary with it. Edwin's just conceited, spent most of the evening bragging about himself and his running. And Portia – I wouldn't want to cross her, to be honest. Got the feeling she didn't want to be there.'

'Or her boyfriend.'

'No. He was an arrogant arse.'

'Speaking of arrogant, how about Anson?'

'Shh,' Jacob hisses. 'Lora's around somewhere.'

'I know,' she whispers. 'But he wasn't like I expected… I don't know what I expected. But he was awful to Lora, wasn't he.'

'I did notice that.'

'He had a thing for Carys.'

'What?' Jacob bristles.

'He just kept staring at her.'

Jacob screws his nose up. 'She's super grumpy today. Has some kind of lung thing, I think, like her old problems. She's got some meds, but Lora was kind of odd about it all.'

'Strange.'

'Yeah. But at least she'll get better soon.'

'Hope so.'

Jacob draws his palm over his chin. 'Only got to put up with *The S Word* now. That's only, like, four days away. Then we can get out of here.'

'What about Raza? Should we look for her?'

'She knows what she's doing.'

'I suppose.'

Jacob mooches around for the remainder of the afternoon, unable to quash his feelings of dismay and revulsion about the Productives he met last night. Carys joins them for the evening meal, subdued and grouchy. Jacob feels uncomfortable discussing their future plans in front of Lora, so they talk of other things that don't matter. He kicks his chair, frustrated with the life they are living in the mansion in all its frivolity and make-believe.

Not long now.

Amy

THE MORNING OF their *S Word* appearance dawns dull and damp. Amy meets the others at breakfast, heavy of heart. It's like she's under a death sentence again, even though she knows they're pardoned. Carys isn't herself and hasn't been since the dinner party.

Coran comes buzzing into the room, fluttering around and straightening things that don't need straightening. 'All ready for tonight?'

'Not really,' Carys mutters.

'Oh, don't be daft now,' Coran says, dusting off an ugly ornamental cat on the mantelpiece. 'You'll be fine, darling.'

'Oh, Coran,' Lora says, glancing up from her paper, 'I need to talk with you about clothes.'

'Oh, yes, you must. I can get these three looking gorgeous for you.'

'I have an idea, actually,' she says. 'Come to my room after breakfast, and we'll discuss it. I've sent for some... things.'

'How mysterious!' Coran grins widely. 'I'll be there.'

THEY'RE TO BE taken to the studios after lunch, where they will be prepared for their appearance. Coran rounds them up with worse grace than usual, and Amy asks what he has for them to wear. He taps his finger to his nose. 'Never you mind,' he says, but his eyebrows are sullenly drawn together. He leads them to the NCV, his face like a storm.

It's not far to the studios. Coran drives quickly, weaving through early afternoon traffic, skipping the odd red light. His patience seems stretched today. He keeps glancing in his rear-view mirror, his brow furrowed. He veers the car suddenly, waiting until the last minute to take a turning. And then he speeds up.

'What's wrong?' Jacob asks, his eyebrows raised. Coran stays silent, his hands gripping the wheel, glancing wildly at the mirror. Amy turns to see what he's worrying about. Another NCV is behind them. Too close. Tinted windows prevent her seeing the occupants.

'I think we've got unwanted company,' she says, her stomach beginning to churn.

Carys and Jacob twist round to see. 'Are they following us?'

Coran nods. 'Seems so.'

'NForce?' Jacob says.

Coran frowns. 'No reason they'd be after us. Let me concentrate.'

A huge bang.

They are slammed forwards, Amy's seatbelt snapping rigid as she crashes against it. Coran freezes, dazed.

'What do they want?' Carys's grey eyes are widened, her mouth puckered as she watches the black NCV behind tail off then speed up. 'Oh no. They're coming again. Coran...'

Bang.

Coran recovers and grasps hold of the wheel again, his jaw tight. 'They want you.'

'What... why?'

He floors the accelerator. Speeds away through another red light, the black NCV left behind, cut off by a white van going the other way. The NScreen gives a shrieking warning about the mounting speed as Coran pushes the car to its limit, swerving it all over the road as he fights for control. *Come on.*

A sheen of sweat breaks out on Coran's forehead. He wipes it with the back of his hand, his eyes intent on the road and his mirror. 'Damn it,' he says, as the NCV catches them easily then pulls parallel to them.

Amy shrinks in her seat.

The black NCV slams into them. Their car shudders, and Amy is thrown against Carys. Coran is jerked sideways, and the car swerves towards an embankment on their left-hand side, leading down to some scrubby wasteland. He battles the wheel and wins, setting them back on the road, but the black NCV hovers next to them, its windows black as night.

'Who is it?' Carys says, but Coran says nothing.

When Amy feels a bang for the fourth time, Coran can't save the car from slewing off the road and down the bank. They gain speed, belting through weeds and bushes, branches scraping at the body panels as they career towards the bottom. There's no time to think. Coran struggles with the wheel, gripping it so hard his knuckles show white, the same shade of white as his face. By some miracle he brings the car into the skid, turns it enough to halt it from its inexorable head-on crash with a tree. The car veers madly as he manhandles it around the tree and out onto the flat ground beyond, and comes to a screeching, bone-jangling stop as he stomps on the brake, the sweat pouring from him.

'All okay?' He swivels, takes them all in, their faces wan and their eyes widened with terror.

Who was that?

His own eyes widen as he looks beyond them. 'They're not giving up.'

Amy glances behind and sees the black NCV crawling down the slope, its progress much more careful than their unwanted plunge.

'Hold tight,' yells Coran and starts the engine, stamps on the accelerator, and speeds off across the rough ground, the black car gaining on them. Jacob grabs Carys's hand and she grabs Amy's as they gawp out of the back window, unable to believe this is happening. *I thought we had a pardon.*

The NCV slams into them once again, and this time Coran's head snaps forward and then smashes back against the rest. Amy spots the blood on his scalp and the panic on his face.

The black NCV swerves around their car, drawing up next to them. This time the front passenger window slides open; a man pokes his head out, his face split in a crazed sneer.

Gardener.

'Who the hell is that?' Coran shrieks, brushing his arm over his bleeding, sweat-soaked brow.

'He hates us,' Jacob cries. 'He's as unhinged as ever!'

Amy shrinks away from Gardener, his face too close to hers, his eyes boring into her, his mouth turning upwards in the terrifying grin of her nightmares.

She tries to see who's driving. She doubts it's Principal, at these speeds. She'd ruin her power suit and stiletto heels. It must be someone else. A disgruntled Think officer, perhaps. Or maybe Gardener's personal driver is simply as insane as him.

Coran pauses, his hands quivering on the wheel. 'What do you think you're doing?' he says to Gardener, but his voice is as shaky as his hands.

Gardener laughs. 'Just playing.'

They stare at him, but his eyes are too empty to read.

'You know who I am?' Coran says, gamely trying to inject confidence into his voice.

Gardener snorts. 'Don't give a shit.'

'What do you want?' Jacob says.

Gardener just stares at him, and he looks away.

'Can't drive,' murmurs Coran. He slumps at the wheel, his face deathly pale. 'Can't—'

'We have to get out of here.' Jacob frantically unbuckles his belt and scrambles over the seat. 'Help me.' Carys and Amy rip off their belts and tug Coran over to the passenger seat, Jacob struggling over him as they do so. All the time, Gardener just sits there, leering.

Jacob presses the accelerator, roaring away, slewing the car and turning back towards the embankment and the road, the vehicle shuddering and screeching but still going. Gardener doesn't attempt to follow them, this time. Amy looks back and sees him hanging out of the window, still staring at them, still laughing at them.

Amy's heart is thumping, adrenaline coursing through her body. Carys's eyes are bright with terror. 'What are they playing at? Have we lost them?'

'Let's get to the studios. We'll be safe there.'

Coran groans, sprawled on the passenger seat, white with shock, his teeth gritted.

Jacob's jaw is tightened as he clutches the wheel hard. 'Coran. You need to tell me the way. The N.Nav… it's broken.'

Coran says nothing. Amy reaches over to him, lays her hand on his shoulder. 'It's okay. You're okay. Breathe.'

His body shudders and trembles as he tries to slow his breathing. 'We're okay.'

As they make their way to the studio, Amy feels as wrecked as their car. *I thought we were free. Safe.*

But she'd not factored in Gardener, and the bitter strength of his hatred.

17

THE CENTRE

AMY

T HE STUDIOS LOOK much like they did that day two years ago when twenty Ashton second years clambered from their coach with bated breath. A let down. This time there are no swarming crowds of wound-up trainees; they will come later when all is ready for the live filming.

The Productive who rushes out to greet them puckers up his face at the sight of the bashed-up car. 'What on earth happened to you?' he says, flinging the doors open. 'Are you okay?'

Amy helps Coran out slowly. 'We should call the NForce.'

Coran is quiet and still, stiff against her hands. He nods, then stops, then looks at the studio worker, then back at them. 'Who *was* he?'

'Mr Gardener. The principal's sidekick from Ashton. He was one of the ones who tried to get us killed in the Think.'

Coran's face falls.

'He can't get away with that!' Carys says, her face red-hot with indignance.

Coran shrugs. 'I don't know.'

'What? Why? Psycho tried to kill us,' Jacob says.

Coran wipes more blood from his face. 'I need to check with Lora.'

'Why?'

Coran is silent.

Jacob bristles and opens his mouth. Amy nudges him. 'Leave it.'

'Why?' he hisses.

'It's because Ashton is in there with Anson and all the Party high-ups,' Carys says bitterly. 'That's why. Right, Coran?'

Coran has the grace to look shamefaced.

'You're bleeding,' the Productive says, taking Coran's arm and turning towards the entrance. 'Don't worry,' he shouts over his shoulder, 'I will make sure he is treated. Wait there.'

Five minutes later, another Productive comes racing out of the building holding an NSlate and bellowing into a headset. 'They're here,' she roars, barely looking at them. They are ushered in through a small stage door and into a narrow, gloomy corridor leading to several small rooms. They're assigned one each, and Amy finds herself anxious and alone, battered and bewildered. She stares around the space. A shabby dressing table stands unsteadily against one wall, a large mirror hung haphazardly above, bulbs lining it, several of them blown. The place has an air of decay and smells musty; this dressing room can't be used very often, certainly not by the judges. She sinks onto the tatty green plush chair, sinking her aching head into her hands and sighing. *Get it over with.*

After a while, another Productive comes in with a tray of drinks and snacks, dumps a mug and a stale-looking biscuit unceremoniously on the table and leaves without a word.

Amy waits.

Later, Coran crawls in, all breathless. His hand is bandaged up and he wears a slight look of martyrdom. She jumps up. 'Are you okay?'

He looks at her, his face tilted, pain washing his features. 'I'm *fine*,' he says, exaggerating the word with a great sigh. 'But darling, I am worried about you. You all. That man… he was out to get you.'

'Yes. We really must tell the NForce.'

He gazes at one of the blown bulbs, his mouth working. 'Listen, child. I have consulted with Lora. She thinks it best, given the circumstances, that it is left. For now, of course. We cannot be seen to persecute the Productives who you… attacked. Do you see my dilemma, sweetheart?'

She gapes at him.

He twists his hands. 'I know it seems… harsh. But we will have words with his boss. He will not harm you, I can assure you.'

'How do you know?'

'I know,' he says cryptically, and then twists, holding something out and getting back to business. Amy watches him as he dumps a garment bag on her knees, screwing up his face and brushing off his hands. She raises her eyebrows.

'It's what Lora has decided,' he says, his nose in the air. 'I, of course, could make you beautiful, but Lora wants simple tonight. She has a… message. For the people. Go on, get it out. It won't take you long to get ready.'

She unzips the bag and shakes the contents out. Her stomach plummets at the sight of an Ashton pinafore, shirt, and cardigan. Coran hands her some plain black rubber-soled shoes and white ankle socks. 'It's not what I would have chosen.'

She shrugs. It really doesn't matter now. If Lora wants them in their training uniforms, that's what she wants. Perhaps it's for the best that they're not dressed in finery tonight; they'll be unpopular enough as it is, despite their rescue of Lora.

'Get it on, and I'll do your face and your hair,' he says, turning to the door. 'Back in five.'

He leaves, and she peels her sweaty clothes off and pulls the shirt and dress on. She'd forgotten how scratchy the material is, how much it chafes on her. She feeds her arms through the cardigan, tugs the socks and shoes on and waits. She feels small again, the little girl ripped from her home and hurled into an unfriendly world.

Coran makes her face up to look even more pale and wan and does nothing much for her short hair. Since the incident with Mercia and the scissors it has grown a little, but still tends to stand in unkempt tufts. He smooths them down with gel and stands back, clicking his tongue. 'Hmm. You'll do.'

'Well… thanks.'

He smiles at her. 'Don't you worry,' he says gently. 'Go get 'em. You'll be fine.'

He leads her from the room to a large backstage space where Carys and Jacob are already waiting, also clad in Ashton uniforms. Carys looks seriously pale, and Jacob slouches on a sofa, pouting. 'Hey,' Amy says.

'Can't believe we have to wear these. I thought we'd left this stuff behind forever,' Jacob mutters.

'Yeah.'

'Are you okay?' Amy says to Carys, touching her hand. She shrugs. 'Coran says the NForce won't be involved.'

'He told me,' Carys says dully.

Jacob slumps, head in hands. 'This is not going to be as easy as I'd hoped. Gardener's still out to get us, whatever they say.'

'Yes.'

They're given a sandwich tea and then asked to walk out onto the stage to go through a rehearsal with the backstage staff. The judges aren't around yet, but they're given lines to say with an autocue and they stand there, bruised and aching, reciting words they don't mean. 'This is just a general guide,' one of the staff, a young Productive in a pink jumpsuit with a headset, says. She doesn't look much older than them. 'You don't have to say it like this, exactly. You will need to ad lib. But don't deviate too much from the script, okay?'

Nobody replies.

There's a lot of sitting around as Productives rush around getting the set ready, sorting lighting rigs, doing sound checks, shouting instructions to one another. There's an air of excitement; an anticipation of something different about tonight's show. Everyone knows the three are to be featured, of course; it's been all over the news for the past few days. They're treated well enough – if not like the judges, at least with something approaching respect. But all Amy wants to do is to go home and go to bed, to nurse her shock and her wounds, inside and out.

Her nerves build as the time draws nearer, her stomach beginning to lurch as she watches the increasingly frenzied activity. There's still no sign of the judges, and Amy guesses that she won't be seeing them until their grand entrance on the show. Coran is nowhere to be found so is probably with Lora, fussing around her, making her even more beautiful. Amy kind of misses his comforting presence, though she is disappointed in him for not reporting Gardener.

Eventually they talk, letting go of their pent-up fear. They share their nerves and promise one another they will suck this up so they can move on. So that they can, eventually, make a difference. Carys's face is swathed in shadow as she makes this oath, her eyes downcast, and Amy reaches out and takes her hand. 'You'll be okay. Just think of the future.'

Carys shrugs.

Jacob turns more upbeat. 'Come on,' he says, draping his arms round their shoulders, 'let's do this. It could be fun!'

Amy tries to smile.

The pink girl comes through to collect them, all bounce and enthusiasm. 'It's time for you to come and wait in the wings. You can watch the judges' grand entrance and meet the players for tonight.'

It's not just them, then. They're a bonus. A sideshow.

They follow the cheerful Productive through another maze of corridors and then out to the west wing of the stage. Close up, it is colossal, the NScreen soaring above, stretched out across the width of the staging area. Amy stares out at the silent auditorium, shrouded in absolute darkness, and remembers how she sobbed when she was faced with it and earned Miss Trainer One's ire and a

Think session when she arrived back at Ashton. She can just about make out faces in the crowd, upturned young faces gaping into the darkness, on the edge of their seats in eager anticipation. They are silent, of course, their Trainers jumping on any movement or hint of a whisper.

She links arms with Carys and Jacob, remembering how far they've come since it was their turn. Since they were the chosen.

She watches as the stage is lit, building the ambience slowly, rapidly crushed gasps echoing through the auditorium as the NScreen flashes with the famous logo. Here they are, then. The ultimate test of them. She crosses her fingers and murmurs words. A prayer, of sorts, to something.

She watches as the spectacle is completed with the arrival of Cadman Showman, jumping onto the stage, whipping up the audience and entrancing everyone, and then the judges, through huge doors in the NScreen. Amy is less awestruck than she once was now she knows them, now she's heard them speak in real life. The whole performance strikes her as an empty sham, a facade plastering over the giant cracks they have uncovered and are now required to paper over so publicly.

The judges' clothes are more flamboyant than ever, their faces made up with flair and precision, disguising who they really are. Portia looks like a fairy, complete with a magic wand and a sparkle-covered face, and Lora is a cat tonight, her white dress trimmed with fur, a headband of cat ears poised on her head and whiskers drawn on her face along with heavily kohled, black-rimmed eyes. Amy can see Coran's handiwork in this. Lora prowls to the front of the stage, stroking the tail curling over her arm. As usual, the audience cheer for her the loudest. She's the beloved one.

Raulf and Edwin are as impressive as ever. Edwin is on rollers, his favoured method of entrance, and when he whizzes round the stage he glimpses Amy watching him from the wing and salutes her, grinning widely. Raulf strides across the stage to his seat, full of power and hypnotising charm, wearing black skinnies and a black waistcoat, shirtless tonight, displaying his well worked out body. Snickers and whoops echo through the audience.

The theme song plays, and the show is in full swing. Amy waits in the wings, feeling like a complete fraud, about to blatantly lie on national TV. But there is no other way out. She glances at the opposite wing: two people stand there, a man and a woman. The contestants for tonight. She feels sorry for them and wants to run over to them, tell them to leave, to go home, that one of them will be murdered. But she cannot.

It seems that the three are to be the grand finale of the show, so they must stand there throughout, watching the whole rigmarole. This time a man named Ash Banker is on trial by *S Word* for working shorter hours than his colleagues, claiming that he is unable to cope with anything longer due to depression. The judges really don't like this and are unrepentantly blatant about it. Cadman works hard to get them to listen to all sides of the story, but they're not having it. They seem snappy tonight, particularly Raulf. Lora keeps riling him up, in a state of intense excitement herself, and he's irritable. It rubs off on everyone, and Ash Banker gets short shrift and a SKIVER from all four judges.

They are less impatient with Cali Cook. She has been sick with cancer and has been receiving treatment for it at the CL Hospital for months now. She didn't manage to make it to her workplace after every chemotherapy session, but she gave it her best shot. She's a chef at a top Centre hotel, and her work is frenzied and frazzled. The video shows her rushing around in her whites, shouting at the sous-chef, whipping up a cake in a huge mixer. It pans round to her sitting in a hospital room with a drip in her arm, her face wan. She wins the judges over at her first sentence, and they pronounce her a Striver. When her wig slips because of the heat on the stage, Lora dashes up to her, sets it straight and hugs her, calling her a warrior, a true Newlander. Cali beams in their adulation, but in the shadow of the stage exit opposite Amy spots Ash Banker slumped on the ground, his head in his hands. Amy wants to save him. To take him with them.

After various entertainment acts, the time finally comes. The three of them stiffen, glance around at one another, then embrace, whispering encouragements. *Hang in there.* Cadman Showman leaps back on stage, applauding the Chefs' Magic Trio they've just watched. 'Wow,' he yells, motioning after the act as they scamper off stage, bowing low. 'Just wow. I've never seen anything like it! How *did* they make Portia disappear?'

The audience shriek and yell, their excitement built to fever pitch. They are ready.

'Now,' Cadman says, holding his hands out to the audience. 'We have an extra treat tonight, as you know. We have a special appearance from some very special people. Lora, would you come here and join me, please?'

Lora rises from her purple chair and turns to the audience. She claws her fingers and scrunches her nose, and they love it. They cheer for her. She slinks round the other judges, purring and mewing at them, batting at them, pretending to pounce on Raulf, who shrinks back and shoves her away, much to the audience's delight. Portia crumples her face at her and swears at her in most un-fairy like language. Only Edwin plays the game with her, barking at her like a dog then scrambling out of his seat and chasing her around on his rollers. The spectators lap it all up.

'Come on, Lora,' Cadman says eventually. 'You have a story to tell us.'

Lora prances up to the stage, swinging her tail. 'Miaow,' she purrs, curling her fingers at Cadman. He smiles, but his face is slightly pained.

'Well then. Tonight, Lora has a story to tell us. A story that will make you gasp. An adventure you cannot imagine. It's not a nice story, not a happy story for Lora, but thanks to our honoured guests tonight, it has a happy ending.'

The audience settle down, shushed by Trainers, shoved back into their seats. For moments, there is silence.

'Lora?' Cadman prompts. He takes Lora's hand.

Lora smiles, swivelling slowly, taking in the whole audience. 'On a fateful day just a week ago, I was travelling to the Northeast Compound,' she begins. A small group of trainees whoop and holler. 'From the Northeast Compound, by any chance?' Lora says, and they cheer.

She gathers herself. 'I was to perform there, in a ballet. I'd been practising for months, and I was all ready. Tolan, my driver…' she pauses. Takes a deep breath. 'He was taking me that day. We got as far as the old ruins of Birmingham. Suddenly there was a disturbance; someone in the road, waving us down. Tolan thought nothing of it and brought the car to a stop. Looked like this guy was in some kind of trouble.'

She comes to another halt and plucks a tissue from her tiny fur-trimmed bag. She dabs at the corners of her eyes, one of which is still swollen and yellowed, obvious despite the cat disguise. 'So Tolan stops the car, and there's this sudden banging, all down the sides, and we see these… thugs… they had cricket bats, of all things, and they were slamming them into the car. It was terrifying.'

The audience inhale sharply.

'So Tolan… Tolan tried to drive away, but he was too late. These ruffians yanked his door open and then… and then…'

She stops. The tears are pouring now, and she makes no further attempt to mop them up. The audience are on the edges of their seats.

'This one guy, he gets his bat and he hits Tolan on his head. He… *killed* him—' she turns to Cadman, implores him with her eyes, '— oh, Cad, I can hardly do this.'

Cadman moves closer to Lora, his eyes soft with compassion. He places his hand on Lora's shoulder. 'In your time,' he murmurs. The NScreen zooms close in on Lora's distraught face, the tears smudging the black kohl, the whiskers smeared.

'Then… they took me. They dragged me to some woods, and they started to…'

'It's okay,' Cadman says softly.

She bats at her tears. 'I hadn't prepared myself for this.' Amy can see she is genuinely distressed. This is not an act. 'They beat me. You can still see my eye.' She touches it gingerly. The audience are with her every step of the way. 'Then…' she gazes at her bare feet, '…they said some things, then beat me further and knocked me out. I was utterly, utterly terrified, Cad. I have never felt anything like that before. It was just horrifying. They were vile. The leader… I could smell him, he was rotten, he was evil.'

'He is an Outsider.'

Amy stiffens.

'Yes. They were lawless Unproductives, like all Outsiders.'

'What happened then, Lora?' Cadman squeezes her shoulder.

'It's a blur. Thankfully. I hardly remember anything of the actual rescue, but there are glimpses of a wild girl with an axe and a knife, and of my three fugitives. They were so gentle. So thoughtful. I remember waking up to one of them, she was smoothing the matted hair from my face. She really did care. They saved me from a fate I don't even want to consider – worse than death.'

'And because of that, you saved them,' Cadman says. 'You repaid your debt, as it were.'

'I suppose so,' Lora agrees, wiping her nose with her sleeve. 'But you know, I was just so grateful. It's all I could think about. I had to get them the pardon—'

Cadman interrupts. 'And that would seem a good point to introduce our first mystery guest of the night.'

The audience gasp, and Amy scans the stage. What does he mean? One of them?

'He is able to be with us tonight, not in person, of course, but through a live link. He is busy meeting at Party HQ, discussing the terms of the new New Day Tax Bill, which will be a privilege for all Productives to pay.'

A louder gasp as the NScreen lights.

Commander Anson sits in state, surrounded by the opulence of a Party HQ meeting room. He sits relaxed in a golden chair with gilt engravings, and he rests his large square hands on the polished teak table in front of him, considering the camera intensely. His eyes are bluer than ever in the carefully created lighting, and his presence as potent. A thrilled sigh runs through the auditorium and is quickly squashed as Trainers lead trainees in a deep bow.

'Commander,' says Cadman reverently, crossing his hands over his belly and bowing his head deeply, 'you were eager to appear on *The S Word* tonight, in order to give your pardon officially.'

Anson nods, and his eyes crinkle. 'I wanted my nation to understand how appreciative I am to the fugitives. You all know of my and Lora's... association.'

The audience twitters, but Productives are quicker than ever to shush their charges, to clip ears and smack heads. You can hear a pin drop.

'Without these children, my beautiful Lora would be gone. So when Lora asked me to show my forgiveness by granting them a full pardon, of course I was absolutely in agreement.'

Cadman stands back from the screen, strokes his chin. 'So this would be the time for us to meet the three fugitives. The saviours.'

This time, the audience are on their feet, screaming, stamping their feet. Amy hears their old names called, shrieked, roared. 'Girl C! Boy T! Girl P!' Again and again. She stares at the others, her stomach queasy.

'Of course,' Anson says, and the kids hush immediately. 'Please do bring them out, and I will speak with them. There is just a small condition for them, and I know they will be delighted by it.'

Amy inhales. What now?

'Girl Clerk, Girl Plumber, Boy Trader, please join us,' Cadman shouts, turning towards them and spreading his hands then sweeping his arms round the auditorium. 'Please welcome Lora Dancer's saviours!'

As they tread gingerly towards Cadman and Lora, the crowd go wild, pumping their arms, shouting their names, screaming and pounding the boards under their feet. Amy is completely overwhelmed. The sea of faces encroaches on her space, a tsunami of them surging forward, gushing over her, trapping her. She holds her arms close around her chest. Carys and Jacob look equally bemused.

'They love you!' Cadman is jumping up and down, lending his fervour, approving theirs. 'Ladies and gentlemen, may I present Miss Clerk, Mr Trader, and Miss Plumber.'

Amy, Carys, and Jacob stand stiffly and gape as the approbation builds to frenetic levels, then begins to ebb away as the audience wear themselves out. Amy does not know how to respond, so she does nothing. She holds herself as still as she can, but she can feel the rumble in her knees.

'Now,' Cadman says, turning to the NScreen, where Anson's face is a picture of benevolence, his applause polite. He temples his hands, leaning his chin on them. 'Over to you, then, Commander.' Cadman gestures to the screen.

'On behalf of the nation,' begins Anson, sitting up straighter and placing his palms face down on the table, 'I pronounce forgiveness for your transgressions. For wilful destruction of property. For attempted murder. For grievous bodily harm. For using drugs on a person without consent. For illegal hacking of computer files. For spreading vicious and heinous lies. For illegally crossing the barriers.' He chuckles. 'I think that's about it.'

The crowd respond, laughing with him.

Amy stands, frozen in place. *This doesn't feel right.*

'You are granted a full pardon,' Anson says, 'on two small conditions. One, is that you renounce all that you originally made up about Newland, and two, that you personally apologise to the most injured parties.'

What?

Amy sneaks a glance at Carys. Her eyes widen, her nose scrunching in revulsion.

Lora prances over to them, swinging her tail around. Her tears are dried, her face a mess of smeared make-up. 'We have a lovely surprise for you,' she breathes, flinging her arm around Jacob's shoulder. 'We thought it would be rather wonderful if you could say sorry in person, so to gain our full forgiveness. In order to facilitate that, I have arranged for some important visitors.'

Amy holds her breath.

'Productives. Trainees. Please welcome Garrett Gardener and Augusta Principal!'

The audience applaud, but at nowhere near the frantic level of their approval for the three of them.

Amy is frozen. So *that's* why he's here in the Centre.

Gardener struts in from the wing, pushing a wheelchair in front of him. Miss Principal is stationed in the chair, her leg in plaster propped out in front of her. *Where Carys shot her. After Gardener shot Sim.* Would she really still be in plaster after three months? Amy doubts it.

She gapes at them and takes Carys's stone-cold hand. 'Be brave,' she whispers. Carys's face is lost in shadow. *Stay quiet.*

Gardener propels the chair over to centre stage, a huge sinister grin on his face. He stops and arranges a blanket over Principal, who casts her cold eyes over the three of them, glittering and exultant. Amy wouldn't be surprised if she brought the flail out and attacked them, there in front of the nation. Despite her injury, she still wears one four-inch-high scarlet stiletto shoe, matching the thin slash that is her hardened mouth.

The crowd are silent, waiting in anticipation.

Carys steps back.

Jacob sidles over to her. Places his hand around her waist, whispers in her ear. She is unblinking. But she says nothing.

Reeling, Amy watches as Lora takes Principal's hand. 'Miss Principal,' she says, bending to her level, 'you of all people have much to forgive. But you have assured me that when these children renounce their lies, you will pronounce your forgiveness, displaying the spirit of our nation because of their redeeming actions.'

Principal glances at them, eyes narrowing as they fall on Carys, then her gaze softens as she turns back to Lora. 'I will.'

'And you also have been hurt badly.' Lora turns to Gardener, who looms over Principal's chair, his feet planted wide and his arms crossed. The sneer hasn't left his face yet. This is the man who hounded them, once again, only hours ago.

'I have,' he says. 'They trapped me like an animal and left me to die.'

Liar. He was fine.

'But you, also, are prepared to forgive.'

'When they apologise, I will forgive.' As he says these last words, he glares at Jacob so pointedly, his gaze so full of rancour, that no one could be in doubt as to his true intentions. Somehow, the camera misses this and focuses on Lora.

'We're going to have a mini *S Word* judgement for you now,' she says, her eyes shining. 'To give you the chance to repent in full.' She claps her hands together and bounces off towards her seat. She prowls around the other judges and bats at Raulf again before she installs herself. Cadman steps forward.

'Lora,' he says, 'we'll begin with you, then, as you are the most affected. Are these children Skivers – or Strivers?'

Lora laughs, a light, tinkling sound. 'Well, Cadman,' she says, loving the charade. 'Only a week back, I would naturally have said Skivers. They'd shirked their studies and turned against our nation. But now they have proved themselves to be good. To be strong. To be examples we should emulate. They are Strivers!'

Her sign lights up and the crowd cheer, working themselves up again. Cadman plasters a smile on his face and turns to Edwin. 'Striver or Skiver?' Amy gets the impression Cadman wants to rush this through. Maybe he thinks it's just as much a sham as she does.

Edwin leaps to his feet. 'I can't say how much I think of these dear children.' He clambers onto his chair, then onto the table in front, and stands tall, turning to the audience. 'They saved my best friend. They are, of course, Strivers!' He flings his arms out, his head thrown back.

Portia is less effusive but goes with the script. They did wrong and would do well to learn from it, she says, but they have proved themselves. They are Strivers.

Cadman spreads his arms, turning to Raulf. 'What do you think then, head judge? Are they Strivers or Skivers? It's three Strivers so far, so they have won, but you must give your judgement, nevertheless. Raulf?'

Raulf sits, coolly collected, stroking his chin and staring into space. 'Without them, Lora would be dead,' he says, and shrieks sound from the audience. 'Wait,' he hisses, pivoting and glaring at the crowd.

He stays silent for moments. The sound of shuffling feet echoes through the auditorium.

'However, they did spread venomous lies about Newland. I won't repeat what they said, but it was malicious. I find it hard to forgive them, but I have to remember their youth. They are not yet Productives, and so I am inclined to give them a chance – so today I will proclaim them Strivers but would warn them to be careful from now.' The camera zooms in on him; his eyes are narrowed, his teeth gritted. He does not like this narrative.

For seconds, silence reigns, but then the audience catch on and begin to pound the boards and shout the three's names once again. Cadman shushes them and turns to the NScreen. 'Commander,' he says, bowing his head slightly, 'they have been pronounced Strivers. All that remains is their apology. Firstly, to these poor people here—' he gesticulates to a smirking Gardener and the hard-faced Principal, '—and then, finally, to you, as a representative of our nation.'

'Yes,' Anson says, linking his fingers and leaning forward into the camera. 'I think we can see here our Newland adage in action: Power to the Strong, Justice to the Good. Girl C, Boy T and Girl P made some very silly mistakes, but they have now proved their strength and their goodness. Power to the Strong! Justice to the Good!' He pumps his hand and repeats the phrase, and the crowd join him, on their feet, their voices swelling through the cavernous space. 'POWER TO THE STRONG! JUSTICE TO THE GOOD!' They shout until their voices crack, Productives and trainees alike.

Amy feels sick.

She glances around at Jacob and Carys, their faces wrinkled in distaste. Carys's face is reddening, the flush spreading to her neck and ears. *Come on. We're nearly there.*

Commander Anson waves his hands up and down, palms turned down. 'Indeed. Now, sit, because I want to hear their apologies. We have shown that justice will prevail when someone is truly good.'

The crowd sit, all on the edge of their seats in eager anticipation, and Cadman invites the three fugitives to step forward.

Carys

I'M NUMB. I sense Jacob's hand on my waist, steadying me, guiding me towards the front of the stage, to Principal and Gardener who wait for us like cats preparing to pounce on their prey. Principal's light blue eyes are hard on me, pupils pinpricked. All I can think of when I see them is Sim. Little Sim, his body so light, his blood-matted red curls dancing in the sultry breeze. Murdered. I grip my name stone in my pinafore pocket so tightly my fingers go numb.

I glance up at the NScreen and look away quickly. Anson leers down at me, his thick lips curled in a grotesque smile. My heart thunders, recalling the way he pressed against me, the revulsion I felt, the disgust that won't leave me. I clench my fists, digging my bitten-down nails into my palms. Jacob and Amy are relying on me. *Just a few more minutes.*

The rage is mounting, like water coming to the boil. My cheeks suffuse with heat, my stomach clenches hard. I swallow over the aching lump in my throat. *You can do this.*

Jacob goes first. He walks right up to Principal, kneels down so their faces are on a level. I don't know how he can do this. 'I'm… sorry,' he says, and I hear the catch at the back of his throat. 'I will never say anything like that again, and I am sorry that… that you got hurt.' He stumbles over his words, and I peer at the useless autocues that no one has stuck to throughout the show. He can't say those words. *Surely.*

'Please forgive me for my weakness and my vicious scheming against you, against Ashton and against Newland.' He says it.

Principal bows her head slowly, her eyes glinting under the spotlight. Gardener barely breaks from his sneer but holds his hand out towards Jacob in a gesture of reconciliation. Jacob takes it, and my heat intensifies. Burns within me, flames flickering at my feet, snaking up my body, licking at me, binding me. I inhale sharply. *Breathe.*

Amy now. She goes through the same routine, and this time, Gardener steps forward, a lascivious sneer twisting his sharp features, and folds her into a too-close embrace. He hisses in her ear, and I can hear his words from here. 'I'll get you next time.' She shrinks from him, almost choking, her sobs spilling from her, and I boil over.

I cannot hold this in. The word tumbles from me, screeching in a rush of righteous indignation and pure, white-hot rage. 'NO.'

Cadman steps back. 'Pardon?'

'No. I will not apologise. I will not, because I have not done anything wrong. It is you… all of you—' I sweep my hands dramatically round, taking in the whole place, '—who have done wrong. Who need forgiveness!'

'Wait…' Cadman falters. Next to me, Jacob kicks my foot, and Amy tries to catch my eye. I look away. Lora stands from her seat, her hands clasped together. On the screen, Anson raises his eyebrows sardonically. The audience are wide-eyed and silent.

I rush on. 'Because what we said is true. There is no Home in Newland. All of you – all you trainees – need to know this, that what they told you is a lie. It's a vicious lie made up to make us bow to their will and do what they want. So that they – the rich people, the Party, the head Productives – they just get richer on the backs of all the murdered people, all the people who were weak. And because they were weak, they were put to death. They are not kept safe in a lovely Home with attentive nurses, like the brochures say. They are—' I stop as a hand is clamped on my arm. Lora.

'Girl C,' she says, staring into my eyes, her face full of hurt. 'What are you doing?'

I take a deep breath. Now I've started, I'm not stopping. I won't look at the others. Won't see the betrayal etched on their faces. 'We found evidence that they are killing off all the sick people. All the elderly people. They are murdering them. This is true. And as for that horrible phrase you were just chanting – do you want to know the source of that phrase? How Commander Lucan, who was a sick, sadistic man—'

Sharp inhalations all over the auditorium.

'—How he found words like those in an old holy book from the Before and twisted them. They meant the opposite. They meant that weak and sick people should be given power and value. Just twisted. TWISTED.' I'm shouting now, my words building to a crescendo as the anger in me intensifies to fever pitch, my mouth foaming in an attempt to get them out, to tell the nation. I open my mouth to spill more, but Cadman and Lora are at my side, taking my arms.

'Stop,' orders Cadman, almost spitting in my face, his eyes narrowed in fury. 'You are making a spectacle of yourself, girl.'

I breathe in.

'Why?' asks Lora, and there are tears forming at the corners of her eyes. Real tears, spilling over, creeping down her ruined cheeks.

I turn to her. Shriek in her face. 'Why can you not see it? WHY? They are deluding you, Lora. You are instrumental in this. You have sent people to be murdered. Oh, yes. It's not just Think criminals and sick people. It's all the Skivers on *The S Word*. This man tonight – Ash Banker – him. He's going to the Think, and in the Think he will be executed. And why? Because he's no use to Newland. Because he wasn't *good* enough. You should be ashamed of yourself.' My words drip with vitriol, my control utterly lost, and I know it, but I cannot stop myself. It cascades from my deepest being in a red-hot rush, pouring through the studio and leaving unqualified havoc in its wake. I sweep my hand over my mouth, purged. And broken. Lora reels, her face draining of colour.

'Have you quite finished?' The words are soft but the tone crushingly formidable. My eyes are drawn to the NScreen, where Anson is standing, his golden chair thrown back, his eyes darkened.

I open my mouth, but Cadman Showman pinches my arm. Hard.

'Whether you think you have or not, I say you have,' continues Anson. 'And I cannot allow this… this *monstrous* language. Girl Clerk, you have just signed your death sentence.'

A loud gasp.

It's Amy. I turn to her, and she looks away, the tears rolling down her white cheeks. I look at Jacob, desperately, wildly, but he stares at the ground. *Please. Stand with me.*

They say nothing.

Then the chaos begins. Small sounds at first; muttering voices, shuffling feet, hushed whispers. Then hissing as Productives attempt to quieten trainees. The voices are mounting.

Anson shouts, 'Get your security Productives. Right now. Arrest her. We'll have no more of this. Take us off air.' He slams his hands on the table, his face purple. Productives around us stir into frenzied action, grabbing NPhones, screaming into headsets. I gaze around wildly. *I need to get away.*

Two large Productives in security uniforms stomp through from the left wing. Cadman whispers to them, eyeing me. Lora stands twisting her hands together, her eyes wide. For seconds, I feel pity for her.

The crowd is rising. Children are standing. Banging their seats up and down. Shouting mutinously at their Trainers. I watch in horrified fascination as a Productive in the front row grabs something from her bag; I recognise it as a flail. She grabs a shouting boy nearby and whacks his shoulder. He roars, and other trainees begin to scream. The auditorium is soon in sheer pandemonium. The two security guards make their way over to me, batons in hand. I freeze. Amy and Jacob look on helplessly.

And then it happens.

A high, loud shriek, cutting through the bedlam, shouting one phrase. Over and over.

'POWER TO THE WEAK! JUSTICE FOR ALL!'

The crowd quietens. Turns to the frantic shouter. The sound is coming from the back of the auditorium. The very back row. It's a girl's voice, strong and powerful. She bellows the phrase, again and again and again, and some trainees catch on. Chant with her. The words spin into a frenzy, discordant and beautiful, and then there's another sound.

A singing of a crossbow quarrel, cutting through the air, inches from my face.

Someone fired an old-fashioned crossbow.

Cadman Showman roars and slams to the floor.

The arrow is embedded in his shoulder, blood pouring from him and creeping over the stage. The guards are distracted, running over to him, and I shield my eyes. Gaze at the back, searching for the shooter.

And there I see her.

Raza.

She opens her mouth. In slow motion, I watch her shriek, cupping her mouth. 'Carys. RUN.'

My adrenaline kickstarts me; my legs pumping before my brain decodes the words. I find myself belting from the stage, through the west exit into the maze of passages. I tear through the darkness, smacking into flustered Productives, flinging them aside. I'm infused with a strength I never knew. I retrace my steps, back to the dressing room and from there to the back stage door of the warehouse. Frantic shouts chase me down the corridors, outraged voices, thunderous footsteps. They're chasing me hard. I slam into the door, hurling it open and then sprinting over the exposed ground outside. I run round the side of the huge structure where there are a number of smaller buildings, which look to be in a state of disrepair but may give me some much-needed cover. I race harder than I have ever raced before, and as I reach the first broken-down shed, the first shot rings through the air.

PART III

RUNNING

18

THE CENTRE

JACOB

JACOB TRADER IS frozen.

He watches as Cadman Showman hits the floor hard, a crossbow bolt sticking out of his shoulder. He watches as the hefty security guys hustle over to him, flustered and mad, bending over, checking him. 'Cadman? Cadman?'

The place is in uproar. Kids are screaming, shrieking at their Trainers. Some are still chanting the phrase Raza started. Jacob searches for her but can't see her anywhere. Productives are hitting trainees, some of them with flails. It's carnage out there.

Slowly, he pivots, looking for Carys, desperate for her.

She's not there.

'Where's Carys?' he shouts at Amy through the commotion. Her eyes are huge. She stares round the stage. Shrugs.

'She's gone.'

Jacob gathers himself. *I have to go find her.* He makes to leave the stage.

Amy lays her hand on his arm. 'Wait—'

'What? Amy, I need to find her—'

'No. No. Look, if you go too, you'll be caught, and you'll be killed. She has a better chance if we… if we keep playing the game.'

He gawps at her. 'What do you mean?'

'Look.' She's flustered. A sheen of sweat glows on her brow. She bats at it, sweeps it away. 'We haven't said anything. We can still be pardoned.'

Jacob shoves her hand from his arm. 'How can you say that? We can't just leave Carys to die!'

'She'll be fine. She's strong. And look, Jacob, if she gets caught, our only chance to save her is if… if we are still in good graces.' She's hissing in his ear now, her hand heavy on his shoulder. 'We can save her if we are together. If you or I are killed, then—'

He shrugs her off, glaring at her.

But he knows she's right.

He slams his head into his hands.

The guards have gone after Carys, angry yells echoing through the passages as they hunt her down. *Run, Carys.* Jacob glances at Cadman. He's very still. Lora fusses over him, sobbing, her cat ears all askew. She catches him looking. 'Why did she…?'

Jacob swallows. 'We don't know,' Amy says firmly, giving him the side-eye. 'We are as bemused as you. She didn't mean it.'

Lora rubs at her eyes. 'But you don't believe that… stuff?'

Amy clears her throat. 'No.'

More Productives stream onto the stage from all directions. All the overhead lights are flicked on, and the battered old warehouse displayed in all its dilapidated glory. Kids are fighting in the aisles, throwing punches at one another; some boys wrestling on the ground. Their Trainers dash round, landing heavy blows and whips with the flail. Some kids are bloody and bruised, some skulk in the corners, eyes wide and mouths agape.

The NScreen is shut down, Anson disappeared from sight. Jacob breathes a sigh of relief. Amy pulls at his hand. 'We ought to help,' she hisses. 'Show willing.' He gawps at her. Still practical, even amid catastrophe.

'What can we do?' he says, scanning the space, sickened by the sights and sounds. He glances at the judges' podium; the other judges have disappeared, left the chaos behind. Medics have rushed in to see to Cadman. Lora still hangs over him, face wan, hair hanging in wet straggles, soaked by her tears.

Jacob grabs the microphone discarded by Cadman on the stage. Bellows into it. 'STOP.'

The auditorium fades to silence. He stands there, every face turned to him; tear-streaked and bloodied and unbelieving and outraged. 'Go home now,' he says, more gently this time, and for some unknown reason, they do as they are told. Kids get up from their fights, dust themselves down, follow their Trainers meekly from the building. In no time, the place is deserted apart from the staff and Jacob and Amy and Lora. The medics bear Cadman away on a stretcher and Jacob and Amy remain, befuddled and exhausted, standing on the stage, staring into nothingness.

Jacob becomes aware of Lora, sobbing next to him. 'Coran,' she's saying. 'Please get Coran.' He motions at Amy, and she runs off into the bowels of the building.

He places his hand on Lora's shoulder. 'Come on. Let's find him. Don't be upset.'

She weeps harder.

He leads her out through the backstage area, and they bump into Amy and Coran, who is bustling with animated outrage. 'Is it really true?' he is saying, and Amy nods, her jaw tight. Coran sees Lora and dashes up to her, throwing both arms around her and holding her tight. 'Oh, my poor, poor darling,' he mumbles into her neck, and she melts against him, wailing, and then, when spent, she snivels, her head against his chest. He pats her back. 'You poor dear girl. What was that silly child thinking?'

Jacob stands in an awkward posture. What are they supposed to do now?

Lora cries herself out then stands away from Coran. 'Let's go home,' she says, and beckons to Jacob and Amy. And he knows that for the moment, they are safe.

He can only hope Carys is.

He's mad with her, but part of him is blown away by her absolute nerve. She looked badass, out there on the front of the stage, yelling her heart out. All he wanted to do was back her up. Join her. But he didn't.

He let her down.

CARYS

I RUN LIKE the wind. The first shed I come to is firmly closed and firmly locked. The shot goes wide, ricocheting off the wall of the warehouse to my left. I tear around the shed and through to a rough passage between various structures. It looks like an abandoned industrial area; small barns constructed of rusty corrugated iron, wooden sheds, the occasional brick-built edifice. Some of it is crumbling away.

The shouts draw nearer. I dart in between two corroded old sheds, almost tripping on the tangled weeds under my feet. I rush to the end of the alley, which is a damaged chain-link fence, coiled barbed wire strung across the top. Parts of the fence are destroyed, gaping holes surrounded by shards of broken wire beckoning to me. I breathe in and shove myself through one of them. The wire mesh grabs at me, gashes at my Ashton uniform and scratches my flesh. I flinch and haul myself through. Shouts are closer now, echoing and rebounding through the close-knit buildings. They're gaining on me.

Another gun shot. The fence behind me cracks and whips round at me, released from its post. Thrashes at my face, drawing blood. I shove it away and run.

The buildings are condensing. More of them look like dwellings now, abandoned houses from the Before. They survived the fires, somehow, but are still in a state of serious disrepair. I shudder, the presence of those who lived here pressing in on me. The guards behind have scaled the remaining portion of fence and tear across the waste ground towards me. 'Stop there,' one of them bellows, but I dart into the empty doorway of a nearby house. The roof is mainly gone, leaving the structure open to the sky, and the windows are long broken, slices of glass lying around on the dirty floors. An ancient shabby red sofa sits incongruously in the centre of the room, a ghostly reminder of what once was. I skirt it and go through to what was once a kitchen and fly out of the back doorway. There are fence posts remaining in the garden, but no fence, so I run at full pelt towards another group of houses behind this one. Behind me, the men scramble through the house in hot pursuit.

My heart is thumping wildly, and I panic as I sense a slight wheeze. *Not now. Oh please, not now.* I ignore it and press on, my long legs pumping madly, eating up the ground. I'm fast. They're not gaining on me now. They stop again to shoot; miss, and shout obscenities at me. I dive into another house and through, this time shoving a broken old kitchen appliance into the path to the back door. It slows them for precious seconds as I bolt down another alley into a street of more ruined homes.

I head for a building I spot in the distance. It's much bigger than the rest; in fact, it doesn't look like a house. A hospital, perhaps, or an old training house – a school? I run for it, skipping between fences and gates lagging off their hinges, ducking down behind old, corrugated iron panels shoved against walls, avoiding the increasingly frustrated security guards. I know it won't be long before more troops are sent; NForce elite officers, possibly. I've been sentenced to death by Commander Anson himself, they won't leave me out here for long. For now, these two are slowing. They scream into NPhones and lumber after me.

I give them the slip around a house just in front of the bigger building I'm heading for. I don't want them to see me enter it. I duck down the side passage and hide behind an old wooden chicken house, any chickens long gone. Most of it is wrecked, but the back wall remains upright and I crouch there, motionless, trying to calm my heartbeat and ragged breathing. They come bumbling around the corner of the house, banging the old walls in temper. 'Where the hell has she gone?' One of them kicks the chicken house and part of it explodes into dusty debris, but my wall stays standing, and I exhale. They tramp through the garden and into another shell of a house, grumbling.

I slink out of my hiding space and back through the side passage then tear across a portion of exposed ground, the weeds as high as my waist in some parts. It's further to the big building than I thought. I freeze as I hear shouts again, turn to see where they are but see them ducking into another place. They haven't seen me. I hunker down and crawl through the thickening weeds, brambles tearing at my bare hands and knees. I crawl swiftly, ignoring the sharp pain of gravel embedding itself in flesh, and I make it to the building, where huge glassless windows gape at me. One door swings on loosened hinges in the wind. The evening is cloudy, and the darkness gives me a helping hand.

The guards are well behind, their torches dancing through the evening murk, scouting the area. 'She's gone,' one of them growls.

'NForce on their way,' says the other, and my heart skips a beat. I crawl right up to the entrance and through the doorway, and they don't see me.

Inside, the hallway of the old building stretches out in both directions, cold and lifeless. A wide stairway sweeps up from the hallway straight in front of me, and next to the stairway there's a bunch of ancient lockers, most of them without doors and some with doors hanging off. If I was Amy, I might just be able to squeeze in one of the bigger ones and hide away. But I'm too tall. I make a split-second decision and start up the stairway. There must be somewhere to hide from the inevitable hunt that will come soon.

I panic, running harder, and I trip, falling flat on my face up the stairs. I grimace as pain floods through my shoulder. I scramble up, throwing a wild glance behind. No guards yet. I push on up the rest of the stairway. At the top, another stairway leads up and a doorway leads through to a landing. I dash up the stairs, this time watching where I am going, moonlight breaking through the clouds for a moment, filtering through the gaping windows and casting patterns of pale light on the ground ahead of me. I crash through the intact double doors at the top and come to a stop, getting my bearings.

The corridor stretches out to my left and to my right. Numerous doorways lead off. I glance into the first room to my left; empty apart from some archaic benches lining the side of the room under some shattered windows. I know what this is; it's some kind of science lab. Old fashioned gas taps languish on the benches. It's got to be an old school, where children once went from their homes. Jacob told me that some kids lived in schools, but only for term times, and had long holidays at home with their families. Most kids lived at home and went to their schools each day. The phantom of what was once here in this place fills my mind: happy shouts, kids running up the stairs, learning their history and safe in their families.

I stand in the doorway, tears swimming in my eyes, but I'm snapped back to reality by the sound of something else. Not the guards shouting, this time. It's the all too familiar whumping of Copter blades. *This is it. They'll pulverise everything.* I have to get out of here. Buildings are not safe – I berate myself for coming here and climbing all the way to the top. *Stupid.* I head back to the stairwell and down to the next landing.

Clumping footsteps on the stairs below. Frantically, I streak through the doorway on the first floor and down the corridor, blindly heading for somewhere to hide. Old classrooms pass me by as I sprint to the very end where a window frame without glass looks out on the night. Harsh lights dazzle me; the Copter is low, scanning the area. I duck down from the broken panes and into the room next door just as one of the guards comes through the doorway from the stairs.

The room is smaller than the others. Cramped. It's some kind of old storeroom. Rickety shelves line the walls – there are even some old books left lying on them, covered in layers of dust. I shrink to the back of the cupboard, desperately searching for somewhere – anywhere – to hide. But there's nothing in here but the shelves.

Heavy hobnailed footsteps tramping towards me. Checking all the rooms. Taking another deep breath, I poke my head out of the door. The Copter is round the other side of the building, its light scouring the ground in front. I turn, searching for the guard; he must be hunting through one of the rooms. I creep out of the store cupboard and clamber through the window frame, looking down.

The ground is too far. If I fall from here, I'll be incapacitated. I can't take that risk. I scout around, my hands gripping the window frame, but there's nothing but rough brick. The chilled night wind rustles my hair. I hear a commotion as the guard stomps out of one of the rooms, and I duck right down, my feet perched precariously on the thin ledge outside. I hang motionless. Waiting.

His footfall fades as he goes into another room further down the corridor. I breathe out slowly, and then I bite on a scream as part of the window frame I am clinging so tightly to snaps and comes away, throwing my hand into space. My body twists heavily and I lurch away from the wall, my feet slipping from the ledge and launching me into space.

I catch myself hard, my fingers seizing the ledge and grappling with it, clutching it tight until I have purchase. My feet slam the wall below, jarring me again. The ledge crumbles under my grasping fingers.

I look down. The ground is closer.

The Copter circles around, ready for another rotation of the building.

I have no choice.

I drop.

The ground below slams into me, jolting my body from head to toe, shock waves running through my feet. I have no time. The Copter is above, the searchlight sweeping the ground nearby; it'll be over me in seconds, and all will be lost. I scramble to my feet, ignoring waves of pain. I can walk. I can run, just about, so I do. I sprint away from the building, narrowly avoiding the light.

That's when the Copter fires on the old school.

The guards are still in there, trapped, but I have no thought for them as I am hurled from my feet and once again slammed to the ground. Behind me, the remaining glass in the windows is blown out, shards of it raining over me. I cover my head with my hands, groaning. I can't hear anything. The world is muted.

The school lights up in an intense conflagration. The heat creeps towards me, scorching my hands, my hair, my face. I roll away, my arms numb. I keep rolling down the slight incline behind the school, gathering momentum and thumping into a thorny bush at the bottom of the slope. In seconds, I heave myself up and round the bush, crouch down and fling my arms over my aching head. The Copter fires again, and the left side of the school is blasted to pieces; the structure groaning as it implodes upon itself in a fiery ball. I lift my head, watching in wonder at the inferno and the collapsing building.

I check myself over. Parts of me ache with pain like I've never known, even from the flail. I grit my teeth as I get up, leaving the shelter of the bush and limping away, heading for a line of trees at the back of the old estate. No one seems to have spotted me. I drag myself as fast as I can through nettles and gnarled remains of trees and bushes and make it to the tree line. Behind me, the entire estate is lit up as the Copter repeatedly bombs the place, leaving no stone unturned, no building unburned.

19

THE CENTRE

Amy

AMY WAKES THE next morning with a feeling of dread heavy in her stomach.

For moments, she buries her head in the pillow, revelling in the softness. Then she sits bolt upright, her hands flying to her mouth, as the events of last night crash into her mind. *Carys. The S Word. The death sentence.*

She throws her clothes on quickly, her discarded Ashton uniform left unwanted in the corner of the room. She wishes she could burn it. Principal's mocking face looms in her head, and she shakes it, chasing the hideous images away. She dashes to Jacob's room, pulling shoes on as she goes. She knocks once and shoves the door open. He's standing by the window, hands in pockets, staring out at the clear morning. He twists when she enters, and she sees he's been crying. He rubs at his eyes and slumps onto the window seat.

'I left her, Amy,' he says, his eyes large and lost. 'I didn't even back her up. What kind of friend – what kind of boyfriend? She must hate me.'

Amy sinks onto the seat next to him, taking his hand. 'She will understand. We had no choice.'

'Perhaps we did.'

'Think about it, Jacob. If you had joined in her rant, or followed her out, you would have been sentenced as well. Like I said last night, she needs us. And that is the reason we could not go with her.'

'I suppose.'

'You've got to get over this. You can't help her by moping around and blaming yourself. You've got to get up and do something.'

'But what shall we do?'

'We go to our original plan. We leave this place. Find the Centre Outsiders camp, where my parents are. Then we rally them and anyone else there. Carys's performance is bound to have stirred unrest – it could all be to our good. We can use it. Get people on side. And then we can find Carys – if she hasn't already found us. I have every faith in her.'

'I do, too. But what if—'

Amy presses his hand. 'Look. We'll cross that bridge if we come to it, okay?'

'Well…'

'For now, we need to get back in the game. Just for another day, while we say goodbye to Lora, and thank you very much. We tell her we're returning to Ashton.'

'But she'll find out, when we don't.'

'Yes. But not until it's too late.'

Jacob shifts, staring out of the window. 'So what now? We go down there, pretend nothing happened? Pretend Carys doesn't even exist?'

'Of course not. We say we disagree with her, that we hate what she did, that we are still incredibly grateful for our reprieve and will not side with her. We are out for ourselves. We have to be the selfish ones here – make them believe it.'

'I don't know if I can.'

'You can.'

Downstairs, they find Coran standing in the den, his back to them, watching the NScreen avidly. It looks like he's watching an action movie of some sort; buildings collapsing in flames, scenes of burnt-out shells, blackened trees. Amy clears her throat. He spins round, his eyes widening, and clicks his fingers at the wall. The NScreen fades to black, and he stands there jiggling from side to side, the tips of his ears reddened.

'What was that?' Jacob asks.

'Oh, well… oh, nothing, really,' Coran stammers.

Something is wrong.

'Coran,' Amy says, stepping forward and laying her hand on his trembling arm, 'let's put that back on, shall we?'

He shrugs.

Amy clicks her fingers, waits for the screen to respond and increases the volume. As she was beginning to suspect, these scenes are not from a film but are footage of something that happened very recently. She perches on the arm of the sofa, and Jacob stands next to her as they strain to hear the words of the newsreader.

"… large scale manhunt. The wanted offender, Girl Clerk of Ashton Training House in the Midlands Compound, was pursued in connection with pernicious and treasonous lies she wantonly spread on a live showing of *The S Word*. Commander Anson was on the show via live link and immediately pronounced a death penalty on Miss Clerk, who had previously been offered a complete pardon for her part in the rescue of Lora Dancer from serious assault by Unproductive Outsiders. Clerk's co-trainees, Boy Trader and Girl Plumber, remain under the terms of the pardon, having declined to take part in Clerk's shocking spectacle. Clerk escaped when an unknown collaborator fired a crossbow, severely wounding Cadman Showman, who is this morning in a serious condition in the Commander Lucan Hospital. As the scenes behind me show, NForce fired on several structures during the manhunt, and it is thought that Clerk is now deceased…'

Amy gasps, and Jacob sinks to the floor, gripping the arm of the sofa.

'… but until that is confirmed, the hunt will continue. In a new directive, Commander Anson has decreed that should Clerk be found, she is not to be killed immediately. His personal assistant gave a press conference earlier and informed us that Anson believes that a public execution would be a positive way to ensure that any further unrest is quashed.'

Coran clicks the NScreen off, his eyes soft on Amy's.

Jacob stares up at her. 'She can't be dead.' Amy cradles him, bringing his head to her shoulder. He sobs against her, broken. 'I should have gone after her.'

'Shh,' she whispers, but the truth is, she feels the same. They should have stood up for her. They left her alone, and now she might be dead.

Jacob sinks his head into his hands. Tears squeeze from between his quivering fingers, and Amy sees how much he loves her. There is nothing she can say.

Coran flutters about, arranging ornaments on the fireplace, straightening cushions. 'Dear ones,' he eventually says, twisting his hands. 'I am so very sorry. She was very stupid indeed, but I don't think she deserves… that.'

Amy gazes at him and sees he is more upset than she imagined. His eyes are red-rimmed and his hair in a tousled mess, as if he hasn't slept. He really does care about Carys. 'Would you help us, Coran?' Amy asks instinctively. 'Help us find her?'

He lifts his shoulders, his eyes darting around the room. 'I can't be seen to do anything rebellious,' he murmurs. 'And I'm sorry, but it looks like she's gone. No one could survive that.' He motions at the blank NScreen, and the images Amy just saw play through her mind; the old houses imploding on themselves, the entire estate lit up. What if she was trapped in one of those buildings? She'd have no chance. Amy hugs her arms, her chest tight with sorrow. When did it all go so very wrong?

Jacob gets to his feet and as if in a daze flicks the NScreen on again. 'Don't torture yourself,' Amy says, but he shrugs her away and slumps on the couch.

Coran nods slightly to Amy, and she knows he will do what he can. He leaves the room, his head bent low, his usual sassy swagger nowhere to be seen.

Amy watches the rolling news in silence, Jacob a valley of gloom beside her. Her stomach is churned into small pieces, tremors rumbling her body. The newsreader reels off a list of other news, but they're the main story. She watches distractedly as the scene cuts to Party HQ and then a stock image of Commander Anson, his silver hair impeccable, ice-blue eyes smiling with warmth into the camera. 'In other news, the New Day Tax Bill was passed today,' the anchor says. 'All Productives are to pay a further three percent from their wages to the Department of Taxes. We go now to Lois Reporter, live from Party HQ Square. Lois.'

A thin woman in a grey raincoat smiles into the camera, framed by a backdrop of the sumptuous Party HQ building. Amy's seen pictures of the Houses of Parliament from the Before, but they were completely destroyed in the riots and the new Party HQ building constructed from scratch. Its fascia is all tinted glass, and it is an impressive edifice. In front of the building is a large square with a magnificent fountain, a bronze figurine of a cherub holding scales the centrepiece. The very centre of justice, where bills are approved that are always for the good of them all. The woman speaks into the camera, motioning back towards the Party HQ building. 'Today, despite the turbulence of the past twenty-four hours, Commander Anson took time to introduce the New Day Tax Bill. The bill was approved and passed in record time. The new taxes will be used to improve Newland's infrastructure: notably our inter-Compound road and railway networks, and to ensure that our health and education sectors continue to deliver the quality we have become accustomed to. As Productives, we are in a privileged position to be able to pay these taxes.'

The studio anchor interrupts. 'What would you say to those who are less than complimentary about the new tax, Lois?'

The woman smooths her dark hair, which is billowing in the wind. 'Well, Elva, I can only repeat that the tax will ensure continued quality in all our infrastructure. Without this extra rise, we would encounter some great difficulty. Those who are opposed should take it up with their local New Day Party representative.'

Amy glances at Jacob, whose eyebrows are raised. 'Those who are opposed should watch out,' he mutters. 'They'll be executed, I should think.'

'Mmm.' She watches the screen.

'Back to the main news story of the day,' says Elva the newsreader, a tiny, neat woman with blonde hair swept back in a tidy bun. She gestures to the studio screen behind her. 'Since the events of last night, there have been scenes of unrest throughout the Centre Compound and the nation at large. Trainees who were attending the live filming were quickly overcome when they began to show rebellion—' Jacob snorts at this, '—and other pockets of insurgence were soon quelled.'

Scenes resembling the familiar images of the riots from Assembly are played across the screen. People holding hastily scrawled cardboard placards ('Power to the Weak! Justice for All!') and people tackling NForce officers with sticks, swiftly overcome. None of the incidents seem to involve more than three or four Productives, so the resistance looks weak. Deliberately so, Amy imagines.

Elva continues, 'The government issued this warning: If any Productives or trainees display any form of mutiny whatsoever, they will be immediately suppressed and taken to their local Think. The Party will not tolerate any form of resistance and will not waste any time in ensuring that Newland remains the peaceful nation we are all so proud of. You are warned that the consequences of any insurrection will be severe. The NForce are at this moment taking extra steps to crush any Outsider uprisings in order to keep the peace. In the coming days, the NForce will subdue suspected Outsider camps.'

Amy stiffens. 'Subdue?'

'She means they're going to bomb them,' Jacob says.

They gaze at one another.

'We have to warn them,' Amy says.

Lora hobbles into the room, her face bearing the effects of too many tears and too little sleep. 'Morning.'

Coran follows her in, skipping around her, asking what she needs. 'Cup of tea? Toast? Morning papers?'

'No thank you, Coran,' she says wearily, rubbing her eyes and clicking her fingers at the NScreen. 'I've already seen the news. I really don't want to think about it all anymore. Please just get me some coffee. Strong. Black.'

'It's coming,' he says and skitters out of the room, leaving Lora standing in front of the fireplace, regarding Amy and Jacob.

'Listen,' she says. 'I'm… I'm sorry about your friend. But look, you were warned. I did say that I couldn't protect you if you didn't uphold your side of it all. And to be honest, I really feel quite let down by you all…' she tails off, tears once again springing to her eyes.

Amy takes a deep breath. 'We didn't know Car… um… Girl C… was going to lie again. It was as much a shock to us. All we want is to be free, and you and the Commander so kindly gave that to us, Lora. We are still so grateful, aren't we, Jacob?' She raises a brow at him.

'Yeah,' he mutters.

Amy nods. 'Look, I don't know what to say. I'm sorry she went off on one, but it's not our fault.' *Be selfish.* 'She's dead to us now.'

A sharp intake of breath from beside her.

'We're really annoyed too,' she continues. 'We just want to get on with our lives. Lora, we'd like to go back to Ashton.'

Lora stares at her. 'After all—'

'Yes. To finish our education and to become Productives. You've given us our freedom and the chance to do that. So would you be able to give us border passes?'

She purses her lips. 'I'm not sure. I'll ask the Commander.'

'The Commander would surely want us to become Productives,' Amy says slowly, smiling at Lora. 'It would be like he's really succeeded with us – show the nation what his forgiveness can achieve, sort of thing. Please, Lora. We just want to leave this all behind us now.'

Lora runs her hand over the mantelpiece. 'I suppose that seems like the best idea.'

Coran breezes in with a tray bearing a coffee pot and mugs. 'Coffee, anyone?'

Amy drinks the hot liquid and muses on her absolute betrayal of her best friend.

20

THE CENTRE

CARYS

HAVE TO get through the barriers.

All morning I've been making my way through the woodland I stumbled into last night. I slept intermittently, curled up in a hollow beneath a large chestnut tree, my body roaring with pain.

Chestnuts lie red-brown and glossy on the ground, split from their decaying prickly cases. I tramp wearily along, heading for the barriers in the distance with no clue how I'll get through. There won't be a Mercia to help me at the last minute this time.

I've had plenty of opportunity to rebuke myself soundly for last night's performance. I completely and utterly lost it. I'd been doing well; keeping it in, ignoring the white-hot fire coursing through me. But Gardener's lecherous paws all over Amy sent me over the edge, and it was like the power of a waterfall, hauling me over the edge, gripping me hard, not letting me go until I crash landed at the bottom. But I still made that split-second decision. It was still my fault.

Eating away at me even more than that is Jacob and Amy's complete disregard of me. They didn't back me up. They just stood there like they were incredibly embarrassed by me, like I was something unspeakable on their shoes. And then they let me go. I ran, and they didn't follow. They left me all alone to die. My stomach twists as I face up to facts: I am on my own. Jacob and Amy made the decision to keep themselves safe.

Unwanted tears prickle my eyes, and I bat them away, rubbing angrily at my cheeks. Now's not the time to wallow in self-pity. Now is the time for survival. I have plans to sneak through the barriers and then to find the nearest Outsider camp. Ideally, I'd like to get back to the Subversives Community: I have friends there. People who care about me.

The afternoon drags on as I navigate my way through a densely forested area to the north of the Centre Compound. I still have miles to go before I reach the border gates; there's no way I'm making it there today. I'm going to need to find myself some food and water and more shelter for the night. Last night and this morning were cool but dry, but this afternoon it's damp. Occasional showers continue through the afternoon, soaking through my thin Ashton uniform, my rubber shoes of no use on this rough terrain. As the damp begins to spread through my body, I wheeze, and then I cough. I have none of the medication from Lora's house with me; I have nothing at all. Shivering, I hug my arms around my chest and trek on as the showers turn to torrents.

In the distance I spot a small group of buildings, a large, partially ruined house along with what looks like rickety barns and outbuildings. I head for it, my hands over my head in a futile attempt at protection from the vicious deluge. Roots and brambles trip at my aching, blistered feet and I heave another long sigh, frustrated at the shortcomings of my body. As well as my chest, my legs and shoulder are in intense pain. I hurry on through the downfall, battered and bruised.

Eventually, I reach the structure, a broken-down house in the middle of nowhere. There is some roofing left on the main house, but the outbuildings are mostly rotten piles of wood with the odd upstanding steel girder gamely attempting to keep the building up. I creep around the outside of the house, checking for Productives, but the place is desolate and silent, beaten by rain and darkness. I find the old front door, rotting and swinging from rusted hinges, and push at it. It swings open with a loud creak, and I enter the house. There is nothing and no one to be seen. I explore the old rooms, such as they are; moss and ivy have taken over, coating the floors and snaking up the crumbling walls, reclaiming the land. An old fireplace sits against the wall in the largest room, the grate rusted and blackened, a few old wood blocks abandoned in the far corner. There's an ancient wrought-iron poker and a worn-down shovel lying loose on the ground, partially covered with foliage. I wonder if I can get a fire going here. If I can find some more wood from the forest area I might just manage; I learned a lot in my time at the Subs. I'm shivering violently. If I stay here with no warmth, wheezing and struggling for breath, I might not make it through the night.

I traipse back towards the woods and scout around for likely looking logs in an area where the trees are so dense the dampness isn't too bad. I find a few sticks lying around and a couple of bigger logs. I also scoop up some loose pine needles, some shredded bark and bunches of fairly dry leaves and grasses. They will do for now. I find some piles of smaller, dry sticks lying under some birch trees, and hope that they will do for getting the fire going. I think about food, and my stomach rumbles. My thirst is raging.

I trudge through the muddy field back to the house, my shoes and socks soaked and useless, grateful the rain is holding off so my weedy pile of firewood doesn't get even damper. I push into the dark house, shivering at the chill. In the room with the fireplace, I contemplate my surroundings. The ceiling in here is mostly intact, which is something. There is no glass remaining in the small window, but the walls are mostly there, with patches of damage and crumbled bricks leaving great gaps for the wind and rain to find their way in. I dump my pile on the floor and sink down with them.

I crave sleep. I lie down, my body wracked with shivers, my mind swirling away.

Come on. I look at my pitiful pile and realise I need more if I'm to have any chance of keeping any kind of fire going. I notice some bundles of newspapers behind the woodpile in the corner of the room and wonder if someone else has been hiding out here recently. They're a little damp but usable, so I shred them and add them to the dry leaves and grasses.

I use the shovel and my hands to scrabble the dirt and old ash away from the fireplace. I heap some of the smaller tinder into a nest then stack up some of the thinner sticks as kindling, then finally place some logs round the edges. Then I find a fairly flat piece of birch wood that will do as a board, and a dry stick for a spindle. I have no knife to make a notch, so I do my best with a sharp stick, but it's less than ideal. I begin rubbing, spinning, over and over. I know how long this can take, but I've nothing better to do. After ten minutes I almost give up, my wrists aching. Maybe everything is just too damp, and I'm on a hiding to nothing. At least the motion of it is warming me. A little. I sit back on my haunches, frustrated.

No. Keep going. I've started fires before, and I know the theory. And I know it's vital.

An ember. A tiny one. I begin to blow at it gently, angling it down to the tinder. It doesn't catch. I puff my cheeks out and carry on, and I get some more. This time, the tinder sparks and catches. I'm going to be okay.

Later, I curl in front of my roaring fire, thawing out, my damp clothes drying on me. I drift off eventually and sleep through most of the darkness of the night, waking with the cold dawn and the smouldering remnants of the fire. Sitting up, I feel lightheaded, but my wheeze is less pronounced. Food and water are the first order of the day. I scold myself for forgetting to find some kind of receptacle for rainwater the night before – the cool dawn sky is suffused with pink, the grey of the storm passed on. No more water.

Still, I drag myself up and clatter round the house, looking for anything of use. Nothing remains in any of the rooms. I pick up the old poker and fold it under my arm, having nowhere to stash it. I need some form of protection. Outside, I find pools of rainwater gathered in sections of broken guttering, swimming with leaves and dirt. I take great gulps, grimacing at the gritty taste, trying not to worry what it will do to my stomach. Rested and strengthened, I leave the house and once again start the long trek towards the barriers. My thoughts stray to Jacob and Amy, but I chase them away, determined to look ahead. *I can do this.*

Later in the morning a watery sun warms me as I walk, and the distance to the barriers decreases. My stomach rolls with hunger and I search through wooded areas for fruit as I go. I spot some crab apples lying on the ground and scoop one up, biting into it and screwing up my face at the bitterness. It is fuel; it doesn't matter. Later, I find wild raspberries growing in an area of scrubby bush land. They are overripe, but I enjoy every second of them, their sickly-sweet juice running down my chin.

The noonday sun is warmer, eradicating my chill. I skip ahead, eating up the miles one by one, finding a patch of wild strawberries and avoiding some shrubs that look similar to elders but I am not sure about. I don't need to go poisoning myself.

Finally, I drag myself through the last of the wooded area approaching the barriers. I have headed for a quieter section a few hundred feet down from the border gates so I can scout the area and grab an opportunity for breaking out. I sink to the damp ground, the mulch of autumn leaves and bark and moss making for a soft place to rest for a while. Keeping the poker by my side, I stretch out, exhausted.

I come to as the sun is low in the sky. I slept too long, and now dusk is approaching. I pull myself up, brushing leaves from my bare legs and shivering. I dance around, getting the feeling back in my feet and warming myself up, and then I edge tentatively towards the border gates, keeping behind trees and bushes and nowhere near the main road. I can hear the traffic from here, though, still heavy at this time of day, trucks heading for other Compounds or returning from a day's work elsewhere.

I stop as a sound reaches my ears and turn to the barriers where the huge NScreens hang, one either side of the gates, broadcasting news from the day. The early evening dusk makes it easier to see what's on the screens. I spot my face; much as expected, and creep nearer, listening to the newscast. They're showing scenes from the bombing last night and proclaiming that I may be deceased "but the manhunt will continue until we are certain". My heart sinks momentarily as I wonder how Jacob and Amy are taking this, but I harden myself. They were no friends to me last night. Why should I care what they think?

I brush tears away impatiently.

More scenes of carnage now, this time of a place I don't recognise, of ruins being blasted into remains of ruins. The newsreader saying that the Party are stepping up their protection for citizens of Newland from Unproductive Outsiders and eradicating any suspected camps. I swallow hard over the tight knot of fear. The camps. The Subs Community. Amy's parents.

I need to get to them. Warn them. If I can find the Centre camp, we can use the radio equipment there to warn Cory. To get them to move on. Fear lends me strength, and I streak through the twilight, heading straight for the border gates. I must do this. This is all my fault – if I hadn't lost my temper on *The S Word*, these innocent Outsiders would be left alone. Commander Anson is doing this because of me. Nauseated, I creep through a cluster of trees to the east of the border gates and flatten myself against one of them, my heart hammering. On the other side of the trees, NForce officers parade the ground with automatic rifles. Far more of them than before. They are there for me.

I peek around my tree to get a better idea of the situation. It looks no better than my first fleeting impression. The officers yell into

NPhones and swipe through NSlates. The giant NScreens scroll announcements punctuated with huge pictures of me: The Wanted.

I scan the ground around and the road ahead. Several NCVs and trucks line the road by the border booths, showing their credentials. Officers are slow to verify them, taking an age over each one, suspicion lining their faces as they check each driver. Other officers search through truck beds and car boots. No stowaways are getting through here.

But there is no other way through the barriers.

I wait, biting down on my already bitten nails. There must be a solution. There must be a way. I wish I had different clothes on; I am so conspicuous in my hated Ashton uniform. I grip my poker and sigh.

I decide to wait until further into the night. Perhaps when it is less busy there might be a chance to sneak through. I retrace my steps until I come to a thicker area of forest and slump to the ground, hungry, thirsty, exhausted and despondent.

I doze fitfully. The autumn chill bites at me and my aching limbs throb. One of my feet pulsates with sharp pain, and I wonder if I chipped a bone in the fall.

I wake abruptly at a sudden crash. Rumblings in the sky. Another rainstorm. Water running from leaves above my head drips on me as I haul myself up once again. The NScreens continue to project their light far into the darkness of the night, the newscasts discussing the New Day Tax Bill and the unrest in the Centre. Productives have been arrested for demonstrating outside Party HQ, and Commander Anson makes it clear that no resistance will be tolerated. I weep, knowing the fate of those unfortunate people.

I steal towards the border gates, unseen and unheard. The thick darkness of the clouded night and the driving rain protects me like a blanket as I creep between trees and around shrubs that seem alien in the blackness, but I'm soon shivering, soaked to the skin in my thin clothes. When I get back to my tree, I see there are still as many officers as before, and my heart sinks. They are on as high alert as they were earlier. The only difference now is that there is no traffic. I curse myself. I could have hidden in a truck, somehow, but I've missed that chance now. It's me and twenty or so border guards with rifles.

Some of them don't look too alert, though. They sprawl around under loose tarpaulin shelters, smoking and drinking, their harsh laughter ringing through the night. Any sound I make is muted by the rain, their voices and the boom of the NScreen newscasts. The wind is whipping up around me, too. They won't hear me, at least. If only I could make myself invisible.

Two or three of them stand to attention at the booth, scouting the area with binoculars. Some of them are on the case, then. They mutter to one another and the occasional laugh floats over to me.

I turn my attention to the colossal NScreen soaring above me. The rain-proof canvas is secured to the barrier by means of heavy-duty bungee ropes woven in and out of reinforced metal eyelets punched through the thick cloth, and then hooked over and under massive, solid bolts drilled into the barrier at intervals. Studying the bungee rope, I get an idea. A mad idea, but it's something. I stand back, scrutinising the mechanism further, biting on the inside of my cheek.

I sidle up to the right-hand side of the NScreen. I stare down the screen towards the border gates – the screen extends right to the gap where the gates are placed, with the bungee rope on that side of it stretched around the corner, firmly hooked around more embedded bolts on the cross section of the thick concrete. I grab hold of the nearest section of the elastic. It's heavily stretched, soaking wet and difficult to get any kind of purchase on, but I manage to slide my fingers round behind it and then, little by little, to loosen it from around its anchoring bolt until it pings up at me, droplets of water flying everywhere, flapping loose in the wind and then sliding through my fingers as it tightens again, the force of the rest of the rope pulling it taut. I slip my cold fingers to the next bolt and repeat the procedure. I step back, studying my work, frowning. The screen soars high above me, pelted by rain; I need to try and loosen all the elastic down the right-hand side and some from the top. Stealthily I climb up, using the bungee rope like a ladder, the tightness of the elastic holding me steady. I get to the top and look down, swaying and clinging to the rope. It's a long way down. No one looks my way, and if they do, I'm well hidden by the brightness and confusion of the tightly pixelated NScreen and the lashing rain. I look up. The barrier towers above me, curving back over me slightly at the very top, coiled razor wire providing an additional disincentive to further climbing. There would be nowhere to find hand or footholds, in any case. The barriers are constructed from smooth grey concrete.

I gather myself and start to move along the canvas, hanging onto the securely fastened bolts, the toughened fabric sagging slightly under my weight. My hands throb, irritated by the damp and the elastic. I get to around two thirds along the screen and then start releasing the bungee rope from the bolts. I jerk violently as the leaden sky crashes deafeningly above me, then illuminates with a flash so bright I can see for miles around. My heart thundering, I move back towards the corner, the rope pulled tight enough to hang from while keeping my feet on the top of the canvas, liberating each anchor point as I go. The wind thrashes at me and the loosened bungees, whipping them around near my face, flaying my bare legs. I make it back to the corner and start downwards now, pinging out the elastic and moving downwards from each released eyelet. I sense a loosening in the canvas and then a pulling as the rest of the screen draws the released portion towards it, the sheer scale and weight of the fabric forcing it away from me. I nod to myself. I keep releasing the bungee, point by point, clutching hold of it hard. I get to the bottom and creep along, unhooking the resistant rope until I reach a point around the same portion as I got to along the top. My fingers are white with the strain and chafed to the point of bleeding.

I leave two eyelets low on the right-hand side hooked to keep the whole thing steady and they pull taut, the top corner of the canvas flapping wildly in the wind. I peer anxiously over at the officers; no one has noticed. They are huddled under their makeshift shelters. No one thinks to look at the NScreens. Thankfully, they are on a level with the border gates and so this section will be difficult for them to spot. Until I finish, of course.

I take a deep breath. The two remaining bolts are at a level with my shoulders. When I release these, the whole thing should yank itself away and start thrashing fiercely in the storm-pounded night, only anchored on its one remaining side. That should get the attention of the Border guards. That's when I slip through.

That's my plan, anyway.

I exhale, and breathe in again, face upturned to the downpour, mouth open, gulping down the pure water. Mustering all my strength for the sprint ahead.

I pull at the bungee. It's so taut it's next to impossible to grip, the remainder of the fabric heaving it away, my grazed and damp fingers useless. The poker is ineffective; it merely slips out of the elastic if I try and wedge it in. I bang it angrily to the floor. The two eyelets are beginning to stretch out of shape and the material beneath is fraying. I watch as the canvas unwinds before my eyes, the sheer force of it doing the job I couldn't. The top portion of the screen starts to whip around forcefully, cracking against the concrete. Frantically I watch the guards, but they're still oblivious.

One of the eyelets snaps. The material tears from the wall brutally, the useless bungee swinging with it, almost hitting me straight in the eye. I back away, panicked by the force. The other one is going. It stretches, creaking as it tries so desperately to cling to its anchor, the fabric above whipping around like a tent loosened from its pegs in gale-force winds.

The images on the screen are distorted, the Wanted picture of me shattered into pieces as it projects over the loosened fabric and the grey stone barrier behind. I smile for seconds at the irony of it, then squeeze my fists hard as I watch the last eyelet lose its fight.

Now.

The entire screen comes belting away from the wall with a power I hadn't imagined, ripping most of the remaining eyelets away and tearing angrily at the resistant bungee rope. I sprint towards the border gates, ducking low through weeds and bushes. The sound of it is terrifying, a loud creaking as elastic stretches and snaps and lashes against the fabric and the unyielding concrete. I watch in wonder as the whole thing appears to take off, thrashing around at itself, then bursting its final eyelets and soaring ferociously through the air towards the gates and the guards. They seem to spot it as one, their mouths agape and eyes widened, paralysed for seconds as it flies towards them in angry twists and spins, frayed and snapped elastic flying at them from all angles, beads of water spraying everywhere. It's like a slow-motion film as they duck and turn and run away from the mad thing, and in those moments I sprint through with all my might, hardly flinching as a rogue elastic whips my ear, covered by the great fluttering fabric dancing through the night sky. Some of them are grabbing hold of it now; bellowing at one another, shouting obscenities. They catch it and it tears them off their feet, slamming them at the ground.

I'm through. I take one last look back at the chaos in my wake, men sprawled on the ground, some grasping hold of the giant canvas with all their strength while being repeatedly lashed with errant elastic. It's almost comical; twenty grown men fighting with an oversized white sheet, and I bite back a huge guffaw of laughter as I run headlong into the stormy night.

I don't look back again.

21

THE CENTRE

JACOB

JACOB MOOCHES THROUGH the day. Lora has promised to get them a border pass by the next morning, so they while away the hours, watching the news and depressing themselves further.

He hates himself. Whatever Amy says about it being the right decision, the best one for them all, it's a decision he regrets; a decision that told the girl he loves that he doesn't love her enough. When he sees the pictures of her plastered all over the place, he is sick with worry and self-loathing. What if she is already dead? He can't stand the thought of it. He'd only just found her, only just found out how deeply he felt, and he went and ruined it all. Amy tries to talk him out of it for a while, but soon gives up. She knows she's not going to persuade him.

He prays for Carys, remembering the tatty old holy book from the Before. He prays that she will be well. That she will escape and that he will see her again.

He hardly sleeps, tossing and turning and then meeting his demons once again in vivid nightmares of Carys burning up in a huge fire and him standing there, doing sod all to help her, watching her die. He wakes drenched in sweat, no more rested than before, and showers quickly, desperate to get their passes and get out of this forsaken place.

He meets Amy at breakfast, and they formulate their plans, such as they are. Lora has told them they can take one of her NCVs to Ashton, so they'll be able get up to the Subs Community as quickly as they can. Jacob's frustrated by the delay, scared they'll be too late. This morning, the news is full of scenes of Outsider camps decimated by fire, or "subdued", as the newsreaders put it. For Productives' safety, of course. They need to protect themselves, in the Compounds. Outsiders are dangerous.

They plan to get on the road as soon as Lora gets their passes to them and drive straight up to the Birmingham ruins. They can't get the vehicle right through to the Bunker, but they can get it within a few miles, and then they can walk; they know it well enough. From there, they can warn the Centre Outsiders camp. With the plan cemented, Jacob heaves a sigh of relief and waits.

Lora doesn't turn up at breakfast. Coran is there, humming and flitting around. He doesn't know where Lora is, he says, his head tilted and his foot tapping. He can't imagine where she might be. Possibly at the council offices, picking up border passes for them, Amy suggests, and he nods, pursing his lips.

Something is wrong.

Jacob waits with mounting impatience, his bags packed with his new clothes and waiting by the door. Coran brings the old NCV from the garage and sweeps it into the driveway with style, and Amy laughs at him showing off, but still there is no Lora.

Lunch time comes, but she doesn't.

Finally, late in the afternoon, she hustles into the den, where Jacob perches on the edge of the couch next to Amy, watching the increasingly distressing newscasts. The Party are mounting a wide-scale attack on suspected Outsider camps. They watch with eyes wide and stomachs tight.

She limps in, her long hair mussed up and her eyes hollow looking. Her black eye looks worse again; the bruises that were yesterday faded to yellow are a vivid purple. She catches Jacob staring at her and brings her hand to her face, touching her eye gingerly.

He gets up and wanders over to her, waiting in expectation. She shrinks away slightly, her hands behind her back. 'Have you got them?' he asks. Amy nudges him and raises her eyebrows.

'Are you okay?' he says instead, and Lora glances at her feet, then looks up again, a smile plastered on her face.

'Of course,' she laughs. 'And I have a really amazing thing to tell you. An offer you can't refuse. But it's not me who's going to tell you – it's my dear friend.' She motions towards the hall, and a shadow crosses the doorway as someone comes in. Someone with a confident swagger and a smiling face.

Raulf Singer.

'So pleased you are still here,' he gushes, sauntering over to them and holding his hand out. 'You are not going to believe what I have to say. To offer you both. It's a chance of a lifetime.'

Jacob looks at Amy, who sinks back onto the sofa, brow creased. 'What do you mean?' he asks.

Raulf pauses, then claps his hands together, laughing out loud. 'I have been asked – from above, of course – to make you a... proposition.'

Another one? Is this another charade, more hoops for them to jump through before they can go free from this place? His stomach twists. He can't do this anymore. He raises his eyebrows at Raulf. 'What is it?'

Raulf clears his throat. 'You know, of course, that poor Cad, Cadman Showman that is, has been severely injured and is indisposed for the foreseeable future.' He looks at Jacob, his blue eyes pinned on his.

Jacob nods. Amy is motionless.

'Well. Sadly, this leaves us with an issue, on *The S Word*. A vacancy, as it were. And at this time, more than any other, it is vital that we should be… politically expedient.'

They watch him and say nothing. Jacob's heart begins to hammer wildly.

'Commander Anson had a most… *imaginative* idea, and when he presented it to me, I was in full agreement. We feel that it would be in Newland's greatest interest, and in fact your own, if you two were to be the interim *S Word* presenters.'

Shock courses through Jacob. Amy shrinks against the sofa, biting hard on her nail.

'What?' Jacob can't come up with anything else.

'Of course, you will have questions, but may I say now that this is not actually an offer, but a directive. You are to be the new presenters until such a time as Cadman is able to take up the reins.'

'But… why?' Amy says, her brown eyes wide.

'There are many good reasons,' Raulf says. 'You have the attention of the nation, right now, and in a good way. They like you. Did you not see the reaction of the crowd at the filming? I was later told how you, Boy T, took up the microphone and spoke with the crowd in the midst of the rather unfortunate event, and how you had a natural authority to which everyone responded. Girl P, you have a sweetness to you, an innocence that people like, but you also have an integrity. You are honest as the day is long. You two are perfect for the role.'

Jacob gawps at him. 'Newland doesn't like my sort.'

Raulf snorts. 'Pfft. That may be the case for some of the less forward-thinking people. The Commander himself informed me of how much he thinks of you, and how he wants to be more inclusive. It will be very good for Newland. We can see how far we've come, then. We know as well as you that our beginnings weren't always completely auspicious. You could change things for us. As for you, Girl P, what better chance to show that Commander Anson is a leader who gives chances, even to those who have gone beyond the pale? Even to those who are illegal? This is a chance like never before to show our… benevolence. Our goodwill.'

'What about Girl C?' Amy says, her voice low.

Raulf rolls his eyes. 'What about her? She made her decision. She wouldn't be right for the role, in any case. Too hot-headed. Not cool in a crisis. We need folk who will think on their feet, with common sense and practicality. From what I have seen, you two fit the bill. Clerk is old news. You must move on. Forget about her. She is probably dead, and if not, soon will be.'

Jacob inhales sharply.

'But… but we haven't finished training,' says Amy. 'We're not Productive yet.'

'Take this as your work experience,' Raulf says. 'You don't need to complete your studies at Ashton. You are already seventeen, are you not, or will be very soon? This high-profile role will take you far into Productivity and launch you into the world of work. Your privileged position will mean you have little trouble finding well-paid work afterwards. You can see the perks, surely.'

'I don't…' Jacob begins, then stops. Words will not come.

'You will be well rewarded, of course,' continues Raulf, spreading his palms. 'You will be provided with luxury accommodation with your own servants – a cook, cleaner and maid – and you will have drivers at your beck and call. You will also be compensated financially, naturally.'

Jacob looks at Amy. Her eyes are pools of fear and hopelessness. What if they say no? 'Can we… can we refuse?'

'That is not an option.'

'But why?'

'I have explained. You are in a unique position for your country, where you can make a real difference. Surely you want to be part of changing views about certain matters, part of heralding in a new age of tolerance and understanding?'

'But what if we do refuse – if we simply go back to Ashton, like we planned?'

'I'll put it this way. If you decide to decline this revolutionary offer, then you will be detained at Commander Anson's pleasure. Also, your friend's… sentence… will come around rather quicker. If you feel able to take us up on this, then the execution will still go ahead, of course, but we will allow more time and allow you to visit her. I think that is very generous of the Commander, under the circumstances. And then, of course, there are the… rationalisations, that are taking place as we speak, of Outsider camps. The Commander has assured me himself that they will be pleased to look the other way a little more if you accept our proposal. That less camps will be subdued.'

Lora is hopping around behind Raulf, beseeching them with worried eyes. Jacob wonders if Anson has taken his anger at Carys out on her. Her appearance might suggest that was the case. He feels sickened.

Amy pipes up again, somewhat feebly, 'But I have no idea how to present a show. I'm nothing like Cadman. He has presence. Power. I'm just a kid.'

Raulf smiles at her, his eyes crinkling right up. He takes her hand. 'It's because of that we think it would work so well,' he says, warmth infusing his voice. 'You two are different from Cadman, but different in a good way. Boy T has the presence you need, and you have the warmth. The reliability.'

Amy remains silent.

'So you're saying we have no choice,' Jacob murmurs.

Raulf nods. 'I'm saying that it is in everyone's best interest. That there is no better way.'

'And when will we…' Jacob trails off, disgusted at the thought of going along with this foulness.

'You start next week.' Raulf stretches his arms high above his head and yawns. 'I'll leave you to make arrangements with Lora here, and later your new driver will pick you up and take you to your new residence. You won't be disappointed.' He winks at Amy, squeezes Lora's arm and waltzes out of the room, his job done.

They freeze in paralysed silence, unable to believe what is ahead.

'It's not so bad,' Lora says, drifting over and sinking onto the couch with Amy. 'It means a steady income and perhaps a positive outcome to all this unpleasantness. You will be famous, and that's such a great feeling, I can assure you. Everyone is going to love you so much! And it's not like you have to do it forever.'

Jacob thinks about the Subs Community, waiting unaware to be "subdued". 'Can we still go back to Ashton – just for a day, to see our friends, to pick up our things?' he asks her, crossing his fingers.

She twists her hands, glances around. 'Oh, well… I don't think… no. That's not a good idea. I'm afraid the Commander wouldn't want that. You must stay here in the Centre. I haven't got the border passes, anyway, because I was told about this before I got them. I'm sorry.'

Amy grimaces at him.

They can't leave the Subs all alone. Jacob doesn't trust Anson to keep to his word, to lessen his attacks, even if they say yes to his horrific proposal. He can't watch as they receive the same treatment as other Outsiders. They need to find a way of getting to them. If they can just get up there, they can come straight back.

So that Carys has more time.

AMY

AMY SITS IN shock, picking at the loose skin around her nails, sweat prickling her brow. It feels surreal, all that has happened and all they are being asked to do. She can't go along with this. They are being asked to collude in the murder of innocent people. To be part of the problem they wanted to solve.

But there seems to be no choice; they are being forced into this against their will, with thinly veiled threats and blackmail. If they run away, the Party will kill Carys and destroy more Outsiders communities. If they refuse, they will be arrested, and Amy knows what that means. If they say yes, Carys gets more time. Not much, but it is something.

But perhaps she is already far away, out of the clutches of the NForce. Perhaps she has defeated all the odds. Perhaps she is free.

If she is, they might be able to disappear as well. They might be able to avoid this unspeakable new situation. They might be able to avoid sending people to their deaths.

They make excuses and get out of the house, wandering the gardens, stunned and helpless. They tramp round the grounds in silence, well aware of one another's thoughts and objections to this vile scheme. Amy feels the sobs building up, all that has been pent up inside for days pouring out in a great sea of emotion. Jacob holds her hand, beating himself up. If he'd gone with Carys, this wouldn't be happening. Amy says that if that were the case he might be dead, too, and where would they be then?

They are trapped. They have no choice but to go along with this odious design that will show the nation how thoughtful their Commander is. How tolerant. How broad-minded.

And all the while, knowing well how underneath it all the man is a cold-blooded killer.

22

THE OUTSIDE

CARYS

IT'S A WASTELAND out here on the Outside, a sterile landscape with no signs of life. It's evident as soon as I escape through the barriers – the fertile, abundant land of the Centre Compound is left behind. Here and there, patches of ruins break up the terrain, old bombed-out farms and villages from the Before. The unrelenting rain drives over the barren land, and I shiver hard as I realise how frozen I am.

Now I'm out, I'm relieved to be free, but as well as being soaked to the very bone, I'm tired and hungry and I have no idea where to start searching for the Outsiders camp. It could be anywhere. I know it's somewhere to the west of the Centre; Jacob found that much out from his limited communications with the man on the other side of the radio. So I'm in the right area, at least. But it's going to be off the beaten track, nowhere near the main road leading up towards the Birmingham ruins.

After my mammoth sprint from the border gates, I am worn out. I slouch, dragging my feet, my pace slowing. For a time, I use the poker as a walking stick, bending low to it, leaning on it until it hurts too much. Out here, there are few verdant wooded areas to hide in. Scraggly grasses and scorched weeds skulk unhappily over the inhospitable landscape, even more ghostly looking through the darkness of the rain-pummelled night.

I drag on. I can't give up now, not when I've come so far. I'm safe; out of the Compound, away from the main focus of the manhunt. I keep walking to the west, searching for any sign of habitation in the distance, any tracks that would tell me of anyone using this as a route. I veer away from the main road. There are no vehicles in sight, no one around at this time of the night, but I should avoid the route anyway. I must find somewhere to shelter again, somewhere I can get warm and dry; I'm well aware I haven't had enough sustenance today, my body is severely weakened. My crazy effort at freeing the NScreen took every last scrap of energy, and the sprint was completed on adrenaline alone. I could lie down here and never get up.

I trudge over the forsaken ground, disheartened, searching for something. Somewhere to stop. The ruins in the distance look like a possibility, but they are a fair way yet. I'm not sure I have the strength left to reach them. And when I reach them, what difference will it make? Out here, there are no easy fruit pickings. At least I can drink, while the rain continues to pound the earth.

Still, I press on.

I pin my eyes on the cluster of ruined houses. Among them are bare trees, lifeless and eerie against the dark horizon. No leaves and twigs to be found there for kindling.

I traipse on.

I will not think about Jacob. Will not think of his arms around me, his lips on mine. Will not contemplate his words of love in the Centre Think, cried out to me in desperation before we were killed. Will not picture his face, those soulful brown eyes, the way one cheek dimples, the way his chin clefts. Will not think of how I felt about him that dark, velvet night we walked back to Arthur Waste's house back in the Midlands Compound, or when we wept together over a book in Daniel's library, or when he lifted me up when I almost collapsed on Remembrance Night. I will not think of him.

I'll not think about my best friend Amy, about how she believes in me, about her compassion and her goodness. About how she rescued me from the Think, how she faced her own fears and changed. How she always helps me be a better version of myself. I will not think of her.

I definitely won't think of how they betrayed me in the *S Word* studios. How they turned their backs on me. How they didn't love me anymore.

I plod forwards.

A howl echoes through the heavy darkness, sending slivers of fear slicing through me. I twirl, scouting the landscape. Nothing. The howl sounds again: closer this time, too near. I don't know what it is. In the dead of night it sounds like a phantom, floating through the ruins ahead, moaning forlornly for its long-ago past when there was life and freedom and the ground was fertile. I stop still, heart hammering against my chest, scanning around me with wild eyes.

Another tortured howl. Then, more than one.

A pack.

Wolves? I've never seen wolves, though have heard they roam the Outside, descendants of dogs from the Before who turned wild and feral after the riots and the Scourge. We're safe from them in the Compounds; no untamed animals cross the barriers. But out here, on my own, in the shadows, I know they are here. They will find me.

There is nowhere to hide. The ruins ahead are unsafe; the place the unearthly howls originate. I turn, wondering whether I should retrace my steps, but I am too far from anywhere. If I go back, I'll have to cross over the main road, and that carries its own risks. No. I carry on. I'll look for a hiding place amidst the ruins.

The yowls increase in volume as I move nearer, creeping now, keeping as quiet as I can. My fatigue is forgotten as I pour everything into keeping alive. I tiptoe towards the first ruin, the remains of a barn, a building once used for cattle, possibly. But there is ground between me and the barn, and in seconds there are the wild dogs, spotting me, baying through the night, calling to their pack. In a few more seconds they are coming for me. Tearing through the open space, ripping up the yards between us, their razor-sharp teeth bared, their slavering jaws tight. Their eyes glimmer yellow, frenzied pinpricks of terrifying light in the black of the night.

I freeze.

And then I run. My legs force me on, propelling me hard across the drenched earth, kicking up great clods of muck, heading to the side of the pack towards the barn. They come to a shuddering halt as they spot my sudden change of direction and correct their course, bolting after me and gaining on me with every step.

I don't have time to think, to plan, to be afraid. I charge ahead, the adrenaline in my bloodstream pumping hard, driving me, stirring me to greater speeds. The ruined barn lies just ahead, its doorway a gaping black space, rotten wood lying on the ground next to it. Inside the shadows lurk, concealing objects that rip my flesh and trip my feet and send me flying flat on my face. The wolves crowd around me, growling and yowling and snapping. Watching me. One of them clamps its jaws round my bare calf and I scream. I pull myself up, kick at it, whack it with my poker, tear through the pack, knocking them away from me with a strength I could never have imagined. Directly in my path is a ladder to an old hayloft. It's partially rotted, but it's my only chance. Another feral beast leaps on me as I bound over the last few feet and onto the first rung. It cracks, breaks away, and I stumble, screaming. hot blood streaking down my leg. I strike out at it with the poker; it lunges, grabs it from me, tears it from my grasp. I have nothing. I grab the next rung up. No time to test it, I heave myself up. It holds. Next one. They gather beneath, nipping at my feet. I kick at them and one of them yelps. I pull myself up to the next rung and then the next. I lift my arms and grab the lip of the hayloft, haul myself up, but the rotten wood is creaking; it's splintering, and flakes drift to the ground, raining down on the growling dogs circling below. I grab a solid beam to my right and heave myself up and over. Around me, great chunks of wood come away, the whole structure shudders. Then settles.

I lie on my back, my heart pumping, my body convulsing.

The pack whine below me.

I stay there, stretched out, until my wild heartbeat slows and I can sit. Great gaps punctuate the old loft, but there's enough of it left to provide a safe place. For now. Old straw lies around the place. I gather it up, intending to make a nest to warm myself, but most of it falls to pieces, brittle with age. I shiver.

I manage to drag some of it over me and around me, but it is less than ideal. At some point, I stop feeling cold and begin to feel numb, then infused with an odd kind of heat. I drift away.

I wake with thin light casting shadows through the barn. I feel odd, like I am not really here. I cough, and cough some more, working up to a spasm of hacking coughs. I am drowning. I'm reminded of my time in the Ashton Think as a second year, so ill I was delirious, and how Principal delighted in my pain. Anger suffuses me and lends me the strength I need to get through this.

I peer over the ledge. The pack of wild dogs have gone. I can see the barn now and the objects that caught me last night, skeletal remains of ancient farm machinery lying abandoned on the ground. I wonder briefly about the dogs. Where do they get their food? They are surviving, somehow. Do they catch wild animals? They looked thin. Malnourished. But they must have a food and water source out here.

I lower myself down the ladder, every part of my body screaming. I know I am ill. I need medication. If I stop now, I know I will die. I let the anger course through me, the anger at all the times I have faced death in only a few months. The anger at Jacob and Amy. The anger will spur me on.

I search the ruins, dragging my leaden feet. There is no sign of the dogs, so something goes in my favour. The sun begins to warm the morning as I make my way through the last of the cluster of buildings, most of them open to the elements. The storm of the night before is forgotten, white fluffy clouds skating through the autumn sky.

In a dark room of the last but one house, I find an old woman sitting in a shabby armchair, her hands on two sleeping dogs. I peer at them. They look like some from the pack who attacked me. I reel back towards the doorway, but she sees me.

'Come in, my dear,' she croaks. Her faded blue eyes are almost hidden under heavily wrinkled folds of weather-beaten skin, and her limbs are resonant of thin twigs under delicate white tissue paper. Her white hair is long, braided roughly down her hunched back. She beams a toothless smile at me. 'It's good to see you,' she says, as if she has known me all her life. As if she has been waiting for me.

I stagger in. She has a fire lit in a tiny grate, and I gravitate towards it, shivers coming thick and fast. Her eyes cloud. 'You are so cold, young one. Here. Sit here.' She gets herself out of the armchair and takes my arm and helps me into it. I slump down, uncomplaining. She fusses round me, somehow making hot tea and pressing an old china mug into my frozen hands, draping a dirty crocheted blanket over me. Washing my wounds, smoothing my brow, scrunching up her face. 'You are fevered.' She fetches a damp cloth. Mops my forehead.

Soon after, I drift into a heavier sleep, filled with dreams of yowling hounds and Jacob coming close to me, arms out, then stepping away at the last minute, cackling. I wake when the sun is high, and the woman brings me some kind of hot soup, and then I talk with her.

My story pours out, and she regards me seriously. She nods in places and scratches her chin. In others, the clicks her tongue and sighs. When I come to last night, she is outraged. 'My dogs would never hurt you,' she says. 'They were just being friendly.' I refrain to mention that they swooped over me, clawed at me, bit me. It is enough that she is here.

I ask her about herself, but she doesn't tell me much. 'Enough to say,' she says, 'that I felt unable to take the Party up on their kind offer of the Home. I moved out here and found my friends.' She strokes one of the dogs at her side. 'I look after them and they look after me.'

Where does she get her food from, I ask, and she smiles at me. The ground may be less than fertile, she says, but she has ways. She has a garden. An old well. And the dogs bring prizes; rabbits and pigeons. She has enough. She is content.

She asks me what my plans are, and I tell her I am looking for an Outside camp nearby, somewhere to the west, and she gazes at me for a few moments. Then, 'They live in the remains of an old airport from the Before, a place the machines called aeroplanes took off from and landed in. If you travel for half a day northwest, you'll see it; there are still remains of an old control tower there. No one'd know they're there. It just looks like more blasted remains of what once was.'

I thank her and tell her I need to go. That they are coming for me. She gives me the blanket and a bottle of water, and I take her hand. 'I… thank you. I don't have enough words.'

She smiles gently. 'I need no more. Go.'

23

THE OUTSIDE

CARYS

I N THE LATE afternoon, I see it. The crumbling remains of an ancient tower, the windows long ago blown. It's like a mirage, shimmering in the desert, a beacon calling to me. I drag my tired feet, huddling further into the blanket. The house, the dogs, the old woman, all seem like a fevered dream now.

As I draw closer, I see more ruins lying around the structure, blasted apart, great hunks of concrete spread over the cracked ground. More haunting are the hulks of the burnt-out air machines, huge cylinders of scorched metal sitting forever discarded on the fractured runways. Once upon a time, Jacob told me, these machines were used for people to visit other countries. They were used when we were free. Each mass of blistered aluminium has stories it could tell, and I gaze over them with a strange yearning.

I reach the main section of the largest structure. Many more shells of buildings lie around the place, but this is the one that seems most intact. Even if I find no Outsiders, at least it will provide some shelter for tonight. My wheeze is acute as I stagger up to a doorway of sorts, sagged under tons of ruptured concrete and steel.

Cautiously, I poke my head in. Nothing to see but more debris and the vestiges of what once must have been some kind of waiting area, metal seats still screwed to the floor but twisted in eerie shapes. The floor is uneven, and I wonder briefly how secure the structure is. If it will all come collapsing down on me, just another means of Death stalking me through the day.

But nothing shifts.

I explore the extremities of the room, if it can be called that. A few doorways lead to passages that snake through more wreckage, but there's not a soul in sight. I find a fairly upright seat and sink into it. Then I shout, 'Hello?'

My words ricochet off broken walls and bounce back at me, mocking me.

'Is anyone here?'

No one answers. I am on my own.

I sprawl over the seat, the aches in my body more intense now I'm still. Shattered and despondent, I close my eyes.

'WHO ARE YOU?'

A hand on my shoulder. A face looming at me, swimming into focus; a round face, short brown cropped hair, a concerned frown. 'Are you okay?'

I shrink back.

'Don't be afraid. I'm Bruce,' says the face. I frown. That rings a bell.

'I… I escaped,' is all I can think to say.

He shushes me. 'Don't try to speak. You're injured. We'll get you to somewhere you can rest and heal. I am a doctor,' he adds, breaking into a gentle smile.

His face swims out of focus again, and I close my pounding eyes.

I WAKE UP to a white room. Cracked polystyrene ceiling tiles soar over my head and a harsh strip light illuminates the room. I'm in a bed, an old-fashioned hospital bed. My wrist stings. I lift it and find a cannula with a drip attached. I sit up, panicked.

The man with the brown hair and the smiling face saunters into the room. 'Ah,' he says, coming over to me, adjusting the drip bag. 'You had a good long rest.'

'Where am I? Who are you? What are you giving me?' The questions come thick and fast now I'm awake and rejuvenated. He smiles. Holds his palms up.

'Okay. One at a time. My name is Bruce Medic. You have pneumonia, I'm giving you intravenous antibiotics and a rehydration drip. You're safe here at the Airport Camp. And I know who you are.'

I raise an eyebrow at him.

'You're Girl Clerk. We have communications linked to the Centre, though they don't know it. We've seen you. All over the news. We were all quite impressed at your little performance.'

I smile weakly. 'Please call me Carys. That's my real name.'

Bruce nods. 'Of course. We're thrilled you are here. There are two people who are particularly interested to meet you – you may remember we made contact with you and your friends through the radio, a week or so back? Your friend – Jacob, I believe he said his name was, though only known as Boy Trader on the newscasts of course – asked about Lois and Alwin. They are here, and they are longing to see you. To find out about their daughter.'

My blood chills. I don't want to talk to anyone about Amy. But I nod at him. He's probably saved my life, the least I can do is be nice.

'Later, then.' He turns his head as he leaves. 'Get some more rest. Get well.'

When I wake later, bandages criss-cross my legs where I was injured from the jump from the school, the farm machinery and the dog bites. The sting of antiseptic ointment is fresh on me.

I drift away again.

TWO PEOPLE ARE in the room. 'Are you awake, dear?' the woman says gently, her lined face uplifted in a genuine smile. I like her immediately. She looks just like Amy. The same shade of dark brown hair, the same petite build. The same warm brown eyes, shining with intelligence and compassion.

Her husband is a stooped man with greying hair and light brown eyes behind old-fashioned round glasses. He smiles tentatively at me, his hand on his wife's waist.

'Hello,' I say, shuffling up the bed. I feel light, slightly fuzzy inside, and I wonder what painkiller they have given me. How do they source medicine out here beyond the barriers?

Lois Retail leans over me and kisses my cheek. She lingers, her eyes swimming, stroking my face then stepping back. Alwin Plumber offers his hand, and I shake it.

Lois twists her hands. 'I'm so happy to see you,' she says, her voice thick with joy.

'I'm pleased to meet you too,' I say, and I really am. Something in me itches with yearning in response to these two. I forget about Amy for now.

'You're feeling better?' Lois asks.

'I am, thank you.'

'I'm pleased.'

I long to melt into Lois's arms, to feel her warm embrace.

'And… Amy?' she asks, softly, almost fearfully, a worried frown creasing her brow. I suddenly feel for her, this slight woman, a woman who defied the authorities and brought an illegal child into the world, a woman who had the courage to bring the child up. And then a woman who had her world torn away brutally; her son murdered, her daughter stolen, and then she and Alwin evicted to an inhospitable land. I can't hold Amy's recent actions against her.

'I left her well,' I say. 'She was… strong. She felt that the best thing to do was to go along with what Commander Anson wanted of us.

It was me who spoiled it for everyone. Who brought trouble.' I hang my head.

'No matter,' says Lois, gazing into my eyes. 'You are here. And you love my daughter.'

I stare at my feet, the sadness in me pushing so hard at my chest that it might burst.

'And she is safe.'

'Yes.'

'Thank you, Carys.' She squeezes my hand, and without thinking I reach my arms to her. She hugs me and I lean against her, my tears spilling over. 'Shh, now.' She rocks me like a baby. Like the mother I never knew; the mother murdered by the New Day Party. 'It's okay. You've got us, now.'

Alwin clears his throat. 'Do you know what Amy's plans are?'

I shake my head. 'I'm not sure what they'll do now. We were all planning to come and find you. Maybe they still will, if they can get through the barriers. It's not easy.'

'And what about you, Carys?' asks Lois, sitting down on my bed. 'What are your plans?'

'I have none, really,' I say. 'But I must try and get through to the Subs Community. The place we were before. They're in danger… and so are you. Did you see, on the news? They're destroying Outsiders camps. It's all my fault—'

'No. It's not.'

'Well, whatever, you need to get away from here. They have so many spies, they know where lots of the camps are – they might know about this one.'

Alwin and Lois say nothing, but their brows are furrowed with worry.

'The radio,' I say. 'Can we try and get through? To the Subs?'

'We can try,' Alwin says, 'but I'm afraid we've not had a lot of luck since Bruce was first able to make contact with your friend Jacob. No one seems to answer.'

I had hoped Cory would be around, would try to use the equipment. 'Can we at least try?'

'Of course. I'll ask Bruce to set it up.'

I SLEEP AGAIN and don't wake until the following morning, when I feel stronger still. Invigorated. I swing my legs out of bed, determination taking hold of me. *The radio.*

Bruce comes into the room, beaming at me. 'You're so much better. The IVs are doing their work.'

'Did Alwin tell you what I said? About trying to contact the Subs, and about moving on?'

Bruce sits on the chair next to my bed. Leans forward. 'Carys,' he says, scratching his head, 'I tried. Last night, when Alwin told me what you'd asked. I did my best, but there was no reply. The channel seemed completely blocked. I'm sorry.'

'Then we need to get to them. Warn them. They don't have links, like you do, they have no idea what is happening in the Centre, or anywhere else.'

'We don't have any fast transport, I'm afraid,' he says. 'We have horses and carts, for working on the land, but nothing that's going to get you up to the midlands quickly. I'm sorry.'

I sit back, fear coursing through me. 'What about you?'

'What about us?'

'You need to move on. You are in acute danger. Surely you know that?'

'We are aware.'

'Then why are you not bailing out of here?'

He lifts his shoulders. 'There's nowhere for us to go. Besides, we're quite safe here. We're tucked away underneath the airport. We dug down and constructed deep bunkers, years ago when we started this community.'

'But you could be killed anyway, surely?'

'I know.'

'So you should move!' A rush courses through me, suffusing my face with hot crimson.

'We don't want to, Carys.'

'But—'

'You are welcome to stay. We'll take care of you, and you can join us, if you like. Alwin and Lois would be delighted.'

'I—'

'You're safer here than back out on the road – you're too exposed out there, and survival is tough in this terrain. You're best off here, with us. Please consider it.' He scrapes the chair back and walks out of the room, rubbing his chin.

LATER I GET up and wander around the small hospital they have here, rooms carved from a basement, dragging my drip stand, my legs wobbly. I leave the complex and explore a corridor leading to more rooms. I head for the room at the end, a huge space with scattered old sofas and tables. People are sprawled around the room, chatting and laughing, children playing on faded coloured mats on the floor. The living space.

I spot Lois in the kitchen area, chopping vegetables and chatting to a tall woman in an apron. 'Hey,' I say, and she whirls at my voice, her face breaking into a gentle smile. She drops her knife and walks over to me, brushing off her hands. 'Lois,' I say. 'Do you think the same as Bruce Medic? That you should all just stay here?'

Lois looks around, her eyes shifting. 'Look, Carys,' she whispers, 'we can't talk here. We should go over there.' She points to an unoccupied corner at the far side of the room. I follow her and sit stiffly on a saggy couch, extending my arm so the drip can flow efficiently. 'There are some who disagree,' she whispers. 'Bruce is generally a good leader. A good doctor. We have much to be thankful for. But he's reluctant to make any kind of change, or to admit we could be vulnerable. We've always been so strong, here in the Airport Camp. No one has ever found us. But some of us are seriously worried; we've seen the news footage. They're not leaving anything to chance, are they? Some of us are planning to walk away from here in the middle of the night.'

I gasp. 'Tonight?'

'Yes. And you must come with us.'

'Where are we going?'

'Anywhere. Somewhere we can cultivate land. We go under cover of darkness.'

'How many?'

'Twelve. Thirteen, with you. Three children.'

I nod. 'You can't persuade any of the others?'

'Sadly, no. We've tried, but they are blind, Carys. They look to Bruce and can't see beyond him. I'm worried for them, but we have to save ourselves. Bruce doesn't want anyone to go, though, so we have to be careful.'

I stare at her, at the fine lines around her dark eyes, the strain marked on her face.

'I'll pack a bag for you,' she says, her eyes darting around the room. 'I'll bring you clothes, and we will go tonight.'

I REST FOR the remainder of the day, conserving energy for what is to come. I hate the thought of being out in the wild once again, but this time I will have company and supplies. It will be different. Perhaps I can persuade them to head for the Birmingham camp, although it would take days. But I hold on to hope.

At eleven, the hospital wing is silent. Lois comes in stealthily, bringing me warm clothes for the challenge ahead; cargo trousers and several top layers including a rain cover, and sturdy walking boots. She removes my IV. 'You're almost there anyway. One or two doses won't harm. Shana has some oral antibiotics packed.'

Shana works in the hospital and is the reason Lois can get me out of here. She waits by the door for us, anxiety etched on her face. 'Hurry,' she says.

'Why are we being so secretive?' I ask. 'Surely you are free to do as you please?'

'To a certain extent,' Lois says, grimacing. 'But Bruce is a little… forceful, at times. He enjoys reigning over his small empire here. He would try and stop us – he has his own little security set-up, see.' She sighs. 'Sadly, even on the Outside, we have those who act in the same way as the Party.'

Still, there is no challenge to us as we walk away from the Airport Camp. Thirteen of us creep through the basement and up through the old waiting room, out into the ghostly ruins of the airport, the blasted doorways of devastated planes yawning at us. I try not to look at them and concentrate on the road ahead. The group is silent, even the little children, who march willingly with their parents, their small faces alight with hope and expectation.

We are all bundled up with warm clothing and backpacks filled with supplies. All we must do now is keep out of anyone's way. We trek towards the northern horizon. It's dry tonight, and clear, the moon casting its silvery light on the scrubby land before us, stars twinkling above. The children turn their faces to the sky, their tiny white teeth glinting in the moonlight.

An ear-splitting bang behind us, and the ground shifts. My heart banging hard, I whirl around and see the sight I so desperately dreaded. Lois cries out and flings her hand over her mouth, her eyes widened in abject horror. The others begin to sob, some to stand frozen.

The airport. Flames lick at the old ruins, the sad planes dying another death, the entire structure collapsing in on itself. We see the Copter now, relieved of its payload, heading back off towards the southeast. From here, the entire horizon seems lit up, and we know that there is no possible way the airport community survived.

Broken, we turn from the inferno and trudge on, faces ravaged in dismay and grief. There is nothing for it but to walk away.

That's when the Copter circles once, then again, then heads our way.

'Run.' Alwin's voice is harsh. We all grab hold of each other, some adults swing the children into their arms and we take off, sprinting onwards towards distant hills. We have nowhere to go; there is nowhere to hide out here in this desolate landscape, dotted only by shells of distant buildings and sickly-looking trees. 'Keep running.'

I hold tightly to Lois's hand and pull her along with me. 'Come on.'

The Copter is dead above. Searchlights sweep the ground, dazzling me. We come to a confused halt, sheltering our eyes. *They're going to fire on us.*

But they don't. The Copter lands, stirring up the dead earth and pelting mud in all directions. I cough, the dust hitting the back of my throat, and step back. The co-pilot is shouting into an NPhone. Something about backup.

'Girl Clerk?' My stomach twists tight. 'If you are here, please step forward.'

Lois squeezes my hand. Whispers in my ear. 'Be strong, Carys.' The words resonate, as if I heard them before, once upon a time, from someone who loved me more than life. I blink and step forward into the blazing light, my hand shielding my eyes.

An NForce officer with an automatic weapon jumps out and ducks under the whirling blades, his narrowed eyes on me. 'Well, well. You got further than I gave you credit for, young lady. Your time is up. Ashley, are the others on their way?'

The co-pilot nods. Shouts out at him, 'Yep. Five minutes.'

The officer grabs hold of my arms and yanks them behind my back. He cuffs me. 'You're caught, Miss Clerk,' he says, his curly hair whipping wildly in the gust. 'Please step into the Copter.'

My heart sunk like heavy rock, I do as he says. Dragging my feet, I stumble into the machine and onto one of the back seats.

'Now. Three more,' shouts the co-pilot, adjusting his headset. The officer goes to the bewildered crowd and grabs three people. A mother with a sobbing child and an older man. 'Get in,' he says shortly, and they stagger over and climb through the open door.

The officer walks back to the others and stands over them, waving an automatic rifle. 'Don't even think about trying to bolt,' he says. 'We have two more Copters on their way to collect you. You should be grateful. You are being taken to the Centre Think. You'll be safe there.'

Grateful? I suppose I am grateful that my travel companions are not dead, fired upon and murdered, like the rest of the airport community. But I know what waits for us all at the Think. I can't imagine why they haven't just got it over with, here in the wilderness where no innocent Productives can witness their mass murder.

The other Copters come into view, cutting through the clear night sky and landing close to us. In no time, the others are rounded up and shoved into the two machines. I get a glimpse of Lois's wretched face as she is yanked along by a hard-faced officer, and I pray I will see her again. That I will see all of them again.

The Centre Think. The place I was so nearly murdered. Do I have to go through it all again? I sigh, exhausted. What do they have in store for me now? What will they ask of me?

All of the time, the small knot of anxiety in me is growing, expanding too quickly as I consider the carnage left behind at the ill-fated airport and what might await my friends at the Subs Community.

24

THE CENTRE

AMY

THE STREETS ARE clean and rain-washed from the big storm the previous night, when Amy gazed out at it from Lora's morning room window, awed by the power of the lightning illuminating the skies above the Centre, hoping Carys wasn't somewhere out in it, frozen and soaked.

Coran dashes into the den, his face screwed up with anxiety. 'I do wish you were staying, darlings,' he says, touching their shoulders. 'But Lora knows best, of course. And you will have your own place. Anyway, I'm to tell you that your new driver is here to take you to your new home.'

Coran leads them out of the mansion and over to a large woman leaning on an old-looking car; nothing like Lora's high-end NCV. 'Crea Driver,' she says, her voice low and strong, her jaw working chewing gum as she slumps against the bonnet. 'Here to fulfil your every wish.' She sweeps her arm towards the back of the car and Amy clambers in after Jacob. Coran throws their bags in the tiny boot and blows theatrical kisses at them.

'I'll see you soon,' he calls as Crea reverses then turns in the drive. 'Don't be strangers.'

Amy will miss Coran.

Crea is an undemanding companion. She drives competently and gets them to their new flat in just ten minutes. 'Here you are, then,' she says, and then speaks into her NPhone. 'Come down and get them.'

A couple of minutes later a short woman in a maid's uniform bustles through a door and skitters over, straightening her frilled apron. 'Mara Maid at your service,' she says, curtsying. Amy rolls her eyes at Jacob. Seriously? They get servants? She shakes her head, trying to stop the buzzing, the deep unease.

'Hey,' Jacob says.

'Nice to meet you,' Amy says.

Mara Maid crumples her brow in confusion, as if not used to being greeted, then leads them through a wide lobby and up some carpeted stairs, then through double walnut doors to their new apartment. It's nice, but not on the scale of Lora Dancer's mansion, and Amy is thankful for that. It felt too pretentious for her there. She could be happy in this place, in different circumstances. Sunlight floods through long bay windows into a small, comfortable living area, and there's a huge kitchen diner and three bedrooms. Amy swallows as she realises if Carys were still here, they'd have one each. *But she isn't.*

Jacob mooches round the place, making appreciative noises to Mara Maid who seems eager that they like it, but Amy can see he is elsewhere. With Carys. With the Subs Community. Anywhere but stuck here in this flat, trapped in this new role he doesn't want.

She stashes her few possessions in her room, a lovely space with a big soft bed and her own bathroom, but she just can't give it the appreciation it deserves. She nods and says thank you to Mara Maid, then tells her they'd like some space and they'll see her tomorrow.

'Mrs Cook'll be in later to do your dinner,' Mara says on her way out.

They hang around like spare parts, severely uncomfortable in this place of comfort. They watch the super-sized NScreen in the living room, scanning for evidence that Anson has been true to his word. There have been no more attacks on Outsiders overnight, so Amy begins to hope. She crosses her fingers. Maybe he was for real? Perhaps they really can keep them alive by taking on this job.

There are no more sightings of Carys, either. Amy's beginning to hope that she is alive and that she is free, somewhere safe and warm. Perhaps things are not as bad as they previously seemed.

Then she remembers what she and Jacob have to do, and her body twists in a great big knot.

THE NEXT COUPLE of days drag in a haze of agitation. They are fed up and bored; there is nothing to do. There are books to read, but they are all Newland books, and once you have experienced Daniel's library, Newland books pale into insignificance. They are poor imitations of the real thing, and Amy wants no part of them. She longs for the glory of the words woven by Ms Austen in *Pride and Prejudice*, and the strange depth of yearning she feels at *The Lion, The Witch and The Wardrobe*.

They are given preparation material for their first appearance on *The S Word*. Old recordings to study, page after page of Cadman's most used phrases, ways to get the audience hooked in, ways to tease the judges. They read it all through and practise on one another in dull, flattened tones. They're taken to see Cadman Showman in hospital, where he is woken from his coma but in a weakened state, yet still finds the strength to congratulate them on their new roles. 'Keep my seat warm for me, won't you,' he quips, smiling feebly. Amy plasters a fake smile on, knowing she will have to be doing that for the next weeks or even months until he is well.

That evening they are watching NBC News when their world is shattered yet again. The newsreader's voice booms, excitable and baritone: 'Early this morning, there was a raid on a suspected Outsider camp at the remains of Heathrow Airport. There was some intelligence to suggest that the wanted criminal Girl Clerk was at the hideout, but she was spotted leaving with a few others around midnight. The camp was then destroyed to ensure there is no resistance from there. The dozen or so Outsiders and Clerk were apprehended around two miles from the airport, where they were found heading north. All the prisoners are now incarcerated safely in the Centre Think where they will face charges of inciting rebellion. Commander Anson has yet to comment, but it is thought that he will announce the date of Clerk's execution in the next few days. Please stay tuned for images of the attack.'

Amy is paralysed, her fists clenched hard. She turns to Jacob. His jaw is set tight, a vein pulsing in his temple as he watches the screen. 'Carys. She's alive. But they caught her.'

'But Jacob, at least she's alive. We weren't sure if she was… that's something.'

'But they're going to murder her. In front of the nation.' Jacob's voice is flat.

Amy grabs his hand. 'But we have time! We can mount a rescue, like we did before.'

Jacob shakes his head. 'This is different. No way can we get to her this time.'

'But we can try.' They have to hold on to hope.

Jacob clenches his teeth. 'And as for that—' he points to the screen, where images of an inferno consuming ruins of an airport flicker, '—they said they wouldn't. That they would "look the other way". But they haven't. They bloody haven't.' His eyes flood with darkness. 'They attacked another camp, Amy, a camp near the Centre…' he trails off and grabs her shoulders. Looks into her eyes.

Her heart thumps hard as she realises what this means.

A camp near the Centre.

Her parents.

Carys was looking for her parents. What if she found them, and they were left in the airport when…

'They might've been with the few that were with Carys,' Jacob says, squeezing her hand. 'Try not to stress.'

But the worry is there, building up then blazing like a fire within, turning quickly to anger. Amy suddenly feels like she understands something of how Carys feels when she loses it. 'We have to get to the Subs. Now,' she cries, leaping up from the sofa. 'If they bombed one camp, they're not going to stop, Jacob. They might've kept their promise about giving Carys time and letting us see her, but they've broken the other one already. We must get up there.'

'You're right. But we need border passes, you know that. They'll be more on it than ever, and we have like no excuse to go out there.'

Amy broods on this, knowing he's right.

Then she has it. 'Coran. He'll help, I know he will, he as good as said it. We get Crea to take us over there – we're allowed to visit, after all, whoever we want to. We visit Coran and we ask him to get passes.'

Jacob looks unsure. 'We can try,' he mutters.

CREA DRIVES THEM to Lora's mansion, chewing away and humming to herself. 'I'll wait here,' she says, screeching to a halt on the driveway outside the majestic front doors. Amy walks stiffly up to the grand entrance and buzzes the NScreen, Jacob slouching after her, his head bent low. Luckily it's Coran's face she sees peering out at her, his eyes brightening and smile widening as he sees who it is.

'Darlings!' he breathes, buzzing the doors wide open and sweeping down the wide hallway towards them, his arms stretched wide. 'You're here to see Lora?'

'No,' Amy says quickly, 'it's you we want to see.'

He blushes red. 'Oh, how *wonderful*. Well, let's see, now. I'll get the maid to bring us some afternoon tea, shall I? Come in, come in.'

She nods mutely and watches him faffing around them, bossing the maid and organising the tea. He pours it out ('Shall I be mother?') and pushes slices of chocolate cake at them. Amy's not hungry, but she takes one and picks at it.

'So,' he sighs, still at last. 'Do tell me all about your new place. Is it amazing?'

'It's alright,' Jacob says, and Coran laughs, hitting Jacob on the arm playfully.

'Ooh, you're so understated. You'll be so utterly fabulous on *The S Word*. I just can't wait.'

Amy smiles politely and puts her cup down. 'Coran.'

'Yes, my love?'

'You sort of told me that you'd help me, if ever I were to need it.'

'I did? Well, yes, that is to say, I will. Of course. What can I help you with?'

'We'd really like to see our Ashton friends. Ans… the Commander… forbade us to go, but we don't see what the issue is. We'll only be gone a day. We miss them… and we have some things we'd really like with us. Things that mean a lot.'

Jacob stays silent.

Coran flutters, his eyes darting left and right. 'Oh, I… I don't know,' he says, stroking his moustache. 'I'm not supposed to do anything in opposition to what the Commander wants.'

'All I'm asking is that you get us border passes, Coran – you can do that, can't you? You're always collecting them for Lora.'

He fiddles with his cake fork. 'I can do that, yes, but if the border guards were to discover that I got two more border passes than Lora uses then there would be a problem. A serious problem.'

'Couldn't you just alter the paperwork – make it seem like there were never extra ones? Fluff it all up a bit? You are her butler, surely you can do something like that?'

'Oh, Girl P,' he says, sighing. 'You are too nice. Too sweet. How can I not? Give me a few hours, and I'll get passes for you. But then that's it, mind. I can't do anything more than that. You do understand?'

'We do,' she says softly, squeezing Coran's arm. 'Thank you. Thank you so much. This means such a lot to us, Coran. You are amazing.'

He preens. 'Well, I know *that*,' he says, flouncing from the room, cake in hand. He turns in the doorway. 'You can wait here. Lora's away tonight with the Commander. I'll be two hours max. Okay?'

'Thank you.'

Jacob raises his eyebrows at her. 'You flirt,' he says, and she laughs.

THEY WAIT IN Lora's morning room, their old den, with mounting impatience. Coran's two hours climb to three before he breezes through the door, waving something aloft. 'Success!' he yelps, dancing from one foot to another, then gathering himself and scanning the room as if someone might be spying on him. 'Here,' he says, pressing the two passes into Amy's hand. 'Now. Not a word. Yes?'

Amy squeezes Coran's hand again. 'You're a superstar.'

'You don't need to tell me that again,' he says as he leads them through to the entrance. 'Now go, and be good.'

'We will,' she says.

They descend the marble entrance steps and walk towards the car. 'I have a plan,' Jacob says. 'Just let me sort it, okay?'

'Yes boss,' she says, saluting him.

He says nothing to Crea until they're pulling up in the street outside their block of flats. Then he says to her, 'Crea, look, Girl P and I want to go explore some bits of the Centre. Maybe have dinner out somewhere. Listen, you take the night off, okay? I'm in the mood for a little drive.'

Crea turns, raises a finely arched brow. 'You can drive?' Her words drip with disdain.

'Of course I can. I drove Lora back to the Centre, remember, when we rescued her?'

'I know that,' Crea says, puffing her cheeks out. 'But do you have a licence?'

'Sure,' bluffs Jacob. 'It's back home. Look, I'll get it.'

Crea shakes her head. 'No need. I won't say no to a night in. I'll have a long soak and a glass of wine or three.'

25

CENTRE THINK

CARYS

T HE CELL IN the Centre Think is colossal. It stretches out before me, my prison for who knows how long. Until they kill me.

There are dozens of people in here. Slumped on the old wooden benches, on the stone floor, propped up against the redbrick wall, arms crossed and expressions stony. I am pushed in here along with the weeping mother and child and the older man who were in the Copter with me. The child wails, clinging to his mother, and she shushes him, stroking his hair. She sinks down onto a nearby section of bench, the boy on her lap, curled into her. Her eyes reflect fear and sorrow.

The door is flung open again and more people shoved in unceremoniously. I turn to see Lois and Alwin standing there, paralysed, their frightened eyes sweeping the murky space. 'Lois,' I cry, rushing over to her. She hugs me tight and then we break away, gazing at one another and then around at all the other inmates.

There is a sudden sound and a flickering as an NScreen lights up, covering most of one wall. The Compound Think didn't have anything like this. I seriously doubt it is for our entertainment and am rapidly proved right as the newsreader I recognise from the other night speaks slowly, her eyes serious.

I watch the news, jaded. Same old. How we were caught fleeing the wreckage of an Outsider camp, subdued by the Party in order to protect good Productives. How we will be given the chance to account for ourselves. My ears prick up as she speculates on when Commander Anson will announce the details and the date of my execution, but I stop listening when it's clear she's merely positing. I'll watch when there's something to tell.

I sit down with Lois and Alwin, exhausted and beaten. 'I'm sorry,' I whisper.

'What on earth for?' asks Lois, her brow creased. 'You have nothing to be sorry for.'

'If I hadn't lost it on that vile show, none of this would've happened.' I stare down at my feet. 'This is only happening because of me. All those people died because of me.'

'No. You came to warn us.' Lois places her hand on mine. 'Some of us listened, some of us didn't. It's not your fault that some wanted to trust Bruce. Please, Carys, you can't blame yourself for this.'

I can, and I do.

There's a shuffle on my right-hand side, then the lightest of touches. 'Carys,' a low voice says, and I whirl round.

A pale, thin face, dark eyes, straggly black hair.

Raza.

'Sorry you got caught,' she murmurs, pursing her lips.

I stare at her. 'You saved me,' I say, daring to take her hand.

She snatches it away, casting her sour gaze to the floor. 'I wanted to cause a commotion. You getting away was a side effect.'

I almost laugh. She can't admit she was helping me, even here in the darkest of places. 'I'm sorry you got caught too,' I say.

She shrugs. 'It was only yesterday. I managed to keep out of their way until then, but I kind of gave myself away. I was looking for someone, and I got clocked.' She leans forward, a knotted curtain of hair falling over her eyes.

'Did you manage to find—'

'No.'

'Oh. I'm sorry.'

'Not your fault.'

I try to draw her further into conversation. 'You were awesome with that crossbow.'

Her lips turn up in a tiny smile. 'I'm sort of okay at that kind of stuff.'

'You got him right in the shoulder.'

'I was aiming for his heart.'

'Oh.'

'Don't worry,' she says, laughing, 'joking.'

'But how did you even get in there? With a crossbow, of all things? Where even were you all that time?'

She smirks. 'Their security at that place isn't all that.'

I think about the battered old warehouse, the uninterested staff on the door. 'True. But… they do sign you in, so how…?'

'Had the crossbow buried in my backpack. They didn't even look; there were these two boys scrapping at the entrance and their Trainers going ape. Pretty lucky, I guess. I just sneaked through 'em.'

She won't say any more. She refuses to be drawn in on anything about her time in the Centre. She is so maddeningly closed. I introduce her to Lois and Alwin, who welcome her effusively. Lois tries to give her a hug, but she is rigid, her arms stiffened by her side. She turns away and sits with her head in her hands, once again blocking out the rest of the world.

JACOB

JACOB AND AMY are approaching the barriers. Amy has their border passes ready, clutched tightly in her hand. They slow as they come to the end of a queue of traffic. Ahead, the border guards are on high alert, searching every vehicle.

'I wonder what happened to the other NScreen,' muses Amy, pointing at the barrier to the right where the screen is missing, rough ends of elastic hanging loosely from seriously heavy-duty bolts. The news is projected onto the wall still but breaks up into oddly pixelated squares over the rough grey concrete.

Jacob peers more closely. Some of the bolts are bent, twisted right out of shape. 'Looks like it tore away, maybe in that storm,' he says, then swiftly forgets about it as they draw closer to the gates. He watches as the NCV in front comes to a halt and two NForce officers rummage right through, lifting up seats, checking out the trunk, peeking behind seats. Questioning the driver closely. Jacob takes a deep breath as the NCV finally moves off through the gates then inches their car up to the booth and hits the window control. The officer looks at him like he is a bit of something nasty on his shoe. He gawps at him for seconds, then a light seems to come on. 'I know you. You're that one from *The S Word*.'

'Yep.'

'Passes?'

Amy leans over and hands the passes to the guard, who scrutinises them closely. 'Hmm. Everything appears to be in order. Now, your business, please?'

'We're picking up some items from our old training house,' Jacob says, crossing his fingers. 'We're living in the Centre now.'

The officer chucks the passes at him. 'You have permission?'

Jacob motions at the passes, and it is enough. The guard inclines his chin. 'You understand that we need to do a thorough search.'

'Mmm.'

Jacob relaxes as the border guards take everything apart, looking for anything that might incriminate. They don't find a thing. The lead guard flashes him a faux smile and waves them through.

'I do hope Coran doesn't get in any trouble.' Amy frowns as she slips the passes back into her bag. 'If they check up...'

'Try not to think about it.'

'Can you switch on the radio? I want to keep up with the news.'

Shrugging, Jacob touches the NScreen and pulls Centre Radio up. He doesn't want to hear them going over and over the same thing. Them. Carys. The airport camp. The New Day Tax. The resistant few. He's heard it all too many times now, but there's nothing else to listen to, so they have it humming away in the background. His grandfather once told him that people used to listen to music on the radio for fun. Now the only tunes they hear are Newland approved classics sung by Raulf Singer and the like on the official Newland music channel. They got forced to have it on in their Ashton common room and forced to analyse it in music lessons. He tries to imagine a free world where music reflects creativity.

The newsreader's voice drones on and Amy falls asleep next to him, her head lolling to the side. Outside, the late afternoon is grey and overcast but dry, and their little red car eats up the miles without complaint. He drums his fingers on the wheel, bored by the monotony of the landscape, the endless ruins.

He straightens as a new bulletin comes in. He turns up the radio and Amy stirs, moaning. 'What is it?'

'Shh. Listen.'

'New reports are coming in of more interventions on Outsider camps,' the newsreader chants. 'After the raid on the airport camp, more intelligence was uncovered about camps scattered across the country, and this afternoon more camps were raided. Productives in Compounds can be assured that any danger from them is being minimised as we speak. The Party seeks your best, as always. I am told that it is believed that most Outsider camps are now eradicated.'

Amy sits bolt upright and turns to Jacob, eyes widened. 'No. That must mean—'

He slams the wheel. 'I know. Look, let's just get up there.'

She nods, sinking her head into her hands. Neither of them dare voice the thought. *What if?*

Twilight draws in as they come close to the eastern edge of the old Birmingham ruins, near the place they found Lora and this nightmare all started. Jacob drives the car in as far as he can, until the road is blocked by great hulks of concrete and they have no choice but to climb out and walk.

Amy stands outside the car, pointing and trembling.

In the distance, towards the northwest, the sky is orange.

'It's just the dusk,' Jacob mutters, clenching his fists.

But they know what it really is.

AMY

THE ORANGE GLOW is too bright.

They tear through the darkened ruins, terrified of what they will find at the end. The unnatural light draws them towards their old home, expanding too much as they get close. They run for thirty minutes, and by then they can see it.

The smoke.

Smouldering ruins ahead of them, ruptured ground, fissures where there weren't any two weeks ago. They leap over them, frantic now, their breath ragged. The landscape is changed. Unfamiliar. Everything has shifted.

Amy stands in a clearing between two undecipherable masses of twisted concrete. 'Where are we?'

Jacob swipes his arm over his sweating brow. 'I think the bunker is just behind that… wreckage.'

They trudge over the inhospitable ground. Rubble and ashes lie everywhere, and Amy is sickened. They pick their way through the debris around the huge pile of concrete and stop short.

Everything is utterly pulverised.

Nothing of the doorway to the bunker remains. The whole structure seems to have sunk several levels and then imploded. Smoke rises from the remains in a horrific symbol of what has happened here.

They stare at one another in sheer horror.

The sobs pound into Amy then rise from her. She sinks to the ground, her head in her hands, choking, screaming, weeping. She looks again at the altered landscape. There is nothing to be seen here of the Subversives Community or any of the people who lived here. Gone. All gone.

Jacob's eyes stream with tears. 'I'll look around,' he cries, and begins to lift sections of rubble, tossing them aside angrily, his jaw tight. Amy joins him, scrabbling through fallen rock, pawing frantically at shards of concrete, ignoring bleeding fingers, her eyes and nose running with mucus, soaking her shirt. Her heart twists as she recognises the futility of it all, and she slams a crumbling brick hard at the ground.

Dear God, she thinks, using the name in the old holy book. It seems more apt than Illumen, somehow. And that book is now ashes, somewhere far below them, torn to pieces. With all the other books in Daniel's precious library; the books that opened their eyes even more to the truth. The books that helped them learn to hope again. The pointless loss of it all is a weight in her chest that feels like it will burst her apart and shatter her body into tiny pieces.

Jacob sits back on his haunches, his eyes haunted. He rubs his hand over his filthy hair.

Neither of them knows what to say.

They extend their search, navigating their way through more rubble to where the back of the ruin that contained the stairs down to the bunker was. Nothing remains of the structure or the stairs. Only broken up hunks of brick and concrete tell them that there was something here once upon a time. Perhaps just hours ago.

Amy thinks about the children. About little Emma and Ella, so vital, so full of life and spirit. Gone. Murdered. Hannah. Esther. The children who drew them here, laughing in joy and excitement in a rainstorm, inviting them into their world of freedom and light.

And Daniel, the old custodian of the best place she ever knew, the library, the place they learned about how to be different. How to be brave. His kindly wife, Kate. Cory, the flawed but fair leader, and the Queen, so broken and so beautiful.

Gone.

Amy shivers, throwing her arms around herself. *This can't be real.* 'Are you sure this is the right place?'

Jacob closes his eyes. 'I'm sure.'

Something catches her eye. A flap of material. Something poking out between some loose rocks on the ground in front of her, something bright and vivid against the chaos. She picks her way over to it and bends down, moving the stones gently, some of them crumbling to dust in her hands. She takes hold of a corner of the material. It's just a scrap, one corner ripped away. She studies it, frowning. It's familiar.

Then she sees it. The clashing purple and orange stitching, now pulling apart in fraying strands. It's a faded, filthy sampler.

It's a cross-stitched cat.

The one Amy promised Esther she would cherish forever. Lost and abandoned here on this desolate killing ground. She brings the sampler to her chest, swallowing hard over an unyielding lump in her throat. *Esther.*

'What's that?' Jacob scrambles over to her, raising his eyebrows. She shows him, and he lifts his shoulders in a question. 'It's that present Esther gave me.' She tells him about the promise. *I didn't keep it with me. I let her down.*

'You can keep it now,' he says softly, crouching down and placing his arm around her quivering shoulder. 'Keep it to remember her.'

Amy searches his eyes and finds them as lost as hers. Burying the sampler deep in her pocket, she gets to her feet. 'What shall we do now?'

'We haven't finished looking. We should expand out more.'

She says nothing and follows Jacob as he continues the fruitless digging. They make a rough circle with their search, enlarging it slowly, stepping over deep crevices and avoiding unsteady structures. All the time, the smoke rises around them and small fires burn, crackling, mocking their pitiful efforts.

Then she hears the sound.

A moaning, a weak wail, coming from her right, not far away. Beyond the circle of rubble they have covered. She looks at Jacob and whirls around, making her way as quickly as she can towards the sound. 'Hello?' Jacob shouts, cupping his hands around his mouth. 'Is someone there?'

The moaning is unearthly but undoubtedly there. They stop, listening. 'It's over there,' Amy says, changing direction slightly and traversing the broken land over to another larger pile of wreckage.

A thin voice. 'Help me.'

She casts some rock aside and sees him.

Cory.

He's in a bad way. His face looks beaten up, dried blood congealing at his temples, swollen bruises around his eyes and his mouth. His brown hair is matted with dust and debris. He lies half-trapped under a heavy boulder, his legs out of sight. He barely stirs when he sees them, but his eyes light up. 'Amy?'

'Cory.' She hunkers down, tearing rocks and stones off him. She can't shift the boulder. Jacob heaves at it, clenching his teeth together. He roars and it budges minutely, but not enough. They haul at it together, putting everything into it, but it's not moving. They sink down, spent.

'D… don't try,' Cory says, his voice feeble. 'There isn't long.'

Amy strokes his matted hair from his brow. 'Don't talk. We're going to get you out of this.'

'No.'

'We are,' Jacob says, his jaw clenched. 'Just give me time.'

'No. Wait.' Cory places a quaking hand on Jacob's arm. 'You have to find her.'

'Find who?' Amy says, staring around at the destruction.

'The Queen. Reia.'

Amy never knew her name.

'I'm so sorry,' Jacob says. 'I don't think anyone—'

'She was with me. We were out here, looking for the twins…'

'The twins?' Amy says stupidly.

'Yes. And Hannah and Esther. They were out on one of their… evening walks. Out to the stables, they headed.' He smiles slightly at this, and she remembers how the twins don't always play by the rules. They like to do what they like doing, and drag the other kids into their schemes. 'They'd not come back for supper.'

'They're out here… somewhere?' Jacob says, getting up and shielding his eyes as he gazes around.

'Yes. And Reia. We were… thrown.'

'We will find them.' Hope infuses Amy as she squeezes his filthy hand.

Cory nods and sinks his head back to the ground. 'Please… keep them safe.'

'We will. And you, too.'

Cory gazes at her, his hazel-coloured eyes soft with pain and sorrow. He shudders, his chest moving too rapidly, up and down, up and down. 'Breathe,' she says. He tries to.

Jacob crouches back down with them and takes Cory's other hand.

'Your story inspired me. You were very brave,' Amy whispers.

Jacob says, 'You gave Carys new life, you know. You gave her a reason. She wasn't the same, after hearing what you said. She felt like she was loved. When you said about her father—'

Cory closes his eyes. His lips part slightly and he breathes, 'Thank you.'

And then he stops breathing.

The sobs rise again, and Amy places Cory's hand on his heart. Jacob gently crosses Cory's other hand over it.

Any wants to bury him. But she can't. He is trapped.

Instead, she places a cross of rough pebbles on his crossed hands, just like the cross of twigs they left on Sim and Aiden, and she whispers words over him, and the sky beyond the smoke is singing with sunset glory. Jacob bows his head with her, and for seconds they stand there.

'We honour you,' Amy whispers.

Jacob echoes, 'We honour you.'

After that, they scramble up over rocks and rubble. They have a mission.

26

CENTRE THINK

CARYS

RAZA'S SCREAM ECHOES through the dimly lit cell, and everyone jumps, jolted from our brooding.

'What?' I rush over to her. She has her hands clamped over her ears and she is sobbing, great liquid tears forming at the corners of her eyes and spilling over, tracks of days-old mascara etched onto her cheeks. She doesn't see me. She holds herself rigid, crying, her eyes pinned on the NScreen.

Slowly, I turn. Focus. I've been ignoring the news since I got here; I just don't want to know. As I turn, my insides twist in a great dance of dread. I know what I'll see before I see it.

I watch in horrified fascination as the images roll over the screen. Images that recall the devastation at the airport and back at the school and the old ruins I hid among. But this time, it's personal, because they are images of a place I called home. Only for months, but it was more of a home than Ashton ever was.

There is no trace of it left. Elva Anchor relays the bulletin with a note of triumph: 'The camp at the ruined city of Birmingham is one of the last major Outsider camps to be subdued. The Party can assure you, good Productives of Newland, that you are safer now than you have ever been from Unproductive Outsiders. Commander Anson himself has issued a statement that he personally ensures that all interventions were necessary to our ongoing freedom and growth as a nation, and that every last one was undertaken with thought for those involved.'

Raza shrieks at the screen, her dark eyes wild with hate. 'You LIARS. You *bloody* MURDERERS.' She spits vitriol, her language worsening as she works herself up. I lay my hand on her arm, and she gazes at me, then her eyes fill again and she falls against me, weeping into my chest. We sink to the ground together, united in horror and grief, and weep for our lost people.

Raza, more than I, has reason to grieve. She lived with the Subs Community for over a year, and although she was known as the prickly one, I know she loved the people there fiercely. She was always protective of the children, concerned about their safety, standing up for them in any kind of altercation. Emma and Ella were her particular favourites. It's like she poured all the love she had for her lost baby daughter Carys into them. I watch her as she rocks back and forth, holding her stomach, wailing like a wounded animal. I stroke her back, my tears soaking her top.

Lois crouches down with us. She says nothing, but she sits with us, stays with us in our darkness.

Raza heaves herself up and over to the bucket in the corner and vomits heavily, purging herself then rubbing her wet sleeve over her mouth. 'The little ones,' she croaks. She slumps on a bench and sinks her head into her hands.

I watch the screen a while more, unable to tear myself away from the unwanted images, the self-satisfied commentary, the sheer hopelessness of it all. I let myself be cradled by Lois, the reality hitting me and overwhelming me. I have the urge to spread myself out on the floor and never get up again.

I did this.

This is my fault.

The cell fades to silence as people take in the events unravelling on the screen and among us. Everyone here has been touched by something of this. I sense a disquiet in the air; a determination that things will change. I wonder briefly if everyone here knows they are going to be drugged and then disposed of somewhere in the bowels of this building. I must tell them, I say to myself, but for now I have no energy.

'It's all my fault.'

Raza whips her head round. 'It's not always all about you, Carys, you know.'

'I didn't say that. I just… if I hadn't said what I said.'

She gets up. Stands over me, her feet planted wide, her bony arms crossed. Her face is whiter than white. 'Did you order the NForce to drop bombs?'

'No—'

'Did you drop the bombs?'

'No.'

'Did you murder those people?'

'No, but—'

'But nothing. You're being a bloody idiot, Carys. You said some stuff. Big deal. That doesn't make you a mass murderer. You didn't do this. *They* did.' She spits the last words.

I gape up at her.

'Stop moping around pretending it's all down to you. You're such a drama queen.'

I almost laugh.

'If you use your anger and grief against them, instead of against yourself, it could be a lot more… productive.'

This time, we both smile, and the tension is broken.

'I just feel so helpless,' I say.

'Yeah, well. We all do. But there's nothing we can do right now. We'll get our chance, I know it. There's no way they're getting away with this. No way.'

'So says Raza,' I say, smiling through my tears.

'So says Raza.'

For the first time, the tension that has always been strung between us like a taut wire is slackened, and I wonder if we might be friends in a different life.

It doesn't hit me until later, and then it slams into me with a force that steals my breath.

I never got to tell Cory that I forgive him.

Jacob

Jacob stands in the middle of the burned-out ruins of ruins and scouts the area, scanning each tiny nook, each crevice, each mass of twisted steel or lump of concrete. They start walking the ground, back and forth, checking, checking again. Cory's words echo in his mind. *Find her.* The Queen, Reia, is out here, and somewhere some of the kids might be too. He closes his eyes against the pounding of his head for a few moments.

He throws a glance over his shoulder at the body that was Cory and thinks about his enthusiasm for the tech he helped him get up and running, how he was like a kid when they got the radio going. He was a good guy, and he didn't deserve to die like that. Rage bites at him and spreads like a fire.

Amy is broken. He looks at her ravaged face and sees a frightened girl who feels alone. He thinks of Carys; if she sees this news she'll be wrecked. She'll blame herself, too, and he's not there to tell her it's okay. To tell her he still loves her, more than ever.

He kicks at a stone, and Amy startles. 'What is it?'

'Nothing. I just… where do we go from here?'

'We keep searching.'

'No. I know. Not that. I mean after… do we still go along with their scheme?'

'Why should we?'

'Because of Carys.'

'Do you really think it will make any difference? They've hardly shown themselves to be honourable to their word, have they?'

'No.' He scuffs at some loose pebbles.

They branch out further, leaving the worst of the smoke behind as the night drapes over them, but the acrid smell lingers in Jacob's nostrils, making his eyes water.

Sobbing. He can hear sobbing. It's coming from way over to their left. 'There,' he says, grabbing Amy's arm and starting for the source. The sobbing gets louder.

A child's voice.

'Emma? Ella?' Amy stumbles forwards, shoving at protruding stone and kicking stuff out of her path. 'Are you there?'

In a hollow behind a more complete building left unhurt by the recent attack, they find them. They're all huddled up against each other, crouched in the rubble, all five of them.

Emma. Ella. Esther. Hannah. Reia.

They spot Jacob and Amy and their eyes get huge. 'Jacob? Is that you?' 'Amy?'

Amy launches herself at them. Falls into them, crying her eyes out. They cling to her like she's the last person on Earth. She could well be, as far as they know. One of the twins breaks free and grabs Jacob's hand, her face split in this huge grin, incongruous in the circumstances. He laughs and swings her up and round, and then she's giggling and asking for more, and Esther is jumping up at him. 'My turn! My turn!' All this time the Queen stares at him with eyes darker than ever.

Amy takes her hand. 'Reia,' she whispers, and the Queen's head whips round.

'How do you know?'

'Cory told us. He told us to look for you, before he…'

Reia goes deadly silent.

'I'm sorry. We got to him, just before… we were with him.'

A pause. 'Then he had a good death.'

'What happened to you all?' Jacob asks.

'The girls here were on one of their little adventures.' Her lips curve slightly. 'Cory and I were in the mood for an evening stroll, and when they didn't come in for supper, we took the chance. We were out here, looking for them, when it happened.' Her face falls into shadow, and she drops her shaven head in her hands.

'No one stood a chance. It was mayhem – one minute we were on solid ground, having a pleasant stroll, the next we were ripped from one another. Cory was thrown right away, and I fell down this crevice that wasn't there before… I managed to haul myself out, but the ground was rocking and there were more forming. I kept calling for Cory, b… but he didn't answer.' Her mouth wobbles. 'It was a nightmare. Everything around just burst into flames and exploded into a million pieces in front of my eyes. It was then that I heard this lot, screaming. They saw it all from over here. After things started to calm down, we looked for Cory, but we never found him.'

Her eyes fill with tears.

'He's much closer to the bunker,' Jacob says. 'He was mostly hidden. You wouldn't've found him from over here.'

'And now he's gone.'

'I'm sorry.'

'I'm glad you were with him. I'm glad you came.'

One of the twins pipes up, 'Why did you go? Where did you go?' And the other, 'Where's Carys?' Hannah and Esther crowd around him, pulling at his hands.

Esther stares up at him. 'Did you find my mummy?'

Jacob's heart breaks as he shakes his head slowly. He lifts her into his arms. 'Come on,' he says, 'let's sit a while, and we'll tell you what we've been up to.'

27

THE RUINS

'WHERE ARE YOU going now?' Reia asks when they come to the end of their account. She's shocked by it but ever pragmatic.

Jacob shrugs. 'We'll have to go back to the Centre. If we can give Carys any chance at all, then we have to do it.' He looks at Amy, imploring.

'I think you're right. I can't see how we can do anything else – because if we just disappear now, they might kill her. I wouldn't put anything past them.'

'Yeah. They might do it anyway, but we can try. Besides, Raulf said they'd let us see her, and that's something. I want to tell her that I'm sorry.'

Reia nods. 'You must do what you think best.'

'But what about you five?' Amy says. 'We could try and smuggle you in—'

'No. Absolutely not. We will find a way, somehow. Join up with others.'

Amy looks at Jacob. *If there are others left to join.*

Reia continues, 'It would be too risky for us, in the Centre, and for you – if they found us with you – it would undo all the work you have done to be accepted. You could use this position for the good, you do know that? You could go along with their sham, while all the time making plans and whipping up support to stop this… this *genocide*… in its tracks.'

Amy mudges on her words for a while.

Then she has an idea. 'I might know somewhere.'

Jacob quirks his eyebrows at her.

'It won't be simple, but if they're still intact, they might help, if we approach in the right way.'

'Wait a minute, you don't mean that psycho guy who tried to kill us?' Jacob says.

'He didn't want to… he stopped, in the end, didn't he? He was doing what his parents asked. And it was through fear. They thought we were Productive spies.'

'As if that's an excuse.'

'I know. I know. But I got a feeling about the boy – Will. He's okay, Jacob.'

Jacob frowns. 'I don't know.'

'Look. This lot need shelter. Food. At least for a time, if not for the long term.'

Reia touches her hand. 'Are you referring to Stephen and Sarah's place?'

'That's it. I know they keep themselves to themselves, and that's why I wonder if they haven't been targeted. The Party may have no idea.'

'You may be right. You can lead us there?'

'I think so…' Amy casts her mind back to the long trek in the burning sun only a few months back, from the ruins of the crypt where Aiden died to the road where Carys collapsed with dehydration, then to the hut they were kept in and given life-giving food and water, and then Will leading them back to the ruins with the horses, Shadow and Rainbow.

Shadow and Rainbow. 'The stables!' she says. 'Are they…?' She gazes off in the direction of the stables and sees no tell-tale red haze. 'The horses.'

Hannah grabs her hand. 'We have to go and get them!'

'Then we should go.' Reia beckons to the children, who follow her readily. Her face softens at the sight of them, and she takes Esther's hand and Ella's hand, the others hanging onto her arms, then sings softly to them as they walk.

Reia and her lost children.

THE HORSES ARE skittish, tossing their heads and whinnying in their stalls. Very much alive. Shadow, Rainbow, and several other horses. Hannah runs to them, whispering and stroking, and they respond to her quickly, nuzzling her hands. 'Saddle them up,' Reia says. 'We can ride them. The girls are so exhausted anyway…'

After preparing the horses, they make their way out of the stable yard with Jacob on Shadow with Emma, Amy on Rainbow with Esther, Reia on a dark brown mare with Ella, and Hannah, who sorted out most of the preparation with very little fuss, at the rear on a grey. They have secured the other horses together and Hannah holds their reins lightly. 'Come on, my beauties,' she says, and they follow her without question.

Jacob scouts the horizon, getting his bearings. 'It's over to the west,' he says, pointing, and Amy nods. If they can find their way through this part of the city, they might see some familiar landmarks that will help them find Will's place. She'll worry about their reception there later.

The night chills as they leave the remains of the blasts behind them. Amy doesn't look back.

It turns out that Shadow and Rainbow are their leaders, instinctively finding their way home. The weary group ride for hours through the still darkness, spurred on by ruins they vaguely recognise. It's a long slog, and they arrive at the outskirts of the city as the dawn breaks and coral chases indigo through the wakening sky. Amy remembers this road: how Will and his brother, Matt, found them here and took it in turns to carry a passed-out Carys to their tiny hamlet. How they were kind.

The settlement is still there. Still intact. No one found them.

The camp is silent in the early morning light, the homes slumbering. A few inquisitive horses greet them, poking their heads out of their stalls as they arrive at the stables and dismount. Their own horses lower their heads, fatigue written across them in the tremble of their legs and their snorted relief at finally arriving. 'What should we do with them?' Reia says.

Hannah gently strokes her grey. 'Leave them to rest a while. Tie them up here for now; they'll be fine.' She fetches a large pail of water and puts it on the ground for the horses to drink, then she whispers to them, stroking their noses and laying her head against them.

'Come on,' Amy says.

'How are we going to do this?' Jacob says softly, glancing around.

'I'm not sure. I think we wait now. Wait for them to wake up and go about their day. We don't want to seem a threat – perhaps if they see us here with the girls, we'll be okay.'

Jacob frowns. 'It's possible. It's also possible that psycho will be out with his crossbow and do away with the lot of us before the cock crows.'

'Hmm.'

Reia sinks to the ground in the centre of the settlement, the girls following, exhaustion etched through their features. They stretch themselves out on the hay-strewn floor, their heads on Reia's lap, and close their eyes.

'You sit,' Jacob says, motioning to the ground. 'I'll keep watch.' He mooches round the place, his arms crossed and his brow creased. Amy is worried, too, but it seemed like a good solution. Back at the bunker site, anyway.

Eventually, the camp wakes and life returns. Curtains are thrown back in the nearby windows and it's not long before faces are peering out at them, shielding their eyes from the early sun. Children see them then run from their windows as if to go and tell their grown-ups. *Not long now.*

They all come together, marching from one of the cottages. Stephen, Sarah, Matt, Will. Stephen holds an old-fashioned rifle and Will has a crossbow, but his arms tremble at the sight of her. 'A… Amy?'

'Wait.' Jacob lifts his palms slowly. 'Please hear us out. We desperately need your help.'

Stephen and Sarah glare at Will. *They don't know?*

Will stares at his feet, dropping the crossbow. It's then he appears to make some kind of resolve. His chin juts out, his eyes pinned on his father. 'It was wrong. What you asked of me. They were never going to hurt us.'

His father is lost for words. Perhaps Will never challenged him before.

Amy scrambles to her feet and walks over to them slowly. 'You need to know that the large camp over to the other side of this old city has been destroyed. Yesterday, by Productives. And that all over the country it's the same story. They are trying to rid the nation of Outsiders. We came to you for a couple of reasons; one, to warn you, and two, because we thought you might offer shelter to these refugees who escaped death—' she lowers her voice, '—but watched their loved ones die horribly.' It comes tumbling from her in a rush, and the faces filled with suspicion turn to horror and then something like pity.

The woman, Sarah, lays her hand on Stephen's arm. 'Do we really have to go along with more killing?' she pleads, gazing into his narrowed blue eyes. He shrugs her off.

Matt, the other son, the tall one, wanders over to Reia and the girls. He crouches down with them and the girls cower away, but he touches their shoulders lightly. 'I'm so sorry for what happened,' he says.

Will looks into Amy's eyes, and something passes through her. A shiver. 'I'm so sorry I tried to…' he trails off.

'I'm sorry too. About leaving you there. I hope you were okay.'

'I was fine. I just broke a little bit there. I'm fine now.'

'I'm glad.'

Stephen steps in now, hostility still radiating from him. 'And the horses you stole?' He stands tall over Amy, glaring down at her.

Amy feels her shoulders sagging in relief. 'Have a look in the stables. You might find more than you bargained for.' Sarah's face lights up, her eyes brimming with tears. *She loved those horses.* For seconds, Amy is filled with guilt. 'Shadow and Rainbow are very well. They have been loved.' She winks at Hannah.

After a mass trek to the stables and gasps of delight from the community, with Sarah insisting on feeding all the new horses and making a great big fuss of Shadow and Rainbow, and some chat about how the new horses will be housed and fed, Matt and Will lead them to a nearby large shed that turns out to be a sort of mess room. People bustle about making breakfast; they are extra guests. Everyone is surprised and some are obviously suspicious, but their story spreads quickly and hostility turns to welcome, in most cases. Stephen keeps his distance, his jaw locked tight.

'Don't worry about him,' Will whispers to Amy as they eat. 'He'll come round. Things have to change round here, and you were the catalyst. We can't just live our lives killing off folk we are suspicious of. No one wanted that, really. I'm glad you're here, and… and I really am sorry. I was weak. I felt so bad about it for months, still do. I always had this sort of half dream, half hope, that I'd see you again. That I could say sorry.'

He looks into her eyes, and she returns his steady gaze.

'I'm glad to see you. We were so angry at you, but you know… one thing I've come to realise, is that we're all flawed. We all make mistakes. Okay, yours was a pretty bad one, in the scheme of it all, but I forgive you.'

'You do?'

'Well...' she laughs, and he bats at her, the tension broken.

'Tell me more about you,' he says, and she settles in to tell her story yet again.

'WE HAVE TO GO,' Jacob says after an hour or so of rest. 'If we don't get back, suspicions will be raised and all could be lost. We've got a hell of a walk ahead, Amy.'

Matt chimes in. 'I can help with that. Will and I will take you with some of the horses.'

Amy exhales. 'That would be brilliant.'

They look round for Reia and the girls, who have been taken elsewhere. Sarah tells them that they are sleeping in one of the cottages. She also says that they are welcome here and will be treated as part of the community. That they are grateful they came, and they have no need to fear. They will come to no harm.

Jacob says, 'You may need to be prepared to move on. Because of the attacks.'

'Surely if they haven't got us yet, they don't know about us?' Sarah's forehead is deeply furrowed.

'Perhaps. But we wanted you to be warned, anyway – maybe at least to prepare.'

'We will. Thank you.'

Amy remembers something. 'The bunker had a farm out on the edges. There are animals – chickens, cows, sheep, pigs – I don't think they bombed out there. Do you think you could send a team out there soon to round them up?'

Sarah smiles. 'Of course. I will lead it myself, with the help of your refugees. We will welcome new livestock round here and care for them well.'

Matt and Will lead them back round to the stables and saddle up four of their horses, all of whom seem ready and eager to go for a long day's trot through the ruins. Stephen follows, and the air seems colder. 'I'm not happy about this,' he begins. 'But it seems my family and community have decided that these strangers should be welcomed. And I suppose that's good enough for me.' His tone is gruff but begrudging. 'Just don't bring anyone else.'

'We have no intention of that,' Amy says.

Jacob leans on the doorpost, looking closely at Stephen. He crosses his arms. 'But… there is a possibility we might be asking for help, somewhere in the future – perhaps quite soon. Things have been left too long. Would you be in?'

Matt and Will look at each other and nod slowly, but Stephen holds them at a distance, standing away from them and stroking his beard. 'I don't want you back here.'

'But we do,' Will says, hardly daring to look at his father. 'I don't want a part of the bad stuff anymore, dad. We could do some good.'

Matt nods. 'I'm with him.'

Stephen grunts and turns away, then walks off, dragging his feet.

'Don't mind him,' Will says.

Mounted on the horses, they take one last glance back at the tiny village of Outsiders, wishing their best to Queen Reia and the girls, and trot off up the road back to the silent city.

28

THE CENTRE

Jacob

It's time Anson lives up to his promise to Jacob and Amy to see Carys in the Centre Think, so Jacob summons Crea.

Will and Matt and their horses made easy work of getting them through the old city, and Amy's awesome sense of direction led them right back to the little red car. They were back in time for dinner, prepared by a tetchy Mrs Cook, who muttered about how they didn't show up for the supper she so lovingly prepared the previous evening or breakfast and lunch today. 'These ungrateful kids today. No manners.'

Crea turns up quickly and hustles them to the car, which they made sure to charge when they arrived back at the flat. 'Where to?'

'The Centre Think, please, Crea.'

She screws up her face. 'Why'd you want to go there?'

They don't reply, and she shrugs her shoulders and starts the car, and soon they're crawling through the streets of the Centre. Jacob can't help comparing these sanitised, well-cared-for streets with the ruins they rode through yesterday, the forgotten ghosts of the past hidden away under the confident smiles and well-spun rhetoric of the New Day Party. He scrunches his nose in disgust.

When they arrive at the Think, they're met with a less than warm welcome. The Productive on the reception desk glances up from tending to her perfect nails, clocks them waiting there, and sighs, puffing out her cheeks. 'Yes?'

'We're here to see Girl Clerk.' Jacob says it with fake confidence, like they have an appointment with a VIP.

She purses her glossed lips at him. 'Who?'

'Girl Clerk. She's in… the Think.'

The girl's mouth turns downward in a visible sneer. 'You can't visit Think inmates.'

Amy pipes up, 'Raulf Singer said he would arrange for permission for us to visit her.'

The girl's eyes widen, and she pauses in her filing, her hands halted in midair. 'Raulf Singer?'

'Yes. He was getting permission from the Commander.'

She stares at them, and her face cracks into a snide grin. 'Yeah. Right. Good one,' she says, going back to her nails.

Jacob goes closer to the desk. Leans over it, placing both hands palm down on the laminate surface. 'Look, um…'

'Aida Admin.'

'Aida. We were guaranteed that we would have access to her. Please can you contact your manager?'

Aida glares at him for a second then shrugs her shoulders and slams her file down. Muttering, she grabs the phone next to her NCom.

They wait as she grumbles into the phone about some kids who are demanding to see a Think inmate. Yes, she knows that's forbidden, and she's told them, but they are spinning some story about Raulf Singer and Commander Anson. Yes, she knows, it's completely ludicrous, but they're insisting on seeing the manager, so he'd better get down here and get rid of them. No, she's not making it up to get back at him for that extra load of NSheets inputting he sprung on her the other day. Yes, please, she really does need him.

Finally, she slams the phone down, brow creased in annoyance. 'He's on his way,' she huffs, and picks up the nail file again. The scraping of the file is maddening in the silence of the echoing reception hall, and Jacob waits in increasing frustration.

A short, round guy comes puffing up the corridor towards them, shoving through the double doors and glaring at them then at Aida. He clutches an NSlate and wears a headset and is evidently a busy man. He's not impressed by their tale either. 'I've heard nothing of this,' he says, scrolling through his NSlate. 'Nope. Nothing on the system. You're having a laugh.'

Jacob's getting seriously wound up. 'No. We were told that we would have permission from the Commander to see Girl Clerk. Can't you ring the Commander's PA? Or just ring Lora Dancer's assistant. He'll tell you.'

The man stares at them with piggy eyes. 'I don't think so. If you can bring me a document signed by the Commander that gives you permission, then I'd consider it. Without that, you've no chance. Now. I'm very busy. Please leave.'

With that, he turns on his heel and storms back through the doors, leaving them swinging in his wake. The girl at the desk snickers at them. 'You heard the man.'

JACOB CALLS CORAN when they get back to the flat. He's delighted to hear from them, of course, and waxes lyrical about how pleased he is that they decided to come back and not abuse the favour he'd done for them. But he's terribly saddened to hear that they haven't been able to see Girl C. Leave it to him. He'll sort it out for them.

CORAN CALLS THEM back after a couple of hours, and his tone is all sheepish; he keeps clearing his throat. He's sorry, but he thinks they got the wrong end of the stick. Raulf tells him that he never promised they could actually visit Girl C, just that they'd have more chance to see her, on NBC and the like, for a longer time, if they chose to accept the Commander's kind offer. 'He said that no Think inmates have ever been granted visitors, and he is not able to make an exception, particularly as the Think is rather crowded at the moment because of the unrest. You understand, darling?'

Jacob doesn't.

He slams the phone down and growls at Amy, who is hovering over him. 'Look. I'm just so hacked off,' he says in apology. 'They've gone back on their word yet again. How are we supposed to believe that they are going to grant her more time? For all we know, she's dead already. They don't hold people in the Think for long. We know that. What if…?' He hurls the NPhone at the wall and sinks to the floor in deep misery.

AMY

JACOB IS DESPONDENT, like he's completely given up. Amy tries to encourage him to keep going. To keep trying.

'What's the point?' he says. 'They're going to do what they want to do.'

'So it's up to us to get her out of there, and to do all that we can in our power to make a difference here.'

'So you're saying we just carry on with this? We go on *The S Word*, plaster on fake smiles and pretend we're, like, stoked to be there? Then we play a part in sending someone to die? Yeah, Amy. Good plan.' He storms out of the room, slamming the door behind him.

He's too shut down to talk to. So Amy dreams plans by herself, plotting to bring the Party down single-handed, to save Carys, to find her parents and to make it all better. *Are you kidding yourself?*

She thinks about the Subversives Community, and the tears spring to her eyes as she pictures the desecrated bunker. She fiddles with the little cross-stitch, allowing hot anger to work its way into her system yet again, allowing it to urge her on. To keep going. Because she will not give up now.

Never.

ᴊACOB

THE FOLLOWING MORNING, Jacob's in the kitchen buttering toast when Amy comes in. She looks at him uncertainly, and he smiles at her.

'You seem a bit better this morning,' she says, grabbing a slice from him.

He shrugs. 'Yeah. Listen. Sorry.'

'You had a right to be angry.'

'I know.' He stares at her, then out of the window at the sun-drenched morning. 'But it's like something shifted overnight. I feel strong again, Amy. Ready. We're going to fight this, and we're not going to stop till we're done.'

Amy turns her face to him and smiles, her face, so wan these past few days, lighting up. 'I'm in.'

'I'm in.' They bump fists.

To JACOB'S SURPRISE and disgust, they are featured on the morning news. 'Girl Plumber and Boy Trader are perhaps somewhat infamous but are to be the interim presenters of *The S Word*. Cadman Showman, recovering in the Commander Lucan Hospital, is delighted with the choice, which Commander Anson himself made. Cadman said on a press release last night that he "can't think of anyone more suited to the task", and he knows that Plumber and

Trader will do him proud. The two trainees showed their firm appreciation and support for Newland and our Commander when they stood solidly against their ex-friend Clerk—'

'Ex-friend?' Jacob snarls.

'—and then confirmed to their host, Lora Dancer, whom they rescued from a serious assault on the Outside, that they were determined to stop the spread of Clerk's pernicious lies and to uphold the values of our great society. The Commander himself will endorse the two via live link on the show this coming Saturday.'

'Ugh,' Amy huffs.

Jacob flicks the NScreen off. 'It's all on, then.'

'Yep.'

'Are you ready?'

'No.'

'But ready to fight.'

'And never stop.'

'Never.'

29

CENTRE THINK

CARYS

'Y ou're going to really love *The S Word* tonight.'

The guard struts into the cell and right over to me. I'm sitting with Raza, Alwin and Lois, and we're talking about how we can get out of here.

'I doubt that,' I say, scrunching up my nose.

The guard laughs harshly. 'Well, whether you think you will or not, you'll be watching it, here in glorious HD, courtesy of the Party. Whoever said we don't treat our Think guests well?'

Raza rolls her eyes.

Over the last days, the cell has been filling up. Occasionally, a guard and a nurse come in and march one or two prisoners away, telling us all that they are to be released. I know exactly where they are going. I live in cold dread of the day they take Raza, or Lois, or Alwin, or me. Yesterday, they took the man from the airport community who came with me in the Copter, and I was sick. But they can't keep up. Too many people are being arrested. I shake my head, reflecting again on how my appearance on *The S Word* has led to all this. People are rising up, unhappy with the state of things. People are resisting, marching against Anson and the Party.

The cell is crowded. It stinks, because the toilet facilities are meagre even for its usual number of temporary residents. Sanitary conditions are poor. Before we're executed, we might all die of some disease spread through us because of the filth. But I'm heartened, too. The people who come in here are riled up. Ready to hear my story.

And I tell it to everyone who wants to hear. I spread it around, not leaving any detail out, hyping things up and stirring them further. Some of them resist. They don't want to know, or they simply don't believe me. That can't be the case, they say, eyes widened in horror. You're making it up to get attention.

Most of them know I'm telling the truth, and the wind of turbulence is growing in here, blowing through the stagnant corners and whipping us into action. We have nowhere to take our determination, but it grows among us anyway like a flood, the waters rising with each new inmate.

That evening, I sigh at the thought of being forced to sit through yet another *S Word*, and slump down on the bench with Raza, my chin propped on my hands, elbows on knees. The familiar theme music starts up, and I swear the Think staff have upped the volume to a stupid level. Everyone groans as the screen lights and we have no place to hide.

I sink my head into my hands, unable to watch. I don't know who is presenting it, and I don't care. I don't want to see the judges again, and I definitely don't want to see some poor Productive booed away for daring to be ill then sent to be murdered.

Someone is shaking my shoulder. Raza.

'What?' I snarl, irritated.

'You have to see this.'

'Why?' I lift my head from my hands and watch the screen, but I can't take in what I see. Can't make sense of it. My head is spinning, and waves of panic and incomprehension hit me. Pound me. 'W… what?'

It's Jacob and Amy.

On the stage at *The S Word,* all dressed up and grinning from ear to ear like they're loving every minute.

'What the hell are they doing there?'

Raza shrugs.

They strut forward like they own the place, and Jacob spreads his hands, his smile wide, his teeth bright white under the studio lights. The crowd are lapping him up, screaming his name, stamping their feet. He laughs.

'Welcome to *The S Word!* My name is Boy Trader—'

'Boy T! Boy T!'

'—and I'm here with Girl Plumber, as your new presenters!'

The crowd go wild, and I go static. Frozen. *What?*

'Yes, that's right! We're here to help out Cadman while he is recovering in hospital, and we're thrilled to be here with you tonight.'

Amy steps forward. She lays her hand on her heart. 'Yes, as Boy T says, we couldn't be more delighted to be your hosts here on *The S Word.* We can't wait to share this experience with you all—' she sweeps her arms wide, taking in the shrieking audience, '—and with the entire nation! We can't wait to get started.'

I sit stock-still as this nightmare plays out in front of me.

Hypocrites.

A voice booms over the crowd. 'Before we start, and welcome our four judges, we have a very special guest with a very special message. Ladies and Gentlemen, please welcome, speaking to you live from Party HQ, Commander Anson!'

This time, the crowd are hushed as they cross their arms over their bellies and bow. I can picture the Trainers in the audience, fiercely watching over their charges and bashing any who resist into submission.

Anson's grinning face appears on the screen, and we all shrink back. Disgust thumps my stomach as I remember his face leering over mine. 'I'm so pleased to see how happy you are,' he says, and the audience are free. They respond to him with warmth and applause. 'This was my dearest wish, when poor Cadman was so wantonly and unfairly injured—' Raza spits, '—that these two… great examples of our country should take his place, temporarily, of course. I am here to endorse them tonight for you. To start this new season off with a bang, as it were. I can promise you they will be a treat. And I hope you can appreciate that I am not the monster I have been made out to be. You can see that I am tolerant of other… *kinds*. Newland is not a prejudiced nation. We are here to embrace every single person who works hard and gets on to their best ability. Boy T and Girl P are shining examples for us.'

He pauses. I realise that I have been biting down on my lip so hard that my mouth is running with blood. My fists are clenched so tight they are numb. I glance at Raza, who looks equally gobsmacked. 'I can't believe this,' I whisper, and she shakes her head.

Anson temples his hands and continues. 'I thought that this would be a good opportunity to make a special announcement.'

The crowd quieten and sit on the edge of their seats.

'As you know, there is a directive that Girl Clerk be executed.'

Fear pounds my chest like a rushing waterfall.

'We at Party HQ feel that it would be for the very best of Newland if she were to undergo a public execution. We can make it into an occasion for Newland, a day to remember where we celebrate all that we are, and to re-iterate that we do not accept the spread of evil lies. Therefore, I proclaim tonight that Clerk will be executed by lethal injection in the Commander Lucan Arena on December fifth. At our Midwinter Festival. Exactly two months from today.'

A hush spreads through the studio and through our cell.

I look at Raza. At Lois. Their faces drained of colour, their hands thrown over their mouths.

I am numb.

On the screen, Anson relaxes back in his chair, a self-satisfied grin spread over his face. The camera pans round to Jacob and Amy, whose fixed smiles are slipping. I watch closely.

Amy collects herself first, but all the make-up and the lighting in the world can't hide the blanch of her cheeks. She clears her throat. 'Right, so, thank you to Commander Anson!' She motions to the screen, then waits for the audience to respond.

But they don't.

Silence drapes the auditorium.

Anson sneers on the screen.

Jacob's face seems paralysed, his jaw slack.

Amy stands awkwardly, twisting her hands, then appears to stand to attention, staring above her at the autocues. She brings her hands to her sides and inhales audibly. 'It's that time in the show when we welcome our amazing judges! Please welcome Raulf, Lora, Edwin and Portia!'

This time, the crowd respond as the screen fades to black, Anson disappearing from sight, and the doors in the screen are flung open with a show of light and sound. The judges process in with their usual style and flair, and the fickle audience forget what has gone before, caught up in the excitement.

Jacob and Amy watch from the shadows, their faces inscrutable.

A shuddering breath next to me. I turn and see Lois, her face drained of colour, her hand over her mouth. 'Amy,' she breathes, and I remember this is not all about me. I lay my hand on her arm, and she turns to me and falls against me. Alwin watches from beside her, his face white.

I blank out the sounds from the screen of betrayal and sit with them while my two so-called best friends talk in language I could never conceive of them using. We rock together, sobbing, and then when it is over we look up.

Everyone in the cell is looking at us. At me.

Raza stands up. Walks to the side of the cell where the screen was lit moments ago and plants herself in front of it, arms crossed in her familiar stance. But this time, it's a fighting posture, not a defensive one.

'Carys will not die,' she states, and the faces gape at her. 'And neither will we. We will not let them do this.'

People begin to nod their heads, to murmur assent.

'We will be the means of change,' Raza continues, her voice hard and her eyes sparkling. 'Jacob Trader and Amy Plumber may have sold out, but we haven't and we won't. If there are enough of us, we can fight this. We can overcome them. We can escape from here and we can do this.'

They look to me for my reaction. I disentangle myself from Lois and go to Raza. I stand with her, mirroring her stance with my arms crossed, and I nod.

The cell breaks out in a clamour of voices. Some are cheering, some chanting our new slogan, 'Power to the Weak! Justice for All!' and some are quiet, their faces veiled with unease and, in some cases, disdain.

An older man with a white beard and a heavily lined face speaks up. 'It's all very well saying that,' he says, his face a mask of scorn. 'But let's be realistic. We are in here for good. Until the end, if she—' he points at me, '—is to be believed, we all end up dead. In a furnace. I, for one, think that is probably true. But there is no way out of here. No way.'

Voices quieten and people break off their excited conversation as hope leaves the room as though air is sucked from its vents. I look at Raza, who gives me an almost imperceptible nod. I take a deep breath.

'Once upon a time,' I say, swallowing over a great lump in my throat and projecting my voice so that everyone is listening, 'I had a good friend. I used to tell him exactly what you said, that there was no way. That there was no hope. But you know what he used to say to me?'

The old man shakes his head. Regards me from faded grey eyes. I wonder what those eyes have seen.

'He said that he doesn't do impossible.'

On the wall the NScreen suddenly flickers on. It's a blurry scene outside Party HQ, where a few dozen people hold cardboard placards high and chant our slogan. One of them looks right at the camera, a tall woman who seems strangely familiar but whom I can't place through the pixellated haze, and she raises both hands high. One by one, the others in the crowd join hands and raise theirs with her at the camera, and they stand silent, a mass of beautiful rebellion, claiming the ground lost for so many years.

A guard runs into the room and flicks the screen off, his face hardened with anger, but something strange is happening in the cell. The hope that fled with the old man's words is flying back in like a hundred butterflies, their vibrant colours punctuating the gloom and lighting up every weary face.

We stand together, resolute, and raise our joined hands at the blank NScreen.

END OF BOOK TWO

ABOUT THE AUTHOR

E.M. Carter is an award-winning author, poet and editor who can't get enough of words. She is the author of the Newland Trilogy (*Repression Ground, Rebellion Ground* and *Redemption Ground)* as well as a writer of several non-fiction books.

Liz was poet in residence for Wellington in Shropshire 2022/2023 and a finalist in the Woman Alive Reader's Choice award 2019. For other writers, she offers a freelance service editing, formatting and designing book covers and interiors. Liz likes to spend her days clad in fairtrade turquoise dresses trying not to eat chocolate and is proud to be a grammar pedant.

For updates and more, visit emcarter.carterclan.me.uk and sign up to her newsletter.

If you've enjoyed *Rebellion Ground,* Liz would very much appreciate it if you could leave a review on Amazon or Goodreads. Thank you so much!

An awakening nation. A deadly appointment. A race against time.

As rumblings increase throughout Newland, Carys, Amy and Jacob find themselves prisoners of the regime in different ways. Midwinter Festival is fast approaching, and with it a deadline nobody wants to think about. From the darkness of a prison cell to forgotten underground tunnels to unexpected visits to places they thought they'd left behind forever, the fugitives must fight to survive where they are and find a way out of impossible situations that threaten to break them.

Meanwhile, scattered Resistance and Outsider groups are coming together to seek justice after decades of oppression. In a frenzied countdown, the Resistance and the young people are caught up in an increasingly dangerous series of events. Can they really challenge the all-powerful New Day Party to bring justice and healing to a broken nation? And can they keep their own integrity in the process?

In *Redemption Ground*, the fast-paced final part of the Newland Trilogy, dive back into a world where equality and justice have been laid aside for power and greed, and journey with tenacious characters who are not afraid to stand up and fight — even in their darkest days.

About Resolute Books

We are an independent press representing a consortium of experienced authors, professional editors and talented designers producing engaging and inspiring books of the highest quality for readers everywhere. We produce books in a number of genres including historical fiction, crime suspense, young adult dystopia, memoir, Cold War thrillers, and even Jane Austen fan fiction!

Find out more at resolutebooks.co.uk

for the joy of reading

www.ingramcontent.com/pod-product-compliance
Lightning Source LLC
Chambersburg PA
CBHW061520210726
48287CB00006B/1754